The Women *of* Great Heron Lake

Deanna Lynn Sletten

The Women of Great Heron Lake
Copyright 2019 © Deanna Lynn Sletten

ISBN-13: 978-1-941212-44-8
ISBN-10: 1-941212-44-1

Editor: Samantha Stroh Bailey of Perfect Pen Communications
Cover Designer: Deborah Bradseth of Tugboat Design

Novels by Deanna Lynn Sletten

Miss Etta

Night Music

One Wrong Turn

Finding Libbie

Maggie's Turn

Chasing Bailey

As the Snow Fell

Walking Sam

Destination Wedding

Summer of the Loon

Sara's Promise

Memories

Widow, Virgin, Whore

Kiss a Cowboy

A Kiss for Colt

Kissing Carly

Outlaw Heroes

The
Women of
Great Heron
Lake

Prologue

Marla sat in the stuffy, closed-up bedroom watching each labored breath her husband took. He was almost gone; she knew the end was near. After over a year of suffering from pancreatic cancer, that had eventually spread, his body could stand no more. She watched his chest rise and fall and listened to his ragged breathing. Yet, she sat silently, waiting.

Gently, she took his bony hand in hers.

At last it happened. He exhaled, a long, final sigh. He was gone.

Marla stood stiffly, walked slowly to the window, and pushed aside the old heavy draperies her husband had always insisted they keep. She unlocked the window and slid it open. Fresh, crisp, spring air floated in, and she inhaled deeply. Marla desperately hoped that his soul would escape the confines of this room on the scented spring breeze.

"Goodbye, Nathan," she said softly.

Marla turned and walked out the door, not ready to notify anyone yet. Walking down the long hallway, ignoring its oppressive dark walls and woodwork, she continued taking deep cleansing breaths. She should be sad, but no tears came. With each step, her spirit grew lighter.

She was free.

Chapter One

Marla

Marla Madison drifted through the crowd of mourners in her home, gracefully accepting their heartfelt condolences. The great room was filled with Nathan's oldest friends and colleagues from the university. Even former students had come to pay their respects to their once beloved English and Literature professor. It was a wonderful tribute for a man who had lived a relatively quiet, private life.

She ran her hand over the skirt of her black Chanel suit, smoothing out creases that had formed throughout the long, warm day, and glanced at her reflection in one of the tall windows. Her short hair was still neat, and her mascara hadn't run—yet. However, her feet ached in her high-heeled pumps and her head hurt, as well. Despite the well-meaning wishes from those who'd gathered, Marla longed to be alone. But she continued to smile politely and nod at each guest and thank them for coming to pay their respects.

Scanning the room, Marla checked to ensure the servers were passing around appetizers and offering beverages to the guests.

She spotted their longtime housekeeper, Florence Cooper, standing stiffly in her black uniform watching the women with a keen eye. Marla should have known Mrs. Cooper would have everything under control.

Marla turned to say a few words to the president of the Great Heron Lake Yacht Club that Nathan had belonged to since he was a mere boy. She caught the eye of her daughter, Reese, sitting on one of the leather sofas by the stone fireplace with her most recent boyfriend, Chad Winters. She could tell from Reese's red-rimmed, blue eyes that she'd had enough. The funeral had been long and the reception line had been endless. Now, with the house full of people, Marla knew that like her, Reese was on her last nerve. Despite being an adult of twenty, Reese was still her father's little girl and today had been especially difficult for her.

Anthony Williams, the family attorney, appeared at Marla's side and gently touched her arm. "Marla. You look exhausted. Would you prefer we wait until Monday for the reading of the will?"

She turned and gave their old friend a wan smile. Anthony had been buddies with Nathan since childhood. They'd sailed, golfed, and even attended college together. But while Nathan had maintained a youthful appearance into his sixties, until he'd become ill, Anthony hadn't been as lucky. At sixty-five, his once thick, dark hair was balding and nearly gray, and lines were etched around his warm brown eyes. He'd also become quite portly, partly due to his eating at the club most nights since his wife had passed away the year before. But he was still the gentlemanly, caring friend he'd always been. Marla appreciated him, especially now.

"No, let's go ahead with it today," she said. "I have a feeling

Reese will want to go back to her townhouse in St. Paul before the weekend is over."

Anthony shook his head disapprovingly. "She should spend time here with you. I'm sure the university would understand if she missed a few more days."

Marla sighed. She wished it were that simple, but she knew that now Reese's beloved father was gone, she'd spend even less time at home. She and Reese had never been able to create the bond mothers and daughters were supposed to have. Especially not the same type of close relationship Reese had enjoyed with Nathan. Father and daughter had connected the moment Reese was born, and it remained that way over the past twenty years. And while Marla was pleased that Nathan had been able to enjoy fatherhood and bond easily with his child at an age when many men were becoming grandfathers, she'd always felt left out when father and daughter were together.

Now, Reese would have an empty spot in her heart that her father had once held.

Marla hoped she'd be able to help fill even a little of that space, but she knew it wouldn't be an easy task.

Marla looked up at Anthony. "I'll say a few goodbyes to our guests then we can meet in Nathan's den."

He nodded and gave her an encouraging smile before turning away.

"Oh, darling! What will you do now without your Nathan? He was the true north that guided your family." In her black sheath dress, dripping in diamonds and white gold, her friend, Victoria Carter, swooped down upon her and gave her a gentle hug. Her husband, Marshall, owned a chain of high-end jewelry stores in the Twin Cities and Vicki modeled their wares quite beautifully. Tall, slender, and with auburn hair and green eyes,

Vicki was gorgeous. Her most recent hospital visit to tighten a sagging jawline had helped to ensure that beauty lasted.

Vicki was her closest friend, even though Marla sometimes felt a little put off by her. They'd met over twenty years before at the Great Heron Lake Yacht Club beside the Olympic-sized pool, both pregnant and feeling like whales. From that day forward they'd been fast friends, golfing together in the women's league, volunteering at the same organizations, and planning school fundraisers together. Their daughters were born within days of each other and had also been friends throughout their school years. But despite their friendship, Marla bristled at the words that had just left Vicki's mouth.

The true north that guided their family? Did her friend really believe that it was Nathan who'd kept their lives running smoothly for the past twenty-two years?

"It will be difficult without Nathan," Marla said softly, keeping her thoughts to herself. "But Reese and I will soldier through."

"Oh, but Marla," Vicki continued in her dramatic way, "Nathan was everything! You two were inseparable. It must be devasting to you. And poor Reese! She was the apple of her father's eye. Poor dear."

"Thank you, sweetie," Marla said, rubbing her friend's upper arm. She watched as Vicki accepted another glass of white wine and sipped it. Her blood-red lipstick made half-circles on the rim of the glass. Vicki loved her wine. Marla wondered just how many glasses her friend had already consumed.

Marla shook a few more hands and visited a moment with her other close friend, Catrina Richardson, another club member whose husband used to golf regularly with Nathan. It didn't go unnoticed by Marla that all their friends were an extension of people who'd known him through his club or his work.

As the crowd thinned, Reese walked over to her mother with Chad in tow. Marla had only exchanged a few words with Chad since they'd arrived late Wednesday night, but she already knew she liked him better than the last four young men Reese had dated. He was from a wealthy family—old money, of course—yet was very down-to-earth and polite. Compared to Reese's former biker boyfriend, and adventure-seeking one, Marla thought Chad might be a keeper.

"When is Florence going to push everyone out the door?" Reese asked, sounding annoyed. "She's good at doing that. I'm so sick of being friendly when all I want to do is be left alone."

"I know, dear." Marla wrapped her arm around her daughter's waist. "But we can't be rude. Everyone means well by being here. Your father would have been honored to see such a turnout of old and new friends."

Reese wrinkled her nose. "Dad would have hated this too. He was happiest in his den, surrounded by his books."

Marla nodded as she studied her daughter. She was such a beautiful girl with pleasing features, a tall, lean body, and long, thick blond hair. But sometimes her impatience and, if Marla were honest, superior attitude, made her seem less beautiful. She'd learned her perspective from her father, who, despite being a good person, could also display superiority over what he called "common people." He was from an older generation and an old money family, and sometimes that outdated attitude came out in him.

Reese pulled away from her mother and headed for the kitchen. Marla knew exactly what she was up to and soon saw Mrs. Cooper round up the women serving food and beverages and sending them to the kitchen. Once the food was gone, so also would the crowd.

Marla shook her head and sighed. Mrs. Cooper had been with the family for fifty years, since she started as an upstairs maid at age twenty. She'd worked her way up to head house-keeper and had since run the home. Even now, long after the days of house guests and weekend parties were gone, and the cleaning had been delegated to a service that came twice a week because of Mrs. Cooper's arthritic hands and bad knees, she still ruled the house with an iron fist. Nathan's family had set up a pension for her years before, and Nathan had bought her a nice cottage on the lake to retire to when she turned sixty-two, but the woman still had not left. She'd been there so long, no one had the heart to tell her to go. And Marla would have felt the same way if Mrs. Cooper hadn't regarded her with disdain over the past twenty-two years.

The people finally filed out as Marla bid several of them goodbye. Soon she and Reese were sitting in the den across from Nathan's antique desk where Anthony sat. He pulled a pair of reading glasses from his jacket pocket and perused the papers he'd taken from his briefcase.

"Well, there isn't much to tell you that you probably don't know already," Anthony said. "Nathan's will is simple and clear-cut. Since Reese had been left an ample trust fund by her grandmother, which she will inherit when she turns twenty-one, Nathan felt that would be more than enough money to provide for her. Reese will take ownership of the townhouse Nathan purchased for her in St. Paul, and her bills and college tuition will be paid for out of an account he'd left for those needs. Otherwise, this house, and all the rest of the money is left to you, Marla."

Reese sat there with her legs crossed, impatiently bouncing

one leg up and down as if she were bored. As Anthony had said, she was inheriting a virtual fortune from her grandmother, and she'd already known that and hadn't expected more. But Marla was surprised to be inheriting the house.

"I thought he'd leave the house to Reese," she told Anthony. "It's been in the Madison family since 1885."

"He and I discussed that at length, and he was firm about giving you the house," Anthony said. "It's yours to keep or sell or do whatever you wish with it. Nathan understood that with his passing, this house would no longer be in the family line. And he also assumed that Reese wouldn't be interested in keeping it."

"Dad was right about that," Reese said. "I wouldn't want to live here anyway, and it's too big and costly to keep up as a summer home. I'm fine with not inheriting it."

Marla turned to Reese. It amazed her at how little her daughter cared about family lineage and responsibility considering how dearly Nathan held on to the past. He'd been proud to live in the family home, which had been passed down for generations, and carrying on the family name.

"Are you sure, dear?" Marla asked.

Reese sighed. "Mom. I'm positive. Besides, you'll be living here for years and I can always change my mind if I want this house later on, which I doubt," she said.

Anthony continued reading the will. A generous donation would be made to the university for scholarship money, contributions would also be given to other charities that Nathan held dear, and there was an added bonus for Mrs. Cooper to thank her for her loyalty. Other than that, the money and possessions had all been bequeathed to Marla.

After Anthony left, the house fell completely still. Reese changed clothes and went for a walk with Chad, and Marla went to the kitchen to see if Mrs. Cooper needed help cleaning up. The women they'd hired to serve were doing the lion's share of the cleanup under Mrs. Cooper's supervision, so Marla left them to their work.

She walked around the empty house, going from room to room. She still couldn't believe Nathan had left her the family's legacy. Built in 1885 by his great-great-grandfather as a summer retreat when the town of Great Heron Lake was first being formed as a playground for St. Paul's elite, the house had grown from a weekend cottage to a mansion of over 6,000 square feet. There were seven bedrooms and eight bathrooms, the great room, family/media room, kitchen, a morning room for Marla and a den/library for Nathan. A game room that held the antique billiards table and the indoor pool built in the 1920s for extravagant weekend parties added to its bulk. The house sat on five prime acres of land with 1000 feet of lakeshore and held tennis courts as well. It was extravagant, absolutely decadent, compared to the scant lifestyle Marla had grown up in, and now, it was all hers.

She wasn't sure she wanted it. It felt like a heavy weight had been dropped on her.

Chapter Two

Marla

Reese left the day after the funeral, just as Marla had expected. She would have liked to have spent a couple of days alone with her daughter, getting to know her better and creating a tighter bond. But Reese couldn't wait to get out of the house. Marla knew it only reminded her of her father and made her sad just being there.

The first few days after the funeral, Marla felt lost. She'd spent most of her time over the past year tending to her husband—doctor's appointments, medications, and, near the end, round-the-clock care. Nurses had been hired to help care for Nathan, but Marla had still spent the majority of her time up in the large, stuffy, master bedroom. It was the least she could do for her dying husband. She'd committed herself to him over two decades before, and she wasn't going to abandon him when he grew ill.

But it hadn't been easy. He'd suffered throughout his illness and it had been difficult for her to watch. Nathan had always prided himself on living an active lifestyle as well as an academic one, but both his body and mind betrayed him in his final months. When he'd retired from the university at the age of sixty-two, he'd looked forward to traveling with Marla, and fulfilling his dream of writing a literary novel. That dream would never come true, though, and Marla knew how disappointed he'd been at not being able to fulfil that last goal in his life.

She spent the next few days splitting her time between reading sympathy cards in her morning room until noon, then taking long walks on the lake trails in the afternoons. The morning room was a space from bygone days when genteel women used it for their daily letter writing or needlework. The term "morning room" had been dubbed the women's domain, and the name had stuck even after all these years of women earning the vote, women empowerment, and equal rights. Marla, who'd graduated college with a degree in finance and who'd worked in investments until she married Nathan had always found the name of her room condescending. Yet, the outdated term remained.

Afternoons and evenings, Mrs. Cooper insisted on serving Marla lunch and dinner in the formal dining room as she'd done all the years she'd served her and Nathan as a couple. But Marla hated sitting alone at the big table, being served. She would have preferred eating in the small breakfast nook or even at the counter in the kitchen. But she didn't have the energy to fight with Mrs. Cooper, so she did as the older woman dictated.

That first week Marla was also busy with appointments at the bank and with their financial manager, Markus Gentry, the man she'd once worked for who'd been the investment advisor for the Madison family for decades. Since Marla had always been the one to prepare the household bills for Nathan to pay, she knew what the expenses were to run the large house. She also knew how much money Reese spent on her father's credit cards.

She discussed what her financial needs would be over the next year with Marcus and they set up a monthly income based on her figures. Of course, she could draw out more if she needed it, for trips or special purchases. She was set for life, and thankful for it. Even if she were an extravagant woman, which she wasn't, there would have been plenty of money to cover her lifestyle for the rest of her life.

But that security didn't help to make her feel any less lonely.

When Marla had met Nathan, she'd fallen for his quick wit and intelligence, not his money. He'd had a warm way about him that belied his older age and status. They both shared the love of literature, spending time on the water, and living a quiet life. Even as he lay ill in his bed, Marla had read to him each evening from his favorite novels, stories written by Tolstoy, Proust, and Minnesota's own Fitzgerald. Now, her evenings were quieter than she liked, filled with nothing but time.

* * *

Two weeks after Nathan's passing, Vicki called and invited Marla to meet her and Catrina at the club for lunch. Marla agreed, relieved for the diversion. When Mrs. Cooper brought her tea into the morning room, Marla told her she wouldn't be home for lunch.

"You should take the rest of the day off and relax," Marla said. "I won't be hungry for dinner after having lunch at the club."

Mrs. Cooper arched one eyebrow at her.

Marla sighed. She knew that look. She'd seen it a million times on the older woman when she disapproved of something.

"Is there a problem?" Marla asked.

"Isn't it a bit soon to be going out?"

Marla smiled and shook her head. "I'm just having lunch with my friends at the club. It's not like I accepted an invitation to a party."

Mrs. Cooper sniffed. "In the old days, no wife would be out galivanting while in mourning for her husband."

"Oh, Mrs. Cooper. We aren't in the 1800s anymore. It won't be disrespectful to Nathan for me to have lunch." Marla gave a small laugh.

"Fine. But I won't be taking the day off. I have other duties to attend to."

Marla watched as Mrs. Cooper walked stiff-backed out of the room. Every gray hair was in place, her light-gray uniform and white apron spotless. Nathan had told Mrs. Cooper years ago that she didn't have to wear a uniform, but she insisted on it.

Marla had never understood why Mrs. Cooper was so cold to her. Everyone in the household was allowed to call her Florence, except Marla. Even Reese called her Florence, and, heaven forbid, would get away with teasing her by calling her Flo sometimes. But not Marla. Once, she'd called her Florence and the woman nearly had a coronary. Her eyebrows had arched up high and her lips had tightened. After that, Marla had given up on trying to win the housekeeper's approval.

At one o'clock, Marla walked into the yacht club's dining room and the hostess greeted her warmly. "I was so sorry to hear about your husband," the young woman said kindly. "Please accept my condolences."

"Thank you, Jeannette." Marla followed her to the table where her friends were seated.

The room was nearly full, as it was most days in the spring through autumn. It was still too early to sail, play tennis, or golf, since the weather was quite cool, but club members enjoyed gathering together in anticipation of warmer days.

Marla nodded to a few women she knew as she passed their tables, and was relieved to finally sit down with her friends. She'd felt as if everyone was watching her, and it made her uncomfortable. Although, it could have been her imagination. Ever since Mrs. Cooper's comment about it being too early to go out after he husband's death, she'd begun to worry that maybe she was right. Would people actually believe she didn't care that her husband was gone if she went out to lunch? But when she saw the warm smiles on Vicki and Catrina's faces, she relaxed.

"I'm so happy you came," Vicki said after hugging her friend. "We've missed you these past two weeks. Haven't we, Catrina?"

"Oh, yes, we have," Catrina said, smiling wide. "I can only imagine how dreary it's been for you, locked away in that house with only Mrs. Cooper for company."

"Catrina! Don't say that," Vicki admonished her.

Catrina smiled devilishly. She was much shorter than Vicki and petite, with dark hair she wore in a sleek bob and chocolate brown eyes framed in thick lashes. Her eyes always seemed to be teasing. At forty-eight years old, she was four years older than Vicki, yet she seemed much younger. Marla guessed it was her small size that contributed to that assessment. But Marla appreciated Catrina's openness. Sometimes she said the most outrageous things, and it always embarrassed Vicki to no end.

Marla ordered a glass of white wine—her friends were already on their second—and sat back, trying to relax. She envied her friends' spring clothes of soft, light colors. She'd been so tempted to pull out her pastel-colored clothing today, but then had settled on wearing navy slacks with a navy sweater and a crisp white blouse underneath. At least she wasn't wearing black.

The waiter arrived and Marla ordered the Caesar salad with shrimp and the others ordered salads as well. After the waiter had left, Vicki asked, "How have you been, dear?"

"Fine," she said. "Busy. There was much to do settling the finances and such, but it's all taken care of."

"I bet it's lonely, though, in that big house," Catrina said sympathetically.

"Yes, it is. Especially after caring for Nathan for so long. I'm not sure what to do with myself anymore. I've been swimming and walking the trails along the lake. And I've had a lot of correspondence to attend to. Honestly, I'm at a loss as to what to do with myself."

The women nodded sympathetically. The waiter brought their food and Vicki and Catrina caught Marla up on what they'd been busy doing.

"The summer kickoff fundraiser for the hospital is going quite well," Vicki said, her green eyes shining. Marla knew how much Vicki loved organizing a fundraiser. "We're having a glamourous ball here at the club on June first. It's going to be fun, dressing up and dancing. We could still use some help, if you're up to it," she said.

"Oh, well, you know how much I love helping," Marla said, hesitating. "But I'm not sure."

"We completely understand," Catrina piped up. "I'm sure you don't feel like working on a party, let alone attending a dance without Nathan."

Marla paused a moment and let that statement settle over her. Nathan was gone. They would never again come to the club on a Saturday night for dinner together, nor would she have him to take her to the fundraisers and dances anymore. Her face must have showed her thoughts because Catrina was instantly sorry.

"Oh, no!" Catrina wailed. "I did it again. I said the wrong thing. Marla, dear, I didn't mean to upset you."

"It's fine," Marla told her friend. "It just hit me that I have no one to go places with any longer. I don't know why I hadn't thought of that before, or why it seems to be such a surprise to me now."

"I'm so sorry," Catrina said again.

Marla gave her a small smile. "Don't worry yourself over it. I suppose I'll experience moments like that for quite some time. Nathan was sick for so long, all I worried about was what he needed to feel better, and now he's gone. It's a big adjustment."

"I'm sure it is," Vicki said gently.

As Marla ate lunch, she felt as if all eyes were watching her. She looked around the room, and saw the other ladies turn away or smile at her. A few of the older men did the same. She suddenly felt uncomfortable. The club had been like a second home to her before Nathan became ill. A place to meet up with friends or attend events. But over the past twelve months, she'd hardly come here at all. She'd felt guilty if she went out occasionally for lunch with her friends and she'd not played golf or tennis that entire time. She suddenly felt as if she no longer belonged.

Leaning closer to her friends, she asked, "Is it just my imagination or are people staring at us?"

Vicki glanced around and scowled at the people looking their way. "You're not imagining it," she said, turning back to Marla. "But it's not *us* they're looking at. It's *you*."

Marla frowned. "Why?"

Vicki dropped her eyes and smoothed the tan cloth napkin in her lap. Catrina looked everywhere but at Marla.

"What's going on?" Marla asked. "I know I haven't spent much time here over the past year, but am I such an oddity?"

Vicki rested her hands on the table and moved in closer. "No, dear. It's not that. To tell you the truth, they're all staring at you enviously. They're a bunch of trophy wives who wish they were you."

She gaped at Vicki in disbelief. "What do you mean by that?"

"Oh, you know the women in this club," Catrina said off-handedly. "Half of them are the younger second wives who, shall we say, didn't exactly marry for love, and the other half are the original wives who are bitter because their husbands hold their money in a tight grasp. We've all joked about it before."

Marla studied the faces around the room. Yes, the three of them had joked before about how often a wife was replaced by a trophy wife. Out with the old, in with the new, and the husbands acted as if it were the most natural of occurrences. And how often had Marla heard some of the older women complain that their husbands were tight with their money? But still, why would they envy her?

Vicki supplied the answer. "Let's face it, Marla. You're exactly what they want to be. You're still young, you have more money than you'll ever need, and you're free to live your life however you wish. You can start over again and marry or play the field. That's what they're all envious of."

Marla was appalled. "They all wish their husbands were dead?" Just the thought of it made her stomach turn. To go through the heartache she'd felt watching her husband fade away wasn't something to wish for.

"Well, probably not all of them," Catrina said. "I'm sure some of them do, though. Mostly, they're just jealous. They'll all get over it, eventually."

Marla thought back to when she'd first married Nathan and he'd started bringing her to the club. He'd been twenty years her senior, and so were most of his friends. His friends' wives hadn't exactly given her the warmest welcome. But then she'd met a few of the younger members' wives, like Vicki and Catrina, and slowly had been accepted by all—or so she'd thought. It dawned on her what people must have thought about her marrying an older man.

"Did people in the club think I married Nathan for his money?" she asked her friends. "That I was a trophy wife?"

Vicki shrugged. "I don't know. I didn't meet you until a year after you'd already been a member."

Catrina grimaced. "I was here when you first came. Some people talked about the age difference at the time. I ignored them, though. That's why I befriended you. You were Nathan's first wife, so I didn't think it was fair of them to call you a trophy wife."

"Catrina!" Vicki admonished again.

"What?" Catrina said. "I'm only being honest. She was much younger than Nathan."

"Oh my God!" Marla was shocked. "How could they think that? I married Nathan because I loved him. His money had nothing to do with it. And now everyone thinks I'm lucky? My husband's dead. How can that be lucky?"

Vicki reached across the table and patted her friend's arm. "I'm sorry, Marla. We should have met you for lunch somewhere else. You know how shallow these people can be sometimes. I mean, they have nothing better to do than gossip. Just ignore them."

Marla took a long sip of her wine and sat back. Her head was spinning. It had never occurred to her that people thought she was taking advantage of Nathan's generosity. They'd been married twenty-two years—nearly half of her life! How could they think it was so lucky to have lost him so soon?

"I feel like I never belonged here at all," Marla said sadly. "I had no idea people thought of me that way."

"Don't take it personally," Vicki said, sipping her third glass of wine. "Honestly, though, you are lucky. Nathan left you that incredible house—one of the best properties on the lake—and plenty of money to take care of yourself. And you're still young and beautiful. I'm sure the women here are shaking in their designer boots, afraid you'll go after one of their husbands." She laughed, then saw the appalled look on Marla's face and stopped. "Sorry." She looked contrite.

Marla picked up her purse and stood. "I need to leave. Please have them put lunch on my tab." She turned to go.

"Don't leave angry. Please?" Catrina said, standing quickly. "We didn't mean to upset you."

"It's fine," Marla said. "I'm just trying to process what you've said. I'll call you both later." She hurried out of there as quickly as her heels would allow.

Chapter Three

Marla

Marla drove home feeling dazed. She parked her car in the garage and headed into the house. The day had grown warmer but the breeze off the lake was crisp. The lake ice had just gone out the week before Nathan passed, so the water temperature was still quite frigid.

She entered the house and went upstairs to change. Walking down the hallway to her room, she didn't even glance inside the master bedroom when she passed it. In the final months of Nathan's illness, she'd moved out of the master bedroom and into the adjoining room. The house had been built in an era when it was fashionable for husbands and wives to have separate bedrooms. There was a bedroom connected to the master that was set up as the lady's room. When she and Nathan had married, they'd ignored that old tradition and shared a room. But during his illness, she could no longer share his bed and had made the room next door hers. Since Nathan's death, Marla hadn't moved back into the master bedroom. She'd always thought it was a dark chamber to begin with. But after months of being enclosed in that room, watching him die, she couldn't bear the thought of sleeping in there any longer.

Of course, her bedroom wasn't any better. It was smaller than the master, but otherwise it had the same dark wood wainscoting and had been painted a dark burgundy above the woodwork. A brick fireplace sat between the two windows covered in heavy burgundy draperies. Nearly every room in the house had a fireplace, most of which had been converted to gas. Marla liked the coziness of a fireplace, but the gloomy rooms throughout the house depressed her.

Slipping on slacks, a light sweater, and flats, Marla returned downstairs. Once at the bottom, she stood there, not knowing what to do with herself. She didn't want to go near the kitchen where she'd be glared at with disapproval by Mrs. Cooper. Marla wished the woman had taken the day off as she'd suggested. Mrs. Cooper, however, did as she pleased. Marla decided to go outside instead and slipped through the great room and out one of the sets of French doors onto the patio.

The patio was made of brick pavers and had planters all around it where the gardener placed flowers in the summer and pine greenery in the winter for the holidays. The pine was now old and tired-looking. It wouldn't be changed to summer flowers until late in May when there was no longer a threat of frost. Likewise, the patio furniture hadn't been taken out of storage yet.

Marla walked down the three steps off the patio and followed the brick sidewalk toward the lake. They had a lovely yard that gently sloped to the water with a sandy shore. Their part of the lake had a natural bay, and farther over was a point where other houses sat. The dock hadn't yet been put in, so she stood on the shore, gazing out over the blue water.

Great Heron Lake was a large body of water that stretched out farther than the eye could see. Nathan had told her it had been named for the many Great Blue Herons that nested there, and still did. She loved spotting them on fallen trees or in the tall reeds near the shore. Often, in the evenings, she and Nathan would take the canoe out to look for the herons and loons, both very majestic yet shy birds that avoided humans.

Marla loved the water. When they were first married, she and Nathan spent hours on the lake in the summer. They'd laze around in the sun on his boat, enjoying the cool breezes on a hot day. They sailed often too, a sport that Nathan relished.

Growing up, Marla hadn't spent any time on the water. No one in her neighborhood could afford the luxury of owning a boat. Her mother had worked as a secretary for a law office, but as a single parent, there had never been enough money to spare. Marla knew that her mother had done her best, though, and appreciated all that she'd sacrificed to make sure her daughter attended college and had a good job. That good job had led her to meeting Nathan.

Marla walked a few steps to the water and reached down, running her fingers through it. As expected, it was icy cold. As she stood, her eyes caught movement far across the bay to the point where she saw a figure walking up to the shoreline, much as she had. She could tell that person was standing in the yard of the cottage she adored. It was a smaller home than Marla's— four bedrooms, three bathrooms, and a cozy living room and spacious kitchen. There was a porch with large windows that ran the length of the front of the house. Once, years ago when it was for sale, Marla had gone to the open house out of curiosity. She loved the unique touches, like the rounded front door painted orange and the stained-glass accent windows. The house had generous windows everywhere, letting in the light and the rooms were painted cheerful, welcoming colors. There had even been a padded window seat with a curtain you could draw across to hide behind. Marla had thought it would be the perfect spot to read Winnie-the-Pooh books to a grandchild. From that day on, Marla had dubbed it the "Fairy Tale House."

But, of course, it would never have been the kind of place that Nathan would want to live in. After all, he had this huge mansion that everyone envied. What more could a person want?

Marla sighed and walked back to the house. She felt lost in her own life. Now that Nathan was gone, she no longer felt she belonged with the country club crowd. But she had no other friends, either. Over the years, her life had changed from a working woman to being a wife, then a mother. Her group of friends had grown smaller. She'd lost touch with her old friends from high school and college. The women she'd associated with when Reese was young were also the country club women. Even fundraising and volunteering work was with those same women. Until this moment, she hadn't realized how small her life had become.

Feeling out of sorts, she thought she'd go into Nathan's study, sit in a soft leather chair, and read one of the many classic novels from the library. Or she could take a swim in the indoor pool. She had many empty hours ahead of her to fill.

* * *

The next morning, Marla sat in the morning room, going through yesterday's mail. Mrs. Cooper brought in her tray of tea.

"Would you like your usual poached egg and wheat toast for breakfast?" Mrs. Cooper asked.

"Yes, thank you." Marla looked up at the housekeeper's pinched face. Marla always wondered why Mrs. Cooper looked like she'd been sucking on a lemon. If the woman smiled, she might actually look pleasant. "Please serve it in the breakfast nook. I'd prefer to eat there instead of the large dining room."

Mrs. Cooper sniffed disapprovingly but said nothing as she walked out.

Marla sat back in her hard desk chair and surveyed the room. It was decorated in Victorian style, with a touch of French provincial. She doubted anything had been changed since it was built in 1885. She ran her hand over the small, white and gold-trimmed writing desk and lightly touched the glass placed over the wood to protect it. It was not her style at all. She would have preferred a larger desk with roomy drawers to store files in. The rugs, nearly covering the dark-stained hardwood floor, had pink and blue roses on a cream background and the upper half of the walls had a hideous wallpaper in a burgundy color with large pink flowers. The lower walls were a mahogany wood wainscoting, like the rest of the house. The chandelier was tarnished brass with tulip-style glass globes and crystal teardrops, a gaslight that had been converted to electric. Frankly, the chandelier was the only thing in the room that Marla liked.

Standing, she walked over to the fireplace which had a dark mantel with a white and gold Baroque-style clock on it. She studied the wallpaper in the corner where the mantel met the wall. It had yellowed over the decades and become dry, peeling up in places. Marla was curious what the wall looked like underneath. Carefully, she picked at the paper with her fingernail, then slowly pulled a small piece up. It came off easily. Underneath was a white plaster wall.

Excited now, Marla pulled at the paper some more. A wave of

satisfaction rushed over her. Finally, with one big tug, she pulled off a huge panel of paper, revealing the white wall underneath.

"What are you doing?" a voice screeched behind her.

Marla turned, feeling her face heat up with guilt from having been caught. There stood Mrs. Cooper looking aghast, like she would have a heart attack on the spot.

Regaining her composure, Marla lifted her chin in defiance. "I wanted to see what was under this old wallpaper."

Mrs. Cooper moved closer. "Old wallpaper? Don't you mean antique wallpaper? It's original to this house. Why on earth would you tear off something as historic as this beautiful paper?"

"It may be historic but it's old, yellowing, and dried up," Marla shot back.

The elderly housekeeper looked insulted, as if Marla had been talking about her and not the wallpaper. "That paper has been here as long as I have, even longer. *It* belongs here!"

Anger coursed through Marla at the woman's insinuation. *She thinks I don't belong here.* "This is *my* house, and I will do as I wish with it," she told her with a firmness that even surprised her.

Mrs. Cooper's lips formed a tight, thin line. "I will call our repairman to come and glue that paper back on," she said. "Your breakfast is ready, as ordered." She turned on her heal and left the room.

Marla stood stiffly, her heart pounding with anger. *The nerve of that old biddy telling me what I can and cannot do in my own house!* She marched over, took ahold of another piece of the wallpaper, and yanked it. Another panel ripped off and fell to the floor. Immature as it was, her action felt satisfying. "Let your repairman put that back up, too," she said to the empty room. Then she stalked out to eat her now-cold breakfast.

* * *

Later, after she'd calmed down, Marla went into the kitchen to apologize to Mrs. Cooper for her angry words. Despite it being Marla's house, she'd always shown Mrs. Cooper respect because Nathan had. The last thing Marla wanted was more tension in the house than there already was.

The older woman was giving instructions to the two women who came twice a week to clean the house from top to bottom. After they'd been sent on their way, Marla approached the housekeeper.

"I apologize for my harsh words this morning," Marla said, as gently as she could manage.

"I accept your apology," Mrs. Cooper said, standing as stiff as ever. "Now, if you'll excuse me, I must call the repairman."

Marla did not like being dismissed like a child. "I'd rather you not call him," she said. Mrs. Cooper turned and stared at her. "I think I'll take down that old wallpaper after all. The room is so dark, and I'd prefer to have lighter walls."

"That paper is original to this house," Mrs. Cooper told her again.

"Yes, yes. I know it is. But just because it's old, it doesn't mean it's nice. I've used that room for over twenty years and I've never liked it. It's time I make it my own. Please don't worry about it, Mrs. Cooper. I'll take care of it."

Marla turned and walked away, feeling the satisfaction of telling her bossy housekeeper who was in charge. But before she made it to the door, Mrs. Cooper spoke.

"I realize I have no say in what you do to this house, but let it be known that I'm completely against any changes you make."

Marla didn't turn around. She nodded, then headed out the kitchen door.

The rest of the morning, Marla ripped the paper off the walls of her morning room. With each sheet that came down, she felt a surge of energy rushing through her. The room was already brighter without the dingy paper. Small strips of paper clung to the wall, and Marla resisted the urge to pick at it with her fingernail. Instead, she'd look for a tool in the garage that could scrape it off.

Maybe I'll even change the room's name to Marla's Office, she thought, taking pleasure in thinking how angry that would make Mrs. Cooper. She might even mention that to her later today. Marla knew she was being childish and churlish, but she didn't care. Tearing down the paper was the most fun she'd had in a long time.

Which didn't say much for her life up until then.

By late afternoon, the floor was covered in discarded wallpaper. Marla went in search of garbage bags and found some in the pantry. One of the cleaning women, Anita, saw her stuffing the paper into the bags and came in to help her.

"I appreciate your help," Marla told her. "But it might make Mrs. Cooper angry."

Anita grinned and shrugged. "I work for you, don't I?" she asked. Then she went back to picking up the mess.

That evening, Mrs. Cooper served her dinner without a word. Marla didn't even try to make conversation. If Mrs. Cooper wished to be surly, so be it.

Later that night, as Marla lay in bed, her thoughts turned to Nathan. She wondered what he'd think of her sudden childish act of tearing down the wallpaper. Would he have been angry? No, she doubted it. He may have tried to talk her out of it, because he loved the house just as it was. Or, he might have suggested they call in a designer to spruce up her room without changing too much. She knew for certain, though, that he would have chuckled over how angry Marla had made Mrs. Cooper.

Nathan had been a kind man, even with his eccentric behavior. He'd been the only son of wealthy parents who'd enjoyed the finest things in life. They'd thought it was very genteel of him to become a university professor, teaching literature to the younger generation. He'd confided in Marla that he'd taken that path because he couldn't bear the idea of sitting in an office, running the family department stores day in and day out. His father had done well managing the family businesses, but Nathan hadn't wanted that life.

The first thing that Marla had noticed about Nathan when they'd met were his warm, brown eyes. They'd been fringed in dark lashes and had a humorous glint in them. She'd been nervous during that first meeting—she'd been only a few months out of college before being assigned as an assistant to the firm's largest investment account. But Nathan's kind ways and sense of humor had helped her relax.

Markus had been her boss then, and the lead advisor on the account. He'd been impressed by Marla's knowledge and dedication and had thought she'd be a good fit working with Nathan. And he'd been right. Nathan had been impressed by her intelligence and expertise. When he'd first asked Marla on a date, she'd declined. She hadn't wanted to cause any trouble between the firm and their largest investor. Then, she'd run into him at a fundraiser for the local hospital. He'd looked quite handsome in his tuxedo, and when they'd danced, she knew there was something special about him. A year later, they'd married. Not once had she thought about his money when deciding to spend the rest of her life with him. She'd only seen those sparkling eyes, his gentle ways, and his intelligence. He was cultured, yet down-to-earth, despite living in a lakeside mansion. He found humor in his way of life, although he enjoyed it too. And he'd been generous to a fault with charities and giving annually to organizations he believed in. They had melded perfectly despite his being twenty years her senior.

But like every marriage, life hadn't always been perfect. Nathan had been very settled in his ways by the time they'd married. While he'd opened up his heart and his life to her, and then Reese, who he'd adored from the moment he'd laid eyes on her, he kept to his rigid schedule of work and time with friends at the club. They had traveled a little, at first. A quick sweep through Europe where he'd shown Marla all his favorite spots connected to literature. China, where he'd taken her to the Great Wall, and Egypt, where they'd spent days in the Cairo Museum, but after a while, the traveling stopped. Nathan hadn't been a fan of beach vacations or cruises. They never left to warmer climates in the winter, even when he was on break. Nathan preferred sleeping in his own bed and spending time with his old friends. When Reese was younger, Marla had been too busy caring for her to think about traveling. But when Nathan retired, she'd thought they might have a chance to go to a few places. And then he'd become ill, and all her energy went into his care.

Marla thought about the day Nathan died, and how relieved she'd felt that he was no longer suffering. Guilt washed over her as it did every time she thought about his final day. She'd loved him, but it hadn't been Nathan lying in that bed in those final days. It had been a sick, old man, someone she barely recognized. And she knew that he wouldn't have wanted to go on that way any longer either. Still, her reaction of relief after he took his final breath haunted her. She thought of it often. More than likely, she'd think of it until the day she died.

Marla pushed away her morbid thoughts, unable to cope with them any longer. Tomorrow was a new day. She would go to a home improvement store and find a nice, light color to paint the morning room. Correction—Marla's Office. She smiled at that as she drifted off to sleep.

Chapter Four

Marla

The next morning, Marla stood in front of her closet assessing her clothes. What did one wear to a home improvement store? She doubted her Chanel suits would be appropriate. Neither would her Dolce & Gabbana floral dresses. She had a few casual dress slacks and blouses or sweaters. Everything looked far too dressy to pick paint samples.

Marla decided on a pair of black pants, a royal blue sweater, and black flats. For the first time in over twenty years, she wished she owned a simple pair of jeans. Nathan had hated jeans on women. He never wore jeans, either, and although he'd never asked Marla not to wear them, she'd chosen not to in order to please him. It was a small thing, just one of his eccentricities. And, to his credit, he never once complained when his daughter wore them, but Marla knew it annoyed him.

Before going downstairs to the morning room, Marla stole a last glance in the mirror. She ran her hands through her short, brunette hair, fluffing the layers. Her face didn't look puffy and lined as it had while caring for Nathan. For months she'd looked much older than her real age of forty-six. She was finally feeling rested after months of sleep deprivation. Digging in the small crystal dish on her bathroom counter, she slipped on a pair of blue topaz stud earrings, and then put her wedding ring on too. She took it off at night because her hands often swelled as she slept. Satisfied that she looked presentable, she headed downstairs.

Marla was at her desk when Mrs. Cooper brought in her tea. The housekeeper didn't say a word, but the look of disgust on her face spoke volumes. Marla didn't react until Mrs. Cooper had left the room, then she broke out in giggles. *My goodness,* she thought. *I'm losing it!*

After breakfast, Marla consulted her phone to locate the nearest home improvement store. She didn't want to buy paint in the local hardware store because people in town knew her—or knew the Madison name. She wanted to avoid answering questions about why a woman of her wealth would be buying paint instead of hiring painters. This was a job she wanted—no, needed—to do herself. So, she mapped out the store, got into her black SUV, and headed out on the highway.

As she pulled into the bustling parking lot, it occurred to Marla that she'd never been in a store like this in her life. Growing up, her mother had always rented places, so the upkeep wasn't their job. Marla didn't know the first thing about painting a room, much less what she needed to buy. She hoped she wouldn't sound ridiculous to the sales clerk.

Walking inside, she gazed around in amazement. The store was huge. Lighting fixtures sparkled to her right, and gardening supplies and plants were displayed on her left. Straight ahead were box fans of all sizes stacked up in the aisle, and a row at least twenty feet long held every type of light bulb imaginable. Marla didn't know they even made that many styles of light bulbs.

"Excuse me," a woman said in an irritated tone, pushing past Marla. Other people stepped around her, and she realized she was standing right in the way. Moving forward, Marla wasn't sure what direction to go. She didn't see a section for paint, but she knew there had to be one.

"Can I help you, ma'am?" a friendly voice asked.

Marla turned and looked at a young woman who wore a blue apron. GWEN was written in a white patch on the apron.

"Yes," Marla said. "Where would I find the paint section?"

The woman smiled at her. "Keep walking straight ahead then turn right at the flooring department. About half-way down, you'll see the paint."

"Thank you." Marla walked in the direction she'd been told. Men and women strode purposefully past her, as if they knew exactly what they wanted to buy and where to find it. Some women pushed carts with children in them, wandering aisles of flooring and tile. Marla smiled at the sight of the children, who looked bored. Had she ever pushed Reese around in a cart? She really couldn't remember. Except for buying her own clothing and personal items, or shopping for clothes for Reese as a child, Marla had never had a need for a cart. Groceries and household necessities were purchased by Mrs. Cooper, although Marla had no idea where or how she bought items. She couldn't picture Mrs. Cooper running from store to store to buy tissues or cleaning supplies. That was how spoiled Marla had become, living with Nathan. She hadn't had to worry about where everything came from. It was just always there.

As Marla pondered how terrible that sounded, she spotted the paint department. She picked up her pace when she saw the rainbow of paint colors. Marla stopped and stared, overwhelmed.

There were shelves for different brands of paint, and what looked like thousands of shades to choose from.

"You look lost," a woman said, approaching Marla. "This display of colors can be daunting, don't you think?"

Marla turned and was greeted by a woman with a warm smile. She was close to the same height as Marla but had a sturdier build. Her light brown hair was short, with layers, and she had kind, brown eyes. Marla noticed the name printed on her apron was ARDIE.

"I feel lost, I'm afraid." Marla smiled back. "I didn't expect there to be so many samples to choose from. I don't know where to start."

"That's what I'm here for," Ardie said. "Tell me what you're painting, and I'll steer you in the right direction."

"Okay. I'm painting the wall of my morn…uh, my office," Marla corrected herself. Saying "morning room" out loud sounded pretentious to her, so she could only imagine how it would sound to Ardie. "I'm thinking a creamy white."

"Perfect," Ardie said. "We have our own brand of paint, which is a little expensive, and two other brands that are just as good." Ardie cupped her hand on the side of her mouth. "Don't tell my manager I said that," she whispered, then laughed softly. Ardie pointed to a display. "Why don't you look at these color samples first. Are you thinking of flat, satin, or semi-gloss?"

Marla stared at her as if she were speaking a foreign language. "Excuse me?"

Ardie gave her a sideways glance. "You haven't painted much, have you?"

Heat rose up to Marla's face. "No. Never."

"We all have to start somewhere, right?" Ardie said. "Go ahead and find a color you like, then I'll explain the types of paint and the supplies you'll need." She patted Marla on the back in a friendly gesture. "Don't be embarrassed. Newbies come in here all the time."

Marla liked how warm and friendly Ardie was. She relaxed and started thumbing through the paint samples.

Within the hour, Ardie had helped Marla load a cart full of paint, brushes, rollers, and drop cloths to protect the floor. Marla hadn't felt pressured to buy anything. Ardie had told her what each item was for and left it to her to decide if it was necessary. She'd been such a great help, and Marla told her so.

"Happy to help you," Ardie said. "That's what I'm here for."

On her way home, Marla realized she didn't have any old clothing to wear while painting. She headed in the direction of the mall and parked outside of Macy's. Once inside, she went to the women's section and looked through the rows and rows of jeans. They had holes everywhere—everywhere!—or crystals or studs on the back pockets. She looked at the price tags. Ninety-five dollars, one-hundred dollars, even two-hundred dollars a pair.

"That's a ridiculous amount of money for pants to paint in," she mumbled to herself.

"Can I help you?" a woman asked.

Marla glanced up. The woman was wearing a Calvin Klein wrap-around dress and stiletto heels. "I'm just looking for a regular pair of jeans," she said. "Like Levi's."

The salesperson raised one eyebrow but otherwise kept her expression neutral. "There are Levi jeans in the men's department," she said. "It's one floor up from here."

"Thank you," Marla said.

She took the escalator up one floor. Men's jeans would be fine with her. When she was a teenager, she'd always bought men's 501 button-fly jeans. They were cheaper than women's jeans and much more comfortable. And they lasted forever.

In the men's department, she searched through as many styles of jeans as the women's department had. It was crazy. She hadn't realized that jeans had become so complicated over the past two decades. Finally, she found a pile of classic 501s. She picked up several sizes and then went in search of a dressing room.

"You want to try those on?" a male salesperson wearing a suit asked.

"Yes," Marla told him. "Is there a problem?"

"Uh, no," he said. "You do know these are men's jeans, don't you?"

Marla laughed. "Yes, I do."

She found a size that fit her well and purchased two pairs.

Once home, Marla put all her painting supplies in the garage then ran upstairs to change into her jeans. She pulled an older T-shirt out of her drawer and put that on, too. Then she rummaged through her sailing sneakers and slipped on an old pair. Looking in the mirror, she laughed. She definitely didn't look like the prim and proper Mrs. Madison anymore. But the jeans were so comfortable, she felt she could live in them.

"What are you wearing?" Mrs. Cooper asked when she served Marla's lunch. "Have you gone to a rummage sale?"

Marla nearly choked on her iced tea. "No. I'm starting the painting project in the morning room. I couldn't wear a designer dress to do that."

Mrs. Cooper's brows were nearly to her hairline. "You know, you could hire someone to paint that room."

"What would be the fun in that?" Marla asked, then took a bite of her sandwich.

"I don't even want to think about what Mr. Madison would

say if he saw you like this." Mrs. Cooper shook her head in disgust.

"He'd probably have a good laugh," Marla said.

Mrs. Cooper left her to her lunch after that.

Marla was excited to start work. First, she moved the furniture away from the walls, then set drop cloths all around on the floor and over furniture. Then, she carried a ladder in from the garage so she could reach above windows, doors, and the crown molding. She took down the heavy drapes and sheers, folding and boxing them. She was going to replace them with lighter curtains after she'd painted.

Taking a roll of masking tape, she began running strips of it along edges of woodwork and around light fixtures to protect everything from paint smudges. This took the better half of her afternoon, which disappointed her. She had so hoped to be painting by now. But she wanted to do it right. Besides, she still had to lightly sand down the walls where wallpaper glue had stuck.

Marla told Mrs. Cooper she'd eat dinner in the breakfast nook because she didn't want to change her clothes. She hoped to begin sanding this evening then be ready to start priming and painting tomorrow.

Mrs. Cooper stared at the work Marla had done so far. "Hmm. Seems like a lot of work just to paint a wall," she said.

"Yes. But it'll look nice when it's done," Marla told her.

"Depends on who you're asking," Mrs. Cooper said.

Marla sighed. There was no pleasing this woman.

It was then that Mrs. Cooper noticed the curtains in the box. She walked carefully on the plastic over to them. "I'll have these sent to the dry cleaners tomorrow."

"I was just going to store them in the attic. But I suppose you can have them cleaned first," Marla told her.

Mrs. Cooper's hand went to her throat as if Marla's words had completely startled her. "The attic? Why, these are very expensive draperies that were made especially for the morning room. Don't you know quality when you see it?"

Marla took a deep breath and willed herself not to respond with a sharp retort. Mrs. Cooper had always looked down on her, but her rudeness was getting ridiculous. "I understand they are high quality draperies," she said, controlling her anger. "But they won't be needed in this room any longer."

Mrs. Cooper turned on her heel and left. Marla wasn't sure how much longer she could be nice to her. She was grating on her nerves. She had put up with Mrs. Cooper all these years because of Nathan. But now, she wasn't sure she could stand to keep the housekeeper around.

Long into the evening, Marla lightly sanded the walls so there was no glue residue left. She found the vacuum cleaner after Mrs. Cooper had left for the evening and vacuumed the layer of dust left over from sanding. It was late by the time she got ready for bed. Her arms were sore and her back ached from standing all day, but Marla felt good about what she'd accomplished. She hadn't worked this hard in decades, and it felt amazing.

The next day, despite feeling a bit stiff, Marla retrieved the can of primer from the garage, a paint brush, the tray and roller, and went into the morning room.

Carefully, she began painting primer around the door, windows, wainscoting, the fireplace, and the crown molding. Half-way through, Mrs. Cooper brought in her morning tea and left without a word. Marla ignored her and kept painting. She had just finished the first coat when Mrs. Cooper announced breakfast was ready.

Marla quickly ate her breakfast, then went back to work.

The primer had dried quickly, so she lined everything in the room one more time. She poured primer into the paint tray, after placing a plastic liner in it, picked up the roller, and took a deep breath.

"Here I go," she said, feeling a little unsure of herself. She dipped the roller into the tray and wiped off the excess, then applied it to the wall, rolling it up and down. Standing back, she smiled broadly. "That wasn't so bad," she said into the empty room. She continued until the entire room was primed.

Anita came into the room for the box of draperies just as Marla was adding another coat of primer to the walls.

"You look like a pro," Anita said with a grin.

Marla laughed. "Thanks." Then she looked down at herself. Smudges and drips of primer were on her shirt and pants. "Oops. I guess I'm a bit messy."

"That's what makes you look professional." Anita winked as she picked up the box of draperies and headed out of the room.

By lunchtime, Marla had primed the room twice and was now ready to trim with the paint.

"You'd better eat in the kitchen, looking as you do," Mrs. Cooper said. "You'll get paint all over the nice furniture."

Marla grinned. "This isn't paint. It's primer."

Mrs. Cooper gave her that evil glare she was so good at then led the way to the kitchen.

The kitchen wasn't a bad place to be banished to. Of all the rooms in the house, it was the only one that had been updated in the past century. It was enormous and even had a small family room attached with large floor-to-ceiling windows. The beech cabinets were stained a rich mocha color and the counters were topped with tan quartz. All the appliances were stainless steel and commercial grade and an island sat in the center with a second sink and extended out to seat up to eight people on the other side. Polished wood flooring and the woodwork and beams overhead were the only original décor in the kitchen.

Marla took a seat at the island. Mrs. Cooper had made her a light chicken pasta and salad and served her a glass of iced tea before disappearing from the kitchen.

Marla was used to eating lunch with Nathan, or going to lunch with friends. It was lonely eating all by herself. She wished she had a better relationship with Mrs. Cooper, so they could share meals together, but she knew that was never going to happen.

Her eyes landed on the small television that was built into the cabinets. She found the remote and turned on the TV, then scanned the channels to find an old movie or show that might be fun.

Television had been another of Nathan's pet peeves. Even though they had a media room that held a huge television screen, they'd rarely ever watched live TV. Nathan thought television programs were trivial and ridiculous. If they watched at all, it was to enjoy a classic movie or a news program. Marla hadn't really missed watching television. She'd enjoyed spending evenings quietly reading a book or playing a game of cribbage or chess with Nathan.

As she scrolled through the channels now, Marla stopped when she saw a home remodeling show. She watched for a while, thinking she might learn a few tips. It was a husband and wife team, and their easy banter made the show fun. They were refinishing an old, brick fireplace, and she loved what they were doing with it. In fact, she loved everything they were doing to fix up the old cottage-style house. By the time Marla had eaten her lunch, she was intrigued by what she'd seen. She wrote down the name of the show and planned on checking to see if there were more episodes on Netflix or online.

For once she was grateful that Reese had insisted they get Netflix so she could watch her favorite shows when she was at home.

That afternoon, Marla painted the morning room the creamy white color she'd chosen. With every swish of the roller, she felt as if she were creating something beautiful. It didn't matter that it was just white. It didn't matter that she was just painting a wall. What mattered was she was doing this herself, creating a room she could feel at home in for the first time since moving here.

That night after she'd eaten a light dinner, Marla went for a relaxing swim in the heated pool. She was going to let the paint dry overnight and add another layer tomorrow. She knew her muscles would be sore, so decided a swim would help to relax them.

It was dark outside by the time she turned on the pool light and entered the enclosed space. Outside, the moon shone on the lake and filtered through the windows. Marla liked leaving the room's lights off and swimming only by the glow of the pool's underwater lamp.

Stepping into the warm water, she could already feel the tension slipping away. She swam leisurely, flipping over from a back stroke to a breast stroke. She enjoyed the feel of the warm water as it glided over her body. Swimming and walking had always been her release. If something troubled her, she could ponder it in silence as she slipped through the water or walked a quiet trail in the woods. Now, as she swam, her thoughts turned to Nathan. It had been nearly three weeks since his passing, and she felt she was doing okay. True, she'd felt lost at first, but only because she'd spent so much time caring for him during his illness. Having that time back to herself, and not knowing how to fill it, had made her feel useless. Working on the morning room gave her a purpose again. She wasn't sure what she was going to do when that was finished, but for now, she felt good about herself. She knew that if Nathan could see how she was handling herself, he'd be proud of her too.

At least, that was what she hoped.

Chapter Five

Marla

"**M**other! *What* are you doing?"
The harsh words sailed across the morning room and
felt as if they actually hit Marla between the shoulder blades.
She turned around from her spot on the ladder and there stood
Reese, arms akimbo, staring at her in shock.

"Hi, sweetheart." Marla made her way down the ladder.
She'd been putting the final touches on the ceiling. All morning
she'd painted, and the room had three coats plus two on the
ceiling. Marla was very happy with how it had turned out.

"Oh my God! You're wearing jeans! Florence was right.
You've lost your mind!" Reese exclaimed.

It not only irritated Marla that her twenty-year-old daughter
was allowed to call Mrs. Cooper by her first name, but also that
Reese was standing there in tight jeans with holes in them and
judging her.

"I have *not* lost my mind," Marla said. "And it isn't Mrs.
Cooper's business what I wear."

Reese pushed back her long, blond hair and studied her

mother. "What kind of jeans are those?" She made a circle around her mother. "Levi's? Are those men's jeans?"

"Yes. I like them. They're comfortable."

"Mom. Men's Levi's? Really? No one wears men's jeans. The least you could have done was bought them in the women's department."

"Forget my attire, Reese. Look at what I've done. Doesn't the room look light and airy now? It was so oppressive before, and the wallpaper was literally over a hundred years old."

Reese crossed her arms and surveyed the room. "Well, yes. It does look better. But really, Mother. Did you have to do it yourself? Why didn't you hire someone?"

"Anyone can paint a room," Marla said, although she knew that without Ardie's help at the home improvement store, she'd have never been able to paint this room properly. "Besides. It was fun. It gave me a project to do."

Reese rolled her eyes. "Well, don't repaint the entire house. Florence will have a coronary. She's called me every day this week complaining about what you've been doing. I finally had to come and see for myself. You know what a drama queen Florence can be sometimes."

Yes. Marla was pointedly aware of it.

"I can't believe she bothered you with all this, but I'm glad you came. Are you staying for dinner? We can eat here, or go out," Marla offered.

"Only if we have an early dinner," Reese said. "I don't want to get home too late."

"Great. Let me clean up and change and I'll be ready in a few minutes." Marla walked past her daughter, but before she was out the door, Reese spoke.

"What are you going to do about that fireplace? Paint it too?

That brick looks old and tired now that the walls are cleaned up."

Marla turned, surprised at her daughter's words. "Actually, I've been thinking about that too. I'd like to change it. I just have to talk with someone first to get a few ideas."

"Hmm," was all Reese said.

Marla cleaned up and changed quickly so she wouldn't miss a chance to spend time with her daughter. When she came downstairs, she found Reese in the great room, sitting on the sofa and texting someone.

"Where would you like to eat?" Marla asked.

Reese glanced up. "Now you look like yourself again," she said, referring to Marla's dress slacks, blouse, and jacket. "Let's just go to the club. It's close and easy."

"Oh." The single word popped out of her mouth before she could stop it. Marla's tone must have sounded strange because Reese stopped texting and looked at her.

"Is something wrong with going to the club?" her daughter asked.

"No, no. I just thought it might be nice to try someplace else."

"I'm fine with it. They have a shrimp salad that I like," Reese said.

"Well, then, the club it is," Marla said sounding cheerier than she felt.

Reese drove. She had a sleek, black convertible that Marla had always thought was an over-priced car for a college student. But then, Reese was a college girl with a trust fund, so she supposed that made a difference.

They pulled into the yacht club's parking lot which was surrounded by lush green lawns. The golf course already looked beautiful and some of the perennial plants were sprouting up.

The lake sparkled under the late afternoon sun.

"Good afternoon, Mrs. Madison," Jeannette greeted them. "And Reese. It's so nice to see you."

"Thank you, Jeannette," Reese said. "Could we have a table with a view of the lake, please?"

"Of course." She led them to the back of the restaurant where the large windows offered a lovely view of the bay. "Jacob will be your server. Enjoy your dinner."

"Thank you, Jeannette," Marla said.

"Good afternoon, ladies," Jacob greeted them. "Would you like to order drinks?"

"Hi, Jake. How's it going?" Reese said familiarly. "I haven't seen you in a while."

The young man beamed. He had thick, dark hair and deep brown eyes that sparkled when he looked at Reese.

"Everything is fine. I've been working here full-time for the past year. It's a nice place to work. How's college?" Jake asked.

The two young people talked a minute then Marla and Reese ordered their drinks. After Jake had walked away, Reese leaned in closer to her mother and said quietly, "I can't believe he's still working here. He should be in college. His parents must be livid."

Marla glanced over at Jake as he placed their drink order. She hadn't been to the club too often since Nathan became ill and hadn't kept up on who worked there. "How do you know Jake?"

Reese sat back in her chair. "He and I went to the academy together. He made good grades. His father is a surgeon. Jake started working here last summer and never left, apparently."

Jake brought their drinks and took their order.

"It looks like he has a crush on you," Marla said after he'd left.

Reese rolled her eyes. "As if I'd date a waiter."

Marla couldn't believe the contempt she heard in her daughter's voice. She didn't want to argue with her though. She spent so little time with Reese that reprimanding her for her attitude wouldn't bring them closer. Marla changed the subject. "How is your friend, Chad? He seemed very nice."

"Oh, he is. We go out from time to time. I'm just not interested in getting serious with anyone right now."

"That's smart," Marla said. She wanted Reese to finish college first before having a serious relationship. Reese was leaning toward a law degree, which was perfect for her. If anyone could argue a case, it was her daughter.

"Will you be coming home for the summer this year?" Marla asked, hopefully. It would be a long, quiet summer if she didn't.

"I don't plan on it," Reese told her. "I've been asked back at the law firm I worked at last summer. It's only filing and doing small jobs, but it'll look good on my application to law school."

Marla nodded. She was disappointed, but she understood how important that was. Still, she'd hoped Reese would spend time at home and maybe even bring a few friends along, too. The place was too large for just her to rattle around in all summer long.

Their food came and they ate as other diners began to fill the tables around them. The golf course wasn't open yet, but the driving range and tennis courts were. A few of the men and women came in, dressed in their sport's clothes. Vicki and her husband were seated at a table across the room from Marla and Reese. Vicki smiled and waved, and Marla waved back, secretly hoping she didn't come over.

"Besides," Reese spoke up, drawing Marla back to their conversation. "You'll be busy with your women's golf league, tennis, and all the charities you're involved in during the summer.

You won't have time to miss me."

Marla pushed her salad around on her plate. "Yes. Well, I'm not sure if I'll play tennis or golf this year. I'll have to see how I feel. And I haven't really been involved with fundraisers or charity work since your father became ill, so I'm not sure I'll be going back to those either."

Reese stopped eating and stared at her mother. "Don't be ridiculous. You've been doing those things for years. Why would you stop?"

"That's just the point," Marla replied. "I've been doing those things since I married your father. I think I'd like to take a break and see if there's anything else I might want to do."

Reese shook her head. "Why change now?" she asked, taking a bite of her salad. "What else would you do?"

Her question irritated Marla. It was as if her daughter had labeled her and put her on a shelf. Like Marla wasn't capable of doing anything else.

"Has it never occurred to you that maybe I no longer enjoy those things? I mean, I'm not exactly the most athletic person on the planet. I only played golf and tennis because your father wanted me to. I had to take lessons when we were first married because I'd never played either before. And as for charity work, while I do enjoy helping others, you can only put together so many balls, carnivals, and silent auctions before it all becomes so routine. Maybe there are other opportunities out there for me to explore."

Reese looked stunned. "You've really been thinking about this, haven't you?"

"I've had nothing but time to think while sitting alone beside your father's bed all those months before he died," Marla said, sounding harsher than she'd meant to.

Reese frowned. "Is that a dig? You knew I would have been right there with you if I hadn't had school. Dad wanted me to stay in school."

Marla's tone softened. "No, dear. It wasn't a dig. I hadn't meant for it to sound that way. I know you loved your father dearly and that he'd told you to stay in school no matter what. I'm only saying that I've thought a lot about my future without your father. It's going to take some getting used to. We did everything together." His way, she wanted to add, but didn't. She'd already upset Reese enough.

Marla signed for their dinner and they left the club. It had grown dark and the temperature had chilled considerably. Reese didn't get out of the car when they pulled up into the circular driveway.

"Thanks for dinner, Mom," Reese said. "I have to head home now."

Marla nodded. "I'm glad you stopped by even if it was to check on me and see if I've gone insane."

Reese laughed. "Well, I'm still not sure you haven't. Please try not to do anything else that will upset Florence. I don't want her to keep calling me, complaining."

It's my house, and I'll do as I wish, Marla thought but didn't say it out loud. There was no sense in getting into an argument before Reese left. She hugged her daughter and waved goodbye as Reese drove out of the driveway.

Walking inside the expansive foyer, Marla kicked off her shoes and put them in the coat closet. The marble floor felt cold under her feet. She walked deeper into the house and stopped when she came to the morning room. It was too late to do any more work. Besides, it looked like it didn't need any more coats of paint, so all that was left was taking down the tape and cleaning up the room. Her eyes turned to the fireplace, and Reese's question drifted through her mind. *What are you going to do about the fireplace?* Marla agreed that it did look old and tired next to the freshly painted walls. But did she want to paint it?

Going upstairs, she changed into comfortable loungewear, then laughed when she looked in the mirror. In college, she'd worn old sweatshirts and boxer shorts to lay around the apartment. After marrying Nathan, she wore beautiful loungewear. It all seemed so silly.

Going down to the kitchen, she was happy to see that Mrs. Cooper had left for the night. She grabbed some crackers from the cupboard and went into the small family room off the kitchen to turn on the television. Sitting back on the cushy sofa, she flipped the channels until she found HGTV. Unfortunately, the show she wanted to watch wasn't on. She did a search and finally found it on Hulu. Marla started watching the first show of the first season and kicked back and relaxed. She loved how cozy this little room was compared to the media room or the great room. Marla decided that this was where she'd always watch television. After years of living the way Nathan had preferred, she was making her own decisions. For the first time in many years, Marla felt normal.

Chapter Six

Marla

M arla spent the weekend cleaning the morning room and went shopping for new draperies. She decided on lightweight blue-gray curtains with a satin sheen. They matched a color in the antique floral rug that she planned on keeping.

Sunday was spent putting up the new curtains and watching more episodes of the decorating show. Mrs. Cooper didn't work on weekends, so Marla was free to roam the house without inquisitive eyes watching her. She also took a long, critical look at her bedroom. Now that the morning room felt cheerier, she wanted the same for her bedroom. It also had the dark wainscoting on the bottom half of the wall, but then someone had painted the upper half a deep burgundy. The draperies and bedspread were also shades of burgundy, making the room gloomy and unappealing. Marla decided she'd paint this room ivory and change the curtains to a soft rose-pink. She wanted a thick, puffy white bedspread with rose throw pillows. She'd also change out the old rug that laid beside the bed on the hardwood floors.

Monday morning, with all her projects in mind, Marla

headed back to the home improvement store, excited to buy the supplies she needed.

"Good morning," Ardie greeted her from behind the counter where she was mixing paint for another customer. "You're back for more."

Marla smiled, surprised but pleased Ardie had remembered her. "My office turned out wonderful," she said. "Now I'm painting my bedroom."

"Great. What color are you thinking of?"

"Another shade of white. I'll go check out the samples. I have another question for you when you're free," Marla said.

"Be there in a minute."

Marla pushed a cart over to the sample display. She sifted through the different shades of white until she found one she liked.

"I'm all yours," Ardie said, coming up beside her. "What have you chosen?" She looked at the sample. "Oh, Ivory Charm. Aren't these names crazy? I'd like a job where I could sit all day and pick silly names for paint."

Marla laughed. Ardie was such an easy person to talk to.

Ardie mixed two gallons of the color then found a gallon of primer for her, too. "Has it been over a hundred years since this room was painted too?" she asked.

"I'm not sure. It seems that way, though."

"That must be some house, being that old. I'll bet there's also a lot of beautiful woodwork in the rooms and built-in bookcases and such."

Marla nodded. "Yes, there are. And most of it is lovely. But the old wallpaper and paint choices are so dark. I want to lighten things up."

"I can't blame you for that," Ardie said. "Everything today is light and airy. That's what people want."

"I had a question for you," Marla said. "I was watching a home remodeling show on TV and they tiled over an old brick fireplace. Can that really be done?"

"What were you watching? *Fixer Upper?*"

Marla nodded emphatically. "I'd never watched it before. They're so good! I love how she decorates."

"Oh, wow. You hadn't seen it before? She's amazing! You know that she has her own furniture collection and Target even carries pieces by her."

"Really? I had no idea," Marla said. She felt as if she'd walked into a whole new world she'd never known existed. "I wish my house was the type that her things would look good in. Like a cottage, or farmhouse. I'm afraid it's too stuffy for her designs."

Ardie smiled. "It sounds to me like you're toning down the *stuffy* elements in your house. And to answer your question, yes, you can tile over a fireplace as long as the bricks are smooth enough to create a flat surface. Did you have any tile in mind?"

"I was looking at the cream or dove gray basket weave tile. It's simple but elegant," Marla said.

"That is nice. Have you ever put up tile before? In a kitchen or bathroom?" Ardie asked.

Marla shook her head. "No. I never painted until last week. Can you imagine me putting up tile?"

Ardie laughed. "I know you can do it. We have some do-it-yourself classes here at the store. Let me see if we have any on tiling coming up."

Marla watched as Ardie looked at a printout. Excitement bubbled up inside her. She couldn't believe she was this excited about learning to tile.

"There's one this Thursday evening," Ardie said. "Should I sign you up?"

Marla nodded. "Yes. My name is Marla Madison. This may sound funny, but I can't wait. I've never learned how to do something like that before."

Ardie smiled as she typed Marla's name into the computer. "I think it's great. Women should know how to do home projects. My husband, Dan, works in construction, so he does all our remodeling. But I know how to do a lot of it, too. Remodeling projects are much more fun than fixing stuff, though."

Marla considered Ardie for a moment. She wondered what her life was like. Probably a nice home in the suburbs with a backyard full of flowers. Maybe a couple of grown children. Grandchildren too. Marla thought that all sounded nice.

"My daughter thinks I'm crazy for doing all this work myself. She said I should hire someone, but I'm enjoying it," Marla said.

"Oh, children think all parents are crazy. My son and daughter think I am." Ardie laughed. "But then, I think they are sometimes too. Have you seen those ridiculous jeans girls are wearing these days? They have more holes than fabric. I'll keep my mom jeans any day over those."

"My daughter wears those. And then she was horrified to see me in men's 501s. She thought I'd lost it."

"Oh, wow. I remember wearing those as a teenager. I loved them. They make men's jeans more comfortable compared to women's," Ardie said.

Marla really liked Ardie. She seemed so down-to-earth. Since marrying Nathan, the friends she'd made were always trying to one-up each other. Who had the biggest house? Who went on the nicest vacations? Who had the smartest children? The underlying contests went on and on. Marla had forgotten how nice it was talking with someone who didn't feel they had to impress her.

"Thank you for all your help," Marla said. "Maybe I'll see you on Thursday night."

"I think I work until nine that night. I'll run over to the tile section if I get a chance. Have a good week," Ardie said.

Marla waved and pushed her cart toward the check-out counters. She couldn't wait until Thursday and the tiling class.

All that week, Marla worked on her bedroom, taping around the woodwork, covering the furniture, and priming the walls. Some people might think this was tedious work, but she enjoyed it. Her mind wandered as she worked, drifting between the past and the present. She pondered her future, and what she'd do with the rest of her life. Should she go back to her old friends and the club activities that were familiar even though she didn't really enjoy them? Or set out on a new course? She wasn't sure.

Nathan hadn't even been gone a month, yet she felt as if he'd been gone for years. His long illness should have prepared her for his death, but it hadn't. Despite what she'd told Reese, she hadn't thought much about what she'd do once Nathan was gone. Working on the house gave her time to sort out her feelings and think about her future.

By the time Thursday came around, Marla had finished painting her bedroom and had it all put back together. The heavy draperies had been replaced with light, flowing curtains. She'd asked Anita on her cleaning day to polish the woodwork so it now shone, good as new. It felt lighter and airy. Marla loved it. Although, she wasn't sure if she should do anything to the fireplace in her bedroom. She'd see how the tile class went and decide afterward.

Marla was nervous the night of the class. She didn't know what to wear, then decided that most people would proba-bly be wearing jeans. She put on the pair she hadn't worn yet, a long-sleeved T-shirt, and a pair of sneakers. She hoped she'd fit in with the group. When she got there, relief flooded though her when she saw the other class members. They were of all ages, male and female, and everyone was wearing their oldest jeans and shirts.

The class was taught by a man named Jeremy, who looked to be in his mid-forties. He gave them all blue aprons, then they each took a spot at one of the two eight-foot long tables that had been set up. Their work began immediately. Jeremy explained the steps for cutting, placing, and putting up tile and how to grout, then seal it. He'd set up a large sheet of plywood, and they each had a turn at cutting and placing tile. He taught them how to use the skill saw for big cuts, and the hand cutter for smaller sections. Marla was surprised at how detailed a person had to be to make the tile fit properly, but she found she liked the precision of it. It was a skill that took some honing to achieve.

By the end of class, Marla felt confident enough to tile the fireplace in the morning room. She discussed her project with Jeremy and he gave her a few tips and pointers, then helped her pick out what she'd need for the project. She was just maneuvering her full cart through the store when Ardie appeared.

"Wow! You really took that class seriously," she said when she saw Marla's full cart.

Marla laughed. "I'm going to tackle a big project, and pretend I know what I'm doing."

"I've no doubt you can do it," Ardie said encouragingly. She walked with Marla up to the check-out counter and helped her unload her cart.

"Don't you have to get back to the paint department?" Marla asked as she paid for her purchases.

"I'm done for the night. I'll go out with you and help load this stuff into your car."

"That's so nice of you. I love the service here," Marla said with a grin.

They unloaded the items into Marla's SUV. "Thank you so much," Marla said. "These boxes of tile are heavy."

"Happy to help." Ardie looked at Marla a moment, as if considering something, then spoke. "Would you like to go out for coffee and chat a while? I mean, if you don't have to go home yet."

Marla was genuinely surprised by her invitation. "I'd love to. Where do you want to go?"

"There's a coffee place just down the street that stays open late. Take a right at the stoplight and go two blocks. You'll see it on the right. It's called Carrie's Coffeehouse."

"Okay. I'll meet you there." Marla got in her car and headed for the coffeehouse. She was excited about spending some time talking with Ardie and learning more about her. It had been years since she'd made a friend outside the circle of the yacht club. Ardie was so warm and down-to-earth—the complete opposite of everyone else she knew—which was refreshing.

Ardie pulled in right behind Marla. Both women got out and headed inside the coffeehouse. They each ordered regular coffee and a piece of the homemade apple pie. Then they took their food to a corner booth in the back.

"Is it weird that I invited you out for coffee?" Ardie asked after they'd settled into the booth. "I was starting to worry that you'd think I'm odd." She made a face.

Marla laughed. "No. It isn't weird at all. I think it's nice. I've really appreciated your help in the store, and I felt as if we kind of clicked."

"That's how I felt," Ardie said, her face lighting up. "And believe me, that almost never happens. But there was something about you that impressed me."

"Really? Was it because I didn't know how to paint a room, or that I took a tile class?"

Ardie shook her head. "No. It was the fact that you decided to learn to do those projects when you probably could have easily paid someone to do them. You're not afraid to roll up your sleeves and get dirty. I think that's great."

"Doesn't that describe everyone who comes into your store?" Marla asked. She wondered if something about her had stood out from the store's regular customers.

"I suppose it does. Except most are already do-it-yourselfers. You seem new to this."

Marla nodded. "I am. I've had a stressful couple of years, and honestly, I think I just snapped one day. I started picking at the old wallpaper that I hated in my office and the next thing I knew it was all over the floor. Needless to say, my daughter and housekee…, ah, I mean, friend, thought I'd lost it."

"I'm sorry to hear that," Ardie said, looking concerned.

"That I lost it?"

Ardie laughed. "No. That you've had a couple of bad years. But you're not crazy. Working with your hands and creating something beautiful is the perfect way to relieve stress."

"It is, isn't it? I don't really have any hobbies, and even though I've played sports through the years, it's not enough to keep me busy. To tell the truth, I've never really enjoyed playing them anyway," Marla admitted. "They were just a way to pass time. My husband wanted me to learn to play them, so I did."

"Really? What sports do you play?" Ardie asked, looking interested.

"Golf and tennis. I love to swim, too, but more for fun," Marla said.

Ardie nodded and took a sip of her coffee. "I was never very good at sports. I played a little softball as a teenager, and I enjoyed track and field, but that's it. Plus, between raising children and working, I've never had time to pursue a sport."

Marla took a bite of her pie. "Tell me about your children."

"Oh, they're both grown and out of the house. My daughter, Melanie, just got married last fall and works as a bank teller. My son, Jason, recently finished his college degree in business management. He just moved out to live with friends in a big house. He's still delivering pizza like he did throughout college but has been sending resumes all over. It's a tough job market out there right now for kids fresh out of college."

Marla smiled. "They sound like they're on the right track, though. My daughter is still in college. She's leaning toward becoming a lawyer, so she has a long road ahead of her."

Ardie's brows rose. "Wow. A lawyer. Is your husband a lawyer too? Those professions tend to run in families."

Marla's smile faded. "No. He was a university professor. He taught English literature. But he passed away a few weeks ago after a long illness."

"Oh, I'm so sorry," Ardie said. "That explains your tough couple of years."

"Thank you."

They sat in silence a moment, each sipping the last of their coffee. Finally, Ardie spoke up. "Is that why you're suddenly taking up house remodeling? Because your husband passed away."

Marla slowly nodded. "I hadn't really thought of it that way, but yes, I guess that is why. After caring for him over these past several months, I felt lost after he died. I suppose I'm taking my anger and grief out on the house." She grinned. "Ripping down old wallpaper has been very therapeutic."

Ardie laughed, then covered her mouth with her hand. "Sorry. I shouldn't laugh, but it really can be."

"It's giving me something else to focus on other than my life. Since Nathan died, everything feels off kilter. My whole life had been centered around his circle of friends and acquaintances. But suddenly, I feel like I don't belong in that group any longer."

"I'm sorry," Ardie said, her expression serious. "I've heard that happens sometimes. I'm sure you'll find you have friends who'll stick by you."

Marla shrugged. "Maybe."

They both stood and threw away their cups and paper plates.

"This was fun," Ardie said. She cocked her head as if assessing Marla. "Are you a reader by any chance?"

"I love to read. I haven't read anything current in a long time, but I love the classics."

"Three of my friends and I get together every other week and talk books. Well, to be honest, we talk about a lot of other things too, and complain about our jobs, but we call ourselves a book club." She laughed softly. "Would you be interested in joining our little group?"

Marla was thrilled by her invitation. She hadn't been invited to join anything outside of her old circle of friends since marrying Nathan. It would be fun, meeting new people, especially if they were going to read and discuss new books. "That sounds like fun. I'd love to."

"Great. We're meeting next Thursday at my house. If you give me your phone number, I can text you the address. The book we'll be discussing is *Before We Were Yours* by Lisa Wingate. It's a really good historical fiction novel."

"I can't wait to read it," Marla said. She gave Ardie her phone number and the two walked outside to their cars.

The night air had grown damp, making it feel even colder out. Marla crossed her arms to ward off the chill.

"You know, I never really introduced myself. You only know my nickname. I'm Ardith Halverson. But everyone calls me Ardie."

"I'm Marla Madison," Marla said, then waited a beat to see if Ardie recognized the last name. She was relieved when Ardie didn't react to it.

"Nice to meet you, Marla Madison," Ardie said with a smile. "I'll see you next Thursday. Good luck with your tile project. Maybe you can bring pictures when it's finished."

"Thanks. See you on Thursday."

Marla watched as Ardie drove off then pulled out and headed in the opposite direction toward home. She was happy she'd met Ardie. She seemed like such a decent person. She was looking forward to meeting her friends and also reading the book Ardie said they'd be discussing. Making a few new friends was just what Marla needed to lift her spirits. She couldn't wait for Thursday.

Chapter Seven

Marla

The next morning Marla came downstairs in her work clothes and went into the morning room where she studied the fireplace. It wasn't too large at five feet tall and four feet wide. A mantel made from the same mahogany as the wainscoting sat on top and there was black tile embedded into the wood floor for the hearth. Marla was going to leave the hearth as it was, so she'd have to be careful not to splatter cement or grout on it. She'd also need to protect the woodwork on both sides of the fireplace. But first, she had to pull the mantel off so she could begin her project.

Mrs. Cooper came in with her morning tea just as Marla walked up to the mantel to see how it was attached. "What are you going to ruin today?"

Marla turned, startled, then saw who it was and let out a sigh of relief. "You scared me. Good morning, Mrs. Cooper."

The housekeeper placed the tray with the china teapot and cup on the desk. "Don't tell me you're going to tear out that fireplace."

Marla refrained from rolling her eyes. "No, not exactly. But I am going to spruce it up."

Mrs. Cooper dramatically placed a hand on her chest. "Those bricks have been there for one hundred and fifty years. They're irreplaceable."

Marla smiled. "They're just bricks, Mrs. Cooper. Don't worry. It will look nice when I'm done."

Mrs. Cooper shook her head disapprovingly and left the room.

"Old biddy," Marla said under her breath.

She poured a cup of tea, took a sip, then returned to the mantel. As she studied it, she realized that it must have been varnished many times over the years. On the left side, she noticed there were slim lines about a foot apart. Marla ran her fingers over the lines, puzzling over why they were there. Had someone once pulled the mantel off and broken then repaired it? She decided she'd have to be careful when pulling it off the wall so as not to break it again.

Picking up the crowbar she'd brought in from the garage, she carefully slipped it between the wall and the right side of the mantel. It only took a small tug to pull that side off the wall a few inches. Encouraged by this, she went to the left side and did the same. It took more strength, but when she pulled, it came away from the wall with a splintering sound. Marla grimaced. Had she ruined it?

She inspected the mantel. It looked fine, except the lines she'd seen earlier had split open. Marla sighed. "I guess I can always get it fixed," she said aloud.

Taking ahold of the crowbar again, Marla placed it behind the mantel and pulled hard. The mantel came off and she fell backward onto the rug. She watched in horror as the mantel hit the tile hearth with a thud. A piece broke away and skidded a short distance.

Mrs. Cooper is going to really have a fit.

Marla stared curiously at the broken piece. It wasn't just a chunk of splintered wood. It looked like a small drawer. And sitting inside it was an old journal.

She tried slipping the drawer into the open section of the mantel and it fit perfectly.

"It's a secret hiding place," she said with glee. She couldn't believe that she'd been in this room nearly every day for years and not once had noticed this drawer.

She took the drawer over to her desk and sat down, then lifted out the old journal. It had a brown leather cover and was the size of a teenager's diary. Opening it, she saw a name and date handwritten in neat script on the top of the first page. *Alaina Clara Madison 1876.*

Marla's heart skipped with delight. This had to be an ancestor of Nathan's.

Turning the page, she read the first paragraph written on July 15, 1876:

> *I was happily on my way to becoming a spinster at the age of twenty-one when my father decided it was time I marry. As this is the beginning of a new life for me, on my wedding day, I wish to keep a record of my life for those who come after me.*

"1876," Marla said quietly, stunned by how old this journal was. She carefully flipped through the pages and saw that all of them were filled with writing. She couldn't wait to read it.

Marla glanced at the mantel on the floor, then the drawer on her desk. If Mrs. Cooper saw this, she'd want to know what was in the drawer. Feeling suddenly protective of it, Marla quickly took the drawer over to the mantel and slid it into the spot it had fallen out of. Then she moved the mantel next to the wall. She was sure that Mrs. Cooper wouldn't bother to inspect it.

"Breakfast is ready," Mrs. Cooper announced from the doorway.

Marla nearly jumped out of her skin. *How does she sneak up on me like that?* "Thank you, Mrs. Cooper. I'll be right there."

Mrs. Cooper nodded curtly and left.

Marla picked up the journal to take with her to breakfast, then decided against it. She'd read it tonight after Mrs. Cooper left. She slipped the journal into the side drawer of her desk. There was a small key in the lock, so she turned it then pocketed the key. The journal would be her secret for the time being.

Marla kept busy the rest of the day working on the fireplace. After taping plastic over the surfaces she didn't want to ruin, she went to the garage and mixed the cement compound. She carefully spread a layer over the bricks for an even, smooth finish. Marla smiled to herself as she assessed her work. She was excited to see how the fireplace turned out. But first she'd have to wait overnight for the cement to dry before beginning to tile.

It was nearly dinner time by the time Marla picked up the mess around the fireplace. She'd skipped lunch so she could work, but now she was starving.

Mrs. Cooper had made a light pasta with chicken and a salad. After announcing that dinner was ready, the housekeeper said she'd be leaving for the evening.

"Thank you for making dinner," Marla said, thrilled that for once Mrs. Cooper was leaving early. "I hope you have a nice weekend."

Mrs. Cooper nodded, then slipped on her coat and left. Marla knew the older woman hated having the entire weekend off. But Marla had insisted upon it not long after Nathan had become ill. She'd had enough on her plate caring for Nathan. The last thing she'd needed was an opinionated housekeeper criticizing her every move. Now, she was glad she'd instituted the change. Marla had a whole weekend to herself without interference from Mrs. Cooper.

Thrilled to be alone, Marla walked through the quiet house to her morning room, retrieved the journal, and went back into the kitchen. After serving up her food, Marla opened the journal and began to reread what she'd started that afternoon.

July 15th, 1876

I was happily on my way to becoming a spinster at the age of twenty-one when my father decided it was time I marry. As this is the beginning of a new life for me, on my wedding day, I wish to keep a record of my life for those who come after me.

My mother passed away when I was a young girl of ten and my father did his best to raise me alone. Between nannies and governesses, I was raised to be a lady as well as educated, so by the time I was sixteen, I took over running my father's house. Not that he asked me to. I slowly took over duties until one day I was the one to give orders to our housekeeper and cook and all other duties that befall the woman of the house, including keeping the household accounts. I love working with numbers and am very good at it. My father saw my potential and eventually allowed me to help with his business bookkeeping as well. As a child, and even as an adult, I enjoyed nothing more than spending time at my father's textile factory and discussing business with him in the evenings at home. It made me feel useful, and he always listened to my ideas with interest and respect.

And then the day came when he realized I was twenty-one years old and not married, and everything changed.

Chapter Eight

Alaina

May 1875

Alaina Carlton sat at her father's large mahogany desk in the library perusing the income and expense ledgers for his business, Carlton Textiles. It was late afternoon and the cool spring air drifted in through the open window, sweeping away the stale smell from months of being closed up. Winters in Minnesota were long and cold, and after months of fireplaces burning to heat rooms and her father's cigars, Aliana was pleased to have the windows open again.

"There she is, toiling away at numbers again," Alaina's father, Arthur, said as he entered the room. "You must have a slave-master for a boss." He grinned at her mischievously.

Alaina smiled up at her father as she brushed aside an errant strand of her chestnut hair. He had just returned from his office at the textile factory and was wearing his typical three-piece suit, a gold watch chain stretched across his ample mid-section. His brown hair and neatly trimmed beard were salted with gray, but behind his spectacles his eyes still sparkled with humor and warmth as he looked at his daughter.

"I'm finishing entering the last of the paid invoices for the month," she told him. "And it's hardly work to me. You know I enjoy helping you with the business, especially the ledgers."

Arthur sat in one of the hunter green padded chairs across from the desk. "Please tell me that you had a little fun today. Did you have lunch with your friend Hannah?"

"No. She had to cancel, unfortunately. Her little boy had a cough and she was worried about leaving him alone with the new nanny. I had a nice lunch with Margaret and Emma instead and we discussed the menu for next week and spring cleaning for the house." Margaret Haas was their long-time housekeeper and cook and Emma McClellen was the young woman who helped clean and acted as a lady's maid for Alaina. She much preferred the company of their down-to-earth employees to that of the society ladies she occasionally attended church fundraisers or had tea with.

Arthur chuckled. "You find a great deal of pleasure in work, don't you?"

Alaina carefully closed the heavy ledger and set aside her fountain pen. She rose and smoothed out her skirt, then walked around the desk and gave her father a kiss on the cheek. "I like keeping busy. And I don't mind at all helping you with the book-keeping." She headed to the liquor cabinet, her skirts swishing over the paisley rug as she moved. "Would you like your usual whisky and water before dinner?"

Arthur stood and walked to the settee. "Yes. Thank you, dear."

Alaina brought his glass to him. She'd poured herself a small glass of sherry, also. She sat in the burgundy velvet chair opposite her father. Alaina enjoyed this time of day with him, as they sat, relaxed, and talked about his work, her day, or the most recent book either of them had been reading. Her father had raised her to be an independent-thinking woman and respected her opinions. She knew that most men did not subscribe to the idea that woman were intelligent, but her father thought differently. He proudly bragged how smart and hard-working her mother had been, and how Alaina was just like her. Alaina had adored her mother and loved being compared to her.

"I've been thinking," Arthur said after taking a sip of his drink.

Alaina's brows rose as she waited for her father to continue.

"I think we should have a dinner party."

"A dinner party?" She gaped at her father, completely surprised. "We've never had one before. Other than inviting the factory manager and his wife over for dinner. Or Hannah and her husband."

"That's why we should have one," he said. "It's time we do a little entertaining. We have this nice, new house and we should show it off."

"We've lived here for four years, Father, and you've never once mentioned you wanted to entertain guests." For years she and her father had lived in a rented house closer to his business in downtown St. Paul, but as the factory had prospered, Arthur had decided to build in a nicer neighborhood away from downtown. He'd bought a good-sized lot in an up-and-coming neighborhood on Laurel Avenue and built a three-story Victorian home. Many prosperous businessmen had followed suit and new houses were sprouting up every year.

"That's even more reason to have a party. It's been too long since either of us has had some fun."

Alaina stared at her father as if he'd lost his mind. He was a man who enjoyed solitude when not at work. His idea of a nice evening was sitting by the fire, reading a book. And she felt the same as he did. They attended church once a week and social gatherings a few times a year when necessary, but no more then they had to. After her coming out year at age seventeen, attending dances, balls, teas, and dinner parties for weeks on end, Alaina was through with endless parties. She liked her quiet life, her work, and running the house.

Alaina decided to humor her father. "Who were you thinking of inviting to this dinner party?"

Arthur stared at the ceiling a moment, contemplating this question. "Well, we should invite your friend Hannah and her husband Matthew, and of course, my factory manager Jerome Campbell and his lovely wife, Lisa." He drew his brows together, pondering some more. "Ah! Our new neighbors, the Garveys. We should definitely invite them to become better acquainted with them."

"Is that all?" Alaina asked, slightly amused. To her, it sounded like her father was making this all up as he went along.

"Well, I was also thinking about inviting one of my best customers, Mr. Madison of Madison's Department Stores. I was just speaking with him the other day, and I think it would be good for business if we extend a warm invitation to him."

Alaina's brows rose again. "Will we also be inviting Mrs. Madison?"

Her father looked confused. "His mother? No. I've never met her."

"Father. I meant his wife. Is Mr. Madison married?"

Arthur looked a bit sheepish. "Oh. Uh, no. He isn't."

"What is this really all about?" Alaina asked, looking

suspiciously at her father. "You aren't playing matchmaker, are you?"

Arthur took a sip of his whiskey then set it on the glass-topped table between them. The Grandfather clock across the room ticked loudly in the ensuing silence. "No. Not entirely, dear," he finally said. "Mr. Madison mentioned he'd met you at the Christmas Ball last year and was intrigued by you. He seems to be a gentleman and is also very wealthy. I simply thought it might be nice to introduce you two properly. And what better way than a small dinner party?"

Alaina sat back in her seat and studied her father. Ever since her coming out year, he hadn't pressed her on finding a husband. And since she hadn't met any promising contenders, she'd been happy to let it be. She knew her father would never even consider a man for her unless he thought him worthy. Obviously, he thought highly of Mr. Madison.

The door opened and Margaret announced it was dinnertime. Arthur stood and offered his arm to his daughter, as he did every evening, and they walked into the dining room together.

* * *

Two days later, Alaina strode purposefully down the sidewalk toward her friend's house which was only two blocks away. The sun was shining, but the spring air was crisp and numbed her cheeks. She wore a cream skirt with gray vertical stripes and a matching jacket that hung long and narrow past her hips. Her blouse was cream colored with no ruffles or bows. Alaina liked simple attire and detested the embellishments that were so popular these days: ribbons, bows, and lace. She was also happy she'd had this skirt made wider at the bottom than fashion dictated, otherwise walking any distance at all would be miserable.

She turned on Holly Avenue and saw her friend's cheery Victorian home up ahead. Stepping up on the front porch that boasted decorative railing spindles and gingerbread trim, Alaina lifted her gloved hand to use the gold knocker and announce her arrival. Within mere seconds, Hannah Anderson answered, looking beautiful but flustered with little Michael in her arms.

"Alaina! How nice to see you. Come in. I had no idea you were coming by today," Hannah said, brushing away a loose strand of blond hair with her free hand.

"I'm sorry to burst in on you, dear," Alaina said, stepping inside and closing the door softly. "But I had to talk to someone before I burst."

"It's not a problem. Let me find nanny and I'll have Mrs. Harper prepare tea for us. Please come in and make yourself comfortable."

Alaina watched as her friend walked away, little Michael waving at her from his mother's arms. The toddler was adorable and looked to be feeling better since the other day. Alaina smiled. When she and Hannah had come out at age seventeen, she'd have never imagined her friend falling so quickly for a man and having a family in such a short time. But here she was with a two-year-old son, a husband, and her own house to manage.

As Alaina sat on the settee in the parlor and pulled off her gloves, she caught sight of a photograph of Hannah and Matthew on the mantel, and it warmed her heart. Hannah was the complete opposite of Alaina—a short, petite, pale blonde with soft blue eyes. Her skin was creamy white and her structure was delicate, whereas Alaina was tall, slender, but sturdily built with straight chestnut hair and dark brown eyes. Two opposites who met in Bible study classes at the church when they were twelve years old and had become fast friends. Alaina and her father had just moved to the St. Paul area where he'd planned on starting his new business. With her mother gone and their living in a new town, Alaina had felt alone even with the new governess her father had hired. But once she'd met Hannah, she felt at home and had been sharing confidences with her ever since.

Hannah swept into the room with Mrs. Harper trailing behind her carrying a tray of tea and biscuits. "Here we are," she said merrily, sitting down across from Alaina in a rose-colored tufted chair. "Thank you, Mrs. Harper. I'll pour the tea."

Mrs. Harper nodded and left the room.

Hannah looked up at Alaina with tired eyes. "Michael has settled down now. I hope he takes a nap. He isn't feeling well and insists on having his mommy all the time." She began pouring the tea, adding sugar into Alaina's cup just the way she liked it.

"I'm sorry he still isn't feeling well. I hope he's better soon," Alaina said, feeling guilty now for barging into her friend's house. Her own problems were nothing compared to a sick child.

"Thank you, dear. I'm sure he will. And I'm happy for the distraction." Hannah sipped her tea and sat back in the chair, looking weary.

Alaina opened her reticule, pulled out a powder-blue envelope, then handed it to Hannah. "It appears we are now having dinner parties, and you and Matthew are invited."

Her friend stared at her in surprise. "A dinner party? Since when do you entertain?"

"Since father has decided to play matchmaker," Alaina said with disgust. "I hope you can attend. It's the Saturday of the twenty-second. We're only inviting a small group and I desperately need you there for support."

Hannah gave her a small smile. "I thought your father had

given up on trying to marry you off. Who does he have in mind?"

Alaina sighed. "A Mr. Nathaniel Madison. He's older than we are, so you probably don't know him."

Hannah's eyes grew wide. "Mr. Madison? The owner of Madison's Department Stores?"

Alaina nodded.

"Of course I've heard of him. He's quite prosperous, you know. He banks at my husband's place of employment. Everyone knows who he is."

"Apparently, I met him at last year's Christmas Ball, and we danced. I hardly remember him. He does business with my father and I guess he mentioned that he was quite intrigued by me."

Hannah's eyes twinkled as she sat forward. "Isn't that exciting? He's quite the eligible bachelor. How lucky you are that he's interested in you."

Alaina set down her teacup. "Am I? Lucky? I like my life as it is right now. I have the freedom to do as I want and I'm allowed to work for my father, which I enjoy. Marriage can be… so sorry to say it, dear, since I know you're happily married, but it's confining."

"It depends upon the marriage and your partner," Hannah said gently. "Don't you want to marry, Alaina? Didn't you dream of someday marrying a handsome man and having a family of your own?"

"Am I so strange that I never did? I mean, I guess I always thought it would be lovely to fall in love with a nice man, but except for you and Matthew, and my parents, of course, I've yet to see a relationship where the woman is treated equally by her husband. I don't want someone to tell me what to do and how to do it. Is that selfish of me?"

"Of course not." Hannah stood and went over to sit next to Alaina on the settee. Taking her hand, she continued, "You just haven't met the right man. Maybe when you do, your ideas about marriage will change. Matthew and I are very happy. Of course, I'm often tired from running the household, managing the small staff, and taking care of Michael. But I wouldn't want to go back to being single, living with my parents."

Alaina smiled and patted her friend's hand. "I know you have a happy life. The problem is, my father has spoiled me. I feel I have a happy life the way it is. Maybe it could be better, as you say, when I find the right man."

They sipped their tea again, each nibbling on a biscuit. When Hannah sighed, Alaina studied her. She really did look weary, her beautiful face drawn and her eyes dull.

"Are you feeling ill?" Alaina asked. "You look so tired."

"I am very tired," Hannah said, then glanced around to make sure no one was within earshot. "I believe I'm expecting again," she whispered to her friend.

Alaina's eyes widened. "So soon?"

"Well, Michael is two years old," Hannah said, defensively.

"Oh, dear, I didn't mean it that way. I'm just surprised. Of course I'm happy for you. How long have you known?"

"Just a while. I think it's been two months. I haven't even told Matthew yet, so please keep it a secret. I wanted to make sure before I said anything. But the way I feel every morning will surely give me away soon."

Alaina held her friend's hand. "I'm sorry you're not feeling well. And here I am, whining about a dinner party. I hope you'll feel well enough to come. If not, I certainly would understand."

Hannah glanced up at her. "Oh, don't you worry. I wouldn't miss meeting Mr. Madison no matter how sick I feel. This is going to be fun." Her eyes twinkled mischievously.

Alaina rolled her eyes. "You can be evil when you want to be, can't you?"

Hannah just grinned and took another bite of her biscuit.

* * *

he day of the dinner party, Alaina bustled about helping with various chores while Emma polished the silverware and Margaret baked and cooked all day. The table was set elegantly with their best china and crystal and everything in the house was polished and shined to perfection. By late afternoon, all that was left to do was for Emma to help Alaina dress before the guests arrived.

Despite her father's offer, Alaina had refused to have a new dress made for the occasion. She wasn't going to waste her father's hard-earned money on some fancy frock that she'd rarely wear. She had plenty of nice dresses from her coming out year that still fit her and had been updated to conform with the latest fashions.

She chose a deep yellow satin dress with silk overlay that had stripes in yellow-gold thread running down the front and the fitted bodice. The overskirt gathered up in back, creating a bustle effect without actually wearing one underneath. The neckline scooped lower than her day dresses and cap sleeves rounded slightly over her arms. When Emma tied her corset, Alaina insisted it not be cinched too tightly. She couldn't care less what Mr. Madison thought of her waist size or if her bust didn't spill over unnaturally. She wanted to be comfortable when she sat and was definitely going to eat the delicious food that Margaret had prepared.

Emma combed Alaina's hair back and left enough strands loose to curl with a hot iron. Soft tendrils touched her neck and forehead. At the last minute, Alaina had her place a delicate comb with a small, diamond encrusted butterfly at the back of her hair. It had belonged to her mother, a gift from her father, and Alaina felt comforted to be including her mother in this evening.

Exactly at seven, Alaina and her father stood at the entrance to the parlor and greeted their guests. Hannah and Matthew arrived first, then Harold and Mildred Garvey arrived, bringing with them an expensive bottle of red wine as a gift. The couple had recently built a house next door. Harold had made his fortune in lumber first in Michigan, then in northern Minnesota. He'd sold out his shares and was enjoying a quieter life in his middle age.

The couples retired to the parlor and soon Arthur's factory manager, Jerome Campbell, and his wife Lisa, joined them. Last to appear at the door was Nathaniel Madison. He was dressed in a three-piece suit, the jacket long and narrow, and carried an expensive bottle of brandy.

"I hope I haven't arrived late," he said, bowing over Alaina's hand. "It was such a lovely evening, I decided to walk here and didn't realize how time had escaped me."

"You're right on time," Arthur said, shaking Nathaniel's hand. "Please. Come join us in the parlor. If we're lucky, perhaps we can persuade my daughter to play the piano for us."

"Oh, Father," Alaina said, suddenly alarmed. "Let's not force my terrible music abilities on our guests."

Arthur laughed. "Darling, you know you play just as lovely as your mother did." He allowed Alaina to walk ahead of him as the two men followed her inside.

The couples mingled over wine and hor d'oeuvres. Hannah

graciously offered to play a tune on the piano, much to Alaina's relief, since she was much more accomplished at playing. Alaina thought her friend looked beautiful in her soft blue watered silk gown that showed off her porcelain skin and bright blue eyes. The Garvey's were a friendly older couple, and Harold had a mischievous sense of humor although he was careful to remain proper in the ladies' presence.

Emma announced that dinner was ready, and the couples paired off to enter the dining room. Mr. Madison offered Alaina his arm.

"May I escort you?" he asked in his rich, deep voice.

"Of course." She was surprised at how much taller he was than her. Alaina was tall compared to the average woman, so it was nice walking beside a man who wouldn't be intimidated by her height.

At dinner, Alaina was certain her father had changed the seating order. Arthur was at the head of the table with Alaina on his right, and much to her surprise, Mr. Madison sat beside her. Earlier, Alaina had changed the name cards so he sat across from her, but someone must have moved them. She glanced sideways at her father, who pretended she wasn't looking his way and turned to speak to Hannah on his left.

Thankfully, Mr. Madison didn't say anything directly to Alaina throughout the many courses of food. Talk was light around the table, keeping to subjects such as concerts they had attended, church functions, and last year's round of winter balls.

"I've been asked to host the first ball of the summer season this year," Mr. Madison said to the group. "I could hardly turn it down. It's for such a good cause. I will be certain that you are all included on the guest list."

"What charity is being supported this year?" Alaina asked.

She was surprised she hadn't heard from friends about this year's ball.

"One that gives support to workers who have been injured while working and can no longer earn a living. I feel very blessed to have the style of living that I do, as I'm sure everyone at this table feels also, that helping those less fortunate is a worthy endeavor."

"I agree," Harold said. "I've known many men who've lost their livelihood working as loggers for my former company, and while we did what we could to help them, I'm happy to hear there are other charities available that want to help."

"Yes. I know the accidents in factories such as my own can be terrible," Arthur agreed. "As much as we try to be aware of safety, mistakes happen, unfortunately."

Alaina nodded. She knew her father felt responsible every time a worker was injured. He'd even created a fund so that if someone had an accident and was out of work temporarily or permanently, he could subsidize their income for at least a short time.

"It sounds like a worthy cause," Alaina said. "I'm sure we would all like to attend and support it."

Mr. Madison smiled over at Alaina but said nothing more.

After dinner, the men retired to the library for cigars and brandy while the ladies enjoyed tea and cakes in the parlor. Alaina sat back in her chair, pleased that the party had gone well. The food had been perfect, and she'd enjoyed getting to know Mildred better, and always liked to spend time with Lisa and Hannah. But deep down inside, it gnawed at her that the ladies had to sit apart from the men after dinner. Alaina would have preferred listening to the men discuss their work, politics, and the economy instead of talk of the latest fashions that the women were discussing now.

Alaina thoughts turned to Mr. Madison and how solicitous he'd been to her all evening. She had to admit he was a handsome man. His thick, wavy dark hair was neatly cut, and she liked that in this era when most men wore facial hair, he chose to be clean shaven. She'd also noticed how kind his deep brown eyes were. But what she'd appreciated the most about him was how polite and interested he'd appeared during the dinner conversation. He didn't appear to be arrogant in any way, despite the fact that he'd been the richest man at the table. That quality impressed her.

As much as Alaina hated to admit it, her father might have been right about this man. He did intrigue her.

As the evening came to a close, the men joined the ladies in the parlor for more small talk, and soon the guests took their leave.

"I had a delightful time," Mildred told Alaina and looked very sincere about it. "I feel fortunate to have such pleasant neighbors. We must do this again very soon. I'll host next time," she offered.

Alaina and her father said their goodbyes to the Garveys, then to Hannah and Matthew directly after that. Alaina thought Hannah looked tired and gave her a warm hug before she left.

"Thank you for coming," she whispered in her friend's ear. "I hope you will be able to rest well tonight."

"I'm glad I didn't miss it." Hannah gave her a smug grin. "I have a feeling that Mr. Madison left an impression on you."

Alaina smiled. "We will see."

Soon the Campbells departed leaving Mr. Madison as the last one to put on his coat and hat.

"I had a wonderful time tonight," he said, once again bowing over Alaina's hand. "Delicious food and interesting company go so well together." He smiled at Alaina and his eyes brightened. "I do so hope you both will attend the June Ball."

"Oh, I'm sure we won't want to miss it," Arthur said, grinning.

With another small smile, Mr. Madison took his leave.

Once the door was closed and the gas lights were distinguished, Arthur and Alaina walked side-by-side up the wide staircase. Margaret and Emma had already left for the evening.

"Well. It wasn't such a bad idea, having a dinner party after all," Arthur said.

Alaina laughed softly. "I had a very good time. But please don't read too much into that, Father. Mr. Madison seems like a nice man, but that's all."

"We'll see," Arthur said. He kissed her on the cheek at her bedroom door and turned to walk to his own room. "We'll certainly see," he said again softly.

Alaina shook her head at her father's words. He was so determined that she fall in love with Mr. Madison. As she entered her room, she allowed herself to think that maybe it wouldn't be so terrible an idea after all.

Chapter Nine

Marla

Marla bookmarked the last page she'd read then gently closed the antique journal. She was completely entranced by Alaina's story. Looking up at the clock, she couldn't believe it was well past one in the morning. She had moved to the sofa while she was reading and now stood and stretched. She would have loved to sit and read Alaina's story all night but knew she shouldn't. Tomorrow would come soon enough.

Marla placed her dinner plate and glass in the dishwasher then began walking through the house, turning off lights. When she went into the morning room to lock away the journal, she gazed around the room. Alaina had lived in this house at some point. Considering the date that she married, she was most likely the first Mrs. Madison to live here. And she had used this very room as her own, just as Marla did.

All the years that Marla had lived here, she hadn't given much thought to the women who'd come before her. Nathan's parents had passed away before she'd met him and he hadn't talked much about his mother, or any of his relatives, so she hadn't pressed him. But since the house was built in 1885, there had been many couples who'd lived here—all Madisons.

It occurred to Marla that she and Alaina had another thing in common. Even though they'd lived over one hundred and forty years apart, they had both married men named Nathaniel Madison. That thought made chills prickle down her spine, but in a good way.

As Marla slipped into bed, in the same room that Alaina most likely used as mistress of the house, she couldn't help but compare herself to her. Alaina had appeared to be a strong, independent woman, even in a time when women were dominated by men. Her father had given her the education and leeway to be her own person. Marla had been like that before meeting Nathan. She'd worked her way through college, with help from her mother, who'd raised her all alone. And Marla had been working in finance when she'd met Nathan. Everything had changed when she married Nathan, and even though he'd given her a good life, she had often wondered if her life could have been different. She could have insisted on working, despite his old-fashioned ideas and the fact that they didn't really need the income. She could have said no to many things, but at the time, she'd thought she was being a good wife. But did she cheat herself out of a fuller life in the long run?

Marla was curious how Alaina's story unfolded. She was certainly going to continue reading her journal to find out.

* * *

Over the next few days, Marla was too busy to pick up the journal again. All weekend she worked diligently on placing the tiles carefully on the fireplace, so it looked professionally done. She

worked days on her project and the evenings were spent reading Ardie's book club selection and taking notes to discuss at
the get-together. Marla enjoyed the book immensely—it was the
first in over twenty years that wasn't a classic or biography. Their
home library was full of wonderful literature, textbooks, biographies, and antique encyclopedias. Being an English professor,
Nathan had felt that the only books anyone should read were
the classics. Marla had never challenged him on that—it was
just another of his eccentricities that she'd found cute at first,
then a little annoying as time went on. It hadn't been worth
arguing about, though. But on Saturday night, for the first time
in her life, Marla opened an Amazon account and downloaded
the book on her iPad. It had been strange but exciting to read a
book this way, and she loved the flexibility of being able to buy
and download a book any time of the day and night.

By Monday, Marla had all the tile placed and on Tuesday she
began to grout. She spent time in the garage with the mantel,
too, adding a new coat of varnish. She'd decided to leave the
drawer loose so it could open and close. She loved the uniqueness
of it and didn't want to varnish it shut.

When she was finally finished with her project on Wednesday, Marla stood back and assessed her work. She loved how
elegant the creamy basket weave tile looked against the dark
wainscoting. The newly refinished mantel topped it perfectly.
She couldn't help but wonder what Alaina would have thought
of her handiwork, changing this room after all these decades.

On Thursday morning, Mrs. Cooper gave it the once-over
when she came in with Marla's tea.

"What do you think?" Marla asked, trying not to smirk
because she was sure the older woman wouldn't like it.

"It looks better than I had anticipated," Mrs. Cooper

admitted. "But I still think it's a shame to ruin the old bricks just because you wanted to change things in here."

"I'm sure you do," Marla said, smiling. "But I love it."

Marla told Mrs. Cooper that she wouldn't be home for dinner that evening and that she was free to leave early. When the housekeeper raised an eyebrow in question, Marla ignored her. She didn't have to explain her comings and goings to her.

That evening, Marla dressed carefully, trying not to appear overdressed but not wanting to insult Ardie by looking too casual. Years of being scrutinized by the women at the club had made Marla self-conscious about the way she dressed. Marla had always found it all so silly and petty, but had followed along with it anyway. She doubted that Ardie and her friends would judge her for her clothing, but she really wanted to fit in. She decided on black dress slacks and a red, short-sleeved sweater and hoped it was the right choice.

Marla drove the half-hour toward a nice neighborhood close to St. Paul and followed the directions on her phone. The day had been sunny, but the temperature was still cool. It was nice that the days were finally getting longer, and summer was on its way. At last, her phone told her she'd arrived and Marla pulled up in front of a 1980s split level house painted dark green with brown trim. There were mature oaks and pines in the front yard and what looked like flower gardens along the front of the house that were waiting to be planted. She liked how warm and welcoming the house looked.

Another car pulled up behind hers as she was getting out. She smiled at the neatly-dressed woman who stepped out of the car, not sure if she was a member of the book club or not.

"Hi," the woman said, a confident spring in her step. "Are you our new book club member that Ardie recruited?"

"Yes, I am." Marla liked this woman immediately. She was tall and slender wearing tan slacks and heels and a brown and tan plaid wrap around her shoulders. Her black hair was cut very short and her skin was a smooth, creamy brown. "I'm Marla Madison." She offered the woman her hand in greeting.

"Toni Moore," she said, shaking her hand. "It's about time we have a fresh face in our group. Let's go inside."

Marla followed Toni up the sidewalk and after giving the door two solid raps, Toni opened it and they walked in. "We're here," she called.

"Come upstairs. I'm just putting out the food," Ardie said.

Toni slipped off her wrap and hung it on an empty hook in the entryway. Marla followed suit with her jacket. They went up the short staircase and through the living room to the kitchen.

"It smells wonderful in here," Toni said. "What did you cook?"

"Hi, ladies." Ardie smiled. "I didn't go to too much trouble. Just tortilla chips and guacamole dip, some beef dip with beans, a cheese and cracker tray, and brownies for dessert."

"Sounds good," Marla said. She glanced around Ardie's kitchen. It was newly remodeled with dark brown cabinets, white granite countertops, and gleaming wood flooring. The flooring ran throughout the kitchen, dining room, and living room with plush rugs laid under the table and in front of the brick fireplace in the living room. The house had plenty of room yet felt cozy.

"The benefits of working at a home remodeling store," Ardie told Marla with a wink. "The discount really helps."

Marla felt her face flush at having been caught studying the house. "You have a beautiful home."

"Thanks. I'll give you the grand tour in a bit. What would you ladies like to drink?"

No sooner had she poured white wine for each of them than the other two came in the front door, hollering up the staircase that they were there. A slender woman with dark blond hair wearing a nurse's uniform walked into the kitchen carrying a tray of vegetables and dip. Behind her was a shorter woman with deep red curly hair cut short, wearing a colorful tunic and blue jeans.

"This is Wanda Graves and Rita Plummer," Ardie told Marla. "Wanda is a school nurse, thus the uniform, and Rita is an artist. She paints beautiful watercolors. Ladies, this is our newest member, Marla."

"Hi, Marla," both ladies said in unison, then laughed.

"It's nice to meet you both," Marla told them. They were a varying array of women and Marla really was excited to meet them all. After two decades of socializing with the same group of people, it was fun meeting women who seemed so down to earth.

"Let's eat first," Ardie said. "Don't be shy. Grab a plate and dig in."

They all did and sat at the dining room table catching up while they ate.

"Where is you husband tonight?" Wanda asked Ardie. "Did you kick him out or is he hiding in the lower level, watching television?"

"Dan's having dinner and a couple of beers with the guys from his crew," Ardie said. "It doesn't take much arm twisting to get him out of the house."

"It took an injunction to get my husband out of the house," Wanda said, then laughed. "I wasn't going to let him get the house when he was the one who left me."

Ardie turned to Marla. "Wanda is divorced, as you could guess. But she isn't bitter at all." Her eyes twinkled.

"No. Not in the least," Wanda said with a smirk.

"Do you work in an elementary or high school?" Marla asked Wanda.

"At a grade school here in the area. I used to work in a hospital, but the school hours were better for me after the divorce. My daughter is seventeen now, but when she was younger, it was nice getting off early each day."

"What about you, Marla? Do you work?" Rita asked. All eyes turned to Marla.

"No. Not really. I had a job in finance before I married years ago, but after that I stayed home with my daughter. I've done a lot of volunteer work through the years, though." Marla suddenly wondered how that sounded to these women who all worked for a living. Did she sound shallow? Spoiled? She hoped not.

"I think that's great," Toni piped up. "I wish I could offer my time at organizations, but I work too many hours."

"What do you do?" Marla asked.

"I'm a real estate agent. I show houses nights and weekends quite often, so I don't have much time for anything else."

"Or for *anyone* else," Rita said with a sly grin. "Toni is a single gal. Do you know any eligible bachelors for her, Marla? We've been trying to marry her off for years." All the ladies laughed.

"I'll keep my eyes open." Marla joined in on their laughter.

"Lord no! The last thing I need is a man who wants me to cook and clean for him. I like my life just as it is, thank you," Toni said.

After they'd eaten, Ardie told them to leave the dishes in the kitchen and she'd deal with them later. They all went into the living room and got comfortable, each with a fresh glass of wine.

"So, who actually read the book this time?" Ardie asked once everyone had either their Kindle, iPad, or paperback out.

"Oh, I enjoyed it very much," Marla said, feeling comfortable enough now around the ladies to speak up. She opened her iPad case and pulled out three sheets of notes. They all stared at her in wonder.

"You took notes?" Wanda asked.

Marla's self-confidence deflated. "Uh, yes, I did. I just wanted to remember some of the main points, themes, and such." She glanced around the group nervously.

"We finally have a serious reader in our group," Ardie said, eyeing the other women. "Isn't that refreshing?"

"I didn't even finish the book," Rita said sheepishly. "Not that it wasn't good, because it was. But I was so caught up in my latest artwork that time just buzzed by me."

"I only got half-way through," Toni admitted. "It's definitely a good story, but I was showing houses nearly every night these past two weeks."

Marla glanced up at Ardie and saw the disappointed look on her face. She guessed Ardie was embarassed by her friends' lack of enthusiasm after inviting Marla to join.

"I guess I went a little overboard about reading this story," Marla said. "I haven't read a new novel in years, and this is the very first time I've ever bought one online. I'm sure that sounds strange, but my husband had been an English Literature professor and he didn't believe anything good had been written since Fitzgerald."

Wanda's eyebrows rose. "As in F. Scott? Wow, that was a long time ago. What did you read all these years?"

"The classics. Biographies. True-life stories. My husband's library is full of great literature."

"Marla's husband passed away recently," Ardie added gently. "She's been exploring new things in her life. We actually met at the store because she'd decided to do some remodeling in their hundred-year-old house."

"Oh, I'm so sorry," the other three women said in unison, looking wide-eyed.

"Thank you." Marla suddenly felt awkward.

"You own a hundred-year-old house?" Toni asked. "Has it been kept up well and where is it located?"

Ardie laughed and the tension in the room dissipated. "There's no hiding what Toni does for a living."

The group talked a while, a little about the book, but mostly more about what was going on in their lives. Marla relaxed again and enjoyed listening to the women, adding a little to the conversation herself. She felt relaxed around these women, as if she'd known them for years. They weren't competitive with each other and truly enjoyed each other's company. Marla found that refreshing.

As the evening grew late, the women began to yawn. "I think it's time for me to leave," Wanda said. "I'd better go home and make sure Miley isn't getting into any trouble."

"Yes. And I have to show a group of houses early tomorrow," Toni said.

"Let's pick our book for next time and decide where to meet," Ardie said. "Who wants to host the next meeting?"

Toni looked up at Marla. "If we haven't scared you away, I vote for your house. I really do want to see it. I love historic homes."

Marla took a breath. She wanted to have the ladies over, but did she dare? Once they saw her house, there was no hiding her financial status and she was afraid they'd act differently after that. "Well, I'd love to have you all there," she finally said.

Ardie seemed to pick up on her discomfort. "We shouldn't

pressure Marla so soon. Let's give her a chance to get used to us first."

"I'd like to see your house, too," Rita said hopefully. "I mean, if you don't mind."

Marla liked this group of women. They'd find out sooner or later where she lived. It might as well be sooner. She smiled. "I'd love to have you all over. I'll get your phone numbers and text the address to all of you."

"That's wonderful," Ardie said. "Your house, your pick for the next book."

Marla thought a moment. "I saw one online that I thought might be good. Have any of you read *Sold on a Monday* yet? It looks interesting."

They all agreed and soon everyone had said goodbye and left, leaving Marla and Ardie alone.

"Sorry you got roped into having the next meeting," Ardie said. "I hope it's okay."

"It's fine. I'm sure it'll be fun. Let me help you clean up the kitchen."

Ardie and Marla talked about tiling the fireplace while they rinsed and stacked the dishwasher.

"What project are you going to work on next?" Ardie asked.

Marla paused. She hadn't thought about it yet. "I'm not sure. There's more painting that could be done. I'd really like to lighten the entire place up. I'm sure I'll be visiting you in the store soon."

After Marla waved goodbye, she thought about how the evening had gone as she drove the thirty minutes home. She'd had such a good time. She couldn't remember when she'd enjoyed sitting around talking to women her own age as much as she had tonight. She'd thought she'd been close to her friends from the yacht club, but their friendship was nothing like the closeness she saw in the group tonight. This group of working women were so different from the entitled women at the club. It made Marla feel like she'd frittered her life away, accomplishing nothing. Sure, she'd raised her daughter and she'd helped raise money for worthy causes throughout the years, but other than that, she'd never felt she'd achieved much. It made her sad. Here she was at forty-six years old, feeling like a failure.

"You're not dead yet," she told herself firmly. "There's still time."

But, time to do what?

When she arrived home, Marla went into the morning room and studied the fireplace. The grout had dried, and it looked beautiful. A small feeling of accomplishment swelled inside her.

Heading upstairs and walking down the long, dark hallway, Marla cringed. She remembered the day Nathan died—just mere weeks ago—and how she'd walked down this hall, despising it. The lighting was poor, and the wainscoting, while beautiful wood, was shoulder height with ghastly wallpaper in a paisley pattern above it. She'd never even think about touching the original woodwork, but the wallpaper just had to go.

Marla smiled to herself. She'd found her next project.

Feeling happier, she turned into her now cheerier bedroom and readied for bed.

Chapter Ten

Marla

The next day, after downloading the new book for their next meeting and assessing the hallway in the daylight, Marla headed out to see Ardie at the store.

"That was quick," Ardie said, smiling when she saw Marla. "I guess you've figured out your next project."

"Yes, I have. I have this incredibly long and dark hallway upstairs that I've hated forever. I'm going to rip off the wallpaper and paint it. I was thinking about a textured paint or would I have to texture the walls? I'm not sure how to do that."

Ardie showed her the choices from easy to more difficult. As they were looking over the different ways to texture, she brought up the night before. "Are you sure you're okay with hosting the next book club meeting? I feel you were pushed into it."

Marla shook her head. "No, I'm fine with it. I really enjoyed last night. I'd like to get to know everyone better."

"I heard from Rita this morning. She was really impressed by you. And Wanda liked you too. Both are excited to see your house."

Marla was still uncertain about the women seeing her house, but she figured they'd find out eventually. She just hoped they'd still embrace her as a friend once they realized she had money. That wasn't always the case, unfortunately, as Marla well knew.

"I'm glad they all want to come. I'm looking forward to it," she said, hoping she sounded sincere.

Marla decided on a light texture using a thicker paint and special paint rollers. She bought two gallons of a soft dove gray color. She also bought a couple of gallons of wallpaper remover and another scraper. "I still have all the wallpaper to rip off first," she said, rolling her eyes.

Once she returned home, Marla ate the lunch Mrs. Cooper had made then changed into her work clothes. She didn't say anything to Mrs. Cooper about pulling down the old wallpaper. The older woman would just cringe and glare anyway. Grabbing the tools she needed, a roll of plastic to cover the floor, buckets for water, and plenty of sponges and rags, she headed upstairs.

Standing at the beginning of the long hallway, Marla stared at the ancient wallpaper. It was yellowed and peeled up in some spots. Looking at how old and tired it was, she felt better about tearing it down. "This *is* my house now," she said aloud. "I can do as I please." She wondered if Alaina had picked out this awful wallpaper, or if some designer had. Of what little she knew of the previous Mrs. Madison, she doubted Alaina would have chosen such a busy pattern. *Maybe she says something about it in her journal,* she thought.

Taking a deep breath, Marla picked at a curled-up corner of paper, pulled slowly, and ripped off a huge section of the dry paper. Just like before, it felt liberating to tear the ugly paper down. With zest, she began peeling it off, excited about starting another new beginning.

Two hours later, Marla was knee-deep in wallpaper and about a third of the way down one side of the hall. She had all the bedroom doors open to let in natural light.

"I should have known," a judgmental voice said behind Marla. She didn't have to turn around to recognize it was Mrs. Cooper.

"Is there something you need?" Marla asked, continuing to slowly rip paper off the wall.

"You have guests. They insisted on coming up to see you."

Marla turned and there, at the head of the hall, stood her yacht club friends, Vicki and Catrina. Both were wearing designer dresses that showed off their still-perfect figures and tall heels, their leather handbags engraved with high-end names hanging from their shoulders.

"Hello, ladies," Marla said cheerfully. "I'm so happy you dropped by." She resisted the urge to hug them both, knowing full well they'd be aghast to have her do so in her dirty work clothes. "Thank you, Mrs. Cooper," she said dismissively.

Mrs. Cooper stood ramrod straight, refusing to leave. "Shall I serve tea to your guests in the great room?"

Marla waved her hand through the air. "Don't bother. I'm sure they've just come from lunch at the club. You may go, Mrs. Cooper."

The housekeeper spun on her low-heeled shoes and left.

Both women stared at Marla as if they were looking at a stranger. She ignored their obvious shock at seeing her working. "I'm going to lighten up this hallway," she explained. "I've hated this old wallpaper for years. It's time to update this part of the house."

Catrina was the first to find her voice. "That's wonderful, dear. But can't you pay someone to do this?"

Vicki cleared her throat. "Of course she can pay someone, Catrina. I'm sure it's not about the money. Perhaps it's more of a therapeutic thing?" She looked hopefully at Marla for validation.

Marla laughed. "Actually, it's just fun. Yes, I could pay someone else to do it, but I like the feeling of accomplishment it gives me. You two must see my morning room. No, I mean my office now. I have to stop referring to it by that old name. It looks light and breezy. I even retiled the fireplace."

Vicki's red brows rose nearly to her hairline. "Really? Tiled? That sounds like a lot of work."

"It was. But it's beautiful. Come. I'll show you."

Marla walked past them, noting that they both gave her a wide berth so she wouldn't dirty their dresses. They went downstairs and into her office.

"Don't you just love it?" Marla asked.

Both women looked around, then smiled indulgently. "Yes. It looks wonderful. You did a beautiful job," Vicki said.

Marla could tell that neither of them were impressed, but quite frankly, she didn't care. She loved how the room looked. "Here, come sit," she said, waving toward the cream settee in front of the fireplace. "Would you like some tea?"

"Oh, no thank you," Catrina said quickly. She and Vicki sat down gingerly, and Marla sat opposite them in a rose-colored chair. "We did just have lunch at the club."

Marla nodded. She'd figured they had. Their dilated pupils looked as if they'd also had a few glasses of wine with lunch, as usual.

Vicki brushed her hair behind her shoulder and cocked her head, looking intently at Marla. "How are you doing, dear?" she asked. "I mean, really. We haven't seen or heard from you since our last lunch and we've been worried about you."

Her patronizing tone irritated Marla. "I'm doing just fine, as you can see. I've been keeping busy with projects and I've even met a group of nice women and joined their book club."

"Oh." Catrina looked surprised. "A book club? Whose club is that?"

"No one you know," Marla said, her words clipped.

Vicki and Catrina not so subtly glanced at each other. "That's nice," Vicki finally said. "You know, tennis is starting next week, and we noticed you haven't signed up. And the ladies' golf league starts soon. We thought you might have forgotten."

Marla let out a long sigh. "I'm sorry. I should have let you know. I'm not playing tennis or golf this year. I've decided to take a year off and do other things to fill my time."

Her friends' eyes widened so large, Marla thought they looked like cartoon characters. She tried hard not to laugh.

"But you've always played golf and tennis at the club," Catrina said. "How can you just give it up?"

"Easy," Marla replied. "I'll just stop doing it. Honestly, I've never actually enjoyed those sports anyway. If I miss them this summer, I can always play next year if I really want to."

Vicki bent forward and placed a hand on Marla's arm. "Dear. I'm worried about you. Making all these sudden changes in your life is unhealthy. You really should reconsider…"

Marla pulled her arm away. "I didn't play those sports last year while Nathan was ill, and no one thought anything of it then. So, I'm not going to this year, either. You can stop worrying about me. I'm fine. In fact, I feel wonderful and I'm enjoying what I'm doing. So please don't concern yourselves."

Both women looked taken aback. "We're just trying to help," Catrina said. "You haven't been the same since Nathan passed. We only want what's best for you."

Marla softened. "Yes, I know. And I do appreciate your concern. But honestly, where were all of my friends, and Nathan's, when he was ill? Hardly anyone came by to visit and I didn't see you two for over a year. So, is everything supposed to go back to normal now that he's dead?"

Both women sat back as if they'd been slapped. Vicki stood abruptly. "I think we should go, Catrina," she said in a clipped tone. "It seems that all we're doing is upsetting Marla. Maybe we can get together another day when you're feeling more like yourself."

"I'm feeling just fine!" Marla blurted out as she also stood. "Haven't you heard me? I'm fine. Just because I don't want to do the same things I've done for twenty-two years doesn't mean I'm not okay."

"That's wonderful," Vicki said tightly. "We'll talk another time. Come along, Catrina." Both women walked hurriedly out of the room and Marla just let them go. No matter what she said, they wouldn't listen to her anyway. That was their problem, not hers.

"Did you manage to alienate your friends now, too?" Mrs. Cooper stood in the doorway, staring hard at Marla. "Honestly. You'd better be careful, or you'll alienate the entire community."

Anger spread through Marla like wildfire. "And *you'd* better be careful because *I'm* the one who signs your checks now, Mrs. Cooper. Remember that."

The stunned look on the housekeeper's face was worth the outburst. She spun around and stormed out of the room.

"How dare that old biddy!" Marla mumbled as she paced her office. "And those two nosy gossips! Trying to tell me what I feel and what I should do!" Marla made a few laps around the room until her anger abated. She stopped and looked around, proud of what she'd accomplished in this room. "I don't care what any of them think. I did a good job in here."

By the time Marla had calmed down and made her way to the kitchen, Mrs. Cooper was already gone for the night.

"I wasn't going to apologize anyway," she said into the empty room. Her mood lifted when she realized it was Friday night and she'd have a Mrs. Cooper-free weekend.

Marla ran upstairs and changed into comfortable loungewear. She'd decided to make herself dinner and sit on the sofa to read more of Alaina's journal. The wallpaper lying in the hallway could wait to be picked up tomorrow. After working all day, then dealing with her friends and Mrs. Cooper, she deserved to have a nice evening.

Once she'd put together a sandwich and a plate of cold vegetables, Marla sat down and opened the journal. She couldn't wait to read more of Alaina's story. She hoped the prior Mrs. Madison had a much better time with friends and staff than she was having.

The next time I saw Mr. Madison was at the June Ball. I'd given in to my father's urgings and had a dress made especially for the event. After seeing the look in Mr. Madison's eyes when I approached him, I was glad I'd made the effort. The evening was magical.

Chapter Eleven

Alaina

June 1875

Alaina's father urged her several times to have a new dress made for the ball, and finally, she gave in. In truth, she was excited about going and did want to look nice. She and Hannah went together to their favorite dressmaker and were fitted for new designs.

The night of the ball, Alaina dressed carefully with Emma's help. Her gown was made of a rich emerald satin, sleeveless and scoop-necked, the most daring dress Alaina had ever owned. She allowed Emma to tie her corset tighter than usual so her nipped-in waist would accentuate her hips as the skirt fell in folds to the floor. Alaina had insisted on a fuller skirt so she could dance without restraint. An additional piece was buttoned onto the back to give the look of a bustle and the skirt fell down into a narrow train. She felt beautiful in this dress and for the first time in her life, Alaina wanted to look good for a man.

"You look lovely," Emma said, after she'd worked for an hour to curl and pin up Alaina's hair.

"Thank you, Emma. It's only because you're so skilled at what you do."

"Nonsense. You're a beautiful woman despite what you tell yourself. Now, what jewels shall we choose for you?"

Before Alaina could answer, there was a knock on her door. Emma opened it and there stood Arthur in his dress suit. "May I come in?" he asked.

"Of course, Father. You look very handsome tonight."

Her father smiled at her, his eyes sparkling with pride. "And you are lovely. Absolutely beautiful. You look like your mother did the day I met her."

Alaina's heart swelled with love for him. She knew how much he missed her mother, as she did, even after all these years.

Arthur lifted a black velvet box and handed it to Alaina. "I thought, perhaps, you might want to wear these tonight."

Delighted, she opened the box to reveal a pearl necklace and pearl earrings with small emeralds on the ear clips. "Oh, Father! They're extraordinary."

"They belonged to your mother. I know that she'd want you to wear and enjoy them."

Alaina hugged her father. "Thank you. They're perfect. I'd love to wear them."

He beamed at her. "Well then, I shall let you get on with it. I believe Matthew and Hannah will be here shortly to pick us up."

"I'll be down in a few minutes," Alaina said.

After he'd left, she had Emma hook the pearls around her neck. They felt cool on her skin as they lay just above her collarbones. Clipping on the earrings, she looked into the mirror and couldn't help but smile. She felt beautiful, which was rare for her. She hoped that Mr. Madison would think she was as well.

Matthew and Hannah arrived in their carriage with their driver and the Carltons climbed inside. Hannah looked lovely in her new royal blue dress which offset her eyes and Alaina complimented her on how beautiful she was.

Arthur winked at Matthew. "We are two very lucky gentlemen tonight, escorting these two beautiful ladies."

It was a nice evening, comfortable enough to wear only a light wrap. They chatted on the short ride to Summit Avenue where Mr. Madison lived. Soon, their carriage was waiting in a long line for guests to be dropped off under the grand Porte cochere. It gave Alaina a chance to study his home. Compared to her house, his was a mansion. It was built of brick in a square shape, but there were turrets on each side to round out the corners. An arched front porch framed the large door, embedded with stained glass. And the house looked to be five stories tall. Alaina couldn't even imagine how many rooms it held.

"It's incredible, isn't it?" Hannah whispered to her friend.

"Yes. It is. I wonder, though. Can you make a castle feel like a home?" Alaina asked.

Hannah giggled. "I'd like the chance to try."

Once it was their turn to alight, uniformed footmen helped the ladies down from the carriage and they stepped onto gleaming oak floors in the chandelier-lit entryway. Beyond that was the ballroom. Dressed elegantly in a black suit with a snowy-white dress shirt, Mr. Madison was waiting to greet them.

The moment Alaina's eyes met his, she knew that Mr. Madison was delighted by her appearance. He smiled, and his eyes brightened as he gazed at her. "I'm so pleased you came," he said, bowing over her white-gloved hand. "You look absolutely stunning tonight."

"Thank you." She suddenly felt shy over his attention.

He greeted everyone in the group, then they moved along to the main part of the ballroom where a string quartet was playing. Floor-to-ceiling windows bowed out on one side of the room allowing the moon and stars to shine in. Two huge gas-light chandeliers lit up the grand space, their crystals glittering a rainbow of colors over the polished oak floors. Tables and chairs were set all around the edge for dancers to rest at and a long table of refreshments was laid out on the other side.

"What a fine ballroom Mr. Madison has," Arthur said, clearly impressed. "I think we could set our entire house in this room, Alaina."

"I have to agree," she said. "And we have a big house by most standards."

"It's simply stunning." Hannah gazed around, mesmerized. "Let's find a table and enjoy something cool to drink, shall we?"

The men escorted the ladies to a table then left to get refreshments. Women in colorful dresses and men in fine suits danced to the music while others wandered from table to table, visiting with friends. Several women stopped to chat with Alaina and Hannah, and to compliment them on how lovely they looked. Arthur and Matthew had just returned with punch and a plate of finger sandwiches when Mr. Madison appeared at their table.

"I hope you're enjoying yourselves so far," he said.

"We are," Arthur told him. "You have a beautiful home, Mr. Madison. So much room to spread out in."

He smiled, clearly pleased. "Yes, there is. This room closes off with doors into two rooms normally and is furnished as a parlor. We moved everything out for the dance."

"The windows are beautiful," Hannah said. "And the chandeliers are breathtaking."

Alaina watched her friend. Hannah wasn't usually taken with

money or possessions. While Alaina knew she appreciated nice things, she was more interested in genuine people. It surprised her how overcome Hannah seemed with Mr. Madison's obvious wealth.

Turning, she was startled to see that Mr. Madison had come to stand right in front of her. "My duties greeting guests are complete. Would you honor me with a dance?"

The quartet had begun a waltz and couples were filling the dance floor. Alaina nodded and accepted Mr. Madison's pro-offered arm to escort her to the center of the room. As she left her group, she heard her father asking Hannah if she'd like to dance. That made her smile. Her father was such a dear, he wouldn't want Hannah to feel left out, even with Matthew standing right there.

"I hope that smile is for me," Mr. Madison said, his eyes twinkling as they turned to face each other. He placed one hand lightly on her back and held her other hand.

"It can be if you like," Alaina said, meeting his eyes. "But to be honest, I thought it was sweet that my father asked my friend to dance."

They began moving gracefully around the floor. Alaina was delighted at how well he danced.

"Your father seems to be a very kind and honest man," Mr. Madison said. "And a very good businessman."

"He is all of that. There isn't a mean bone in his body. And he places family above all else, which is an admirable trait."

"What about you, Miss Carlton? Are you as sweet-natured as your father?"

Alaina almost stopped short at his question, then remembered they were dancing and continued to follow his lead. "Are you insinuating that I'm not?" she asked.

Mr. Madison chuckled. "Not at all. I'm sorry. I tend to tease, and most people don't know how to take it. I'm sure you are a lovely woman in both beauty and actions."

She assessed him a moment, wondering if he was teasing again. She hadn't expected him to have much of a sense of humor, considering how hard a worker he was. She'd thought he'd be the serious type. She gave him a small grin. "I appreciate your assessment of me, but I will admit that I'm not always sweet natured. I can be quite stubborn at times."

"I appreciate your honesty. It's refreshing."

After the dance ended, Mr. Madison escorted her to her table, but Alaina was asked to dance by another man before she could sit down. Throughout the evening, men she'd met a few years prior during her coming out year asked her often to dance, as well as Mr. Madison, who danced with her several times. By the time she danced with her father, she was warm and parched from so much activity.

"I think I might faint," she teased her father. "Please say no to any other man who asks me to dance. I need to sit and have something to drink."

Arthur chuckled warmly. "It seems you are the belle of the ball tonight. So many suitors wanting to spend time with you."

"I hardly think I'm the belle of the ball. I'm sure they're all just being polite."

Arthur shook his head. "Take the compliment, dear. You're beautiful tonight and all the men see it. They are lucky to be in your presence."

Alaina leaned over and kissed his cheek. "Spoken like a true father," she said.

When she finally sat down, Mr. Madison joined her, and they had punch and nibbled on a plate of finger sandwiches and fresh strawberries.

"Are you enjoying yourself?" he asked.

"Yes, I am. You've put on a lovely ball. It will be the talk of the town for weeks."

"I can't take all the credit, I'm afraid. Frankly, I just opened my house for it. The ladies of the charity organization did all the work."

"Well, it was generous of you to allow us all inside your beautiful home."

He nodded his appreciation. "Would you take a walk with me? We could get some fresh air in the garden. The paths are lighted outside."

Alaina hesitated. She didn't want to insult Mr. Madison, who'd been nothing but kind to her, but she also didn't want tongues to wag because she'd gone off alone with him.

"I can see that makes you uncomfortable. I promise, I'll be a complete gentleman. I'll even let your father know where we're going, and we will stay within sight of the ballroom."

Alaina nodded. She felt she didn't have to worry that he'd be improper. It did surprise her that in the short time she'd known him, she actually trusted him.

Mr. Madison offered her his arm and they walked toward the open doors to the garden. On their way out, as promised, he informed Arthur where they were going.

Arthur nodded and waved them on. "Enjoy your stroll."

Alaina was encouraged by her father's trust of this man. She relaxed as she walked beside him. The cool evening air felt refreshing as they drifted out to the garden.

"Do you like the house?" Mr. Madison asked. "I'd love to know what you think of it."

"It's a fine house," she said. "But I hardly know anything

about it."

"Ask me anything."

"Well." She thought a moment. "Is it really five stories? And how many rooms are in it?"

"Yes. It's five stories. The main floor has the usual: a parlor, morning room, a library which is also my office, the kitchen, a grand dining room and a smaller one that I prefer since I eat most of my meals alone. There's also a room off the kitchen for the head housekeeper, and the rest of the staff have rooms up on the fifth floor."

"I see," Alaina said, wondering how much staff he actually needed but didn't want to pry.

"The second floor has several guest suites and the third is the family floor with several bedrooms, as well. The fourth floor has rooms that could be used as nurseries and where nannies could live near the children. There is also a large, sunny room that would be a wonderful playroom for children."

Alaina's brows raised. "You must be planning on raising a large family."

Mr. Madison chuckled. "No, not particularly. But this house is an investment like all my properties, and I built it to include everything a family would want." He looked directly at her. "If I'm blessed with children, then I'm prepared, though."

A blush crept up Alaina's neck and into her cheeks. Was he insinuating that he'd like to have children with her?

They stopped walking and he turned to her. "Your father tells me that you enjoy helping him with his business ledgers. And that you are very astute at running the house and household accounts."

"Yes. I do enjoy doing all of it. I particularly find pleasure in discussing his business with him. I find it all interesting."

"I think that's wonderful. I don't know many women who take an interest in business or figures."

"Well, that may be because women aren't usually allowed to participate in those duties," Alaina said.

"Yes, of course. Well said." He grinned. "You are an extraordinary young woman. May I be honest with you?"

"Yes. Please do."

"I found you very interesting when we danced last year at the Christmas Ball. We talked about your father's textile business and what products were the best sellers. I was amazed at how knowledgeable you were. And I even took your advice and stocked my stores with some of the products you suggested, and they sold well. You understand what the public needs and wants. That is a wonderful quality."

Alaina barely remembered their conversation and was surprised he'd taken her words so seriously. Most men she knew wouldn't have listened so intently. "Thank you."

"I've thought of you often since then, and I was the one who prompted your father to have a dinner party and to invite me. I'm sorry for being so forward, but I wanted to meet you again. And that evening, I wasn't at all disappointed. You were as interesting and beautiful as I'd remembered."

Alaina's eyes dropped at his candied words. Beautiful? She never thought of herself that way. Handsome, comely, maybe. But beautiful? No. Hannah was a beauty, not her.

Mr. Madison touched her under the chin and raised her eyes to his. "Don't look away. Please. You are beautiful. And I also have noticed that you aren't silly and giggly like many young women. You're serious, but in a good way. You're responsible, and you have a good head on your shoulders. I can tell that just from the short time I've known you. I admire all of that about you."

She gazed up into his dark brown eyes, aware that his finger still touched the underside of her chin. They were so close, she could see how thick his lashes were and how the skin around his eyes crinkled ever so slightly when he smiled. "I appreciate your honesty, Mr. Madison." Alaina was astonished that he'd noticed those traits in her after such a short acquaintance. But she was flattered, too, by his kind words. No man, except her father, had ever noticed or appreciated her in such a way before.

"Please call me Nathaniel. And may I call you Alaina? If I get my wish tonight, and you will allow me to court you, then I feel we should be on a first name basis."

Alaina's heart beat faster. Court her? He was serious about beginning a relationship with her. "I...I'm speechless."

Nathaniel smiled then, his eyes sparkling with delight. "Well then, that's a start." He bent down and placed a chaste kiss on her cheek. "Do I have your permission? To court you?"

Alaina swallowed. His kiss had been like one an uncle or friend would give, yet it had made her heart dance. "Yes. I would like that."

A year later, they danced again in that very same ballroom as friends and family watched, celebrating their wedding day.

Chapter Twelve

Marla

As Marla worked on the hallway wallpaper the next day, she couldn't stop thinking about Alaina and Nathaniel. Last night, after reading about the ball and their being married a year later, she'd thought of her own marriage to Nathan. They, too, had only known each other a year before marrying. It seemed like a small coincidence, but it made her feel somehow connected to the first Mrs. Madison.

Curious, Marla had gone online and searched for homes on Summit Avenue in St. Paul to see if she could find Nathaniel's mansion. She finally found it on Zillow and was able to look at photos. It was an incredible home, with beautiful woodwork, large, open rooms, and fireplaces everywhere, much like her own home. It sat on a large lot with a garden in the back that allowed privacy despite there being houses on each side. And the last price it had sold for was incredible. It was strange, though, to realize it had once been owned by her husband's great-great-grandfather. Yet, she'd never known about the house or the original Nathaniel Madison.

Marla's curiosity grew about her husband's family. Nathan had never spoken much about his parents or grandparents, all of whom had passed on before Marla had married him. Nathan had been forty-four when they'd married and she'd never given much thought to his parents. He'd casually mentioned a couple of times how the men in his family had died young, but she'd never questioned him on that, either. Now, she wished she had.

Of course, Mrs. Cooper would probably have met Nathan's parents and maybe even his grandparents, but Marla wasn't ready to ask her. After their little dispute on Friday, she figured she'd have to wait a while for Mrs. Cooper to cool down.

With that thought in mind, she was surprised when her phone rang and saw it was Reese.

"Hi, sweetheart," Marla said, genuinely happy to hear from her daughter. "I'm so glad you called."

"Hi, Mom. How are things going there?"

"Everything is fine, dear. I've been very busy, working on the house. How is school?"

"School's fine. I'm looking forward to finishing in May, though. It's been a long year."

Marla thought Reese sounded tired. She understood how she felt. Between her father being ill, and then his passing, and with her having classes on top of it all, it had been a trying year. "Are you coming home for spring break? Or do you and Chad have plans?"

Reese sighed. "A group of us were thinking of going to the Caribbean. A friend of mine's father has a huge yacht and we thought we could take off from Florida and island hop. It would be nice to go somewhere warm."

Marla nodded. She'd love to go to the Caribbean. It looked so beautiful in pictures. But Nathan hadn't liked the idea of island vacations, so they'd never gone. "That sounds wonderful, dear." She tried hard to sound excited for her. In truth, Marla would have loved to have Reese come home for a few days, but she knew her daughter would find that boring.

"So, I hear you had another go-around with Florence," Reese said, sounding slightly amused.

"Ah, I see. That's why you called. The old biddy complained to you again." Marla was disappointed. She'd hoped that Reese had called to catch up with her. She should have known that wasn't the case.

"Did you really threaten to fire her? She told me you said she was no longer wanted there."

"Fire her?" Marla's pulse quickened with anger. "She's either crazy or going senile. She was quite rude to me in front of my friends and again after they'd left. I only reminded her that I now sign her paycheck."

"Mom! That's terrible. What could she have possibly done to deserve you saying that to her?"

Marla closed her eyes and counted silently to ten. She hated when Reese took Mrs. Cooper's side. Taking a deep breath, she finally said, "Mrs. Cooper can be intolerable, and you know that. Even your father knew that. Why do you think he tried to get her to retire twice? And then he put her in the will to get rid of her a third time, and that didn't even work."

"Mom. She's a lonely old woman. What is she going to do if she doesn't run the house? She has no husband, no children, and probably no friends. Her whole life has been serving the Madisons. The least you could do is be nice to her."

"So I should just let her insult me, as she's done since I moved in here? It's not my fault she has nothing else in her life. And quite frankly, Reese, I don't understand why you always take her side over mine. I'm your mother, for Pete's sake."

There was a long, silent pause on the other end as Marla waited for her daughter to respond. For a moment, she was afraid she'd gone too far. But then, she decided she was right. Her daughter should be on her side.

"Mom," Reese began in a calmer tone. "I do know how difficult Florence can be. And you're right. She is rude to you at times. But she's always been nice to me. Always. I'm sorry it feels as if I take her side. I don't mean to. I just don't understand why you two can't get along."

Marla let out a long breath. She hadn't even realized she'd been holding it in until she sighed. "I know she's always been kind to you, Reese. And I appreciate that. But she has never liked me, and she's made it very clear she's never approved of me. I put up with it when your father was alive, but I don't know how much longer I'll be able to now that he's gone. She has plenty of money to retire on, and that nice cottage your father bought her. What more could she possibly want, especially since she doesn't even like working for me?"

"I don't know, Mom. But could you just try to get along with her? Otherwise, I'll keep getting calls from her, and that's annoying. By the way, I hear you're tearing apart the upstairs hallway now." Reese let out a chuckle.

Marla couldn't help but smile at that. "Yes, I am. And it's going to look so much better when I'm finished, just wait and see. And I'm going to continue sprucing things up around here for as long as I want. So, you'd better get used to Mrs. Cooper complaining to you."

Reese laughed. "Okay, Mom. As long as it makes you happy. But for the life of me, I can't figure out why you want to do so much work on the house."

They talked a little longer then Reese had to go. Marla was glad they ended their conversation on a good note. She hated arguing with her only daughter. And she wished that Mrs. Cooper wouldn't try to pit them against each other.

Ugh! Another thing I need to discuss with the crabby house-keeper. To stop calling Reese and complaining.

Marla spent the rest of the weekend tearing down wallpaper and cleaning up her mess. Once it was down, she scrapped off the remaining paper and any glue that was still on the walls, then prepared it for painting. In the evenings, she started reading the new book club selection, reluctantly leaving Alaina's journal locked in her desk. She would continue reading Alaina's story after she'd finished the new book.

On Monday, she was ready to prime the hallway walls. She came downstairs in her work clothes and ran into Mrs. Cooper, who was bringing her tea tray to the morning room. Secretly, she'd hoped that Mrs. Cooper would have quit. But she knew it wouldn't be that easy to get rid of her.

"Good morning, Mrs. Cooper," Marla said in as cheery a voice as she could manage. "I thought I'd take my tea in the breakfast nook. I have a lot of work to do after breakfast."

Mrs. Cooper nodded curtly and turned to go to the breakfast nook with Marla right behind her. She set the tray on the table and was about to go into the kitchen when Marla stopped her.

"Mrs. Cooper? May we speak a moment?"

The housekeeper turned, a sour look on her face.

"I'm afraid we ended last week on a bad note. I truly want to get along with you, especially now that it's just the two of us here. Can we please come to some sort of an understanding?"

Mrs. Cooper's brows rose a fraction of an inch.

Marla knew this was one of the tactics she used to make

her feel uncomfortable. "I'll try to stay out of your way if you stay out of mine. Would that work for you? We'll both keep our opinions to ourselves, and that way we can get along."

The housekeeper raised her chin a bit and looked down her nose at Marla. "I'll be happy to stay out of your business. My comments about the changes you're making to the house were only for the good of this fine, old home. But I see they are not welcome, so I will mind my own business from now on."

Marla wanted to roll her eyes. She would never get an apology out of her, but maybe they could at least coexist. "Thank you. And would you please not call Reese every time you don't like something I've done? I'm pleased that you have a close relationship with her, as is she, but we shouldn't be bothering her with our disagreements."

Mrs. Cooper squared her shoulders. "Fine." And with that, she left the room.

"Fine," Marla said under her breath. Dealing with Mrs. Cooper was like dealing with a petulant child. Hopefully, things between them would settle down.

I just have to make sure she leaves early next Thursday before the ladies show up, she thought. The last thing Marla needed was a snooty housekeeper here when the book club women arrived.

Marla wondered how Alaina would have handled someone like Mrs. Cooper. She probably would have fired her on the spot. With that lovely thought in mind, Marla sat down to drink her tea and plan her day.

* * *

That week was spent priming and painting the hallway walls. It seemed to have taken forever to tape around the woodwork before she could begin priming. And the walls had been so dry, they'd needed several coats of paint. That meant extra trips to the store to buy paint. Marla hadn't minded that, though, because it gave her a reason to visit with Ardie.

In between painting, Marla took a break to walk along the lake and enjoy the spring weather. These walks gave her time to ponder where her life was heading. She'd been so organized and busy when Nathan was alive, but now, she felt like it had all scattered in the wind. While she enjoyed putting her energy into redecorating the house, for now, she knew she couldn't do that forever. At some point, she'd have to find a satisfying way to spend her time. She just had no idea what that would be.

Often, after her walk, she'd stop and gaze across the bay at the little cottage house. Because the trees were still bare, she could make out the roof and porch, and it reminded her again how charming the house was. She could picture herself living there. It would be so much nicer to be in a smaller, cozier home that didn't require a housekeeper or staff to run it. But the thought of selling Nathan's family manor was daunting. It would be like selling off the Madison name to the highest bidder—disposing of the family legacy. Would she regret it in the future? Maybe Reese would decide she wanted it after all, years from now. Yet, living in this huge house, alone, for the rest of her life, wasn't something Marla wanted either. Marla knew she didn't have to make any life-altering decisions yet, but she kept these thoughts in the back of her mind.

In the evenings, Marla sometimes swam in the indoor pool or sat in the little family room off the kitchen and read. She was almost finished with the book club selection and had enjoyed it, despite it being a sad story. She couldn't wait to discuss it with the ladies. She liked having a group of friends she could do more with other than gossip or play tennis or golf. And, it was more than that. The camaraderie between the women was wonderful. She hadn't felt that way with a group of friends since college, and it felt good.

By Thursday—book club night—the hallway was finished. Marla had gone to the grocery store that morning and purchased a few items to make snacks for the group. She casually mentioned to Mrs. Cooper that she wouldn't need to cook dinner that night and could leave early.

The housekeeper looked at her curiously. "Are you eating out?"

"No. I'll be home. I'm having a few friends over," Marla answered. She'd thought about lying but then decided that was ridiculous. After all, this was her home. Why on earth should she lie to her housekeeper?

"Then you'll need me to make hor d'oeuvres," Mrs. Cooper said. "Unless you have suddenly developed a talent to cook."

Anger simmered inside Marla. Just a week after their discussion about being civil to each other and still Mrs. Cooper was being rude. She took a deep breath, let it out, and spoke in a controlled voice. "Thank you, but we won't need anything fancy. We'll be fine with the snacks I bought."

Mrs. Cooper looked aghast. "You're going to serve your friends *snacks*? You mean like potato chips out of a bag? I simply can't allow that. We've always entertained properly in this house. I can't have the members of the yacht club thinking that I chose to serve *snacks* to your guests."

The snide way the housekeeper said *snacks* nearly made Marla laugh out loud. Did the woman really think Marla was that incompetent? Well, probably.

"Please don't worry about it, Mrs. Cooper. These friends

won't tattle on you at the club. They're a group of women you've never met before, and they will be fine with *snacks*."

Mrs. Cooper sniffed. "I see. Well, then, I guess since I won't be needed, I might as well take my leave now."

Good, Marla thought, but said politely, "Have a nice evening, Mrs. Cooper."

After she'd left, Marla went right to work in the kitchen. She made some beef topping for nachos and grated cheese to sprinkle on top. She'd put the beef and cheese on tortilla chips and microwave it as soon as the ladies arrived. She also put guacamole sauce and salsa in bowls in case they'd prefer to dip their chips and also made up a plate of cookies she'd bought at the bakery. She hoped it would be enough. Ardie had said to keep it simple, so that was what she did.

At five-thirty, the doorbell rang, and Marla ran to answer it. Ardie stood in the doorway with wide eyes.

"Hi, Ardie. I'm glad you were able to find the place easily," Marla said. "Come on in. You're the first to arrive."

Ardie walked in and gaped all around her. "Okay, I have to say it. Wow! I figured you lived in a nice house but hadn't thought it would be this nice."

Marla smiled. "I know. It's a bit over-the-top."

"A bit over-the-top? It's a mansion!" Ardie gawked at Marla, then broke out laughing. "I'm sorry. I shouldn't be laughing. But this is a total shock to me. And now I'm trying to picture you doing all that painting and tiling. You could have hired someone to do it."

"Yes, I could have. I didn't want to, though. I wanted to do it myself. And I didn't grow up rich. Not at all. So please don't judge me because of this house." Marla was worried by Ardie's reaction. She didn't want to lose her as a friend.

Ardie smiled warmly. "I didn't mean to make you feel uncomfortable. This house was just a shock. It's beautiful. I hope you'll give us a tour."

Marla nodded and then the doorbell rang again. She opened the door and there stood Wanda and Rita, both with the same shocked look on their faces as Ardie.

"See. I told you we were at the right address," Wanda said to Rita. She turned to Marla. "You forgot to mention you lived in a mansion."

Marla bit her lip. "Sorry."

Wanda laughed. "Don't be sorry. Good for you! I can't wait to see the rest of this place."

"It's lovely," Rita said, looking around in awe. "And we're only in the foyer."

Marla smiled. She ushered them in, and they went to the great room.

"Oh my God! You live on the lake, too?" Rita walked over to the French doors and the others followed. "I knew Great Heron Lake was nearby. I had no idea it was in your backyard."

The doorbell rang again and Marla went to open the door. She prepared herself for Toni's reaction. But Toni only smiled, said hello, and handed Marla a covered casserole dish.

"I brought my special layered taco dish. I hope you don't mind. I actually had time to make something for a change," Toni said. She glanced around, taking in the foyer and the great room. "This house is spectacular."

"Thank you," Marla said. "You don't seem surprised like everyone else."

"Oh, I was when I looked up your address. Seeing it was on Bellwood Avenue, I knew it was going to be special. Any house on this street is a realtor's dream."

Marla laughed. "I'd forgotten you'd be able to look it up. Come in. The ladies are enjoying the lake view." Marla set Toni's dish on the dining table and headed for the kitchen. "I'll be right back," she called out.

"Are you going to the kitchen?" Wanda asked. "Can we see it?"

Marla chuckled. "Sure. Come along."

Everyone marveled at the large, beautiful kitchen and family room.

"This room was remodeled a few years ago, but the rest of the house has barely been touched since it was built in 1885," Marla said as she placed her nacho dish in the microwave. "Of course the plumbing and electrical has been updated because it used to have gas lighting, but other than that, it's pretty much the same."

"1885," Toni repeated, looking around in awe. "Amazing. Has it been in your family the entire time?"

"My husband's family, yes. His great-great-grandfather built it."

"Incredible. What history this place must hold," Toni said.

They went back into the dining room once the food was ready. Marla poured the wine and they all sat down to eat.

"Marla has been remodeling the upstairs hallway this past couple of weeks," Ardie said. "I have the inside track because I sell her all her supplies." She laughed.

"There was the most awful wallpaper up there," Marla explained. "And it was as old as the house and looked it. I pulled it all down and painted the walls with a textured look. There's dark wood wainscoting along the bottom and the new color complements it now."

"But shouldn't you keep the original wallpaper in a house like this?" Rita asked. "It's antique."

"It won't devalue the house at all by removing it," Toni offered. "Many people update older homes like this. In fact, it helps to do updates in order to sell. It may sound good to say it has the original wallpaper, but most people won't like it anyway. The floors and woodwork, however, are important to keep as is."

"I'm not touching the woodwork," Marla said. "The wainscoting and crown molding you see in here is throughout the house. A crew comes in once a year to clean and polish it all. It's beautiful. But the walls above it in many of the rooms were awful. I changed my bedroom upstairs, and my office down here. I wouldn't mind lightening up the other bedrooms, but I'm not sure I'm ready to take on that much work."

"How many bedrooms and baths does this house have?" Toni asked.

"Uh oh. Toni is calculating the value of your house in her head," Ardie said, grinning. "She's done it for all of us, so don't be insulted."

"I don't mind," Marla said. "There are seven bedrooms and eight bathrooms plus a maid's bed and bath downstairs behind the kitchen. There's six-thousand square feet in the house, and an indoor pool. The house sits on five acres of land with one-thousand feet of lakeshore."

The women stared at her with wide eyes. "Six-thousand square feet!" Wanda exclaimed. "Don't you get lost in here?"

They all laughed. The talk turned to other things as they ate, then afterward, Marla gave them a tour. The women marveled at how spacious the house was and all the bedrooms and bathrooms upstairs. They complimented Marla on how well the upstairs hallway turned out.

"With a little help from me," Ardie had said with a glint in her eye. Everyone laughed.

When they walked into the library downstairs, they all stopped and stared in awe at the three walls covered in floor-to-ceiling shelves full of antique books. A brick fireplace was on one wall between the bookshelves and at the far end tall windows overlooked the lake. A heavy, antique mahogany desk, polished to perfection, sat in front of the windows.

"Look at all these books!" Wanda exclaimed. She went up to a shelf and touched the spine of one. "Are they all leather bound?"

"No, not all of them," Marla said. "But there are many first editions of several classics. I think they've been collecting these books since this house was built, maybe even before that. It is impressive."

"Is this your office?" Rita asked, glancing at the heavy desk.

"No, it was my husband's office. I'll show you mine." She led the way to the morning room which was on the opposite side of the house.

"It's beautiful," Rita exclaimed. "Very feminine."

"You did a wonderful job tiling the fireplace," Ardie told her, examining her work. "I love this room. It's so cozy."

"Thanks." Marla was thrilled by Ardie's praise. She'd worked hard on this room and was happy it had turned out so nice. "And look what I found when I took down the mantel." She walked over to the fireplace and carefully pulled out the secret drawer.

"I've never seen anything like that before," Rita said, mesmerized. She looked up at Marla with a glint in her eyes. "Was there anything hidden in there?"

Marla went to her desk, unlocked the drawer, and pulled out the antique journal. "This was in there. It's a journal written by the very first Mrs. Madison to live in this house."

All the women circled around her to admire it.

"Have you read any of it?" Wanda asked.

"I have, but only some of it. It's really interesting. She starts with how she was introduced to the very prosperous Mr. Nathaniel Madison and then goes on to their getting married. Before that, she'd worked alongside her father in his textile business in St. Paul and did his bookwork. She was very forward thinking for that time period. But Mr. Madison was handsome and persuasive. And rich. I stopped reading just as they had married in 1876."

"Wow. It's like a novel. I'd love to hear more," Rita said.

Wanda looked around at the group, a mischievous spark in her eyes. "Let's ditch the book we were going to discuss and read the journal. I'd like to learn more about this Mrs. Madison too."

Marla stared at the women, surprised. "Are you sure?"

"Would you mind sharing your journal with us?" Ardie asked hopefully. "You could read the next few pages to us. But only if you want to."

"Oh, no. I don't mind at all. I just don't want to bore you."

"Bore us? Are you kidding?" Toni said. "This sounds like the best story I've heard in a long time."

They went into the great room and everyone got comfortable on the leather sofa and chairs. Marla turned on the gas in the fireplace to take the chill off the big room. She sat in one of the wing chairs and opened the journal to the next page where she'd ended, then began reading.

We married on a warm day in July surrounded by friends and family at Nathaniel's church. I wore a beautiful gown of satin and lace, and my dearest friend, Hannah, stood beside me as my matron-of-honor. That evening, the reception and dance was like a dream. Beautiful flowers of white, pink, and red were everywhere, and the crystal chandeliers above sprinkled a rainbow of colors over the dance floor as Nathaniel and I danced our first dance as husband and wife.

Chapter Thirteen

Alaina

July 1876

Alaina and Nathaniel hosted the most talked about wedding of the season. Although Alaina would have been more comfortable with a small wedding, Nathaniel insisted she have one she could be proud of because he only wanted the best for her. She'd agreed because she'd felt honored that this fine, upstanding, and generous man wanted to give her the most beautiful wedding ever, and provide her with everything a woman could want or need. Alaina had never imagined she'd find a man who'd love her so completely that her happiness was his main objective.

From the moment she'd accepted his proposal, Nathaniel had made sure she was included in every decision about the wedding and his house. He'd shown her the room that would belong to her, which she'd noticed had a connecting door to the master bedroom, and told her to decorate it in any color that pleased her. He'd brought in a decorator to show her fabrics, wallpaper, and paint colors so she could choose what she liked.

Nathaniel also told her she could change anything she'd like in the parlor and her morning room, the dining room, and the breakfast nook. Alaina was overwhelmed by it all. She made few changes to any of it, because she thought the house looked beautiful as it was, but she'd appreciated his concern to make his house her own.

They were married on July 15, 1876 in the beautiful Lutheran Church he attended with the pews full of family and friends. The sun shone through the stained-glass windows sprinkling the white marble floors with a kaleidoscope of colors as the bride, in a gown of satin and lace, walked up the aisle on her father's arm, wearing her mother's pearl necklace for luck.

Hannah looked beautiful in a frothy blue gown as her matron-of-honor. She'd given birth to a nine-pound, six-ounce baby girl in early December and had named her Meredith Alaina, Merry for short because she'd been born during the holidays. Matthew sat in the pews holding little Merry as Michael sat between him and the nanny to keep the boy out of mischief.

Alaina remembered little of their vows. When she gazed into the warm brown eyes of her new husband, she was content with the choice she'd made to marry him. She trusted him, and that was the most important thing to her.

The couple spent their first night as man and wife in his home on Summit Avenue, going up to their rooms late in the evening after their wedding reception. They were to depart on the train the next morning to a resort north of St. Paul on Great Heron Lake to spend a peaceful week away from the city.

That night, as Alaina prepared for bed, she was suddenly nervous. A few well-meaning married women from her church had taken her aside to explain her marital duty. They felt it was their responsibility since Alaina's mother was no longer alive.

The way they described being "intimate" was enough to scare any young woman away from the marriage bed. "It's your duty to your husband to lay there and be quiet as he performs the act. Say nothing and do not complain," one woman told her. "It is painful and embarrassing, but you must give in to your husband's needs," another had advised.

Alaina had a good idea what the "marital act" was, but their advice had more than upset her. When she'd finally drummed up the courage to ask Hannah just how awful it was, her friend smiled and her eyes sparkled.

"If you and your husband care deeply for each other, it is a beautiful way to express your love," Hannah had told her. Then she'd whispered, "And fun, if he knows what he's doing."

Alaina decided to ignore the older women's advice and believe her friend, but as the time drew near, she found herself feeling anxious.

Her maid and friend, Emma, had come to work for Alaina now that she lived with Nathanial, and had helped her out of her wedding gown and into a nightdress. She'd combed out Alaina's hair, so it hung straight down her back, then hugged her and said, "Don't be nervous. He loves you. That's all that matters."

Soon after, as Alaina sat on her large bed with the emerald-colored coverlet and matching canopy high above on the four-poster bed, there was a knock on the door between their rooms, and it opened ever so slightly.

"Come in," Alaina said, her voice nearly shaking.

Nathanial, dressed in a nightshirt and robe, came in and smiled, and suddenly, Alaina's nerves calmed. She trusted Nathaniel. He'd been nothing but kind and considerate to her, and when they'd shared a few stolen kisses during their courtship, she'd felt a flutter in the pit of her stomach. She did love him, and she believed that he'd be kind to her in every way.

"I only wanted to come and say goodnight to my beautiful bride," he said, sitting on the bed beside her. "It's been a long day, no, a long week for both of us. And our train leaves early tomorrow." He took her hand in his. "I thought perhaps, if you don't mind, we would wait until we are settled and rested in our rooms at the lodge before we," he hesitated, then cleared his throat. "Before we enjoy the benefits of marriage," he finished, finally looking into her eyes.

Alaina let out a sigh of relief, then quickly placed a hand over her mouth, realizing how her sigh must have sounded to Nathaniel. But he only laughed, and she did also.

He kissed her softly on the lips. "I want our first time to be perfect for you," he said. "We are so compatible in every other way. I'm hoping we will be in this way as well."

Alaina swallowed hard and nodded. She was both relieved and intrigued by her new husband that he'd be considerate enough to wait. It showed what a true gentleman he was.

Nathaniel kissed her again, this time surprising her by gently parting her lips with his tongue. She enjoyed the soft, warm feel of his lips and wasn't at all bothered when his tongue explored hers. Her stomach did more than flutter at the feel of his mouth over hers and his arms around her, holding her tightly. He ran his fingers through her hair, and she found her own hands exploring the tautness of his back. When at last he pulled away, he gazed into her eyes and the heat coming from them made her heart flip.

"Goodnight, my dear," he said.

"Goodnight," Alaina said, nearly breathless. As she watched him leave, she suddenly wished he'd stayed. She now couldn't wait to find out what this mysterious act was that would truly make them husband and wife.

* * *

The train trip north was short and soon they arrived at the lodge that sat on the shore of Great Heron Lake. The Evergreen Inn wasn't a typical lodge as Alaina had imagined. Styled like a hunting lodge, it boasted tall, beamed ceilings in the main room, a huge stone fireplace, and the typical stuffed deer, moose, and bear trophies hung on the walls. But that was where the rustic look ended. The lodge had a beautiful dining room where three meals a day were served, and the rooms were comfortable and modern. The best feature of the inn were the large windows in all the rooms that allowed magnificent views of Great Heron Lake, a grand body of water that seemed to go on forever.

The Madisons were given a suite of rooms on the second floor overlooking the lake. Alaina and Nathaniel each had their own bedroom with a sitting room between them. Emma had come along to attend to Alaina's needs as had Nathaniel's valet, John Laraby, a middle-aged man with a calm and polite demeaner. He'd been working for Nathaniel for several years and Alaina felt comfortable in his presence. Both personal attendants were given rooms down the hall from their employers.

Their first day there, Alaina and Nathaniel strolled along the boardwalk that edged the lake and drank iced tea under a table umbrella on the brick patio. Alaina marveled at the expansive, tall pines that covered the landscape and the beautiful birch and ash trees that shaded the rolling lawn. Eagles soared overhead in search of a meal. Men rowed out in wooden boats and fished, bringing in large walleye, bass, and small crappie. It was rustic, yet charming, and Alaina found herself feeling refreshed and relaxed just sitting and watching the calm blue water.

"Do you like it here?" Nathaniel asked her as they enjoyed their drinks in the shade of the sunny day.

"Oh, yes. It's beautiful," she said, smiling over at him.

Nathaniel lifted his arm and pointed out toward the lake. "Do you see the heron flying there over the water? It's a great blue heron. The lake is named for these amazing majestic birds because so many make their nests here."

Alaina looked where he'd pointed and watched the heron as it lifted higher into the sky. "It's incredible. I've seen them by the river before, but never close up. Maybe we'll get a chance to see more while we're here."

He smiled over at her, then reached for her hand. "I'm sure we will. Anything for you, darling."

Alaina felt a blush rise up to her cheeks. She knew that if Nathaniel had his way, he'd make the herons come parade in front of her just to please her. She felt deeply fortunate.

They dined that night with the other guests, sitting six to a table in the spacious dining room. There were several choices of dishes, the fish-of-the-day being the most popular, along with steak, roast, potatoes, glazed carrots, and fresh blueberry pie for dessert. They drank wine with dinner, then went outside to enjoy their tea under the stars.

"Look at that moon," Alaina said, gazing up into the sky. "It's so beautiful, reflecting off the water. And the stars. It's a perfect night sky."

Nathaniel gently took her hand in his. "It's a perfect night." He smiled at her.

Alaina nodded, enjoying the warmth of his hand over hers.

Later that night, after Emma had helped her dress in a soft linen nightgown with embroidery along the scoop neckline and cuffs, Alaina waited in her room for her husband. When he knocked on her door, her heart pounded in her chest.

"Come in," she said, nervously smoothing her hands over the counterpane.

Nathaniel was still wearing his trousers and shirt but had shed his shoes, jacket, and tie. He carried a silver bucket that held ice, a bottle of champagne, and two glasses. "I thought it would be nice to enjoy a glass of champagne to celebrate our marriage." He set the items down on a small table near the bed and poured two glasses.

Alaina accepted the glass as he sat on the bed near her.

"To us," Nathaniel said. "And to a long, happy marriage."

They clinked glasses and Alaina took a sip. The champagne was sweet, and she felt the liquid warm her from the inside as she took more sips.

Nathaniel reached for her hand and held it gently. "I understand if you're nervous, but I hope that will soon pass. You can trust that I will never do anything that will make you feel unsafe. I have opened my heart to you, Alaina, and I hope we can feel comfortable in all aspects of our relationship."

Alaina wasn't sure how to respond. She was nervous yet filled with anticipation for what was to come. "I hope we can too," was all she could manage to say.

He leaned over and ran his fingers slowly through her hair, bringing her closer to him. Their lips touched gently, then he pulled back and gave her a small smile, his brown eyes warm with tenderness. "Will you unbutton my shirt?" he asked.

She nodded, and with trembling fingers, slowly unbuttoned his shirt. Underneath, he wore a white undershirt that scooped at the neckline. She saw dark, curly hair on his chest, and blushed at the sight of it. Never had she seen a man without a shirt on.

Nathaniel pulled off his shirt and dropped it to the floor. He drew closer to her, bending down to kiss the delicate spot at the base of her neck. Sweet chills ran up her spine at the touch of his lips. How could anyone think that this was something to just bear? The feelings that were welling up inside her from his touch and his kisses were delightful, not horrid.

Soon his undershirt and pants were shed, and he'd joined her under the bedsheets. They kissed, more passionately then he'd ever kissed her before, and Alaina's body cried out for more. When he began to unbutton the back of her nightdress, she didn't stiffen with fear. She allowed him to do so, and soon, she lay there, naked in his arms, unashamed. He caressed her and kissed her everywhere, making her feel loved and cherished. She touched him also, tentatively at first, becoming more eager as he brought the passion out in her. When at last they came together, he was gentle and loving through it all, and despite the initial pain, Alaina soon learned his rhythm. This wasn't the wifely duty she'd feared. Their union was one expressing love for each other, and she was overwhelmed with emotion and desire.

Afterward, Nathaniel curled his body around hers and kissed her ever so gently. "We're perfect together," he whispered. And Alaina felt it was true, as they fell asleep in each other's arms.

* * *

The newlyweds enjoyed their carefree days together on their honeymoon and their nights in bed. Alaina couldn't remember ever being so happy and was surprised that being married to Nathaniel made her feel completely whole. He was kind, gentle, and loving to her the entire time, and she hoped that they would remain this way long after they returned home to their everyday routines.

On the last day of their vacation, Nathaniel ordered an open carriage and asked Alaina to wear something that was easy to walk in and that she didn't mind getting dirty. She'd thought it an odd request but slipped into a simple skirt and blouse and a pair of low-heeled leather boots she'd brought along for walking.

Nathaniel drove the carriage down the dirt road, expertly maneuvering the two horses. The day was warm; the sky, clear and blue. Alaina held onto her wide-brimmed hat as they rode along, the breeze refreshing as it caressed her face. After a time, the road narrowed considerably, and Nathaniel stopped the carriage in a wooded area.

"Here we are!" he exclaimed excitedly.

He helped Alaina down from the carriage and she looked all around her. "Where are we?"

Nathaniel laughed happily. He crooked his elbow and offered it to her. "Let me show you."

She took his arm and they began walking down a rough path in the woods. Tall white pines, jack pines, and evergreens were on either side of them with a few birch, ash, and oak trees sprinkled in. Ferns and moss grew on the ground in the shade. Alaina could smell the pine scent and thought she detected the aroma of cedar as well.

Just as she was about to ask again where they were headed, they came to an open field. There before them was the lake, wide and deep, sprawling out underneath the blue sky.

"Oh my," she exclaimed. The view was breathtaking.

"It's magnificent, isn't it?" he asked, leading her to the sandy beach beside the water.

"It's gorgeous," she said. There was a natural cove and far across the water land jutted out into the lake. To her left, more open land with beach seemed to go on for miles. It was all virgin forest, untouched yet by man. "Is this still Great Heron Lake?"

"Yes, it is. We're quite a distance from the lodge, so you can't even see it from here. If you look closely, you can see a home built on the land across the bay, but other than that, no one has built here—yet. It's prime lakeshore just waiting to be developed into a rich man's paradise."

Alaina stared at him, wondering what he meant. "A rich man's paradise?"

"Yes, my dear. This area is slowly becoming a favorite of the well-to-do families who live in St. Paul and want a vacation spot. The owner of the lodge confided in me that he was going to add on cabins to meet the demand of reservations. There is also talk of starting a summer yacht club here, to bring in even more residents and tourists. And this land you're standing on right now is in a prime location."

Alaina heard the excitement in his voice and smiled at him. He looked so happy, like a little boy at Christmas. "So, who owns this land?"

He grinned even wider. "I do. We do. I just purchased it this week. Everything you see from left to right is ours."

Alaina was stunned. She couldn't remember when they'd been apart long enough for him to run off and purchase land. "That's amazing. What do you plan to use it for?"

He took her hand in his. "Hopefully, one day, we'll have a beautiful vacation home right here where we stand. We can bring our family here every summer and entertain our friends. And possibly, at some point, I can sell the land to our left to the people who want to start the yacht club. That's why I had to snatch up this land quickly. There's money to be made here and I plan on making a huge profit. It may be a few years before growth happens in this sleepy area, but I don't think it will be too long. It's a wonderful investment."

She gazed out over the lake and thought about them having children and bringing them here for the summer. It was a beautiful spot to unwind and relax. The children could swim in the crystal-clear water and build castles in the sand. It did seem like a nice dream.

She turned again to her husband, impressed by his foresight. "You're a smart man to see what others will want in the future," she told him.

He beamed at her, obviously pleased with her compliment. "I built my fortune from nothing by seeing a need and filling it. So far, it's worked well for me. I love that you can see it too. You have a keen sense of business, and that is but one of many things that I love about you." He kissed her sweetly, and they began the trek back to the carriage.

"How many years before you build?" she asked, curious now about their prospective summer house.

"I'm not sure. Five. Maybe ten. No longer than that. As long as the economy continues to thrive in our area and I can continue to build stores in other cities, there will be plenty of money in the upcoming years." He wrapped his arm around her waist and looked down at her, his eyes bright. "And as soon as we have children to bring here. They are going to love it, I'm sure."

Alaina nodded. With their eager lovemaking, she suspected it wouldn't be long before children came along.

Chapter Fourteen

Marla

The women sat quietly in the great room as Marla marked the page and closed the journal.

"What a story!" Wanda said, glancing around at the other women. "So interesting."

"And so romantic," Rita said, looking dreamy. "He pursued her like a hero in a novel and won her in the end. And he's rich! A dream husband."

"Think about how a woman's life was in those days, though," Toni said, shaking her head. "She was told horrendous things about the 'marriage act.'" She used finger quotes. "How awful to believe that sex is scary and terrible."

"But she found out it wasn't after all. Alaina was a very progressive woman for her time," Ardie added. "I just love this story."

"Me, too," Rita said, brightening. "Let's forget about reading a book for the next few weeks and just read this when we meet. I want to continue hearing about Alaina's life."

"I'm for that," Wanda said.

The other women agreed, and it made Marla smile. She was thrilled they'd enjoyed Alaina's story so far and was more than happy to share it with them.

After agreeing to meet at Rita's home in two weeks, the women began to leave. Ardie was the last one there and offered to help Marla clean up the dishes.

"Don't worry. I can do it. There isn't much," Marla said.

Ardie looked at her and grinned.

"What?" Marla asked, puzzled.

"You completely amaze me," Ardie said. "You have all the comforts available to you yet you're willing to get your hands dirty and do the work around here yourself. And you're not spoiled in the least. How in the world did you live like this for so many years and not become a snob?"

A laugh escaped Marla's lips and Ardie joined in. "I don't know the answer to that, but I'm glad you don't think I'm a snob," she said.

"Well, you're a stronger woman than I am. I'd become a snob right away, and insist everyone do all the work for me." Ardie's eyes twinkled.

"I highly doubt that."

"I'd like the chance to try," Ardie said.

As Marla walked her out, she said, "I grew up with a single mom who had to stretch every dollar. I guess it's still a part of me. My husband didn't think twice about spending money on frivolous things, but I was careful. He used to tease me about it."

"I know what you mean. My husband and I do okay, but I remember our younger years when there was never enough money. I'm still careful and look for good sales. If I were a millionaire I'd still watch my spending."

"Like Alaina," Marla said. "She married money but was

hesitant to overspend. She was a smart woman."

Ardie nodded. The two women hugged and Ardie slipped behind the wheel of her car. Rolling down the window, she said, "I'm so happy you're in our group, Marla. We all get along so well. It's fun being with you."

Her words warmed Marla's heart. "I'm happy to be a part of it too. I'm sure I'll see you at the store soon. I'll need a new project now that the hallway is finished."

Ardie waved as she drove off into the night.

After cleaning up the dishes in the kitchen, Marla slipped on a thick sweater and walked outside into the moonlit night. The air was still, and the water lay as smooth as glass under the stars. Soon, the workmen would come and put in the dock and the gardener would plant the annuals and tend to the perennials as they came up. Marla had never been very good with plants, so she was more than happy to let the men do their job. The most she did was decide what to plant in the pots that decorated the patio and front steps.

She wandered out to the shoreline and stood there, listening to the silence of the night. When it grew warmer, the sound of frogs and crickets would fill the air. Fireflies would flit around, and the mosquitos would come out to feed. But now, everything was cool and quiet. Light from homes along the lakeshore reflected off the water, and across the bay, she saw a light on in the cottage that intrigued her so much. At that moment, she thought about Alaina and Nathaniel, standing on this very shoreline, looking out over the vastness of the lake where no houses, save the one, littered the shore. What had that been like, to be here before trees were taken down to make room for sprawling lawns and enormous homes? It was still beautiful today, but it must have been absolutely gorgeous in Alaina's time.

Marla let her mind wander to memories of the many evenings she and Nathan would sit out on the patio with a drink and enjoy the beauty that surrounded them. They had a comfortable relationship, the type where they could finish each other's sentences or even guess what the other was thinking. She hadn't thought much back then about having a purpose in her life. She'd had Nathan and their friends and activities to fill her hours. But now, everything was different. She yearned for more. Much more. She just wasn't sure what it was she wanted.

After a while, she made her way back to the house and to her lonely bed.

* * *

The next morning, as Marla awoke, she gazed around her bedroom and thought about how this had once been Alaina's room. And the master bedroom where her husband had died was where Nathaniel had slept. Had Alaina been the one to choose the original colors in this room? It seemed likely, since she would have been the first wife to live here, but the original shades in here didn't fit with what she knew so far about Alaina. She had chosen a rich green for her room in the Summit Avenue house. Why on earth would she have had her room painted a dark burgundy here? Maybe Marla would find her answers as they continued to read the journal.

Marla showered and dressed, then walked down the hall, slowing as she passed Nathan's bedroom. She opened the door and tentatively glanced inside. Everything had been tidied up after he'd passed. The bed was made and there were no remnants of his long illness. But the room smelled stuffy and the heavy draperies and dark wall coverings made the room feel oppressive.

Marla hadn't given much thought about the bedroom before Nathan had grown ill. Since Nathan had occupied that room for several years before meeting Marla, she figured that explained its masculine décor. But now, after having spent months in the room watching her husband wither away, she had trouble even walking inside. For a moment, she wondered if she should redecorate the bedroom and lighten it up. But as soon as the thought entered her mind, she dismissed it. She'd never sleep in that room again anyway. It held too many sad memories.

Closing the door, she headed downstairs and skipped going into her office, opting for the kitchen instead. As she passed the French doors in the living room, she noticed it was cloudy and rainy outside. She sighed. At least she could always use the indoor pool if she wanted some exercise.

"Oh. Good morning." Mrs. Cooper looked up over her half-moon reading glasses. She sat on a stool at the counter, a newspaper spread out in front of her. She quickly closed the paper and stood. "Your tea isn't ready yet. I'll bring it to you in a moment."

"Good morning, Mrs. Cooper," Marla said, giving her a small smile. "Don't bother yourself. Please, keep reading the paper. I can make my own tea. Would you like some too?" Marla walked to the stove and clicked on the gas under the kettle.

Mrs. Cooper looked stunned. "You don't serve me tea. I serve you," she insisted. She walked over to the cupboard and pulled down a tea cup, saucer, and a plate. "I can start your breakfast now if you'd like."

Marla watched her, holding back a chuckle. Mrs. Cooper didn't like anyone in her kitchen, let alone doing her job. It all seemed so silly now that Nathan was gone. Marla didn't need to be waited on hand and foot.

"That will be fine, thank you," Marla said, giving in. She

walked over to the attached family room and looked out the window. "It's a gloomy day outside." When Mrs. Cooper didn't comment, she continued, "I'm not sure what I'll do with myself today. Can you think of any more projects I could do in the house?" She held back a grin, knowing she was annoying the older woman. But when she turned to see her expression, she was surprised that Mrs. Cooper was only looking at her curiously.

"Are you asking my opinion?" the housekeeper said.

"Of course. If anything needs refinishing or fixing, you would be the one to know."

"Well, if you don't mind my saying, the maid's room off the kitchen looks rather shabby. It wasn't remodeled when the kitchen was. It had been made a bit larger long ago, but they didn't do much to cheer it up. If someone were ever to live in there again, it wouldn't be very comfortable or nice."

Marla stared at Mrs. Cooper, speechless. She would never have expected her to make a suggestion like this in a million years.

The older woman's face turned sour. "Have I overstepped?" she asked.

"Oh, absolutely not. I think it's a wonderful idea. Let's have a look at it after breakfast and we can decide what can be done," Marla said.

Mrs. Cooper nodded and placed Marla's tea on a tray. She walked past her on the way to the breakfast nook. Marla followed dutifully.

After breakfast, the two women went to inspect the maid's room. Marla couldn't remember how long it had been since she'd seen it. The room used to belong to Mrs. Cooper, but when Nathan had bought her the cottage, she'd moved in there. No one had occupied the room since.

After pulling open the heavy draperies, they both studied the room in silence. It looked as if it hadn't been remodeled since the 1960s. There was gold carpeting and flowered wallpaper on three of the walls. The other wall had cheap dark paneling. A short hallway led to the small bathroom and there was a walk-in closet too. Nothing about this room looked like it belonged to this elegant house.

"You're right. It's ghastly," Marla said. "How did you stand living in here all those years?"

Mrs. Cooper pursed her lips. "It wasn't that bad years ago. This was the style. But I agree, it looks terrible now."

"Why is there no wainscoting in here? It's everywhere in the house."

"I suppose they didn't need the maid's quarters to be as fancy," Mrs. Cooper said. "The roof leaked in here around 1975, so that's when they expanded the wall and put up the paneling. Otherwise, it's been the same for decades."

"Well, I'm afraid this is far beyond my capabilities," Marla said. "I think we should hire a carpenter to fix up the room and completely remodel the bathroom. This room should look like the rest of the house, don't you think? With wainscoting along the lower walls and crown molding. Maybe even a bigger window, perhaps one with a window seat."

Mrs. Cooper nodded. "That sounds like a good idea. You never know when you may need this room again. People today wouldn't put up with a shabby living space like this."

Marla turned to her, suddenly intrigued by her once-foe who now seemed on her side. "How long have you worked for the Madison's, Mrs. Cooper?"

"Since 1969," she said proudly. "I started as a maid and worked my way up to head housekeeper. Of course, that was when they had a full staff. Nothing like today."

Marla ignored the jab. "You must have known Nathan's parents quite well. And his grandparents. Were they still alive and living here?"

"Mr. Madison's mother hired me. She was a lovely woman. Very kind. And his father was quite the gentleman, too. Nathan was only sixteen when I came to the house. He was a quiet young man, always reading when he wasn't out with friends at the yacht club. The grandparents had already passed on by the time I was hired."

Marla noticed how her eyes softened when she spoke of young Nathan and his parents. She wished she could have met them. "There's a lot of history in this house. I hadn't considered it before since there were no other relatives around. Now, I'm beginning to appreciate it," Marla said.

"Well, if you ever want to see what the family looks like, there are portraits in the attic. I helped carry them up there myself, years ago. They used to hang in the upstairs hallway, but Nathan's mother thought they were a bit creepy and had them taken down. She was the one who placed the paintings that hang up there now. That is, the ones I believe you might hang back up." Mrs. Cooper sniffed, returning to her old self.

"I think I will. Most of them are quite lovely," Marla said sincerely. The hallway paintings were a mixture of landscape watercolors, a lakeside shore, and one of the yacht club. "I'm assuming they were done by a local artist."

"Yes." Mrs. Cooper hesitated, then added, "Nathan's mother painted them."

Marla's eyes widened. "Really? I had no idea. Nathan never said a word about them."

"I suppose they'd been hanging there so long, he hadn't

really thought much about them," Mrs. Cooper said.

Marla sighed. There were so many things she didn't know about this house, the family, or their past. It was both maddening and sad.

"Well, I'll have to look at the portraits in the attic sometime," Marla said. "But first, I'll see about finding someone to remodel this room."

Mrs. Cooper closed the drapes again, although Marla didn't understand why she didn't leave them open, and they snapped off the light. As they walked back through the kitchen, Marla spoke.

"Thank you for telling me about the maid's room. This will be a fun project that really needs to be done."

Mrs. Cooper nodded, then went back to stacking the dishwasher. Marla had been dismissed.

With a wry grin, she headed to her office. It was getting easier to think of the morning room as her office now, and that made Marla happy. As she sat at her desk, she thought about who she could call to remodel the bedroom and bathroom. Then she remembered that Ardie had said her husband worked in construction. She thought Ardie might know someone through her husband who could do the project, or even from working at the store. She picked up her phone and called her, hoping she wasn't bothering her at work. Ardie answered on the second ring.

"Hi, Marla. What's up?" Ardie said, sounding chipper.

"Hi. I hope I'm not bothering you, but I had a question," Marla said.

"I'm on break, so it's no bother. Shoot."

Marla told her what she was looking for.

Ardie laughed. "You mean you aren't going to tackle this yourself?"

"No, this one is too big for me. But I might do the finishing work. We'll see."

"My husband, Dan, is a foreman of a crew that works for a contractor. His name is Roger Simms. He's a great guy, and honest, too. I can give you his number and you can see if he'll come out and look at the project."

"That would be great." Marla wrote down the contractor's number. "Thanks, Ardie. You saved me again. Maybe we can go to lunch sometime. It would be fun to sit and chat."

"I'm game any time you want to go," Ardie said.

After hanging up, Marla sat at her desk and smiled. She was happy. Really happy. She'd made new friends, had projects that kept her busy, and might even have won over Mrs. Cooper. Well, at least for today. She'd take it. Picking up her phone again, she dialed Roger the contractor, ready to delve into a new project.

* * *

Two weeks later, the ladies met at Rita's Craftsman-style home. Her home was as vibrant and colorful as Rita, with vivid red, green, and yellow everywhere, mixed in with natural shades of tan and cream. It worked, though. Rita had a style all her own, and it blended well with her personality.

Rita's paintings hung everywhere. Marla marveled at how beautiful her landscapes and still-life watercolors were. She had numerous canvases of the North Shore and Lake Superior, as well as local ones of the Mississippi River winding through the Twin Cities. Her still-life paintings were also incredible. She'd done one of antique tea cups on rustic shelves, and another of a green pie cupboard with ivy winding down from the top and a cat curled up on a shelf. The detail in the paintings was amazing.

She was truly talented.

"I'm not a great chef," Rita said the moment they walked in the door. "So Dominoes is cooking tonight."

They all laughed and enjoyed the pizza and cheesy sticks. She'd set out raw veggies and dip too and poured them each a glass of red wine. Her husband, Jerry, wandered in from the family room to steal a piece of pizza and grab a soda from the fridge.

"Don't mind me, ladies," he said with a grin. "I'm heading back to watch the game. The pizza was too tempting, though."

"What game is on tonight?" Wanda asked, looking confused. "The Twins aren't playing."

"Any game will do." He winked then headed back out of the room.

"I swear, he'd watch little league if that was all that was on. I caught him watching a dog show one day. He said it was like a sport," Rita said. "But he teaches all day, so I guess he deserves to watch mindless TV at night."

"What does he teach?" Marla asked, perking up.

"Graphic design at the high school. He's an art teacher, too, but these days everything is on the computer."

Marla nodded. She remembered how Nathan would come home from teaching college and just want to sit and unwind reading a book. After lecturing all day, he didn't really feel like talking. That had been fine when they'd first married, she'd even thought it was romantic to sit quietly together, reading. But over the years, she'd wished he'd communicated more.

After they'd eaten, Ardie spoke up. "I can't wait to hear more about Alaina's life. Did you want to read again tonight, Marla? Or should someone else?"

"Either way is fine with me," Marla said, pulling the journal out of the side pocket of her purse.

"I will," Rita offered excitedly. "If you don't mind me handling the journal. I'll be very careful."

Marla handed her the old book. "I know you will be." She gave her a warm smile.

Everyone got comfortable in the living room and Rita turned the page to the bookmark. She began to read.

I was surprised at how little my life changed after I was married. I was pleased as well. Marriage was not a cage for women as I had once believed. I was free to spend my days as I wished, even encouraged to do so by my husband.

Daily, I spent time at my father's home working on the factory or household ledgers. Sometimes, I lunched with Margaret and Emma who would accompany me to the house. Other times, I'd join Hannah for lunch or even ride into St. Paul and visit my father at the factory. Of course, I had many duties at my new home, conferring with the housekeeper, Tilda Hanson, and setting up a weekly menu for dinner. But for the most part, Mrs. Hanson ran the house and I was happy to let her. In truth, I preferred helping with my father's business over worrying about menus and household linens or groceries. And since Nathaniel worked long hours, he was happy that I was able to fill my days with activities that pleased me. But my nights were for him only.

Chapter Fifteen

Alaina

Autumn 1876

Alaina rode in the carriage the short distance to Hannah's home. It was a beautiful autumn day, and she would have preferred to walk, but Nathaniel asked her to let their driver, Sven Hanson, take her on her outings, so she gave in to his request. Besides, Mr. Hanson was always so eager to drive her and pleasant to be around, so she didn't mind too much. He was the husband of their head housekeeper, Mrs. Hanson, and both had been very welcoming to Alaina. While she missed the familiarity she'd had with Margaret at her father's home, Mrs. Hanson and the other staff—and there were many—had done their best to respect her role as Nathaniel's wife, and she appreciated it greatly.

She arrived at Hannah's a few minutes before noon and was greeted at the door by Mrs. Harper.

"Mrs. Anderson is in the parlor," the housekeeper told her, and Alaina went in directly.

"Ah, there you are," Hannah said, giving her a hug before sitting back down on the settee. She wore a yellow floral cotton dress with a lace insert at the neck and lace edging the sleeves. Yellow usually brightened the color in Hannah's fair skin but today she looked pale. "The children are taking a nap, thank goodness, and all is quiet around here. That's a rare occurrence." Hannah made a funny face.

Alaina laughed. "I'm sure they keep you busy. I had hoped to see them, though, but maybe next time."

Mrs. Harper announced that lunch was served, and the two women walked into the dining room and sat. Alaina had noticed the last few times she'd visited that Hannah looked tired. She also knew that her friend was desperate to lose weight that she'd kept on since the birth of her daughter last December. Hannah looked fine to Alaina, but her friend was used to having a tiny waist and complained about being thicker in the middle.

"I hope you don't mind a light lunch," Hannah said. "When it's warm out like this, I don't seem to have an appetite."

"It all looks delicious," Alaina said. Mrs. Harper had served chicken broth with vegetables and there were small, thinly-sliced ham and turkey sandwiches. A bowl of freshly cut strawberries sat on the table also with whipped cream to spoon over them.

"How have you been feeling?" Alaina asked her friend as she watched her pick at her food.

Hannah looked up at her. "I'm fine. I'm a bit tired, though. I've been busy lately, working at the church's Ladies' Aid Society. We're making quilts for the poor for this winter. There are so many families in need right now. We're also selling quilts to raise funds so families in need can buy food supplies for the upcoming winter."

"That's wonderful work," Alaina said. "Very rewarding."

Hannah nodded. "Yes. I feel that Matthew and I are so fortunate, and I should give back in some way." She gave Alaina a little smile.

"What? I know that look. You have a secret. Are you expecting again?"

"Heavens no!" Hannah grinned wider and leaned in closer to Alaina. "I know I shouldn't be happy about the misfortune of others, but I can't help it. The vice-president at the bank Matthew works for passed away last week. Matthew has been working closely with him for two years now."

"I'm sorry to hear that," Alaina said. "But why are you grinning?"

She spoke softly. "We think he might be offered the vice-president's job. It's not been mentioned to him yet, but he knows the job completely. This would be such a boost for our family. I know that sounds terrible to be happy, and the poor man died and all, although he was quite old and had lived a good life. But it would be so wonderful if Matthew gets the promotion."

"I'm so happy for you," Alaina said excitedly. "I don't see why he wouldn't be offered the position. Matthew is a hard worker and a good man. I'm sure he has a good chance."

As they each dished up strawberries and cream, Alaina asked, "Does your ladies' group need more help with quilting? Nathaniel has been encouraging me to participate in charity work. And I know I should. It would be fun if you and I worked together." Alaina hadn't thought of where she might volunteer and she was already so busy, helping her father and running the house. But she thought it might please Nathaniel if she volunteered in a church group.

"We can always use an extra set of hands," Hannah said, brightening. "And you're more than welcome to join. It used to be your church too, after all. But aren't you involved in planning the Christmas ball this year? That's such a high honor."

Alaina nodded and sighed. "Yes, I'm on the committee. And I should be thrilled that such distinguished women asked me to help organize it. But frankly, I'd rather use my time for a better purpose than deciding on decorations, food, and music for an uppity event."

Hannah raised her brows. "Uppity? It's the event of the season. And it's a charitable event as well."

"I know it is," Alaina said. "But honestly. Why don't we all just donate money to the charity plus the money it costs to put on the ball. It seems wasteful for all of us to buy new dresses and go to a fancy ball when that money could help feed families or heat homes."

"You never minded attending the ball before. In fact, it was after such an event that you and Nathaniel began courting," Hannah reminded her.

Alaina conceded. "Yes, you're right. Don't mind me. I'm just being cantankerous. Let's change the subject." In truth, Alaina was uncomfortable around the wealthy society women Nathaniel wanted her to socialize with. She had never been a woman who relished excess. She and her father had lived a comfortable life since his factory had become successful, and she'd always appreciated that, but she'd never wasted money. Now, she was around women who spoke of nothing but waste with their fancy gowns, expensive furniture, and exorbitant amounts spent on entertaining for no reason other than to overeat and gossip. It all seemed so extravagant to Alaina.

Her friend considered her a moment then gave her a small smile. "Are you any closer to becoming a mamma?" she asked hopefully. "I think it would be wonderful for our children to grow up together and be the best of friends."

Alaina laughed. "No, not yet. But it would be fun if our children were close in age. Nathaniel is hoping we are blessed with children soon. I am too, of course."

Hannah glanced around to make sure Mrs. Harper wasn't in the room. "I adore my children," she said in a hushed voice, "but I think two are the most I want to have. Matthew is in agreement, thank goodness."

Alaina stared at her friend curiously. "How does one go about controlling that?" she asked.

Hannah blushed, then giggled nervously. "There are ways. And when you and Nathaniel decide you've had all the children you want, we can discuss it."

Alaina found that humorous. She knew her friend enjoyed being intimate with her husband, so she couldn't imagine how they'd prevent having another child.

Suddenly, Hannah let out a laugh. "Look at us. Two society ladies talking about balls and volunteering and children. We've come a long way from the two little girls who played with tea sets and dolls and who giggled in dance class when we had to waltz with boys."

Alaina joined in on her laughter. Hannah was right. They'd grown up and become much more than either of them would have ever imagined.

She left in the late afternoon after hugging Hannah close and making plans to meet up at the church the next week. Although they'd had fun together as they always did, Alaina was still worried about Hannah's health. She'd looked so tired by the end of her visit. But she supposed that with two children and a busy life, it was probably normal to be tired. At least, that's what Alaina hoped was the problem.

That evening, as she and Nathaniel ate dinner in the small dining room, which was much cozier than the formal one, she mentioned she'd be joining Hannah in making quilts for fundraising at her former church.

"That's quite commendable," he said as he cut his steak into bite-sized pieces. "But I had thought you'd volunteer with the ladies at our church. It would be the perfect way to get to know them better."

Alaina studied him, gauging his reaction. True, he'd suggested she volunteer at their church, but she'd thought volunteering was more about doing good works than socializing with the right people. She was disappointed that he didn't seem pleased by her announcement of doing good works. "I hadn't thought it mattered where I volunteered," she said, carefully. "And I thought it would be enjoyable to work alongside my dear friend at my old church where I know so many others."

Nathaniel nodded as he chewed. After taking a sip of wine, he said, "I certainly understand how you'd prefer to stay with what's familiar. But I do hope you'll make an effort to get to know the ladies at our church, also. Many are wives of prominent businessmen and local politicians. Important people who might become good contacts in the future. Maybe you can invite some of them to tea one day, or we could have a small dinner party. I suppose, now that we're married, we should entertain more than I did before."

"Yes. That would be nice," Alaina agreed quietly, but she honestly didn't feel that way. She disliked entertaining. There were so many other things she'd rather do than sit and make silly small talk with women. Changing the subject, she asked, "How was your day at work? I'd love to hear what you did."

Nathaniel smiled at her for the first time that evening. A real smile, not the small one he'd given her when he'd arrived home. "I had a very good day. I made deals with several small millinery shops to supply high-quality women and men's hats for our stores on a regular basis. And I spoke with a furrier who creates the most beautiful beaver and raccoon coats. I'm sure we'll come to an agreement soon."

"It's wonderful that you're able to entice so many high-quality suppliers for your stores," Alaina said, imagining how rewarding that must feel. "Think of all the jobs you create when you set up contracts with the smaller shops. I'm sure they, in turn, must hire people to fill those orders. Just like my father's factory. The more businesses he supplies, the more employees he needs to hire."

Nathaniel raised a brow, considering her comments. "You're right, of course. How clever of you to realize the impact on the economy just one transaction can make. And as my stores grow, so does the need for employees. I'm looking at opening a store in Chicago next year. I have the land already, and if we have a good end to this year, I'm sure it will happen. It's exciting times for the business."

Alaina loved hearing about Nathaniel's business and wished she could, in even a small way, be a part of it. When they did entertain his store managers and larger suppliers, she listened intently to their conversation, absorbing everything. Their talk of business was so much more interesting than what the wives discussed. But for Nathaniel's sake, she always played the most gracious hostess, so he'd be proud of her. Still, she yearned to be more useful in important matters other than just entertaining and charity work.

* * *

Winter soon came and the days grew shorter and colder. On a brisk, windy day, Alaina had Sven drive her the short distance to her father's house and told him he could pick her up after one in the afternoon. He nodded and smiled as he helped her out of the carriage then drove away. Alaina liked Sven. He was a sturdily-built man with light blond hair and bright blue eyes. He had an easy smile and was always happy to drive her or help her in any way. Today, she figured she'd work on the ledgers then lunch with Margaret before returning home. After entering the house and hanging her coat in the closet, she was surprised to find her father bundled up under a blanket in his favorite chair near the fire, drinking hot tea.

"Are you feeling poorly?" Alaina asked, hurrying to his side. Her father never missed a workday unless he was extremely ill.

"Nothing but a stomach bug," he said, his voice tired. "Don't fuss over me." But then he winced after a sip of his tea and Alaina couldn't help but worry.

"Has the doctor come by to see you?" she asked. She noticed he looked pale and his eyes were dull.

Arthur took another sip of tea. "There's no need to call for a doctor, dear. It's just a stomach ache. Probably something I ate, nothing more. I felt too uncomfortable to go to work, but I'm sure I'll be fine by tomorrow. Margaret is making her chicken broth for me and you know that's as good as medicine."

Alaina knew better than to press him. He could be very stubborn when he didn't feel well. "I'm glad you're taking care and staying home today. There's a bite to the air outside."

"Are you here to work on the ledgers?" he asked, apparently wanting to change the subject.

Alaina nodded.

"I brought home the latest invoices yesterday, so you have

plenty to do. Don't mind me. I'll just sit here and enjoy the warm fire."

She smiled at her father all bundled up in his chair. He was such a dear. Since she'd married, he'd come to the house almost weekly for dinner and he and Nathaniel got along well. Alaina was pleased that they did. She would have missed her father dearly otherwise.

Alaina worked on the books for two full hours before she realized it was nearing noon. She carefully closed the ledger and put away her pen so it wouldn't leak on the desk's blotter. Then she rose, stretched, and smoothed her wool skirt. Seeing that her father had fallen asleep, she quietly left the room and made her way to the kitchen.

"I thought I'd join you for lunch," she told Margaret as she entered. The housekeeper had anticipated she'd eat with her and had already made up a plate for Alaina. The two women sat, and Margaret filled Alaina in on all the gossip in the neighborhood and how her own family was doing.

"I'm worried about your father," Margaret said in her thick German accent. "He's had stomach pains for a fortnight, but he refuses to call the doctor. He barely has an appetite and has lost weight, too."

Alaina frowned. She'd thought her father had looked thinner. "Is he missing work?"

"No. But you know your father. He'd go to work if he was dying. I was surprised that he stayed home today. He said he felt uncomfortable. I'm worried he has something worse than a simple stomach ache."

As far as Alaina had heard, there was no influenza spreading in the area. She hadn't heard of anything contagious for a while. Earlier that week at the church when she and Hannah were quilting with a group of ladies, no one expressed concern about any illnesses. She hoped that her father hadn't contracted something dangerous. "I'll talk to him again about seeing the doctor. It may be just a stomach ache, but he should have it checked."

Later, when Alaina brought up the subject with her father again, he waved away her concern. "I'm already feeling better after resting today," he told her. "Don't worry about me, dear. I'll be fine. Now, sit and tell me what you've been doing to keep busy, besides working on my ledgers and running two households." He chuckled.

Alaina didn't say another word about his feeling poorly, and the next day when she stopped by the house before going to the church to quilt, Margaret told her that Arthur had gone in to work. Both women decided he must be feeling better, but Alaina made the housekeeper promise to contact her if her father felt ill again.

That evening, after sitting together in the library, each reading quietly, Nathaniel joined Alaina in her bedroom and curled up beside her. Alaina's mind was filled with all she'd done that day and her schedule for the next, but she soon relaxed in Nathaniel's arms. As she gazed into his warm, brown eyes, she was thankful she'd found a husband who understood her and allowed her to be who she was. She hoped as the years went by, it would always be that way.

Chapter Sixteen

Marla

Rita stopped reading and marked the page. Everyone sat silent, absorbing all that she'd read.

"I'm worried about Hannah and Arthur," Rita said, breaking the silence. "Alaina seemed to think something was wrong with both of them. I hope nothing is. I really like them both."

The women stared at each other. "We're really getting involved in her story," Toni said. "I've never felt so connected to a story like this before."

"Probably because this isn't fiction. They were real people who lived real lives," Ardie offered. "I'm a little worried about Alaina and her marriage. It sounds like Nathaniel is slowly trying to manipulate her, in spite of what Alaina thinks. It's subtle, though."

Marla nodded. She remembered how her Nathan had slowly moved her away from her old life and into his. "I agree. The way he didn't like how she chose to volunteer at her old church instead of at his." She bit her lip. "Maybe we're just reading more into it, though."

Wanda spoke up. "Doesn't surprise me. Didn't rich people in those days marry well to breed but keep other women on the side for fun?"

Toni snorted. "Breed? Well, that's one way to look at it. I think some still do."

The other women laughed.

"Hey, I'm not kidding," Wanda said. "Nathaniel will probably leave her for some twenty-something girl as soon as he gets a male heir out of her. That's what men do. Then, and now."

Ardie gave her friend a sly smile. "And your opinion isn't prejudiced at all by the fact that your husband left you for a younger woman, right?"

"Not at all," Wanda said seriously. Then she broke out in a smile. "I'm completely over it. I'm not bitter at all."

The women burst out laughing.

"Okay. I'm not as bitter as I was. I'm working on it." Wanda grinned.

"It was his loss," Marla told Wanda. "I'm sure there's a guy out there who's just waiting for a woman like you with a great sense of humor."

"Yeah. Because that's what men want—a sense of humor. Besides, I'll never find a man working as a grade school nurse. I'm too old for the younger teachers and the last thing I need is a divorced man. Talk about bitter."

Rita shook her head. "There are men out there, I'm sure. We could find both you and Toni a great guy. And you, too, Marla. I mean, when you're ready."

Toni raised her hands as if to ward off a blow. "Leave me out of it. I'm not looking to be tied down with some guy who'll try to tell me what to do."

Rita ignored her cynical attitude. "We should take a girls'

vacation this summer. Somewhere fun. Like Hawaii. Or a cruise. I'll bet there are a lot of single men on a cruise."

"I'll go on a vacation any time you want, but leave the men out of it," Toni said, shaking her head.

Marla smiled at her friends. She loved listening to their silly banter. These were the type of friends she'd missed out on having over the years. She caught a glimpse of Ardie across the room and saw her roll her eyes good-naturedly at the women as they chattered on. This only made Marla smile wider. They were a wonderful group of women and she enjoyed spending time with them.

On the way to their cars, Ardie said to Marla, "Dan tells me his crew starts work on your house this Monday. Are you ready to live with noise for a while?"

"It won't bother me, but I'm not sure how Mrs. Cooper will be able to stand it. It was her idea to fix up the room, though, so that's the price she'll pay."

"Mrs. Cooper?" Ardie asked, looking confused.

"Oh, yeah. I guess I've never mentioned her before." Marla looked sheepish. "I was a little embarrassed to say I have a house-keeper. And what's worse, she can't stand me, but I still keep her on."

"I'm not surprised you have a housekeeper with that big house. But why on earth do you keep one who doesn't like you?"

Marla sighed. "She's been with the family since 1969. My husband tried to entice her to retire twice. He bought her a nice little house on the lake and gave her a pension. But she has stayed put. She was even in the will, and still she won't quit. She was loyal to my husband and adores my daughter, but not me. But I'm scoring some points with her over fixing up the maid's quarters. Maybe I'll win her over."

Ardie laughed. "Maid's quarters. I can't even imagine having such a thing. I'm sorry, Marla, but I can't relate to your life at all. But I'm so happy we're friends."

"Me, too," Marla said. "I'll probably see you tomorrow. I've figured out my next project and I need paint. I'm thinking a soft sage color. Or maybe a lemon yellow."

"I'll be there all day." Ardie waved and they both slipped into their cars and drove off.

That night after Marla had crawled into bed, she thought about Alaina and how similar their lives were, despite the years that separated them. Marla had been an independent woman with a single mother who'd raised her. Alaina had a mind of her own and a single father. Both had married a man they'd fallen in love with who was well-to-do. And it seemed as if Alaina's life changed as her husband encouraged her away from her old friends and toward new ones. That had definitely happened to Marla. Her friends from college and work had slowly disappeared as Marla became immersed in Nathan's life and friends. The connection between her and Alaina was almost eerie.

She wondered what other things she'll learn about Alaina as they read through the journal.

* * *

The next morning as Marla walked down the hallway to go downstairs, she wandered into what was once the nursery, many decades before. The room was large, with a brick fireplace, the usual dark wood wainscoting on the lower section of the walls as well as the dark wood flooring. A large rug with a leaf and tree design that had faded over the years filled the center of the room. The wallpaper was decorated with pictures of rabbits, ducks, and other animals wearing hats and coats and walking with canes or pushing baby carriages; images from an old children's storybook. It had yellowed with age and was peeling away at the corners. Marla found the wallpaper terrifying. The old depictions of the animals would give a child nightmares. They did for her. She wasn't sure who had first used the room as a nursery, but she had never used it for Reese. There was a room connected next door for a live-in nanny—which, to Nathan's surprise, Marla hadn't wanted—and another room on the other side which she'd used as Reese's room. It had been painted a soft pink years before and had sweet priscilla curtains on the windows. Through the years, Reese had changed the room to colors she'd liked better, but now it was the same as it had been when she'd left for her dorm room in college.

Marla decided the nursery would be her next project. Then, perhaps she'd fix up the nanny's room, which had its own bathroom, and work her way down the hall. A smile touched her face. She was excited again about transforming a useless room into something fresh and new.

"What are you doing in here?" Mrs. Cooper asked from the doorway. She was carrying an armload of clean, folded sheets.

Marla nearly jumped out of her skin. "You scared the life out of me." She turned toward the housekeeper. After taking a calming breath, she said, "I'm sure you're not going to like it, but I've decided to redecorate the nursery. It hasn't been used in decades. It needs a facelift."

Mrs. Cooper walked further into the room and glanced around, her expression unreadable. Marla thought for sure she was thinking about the antique wallpaper and how terrible it would be to tear it down.

"I know the paper is old, and may even be worth something

to someone," Marla said quickly. "I was thinking I should pull it down carefully and save it, not rip it down like in the other rooms."

Mrs. Cooper turned to her. "I'd just tear it down. It's terrifying. I'm so glad you didn't make Reese use this room as a child." With that, she headed out of the room.

Marla stared after her, rooted to her spot, stunned. Finally, she couldn't hold it in. She blurted out a laugh that echoed in the empty room. "That's the second thing we've agreed on," she said aloud. "Maybe we'll get along just fine after all."

She arrived at the home remodeling store right at noon and went directly to the paint department. Ardie was just finishing up with a customer.

"You're timing is perfect. You can buy me lunch," Ardie said, smiling.

"I'd be happy to." The two women went to the little coffee shop next door in the strip mall and ordered coffee and sandwiches.

"You couldn't have timed that any better," Ardie said. "But I was kidding about you buying me lunch."

"I'm happy to do it." Marla stirred sugar into her coffee. "You would never believe what happened this morning. So far, my housekeeper has been against my remodeling anything in the house, except the maid's quarters. Today, she actually agreed with me that the scary bunny paper in the nursery had to go. That wallpaper has to be as old as the house, yet she hated it too. Said to tear it down and throw it away."

"You're winning her over. That's great," Ardie said.

"So, what's going on in your life?" Marla asked.

"Well, my husband is starting a new job at a very rich person's house on Bellwood Avenue next Monday," she said with a smirk.

"Oh, and my son found a job. I'm so excited for him. He'll be starting as a teller at a bank but with his degree, they want him to work up to lead teller within a few months and then possibly a loan officer. It sounds like he'll have plenty of opportunities there."

"That's wonderful!" Marla said, genuinely excited. She lifted her coffee mug and they clinked them in a toast. "It's just like Hannah's Matthew in Alaina's journal. I can't wait to find out what happens with them next."

"Me too," Ardie said. "It's so interesting. Someone should turn it into a novel for people to enjoy. It's a great story."

Marla's brows raised. "That would be interesting. But let's first see how it turns out. We don't know if Alaina gets a happy ending."

"So you don't know anything about your husband's family? You never heard about Alaina before this?" Ardie asked, looking intrigued.

Marla shook her head. "No. Not a word. Nathan never talked about his family and his parents had passed on before we were married."

"That's interesting," Ardie said. "I mean, a lot of people don't keep track of their family's past, but you live in the same house as generations of his family. It seems there'd be photo albums or at least portraits of family members."

Marla thought a moment. "Mrs. Cooper said that years ago family portraits hung in the upstairs hallway, but then Nathan's mother put them in the attic and hung other paintings on the walls instead. Maybe I should snoop around in the attic. I've been up there before, but I've never looked around. It's kind of creepy." She pretended to shiver.

"Maybe it would be fun if we all go up there sometime. That

way it won't seem scary. If you don't mind us poking around up there."

"I wouldn't mind at all. It might be fun," Marla told her.

The hour was almost over, so Marla paid the bill and they headed back to the store. She'd decided on a sage color, so she searched the paint samples and found the right one. She filled up her cart with primer, more roller brushes, roller trays, and the paint.

"I'll see you soon," Marla said after Ardie gave her the two gallons of paint. "I want to tile that fireplace too, so I'll be in for new tile."

"That place won't look the same once you're done with it," Ardie said, laughing. "Have fun."

"Oh, I will. I can't wait to tear down the creepy bunnies."

Later that afternoon, that was exactly what Marla did. She tore the paper off, then used her tools to scrape off the stubborn paper. Halfway through ripping it down, Anita appeared in the doorway with a roll of garbage bags.

"I was asked to come up here and help you pick up your mess," she said, giggling. "Mrs. Cooper said you would be knee-deep in wallpaper by now."

Marla grinned. "I could use the help. Thanks. For once, Mrs. Cooper is on my side."

Anita snapped open a bag and started stuffing it with wallpaper. "She said she hated this paper. I was surprised by that. She's always telling us to be careful not to ruin anything in this house because it's all vintage."

"She has that right. Everything is vintage. But some of it is just old."

They worked until five o'clock then Anita took off. She'd picked up all the paper that had been taken down so far. Mrs.

Cooper came in to tell Marla she was leaving for the weekend.

"There's a sandwich in the refrigerator for you, and some cut-up vegetables," she said.

"Thank you." Marla brushed away a strand of hair that had fallen in her eyes. "What do you think of this room so far?"

The older woman surveyed it carefully. "It's much better without the wallpaper. That rug could be rolled up and put in the attic too. The room could use a new one."

Marla nodded. "I agree completely."

"What color are you going to paint it?" Mrs. Cooper inquired.

"I chose a soft sage color."

"Good choice. It would be fine for a boy or girl. It could be used as a guest room too, if it's not used as a nursery." She glanced over at the fireplace. "Will you change that, too?"

"I was thinking of tiling over it. I haven't chosen a tile yet, though." Marla waited for Mrs. Cooper to make a snide remark.

"Maybe something simple, and light," she said. "It'll soften the look of the room. And new curtains, too."

Marla stared at her, trying hard not to let her mouth fall open. Was the poor woman feeling ill? Had Marla knocked all the fight out of her?

"Well, good night." Mrs. Cooper turned and left.

"Goodnight," Marla called after her. She was too stunned by Mrs. Cooper's approval to say much else.

That weekend, Marla worked non-stop on the nursery, preparing the walls to paint. Sunday night, as she was about to collapse in front of the television in the family room while she ate dinner, her phone rang. To her amazement, Vicki's name popped up.

"Hi, Vicki. What a nice surprise."

"Hi, Marla. I hope I'm not imposing on your Sunday

evening," she said, sounding distant.

"No. Not at all. I was just taking a break from working on one of the bedrooms. What can I do for you?" After her last conversation with Vicki and Catrina, she doubted she'd called just to gossip.

"The members of the yacht club would like to honor Nathan with a plaque for being a life-long member and for all the Madisons have done to support the club over the years," Vicky said. "We're going to have a little ceremony during the June Ball, and I wanted to invite you and Reese. I'm assuming, since you haven't bought tickets, you hadn't planned on attending. But I hope you'll reconsider so you can be present for this honor for your husband."

"Oh. Well, that's very nice of the club to do that," Marla said, at a loss for words. It was the last thing she would have expected from the club. When she didn't say more, Vicki continued speaking.

"I know things have been difficult for you since Nathan's passing. And you're still trying to find your bearings. But I do hope you still consider me and Catrina as friends. We've made so many memories together, I'd hate to think we've lost all that."

Marla suddenly felt guilty. She hadn't meant to be short with them that day at her house. Vicki was right—she was still trying to find her way without Nathan in her life. And leaving the club and everyone behind probably wasn't the best solution. "I do still think of you and Catrina as friends. And I'm sorry I snapped at you both. You're right, it's been difficult since Nathan's passing. I'm just trying to find my way without him in my life."

"I'm so happy to hear that, Marla," Vicki said, sounding cheerier. "I do value our friendship. And Catrina does too. She'll be relieved to hear that you aren't really mad at us. As for the ball, I do hope you'll come. We'd love to have Reese attend, as well. I'll be extending the invitation to her, too. And you'll be the club's guests. No need to buy tickets. Please feel free to bring someone. Reese too. Is she still dating that nice young man? What was his name?"

"Chad Winters," Marla said. "As far as I know, yes, she is."

"Ah, yes. He seems like a very nice young man. And from such a fine family, too. Very wealthy."

Marla winced. Wealthy. She couldn't care less if Chad had money or not as long as he was good to Reese. But of course, his being wealthy would mean something to Vicki. Marla took a breath and held her tongue, not wanting to snip again at Vicki.

"I'll email you the details about the ball. Of course, you've been to so many of them, you probably know all the details by heart. I can't wait to see you, dear. Talk to you soon." Vicki sounded like her old gleeful self again.

"Yes. Goodbye," Marla said before hanging up. She didn't feel as cheerful as Vicki had sounded. Marla wasn't at all sure if she would be happy seeing everyone at the club again.

* * *

The next week was a busy one with Dan's crew starting work on the maid's quarters and Marla spending her time upstairs painting the nursery. Ardie's husband was pleasant and efficient, and the crew members were good workers too. They'd immediately laid a heavy drop cloth on the floor leading from the outside door to the maid's room and had hung plastic in the doorway to protect the kitchen from any mess. That particular action had made Mrs. Cooper quite happy. Even with the loud noise off the kitchen, Mrs. Cooper had no complaints. This both surprised and pleased Marla.

Marla had visited the store again and found a beautiful Grecian-white marble tile to place over the brick fireplace in the nursery. It would go well with the black marble tile hearth. After a week-and-a-half of painting, tiling, and listening to sawing and pounding coming from the room downstairs, Marla was relieved at last to leave the house and go to Wanda's for their book club meeting.

Wanda lived in a nice, 1980s style neighborhood of split-level homes with mature pine, oak, and birch trees in the yards. Wanda had said once that she'd won the house in the divorce settlement and it had been paid off, so it was the second good thing she got out of the marriage—the first being her now seventeen-year-old daughter, Miley.

Ardie pulled in behind Marla and the two women walked up the sidewalk together, each balancing a casserole dish of food.

"How's the work going in the maid's quarters?" Ardie asked. "Dan says they're almost finished."

"They've been wonderful. Dan is so nice. He's like a big cuddly teddy bear."

Ardie chuckled. "Wait until hunting season when he grows a beard. He becomes a grizzly bear then."

Marla smiled as she tried to picture him that way. "They're doing a great job. That room is going to look so nice when they're finished. And even Mrs. Cooper is happy. Did you hear she made sandwiches for the crew for lunch the other day and even baked cookies? Who knew she could be so friendly?"

"I'm glad it's working out well. I feared something might go wrong, and you'd never talk to me again."

"I knew that wouldn't happen. I trust your judgement," Marla told her.

Wanda's kitchen was upstairs, a warm, inviting space with a tiled fireplace in the attached dining room next to the big oak farm-style table. Everyone had brought food that was Italian-themed, and they stuffed themselves on lasagna, meatballs, and crusty garlic bread. Then they gathered in the living room on her cushy sofa and chairs to hear more of Alaina's story.

"Do you mind reading tonight?" Wanda asked Marla. "I hate reading aloud. I don't have the voice for it."

"I don't mind," Marla said. She pulled the journal out of her bag and opened it.

The winter of 1876-77 was a busy one as I split my time between volunteer work, my father's ledgers, and running the household and staff. The Christmas Ball was a success as was the New Year's Eve party we hosted for the managers of Nathaniel's stores as well as the owners of businesses he purchased merchandise from. My father looked weary the night of the party, but refused to let me coddle him and seemed to have a good time. I worried, though. I had never seen him look anything but robust and full of energy. I was concerned about my dear Hannah, as well. She was no longer the energetic, spirited woman I had grown up with. She always looked pale and drawn. But she continued to help with the quilting and other church work for the poor and never complained. I, on the other hand, was restless. Despite being busy with meaningful work, and happily married to Nathaniel, it felt as if I were waiting for something to happen. Something big. And in the spring of 1877, I finally realized what it was I'd been waiting for.

Chapter Seventeen

Alaina

May 1877

"I believe I'm expecting," Alaina whispered to Hannah as they sat at a table by themselves, working their needles in and out of the cotton fabric in neat, fine stitches.

Hannah gasped and her blue eyes sparkled for the first time in months. "Are you sure?"

She nodded and couldn't help but smile brightly. "I'm almost certain. My monthly is late and I've felt a bit ill every morning. I've made no mention to Nathaniel yet, and won't, until the doctor has confirmed it. But I was just going to burst if I didn't tell someone."

Her friend rose and hugged her. "I'm so happy you told me first!"

"What are you two chattering about?" Ellen Parsons asked from across the room. Both women had known her since they were young and neither of them particularly liked her. She was nosy and gossiped endlessly.

"Never mind us," Hannah told her before sitting down again. She turned back to Alaina. "This is going to be so much fun," she whispered. "We can make little nightgowns and booties, and even make a little quilt for the crib." She stopped talking and her smile faded.

"What is it?" Alaina asked, suddenly concerned.

"Oh, I was just thinking that we don't need to do those things anymore. I forget that you're married to a man who owns the most successful department stores in the city, and you can afford to buy anything you need. And ever since Matthew's promotion to vice-president of the bank last year, we're doing quite well also. I suppose sewing a baby's layette is beneath us at this point."

"Not if we enjoy doing it, it isn't," Alaina said. "And I'd love handmade items we made together for my baby." She smiled again and so did Hannah. "Let's just pray I'm not wrong and that a baby is on the way."

Alaina learned she was expecting a baby two weeks later after visiting the doctor. She was due in early January of 1878. When she broke the news to Nathaniel, his eyes lit up and he hugged her tightly, then pulled back, fearful he'd hurt her. Alaina laughed with joy.

"You can't hurt the baby, silly," she said. "He or she is just a peanut at this point."

"You have made me a very happy man," Nathaniel told her, kissing her gently. "Now, you must not overdo it. I don't want you running about as you normally do. You must take care of yourself."

"I'll be fine," she said. "The doctor said I could continue my daily routine as long as I don't lift heavy items and I get enough sleep at night. I've been a little ill in the mornings, but he said that will pass."

Her husband looked at her seriously. "Please promise me you'll take good care of yourself. I don't want anything to happen to you or our baby."

She nodded. She understood his fear. While it wasn't discussed in polite society, one heard often of women losing babies or dying in childbirth. "I will take care of myself and our child," she promised. *Our child,* she thought afterward. Those two words made her so happy.

For a time, Alaina continued helping at the church alongside Hannah and working on the ledgers at her father's house. Arthur was thrilled to hear he'd be a grandfather. He also insisted that Alaina take good care and offered to bring the ledgers to her home if that would be easier for her. But Alaina shook her head.

"It won't hurt me to come here once or twice a week and work," she told him. "I like getting out of the house and visiting with Margaret. But I promise, if it becomes too difficult, I will let you know."

"I can always hire a bookkeeper, you know," he offered. "After all, once the baby is born, you'll be too busy to bother with this."

"Oh, no. I love doing this work," she insisted. "As long as I'm able, I'll be your bookkeeper."

Arthur smiled warmly at her. "Your mother would be so proud of you. You really are an amazing young woman." He hugged her tightly.

Alaina wrapped her arms around her father, her heart warmed by his obvious love for her. She could feel how thin he'd become, and wondered why. He hadn't looked like he'd lost much weight, although his beard did a good job of hiding any weight loss in his face.

"Are you feeling well?" she asked, studying him closely when she pulled away.

"Now don't go worrying about me, dear. I've lost a bit of weight, but I could stand to lose it. Margaret's cooking was making me too plump as it was. Only worry about yourself and the little one."

Alaina didn't say any more about it, but she was worried.

The next two months, Alaina felt well enough to continue all her activities. By the middle of the third month, she was no longer feeling sick in the mornings and her appetite increased.

Nathaniel treated her like she was a royal princess and often brought home gifts. A sterling silver vanity set with her name engraved on it, a decorative gold hair comb encrusted with garnets, a delicate gold chain bracelet. She felt pampered and loved, overwhelmed by how generous he was. And although he rarely visited her at night now, insisting she needed her sleep, occasionally he did curl up in bed beside her, holding her. His arms made her feel more cherished than any gift he could give her.

Near the end of her third month, she had word from Hannah that she wouldn't be joining the ladies at the church that week. Concerned that she might be ill, Alaina dropped by her home to check on her. Mrs. Harper showed her upstairs to Hannah's bedroom.

"I'm so sorry to bother you, dear," Alaina said, finding her friend in bed, looking ghostly white. "I was worried when your note said you weren't coming to the church today."

Hannah gave a weak smile. "I'm the one who's sorry. I just didn't feel up to going anywhere today. I'm afraid it will be a few weeks before I'm strong enough to help with the quilts again."

Alaina frowned. She'd been worried about Hannah's health for months, but now she was even more scared that something was wrong.

Hannah laughed. "You can put away that worried frown. I'm not ill in a bad way. In fact, this may be a blessing in disguise. I'm expecting."

Alaina's eyes widened. "You are? That's wonderful! But I thought you were trying not to have another child."

Hannah shrugged. "It's not always easy to control. But once I was over the initial shock, I was thrilled. Now you and I will have a child near the same age. What fun will that be? They'll grow up together, and maybe even be best friends. Wouldn't that be lovely?"

Alaina sat on the bed beside her dear friend. "Yes. That will be perfect. Now we have two layettes to make. That will keep us very busy."

Hannah nodded. "As soon as I get over this initial phase of morning sickness. It's terrible, isn't it? I feel so weak. You were so much stronger during your first few months. I wish I had your stamina."

"You'll be fine in a few weeks. What did Matthew think of the news?"

Hannah bit her full bottom lip. "He was surprised, but he got over it quickly. He immediately said we must hire a second nanny to care for the baby so our other one can watch the older children. I'm afraid we're growing out of our small house. It might be time to move."

"But you love this house," Alaina said.

"I know. But it might be fun to move to a bigger one. Maybe closer to you."

Alaina smiled at her friend. "That would be nice. To be within a short walking distance of each other."

Hannah's eyes brightened. "Isn't it amazing how wonderfully our lives have turned out? We're both married to kind and successful men and live prosperous lives. Who would have thought that this was how our lives would have turned out when we met at twelve years old?"

Alaina thought back to that first day she'd met Hannah, both wearing their ankle-length dresses with neat pinafores over them, their shiny black button-up boots peeking out from underneath. Snow White and Rose Red; that was what Hannah's mother had called them. Who knew then that they'd have remained friends all these years?

"Yes," she answered. "We are truly blessed with our lives."

Over the summer, Hannah and Matthew did move into a larger home, but it was on their very same street of Holly Avenue. A wealthy man who'd made his money in silver mining had built the house for his wife, but she'd died unexpectantly before it was finished. Since his heart was no longer in it, he sold it to Matthew for a decent price and they moved in during the warmest days of August. The Victorian home had three stories with five bedrooms on the second floor and three bedrooms on the third, accommodating their growing family and staff. A beautiful three-story turret rose up on the right side of the house, and Hannah claimed the lower floor of it for her morning room.

Alaina marveled at the beauty of Hannah's home when she visited the first time. Stained glass accent windows allowed a rainbow of color in various rooms while the beautiful mahogany woodwork throughout shone, polished to perfection. They sat many hours in the rounded morning room on the new rose settee and chair, embroidering the yokes of tiny white nightgowns and adding lace to hems and sleeves.

Alaina continued to worry about her friend, though. Hannah's morning sickness had subsided, but she complained of feeling tired and weak. They no longer volunteered at the church together, although Alaina did begin to volunteer time at her and Nathaniel's church to please him. She was slowly making new friends with the women there and also the wives of Nathaniel's business associates. They entertained often, usually small dinner parties, and soon Alaina felt comfortable around Nathaniel's many friends and their wives. She dressed the part of the successful merchant's wife, wearing new gowns that he insisted she have made by the most expensive designer in town, and dripping in jewels he bestowed upon her as gifts. But even though she was growing used to her new life, Alaina felt most comfortable wearing her no-frill clothing and sitting at her father's desk working with the ledgers or in Hannah's morning room stitching tiny gowns.

By September, Alaina was growing large and Nathaniel insisted she cut back on her daily routine. She felt completely healthy, only more tired than usual, but she finally gave in to his demands because she didn't want to upset him. Arthur agreed with her husband, and he hired a bookkeeper to work with the ledgers and deposits. Giving up that work was the most difficult part of being pregnant for Alaina. She liked feeling useful and now all she felt was large and useless. But she did have to admit that when the baby came, she couldn't be running to her father's house nearly every day to work and lunch with Margaret. Yet, she knew she would miss it.

Six days after they'd celebrated the new year in 1878, Alaina went into labor. The doctor and midwife were sent for, Emma stayed by her side, and Alaina's father came to sit with Nathaniel to await the birth. By evening, the baby was born; a round little boy weighing eight pounds, six ounces. Smiling up at her husband and father, Alaina announced the name they'd agreed upon—Arthur Tobias Madison—much to Arthur's delight.

Nathaniel beamed with pride, kissed his wife sweetly on the cheek, and presented her with a ruby and diamond necklace and earrings for giving him an heir.

* * *

Alaina had never known she could love anyone or anything as much as she did little Arthur. Her heart swelled with pure joy each time she held the tiny infant and she insisted on spending as much time as possible with him despite their having hired a wet nurse and nanny.

"You should rest and leave the work of the baby to the hired help," Nathaniel admonished her every time he saw her rocking the child or carrying him. "You've been though a great ordeal. You need to heal."

Alaina would smile and shake her head. "I'm fine. I'm stronger than you think. I laid in bed for three days and I can't bear to lie around any longer." Alaina knew that Nathaniel didn't understand her desire to be with her baby, or her need to be useful. She'd reluctantly give up little Arthur to the wet nurse when he needed to be fed but then would take him afterward and rock him to sleep in her arms. She didn't want to miss a single minute with him, this little treasure she and her husband had brought to life.

Hannah sent a note explaining she wasn't feeling well enough to come and visit the baby but sent over a box full of the lovely gowns she'd made as well as a baby quilt in blue and white with embroidered baby animals on it. Alaina loved her gifts, especially because they were from her dear friend. Business associates and friends had sent gifts too: silver engraved cups, baby rattles, lovely layettes in blue and white, soft blankets, and knitted baby booties. But it was the quilt from Hannah that Alaina treasured the most.

Her father brought a wooden rocking horse on one of his many visits, which made Alaina laugh.

"He's too young for that," she'd told him, kissing his cheek and noticing he'd lost more weight.

"I know, dear. But an employee of mine makes these and I couldn't resist. Little Arthur will grow into it and will wear it out, just you wait and see." Arthur smiled brightly at his namesake and held him lovingly in his arms. He'd been so honored that his daughter had chosen his own name for her firstborn, and now, as Alaina watched him cuddle the tiny baby as he walked around the room, she was so happy that she had. Her father looked ghostly white, his eyes sunken into his once full face. Something was wrong, but he wouldn't tell her what. As soon as she was able, she was determined to speak with Margaret and get to the bottom of his illness.

The days went by quickly and the cold winter air warmed enough to clear the roads of the mushy snow and slippery ice. Alaina rose early one morning in late February, determined to visit both Hannah and her father's house so she could speak to Margaret about his health. When she entered the smaller dining room to breakfast with Nathaniel, she was greeted with a frown on his face.

"Good morning, dear," she said, ignoring his displeasure and offering him a soft kiss on the cheek.

"You look like you're planning on going out today," he said, setting down his newspaper.

"Yes." She accepted a plate of eggs and a muffin from a young maid who Tilda had recently hired to help in the kitchen. Searching her mind, she remembered her name. "Thank you,

Mary." She turned to Nathaniel. "I thought I'd ask Sven to drive me to Hannah's home today. I want to check on her to see how she's feeling."

Nathaniel watched her, his brows coming together. "I'd prefer if you'd stay at home a while longer. You need to worry about your own health first before worrying about the health of others."

Alaina froze, her fork in midair. She'd never heard her husband speak so sternly to her before, like she was an errant child. Taking in a calming breath, she set her fork down and smiled at him. "I feel fine. Please don't worry about me. It's been weeks since little Arthur was born, and I'd like to get out for a bit."

"Have you grown tired of the baby already?" Nathaniel asked.

Alaina was stunned. "Of course not. How can you even ask such a thing?"

Nathaniel cleared his throat. "I'm sorry," he said, looking contrite. "That was cruel. Of course you've been a doting mother since his birth. I just feel you should spend a little more time at home before you begin calling on friends again."

Alaina folded her hands in her lap and sat back, studying her husband. She didn't understand why he suddenly felt she should be homebound. Mary came in again and asked if she'd like more tea, and she accepted. After she'd gone back to the kitchen, Nathaniel spoke again.

"Please ignore my sour mood, dear." He reached over and patted her hand in her lap. "I've been much too busy at work and I shouldn't take it out on you. Go along and visit your friend. I'll tell Sven to have the carriage ready for you." He stood and bent to kiss her on the cheek, then left the room.

Alaina's eyes followed him out. She was confused over his behavior. Perhaps he was just being cautious. She should be pleased that he worried about her well-being. Still, his attitude was strange. Sighing, she gave up on figuring out why he was behaving oddly and ate her breakfast. She had much to do today.

Chapter Eighteen

Marla

"You see? Nathaniel is turning into a brute. Just like all men." Wanda scrunched her nose as if there were a terrible smell in the room. Her blue eyes sparked with rage.

Ardie laughed softly. "Calm down, Wanda. The man's been dead for decades."

"Wanda's not too far off the mark, though," Toni said. "He claimed he had an open mind when they married. He told her he liked her independent streak. And now that she's had an heir for him, he feels he can push her around. It's maddening." She sat back and smoothed out her slacks. "That's why I never married. No one owns me."

Rita chuckled. "My husband would say I own him. He does my bidding, not the other way around."

"We have to consider the time period, I suppose," Marla interjected. "Men thought of women as their property."

"True," Ardie agreed, and the other women nodded. "How horrible, though. To have to ask your husband just to go out to see a friend. Thank goodness some things have changed."

Marla nodded but kept silent. She understood how Alaina felt. When she'd married Nathan, she'd been an independent woman. But after years of marriage, that had changed without her even realizing it. Maybe her husband and the original Nathaniel weren't so different after all.

"You look deep in thought," Ardie said, tapping Marla on the arm.

Marla glanced up. She didn't dare share her thoughts with them. She was afraid they'd think she'd been weak in her marriage, and they all seemed so strong. "We should take a walking tour of the houses on Summit Avenue and the surrounding area," she blurted out, surprising herself. "I'd love to see Alaina's house, and Hannah's house, if they still exist."

Toni brightened. "What a great idea. Many of them still do exist around there, although they were such grand mansions that several have been turned into condos or townhouses. There's actually a map online telling about each house and who built it. F. Scott Fitzgerald's homes where he grew up are in that area, too."

"Oh, that would be fun," Rita clapped with glee. "Let's do it. I'm free Saturday morning if you all are."

They made a plan to meet at a cafe on Grand Avenue near Summit for breakfast and then would tour the area. That night, when Marla got home, she searched her computer for a walking tour map of the Summit Avenue area. It wasn't hard to find. Then she searched on Google Maps to see if she could find where the first Nathaniel Madison lived. After a half-hour of pushing the little man up and down Summit on the map, she finally saw a house that fit Alaina's description. Five stories, turrets on each end, and a portico on the left side.

"That has to be it!" she exclaimed to the empty room. She

marked down the address on the map she'd printed out, then looked for the two houses Hannah lived in on Holly Avenue. She couldn't wait until Saturday. It was going to be fun to see the past come to life.

* * *

Saturday dawned a beautiful, sunny day with forecasted highs in the low seventies. The ladies met at nine a.m. at The Uptowner Café on Grand and were escorted to an empty table.

"This place is cute," Rita said as they squeezed into a red padded booth. "It reminds me of the old diners from days gone by."

Ardie chuckled. "And you fit right in with your cuffed jeans and high-top sneakers," she told Rita.

Rita beamed. "You said to dress comfortably, so I did."

They each ordered a big breakfast because they knew they'd be walking for several hours. After the waitress left, both Marla and Toni pulled out their maps and piles of papers that described each house on the walking tour.

"It's strange how you can live in a town all your life and never bother to visit the popular sites," Toni said. "As soon as I started researching this area, I was amazed at all the history here. And tourists come from all over the country to walk down these streets and admire the homes."

"Yeah. It's crazy," Wanda agreed. "I'm sure Fitzgerald has a lot to do with the interest in the area, but it's full of interesting history."

"I can't wait to see Nathaniel and Alaina's home. And Hannah's," Ardie said enthusiastically. "History is coming alive today."

They filled up on waffles, pancakes, eggs, omelets, and bacon, then headed out into the beautiful spring day to start their walk.

"Let's start our walk from this end of Summit," Marla suggested. "Many of Fitzgerald's homes are close by, and Nathaniel's house isn't too far from here either. Then we can go up to Laurel and Holly Avenues and look for Alaina's dad's house and Hannah's."

"Sounds like a plan," Ardie said.

Rita's camera hung from around her neck over her red flower print tunic top. "I thought it might be fun to paint a house or one of the neighborhoods if I get a good picture," she said to Marla as they walked up the block from Grand to Summit.

"That would be fun." Marla only had her phone to take pictures with, but she was fine with that. Her daughter always told her she took terrible pictures anyway.

The group turned right on Summit Avenue and after walking for several blocks, they came to Summit Terrace, the first set of homes where F. Scott Fitzgerald had lived. The ladies stopped to admire the row houses built in 1889 that were numbered 587 – 601 on the street. They were made of brick and had a Gothic look. Fitzgerald had lived in number 599 with his parents in 1918, and had completed his first novel, *This Side of Paradise*, in a room on the third floor.

"I can just see him now," Rita, the dreamer in the group said, "jauntily walking out the door and down the stairs, heading out to meet up with old friends at a local watering hole."

Marla smiled. She could imagine it too, in this old-fashioned neighborhood with tidy lawns and huge oak trees. Men in three-piece suits and women in long skirts and shirtwaists, wearing hats and gloves as they went visiting.

As they continued walking down the quiet street, they were

amazed at the variety of homes. Queen Anne, Gothic, Victorian, Italianate Cupola, Tudor, and Georgian Revival. Some were as tall as five stories, with watch towers, turrets, widow's walks, porticos, gingerbread trims, and leaded or stained-glass windows. The details were astounding, and the women stared in wonder as they made their way down Summit.

Halfway down the long street, they all stopped walking.

"Is that it?" Wanda asked in a hushed tone.

"Yes, I think it is," Ardie whispered back.

"Why are we whispering?" Toni asked. Everyone laughed then and started talking in a normal tone.

"Nathaniel Madison's house," Marla said as she gazed at the five-story brick home. She couldn't believe she was standing in front of the same home Alaina spoke about in her journal. It wasn't marked on the map or described in the papers they'd printed out. Marla wondered how an important and wealthy man such as Nathaniel, one of the first to build his mansion on this avenue, could be left out of history.

"It looks exactly how I imagined it from Alaina's description," Ardie said. "And it hasn't changed a bit in over one-hundred and forty years."

Marla nodded, but she thought that it had. She suspected there had been open lots around it when Alaina had lived here, and the lot behind the house had been empty too, because they'd used it as a stable for the horses and a carriage house. But the house was there, intact, and looked to have been kept up beautifully. Marla was pleased this mansion hadn't been turned into apartments or townhouses. While it might have been remodeled inside, for all she knew, it still looked like Alaina's home on the outside.

Toni tapped Marla on the shoulder and held out her phone.

"I found this on Zillow. The house sold for an outrageous price five years ago, but this is what it looked like inside."

The group gathered around Marla as she scrolled through the pictures. The floors were still polished hardwoods throughout and the wainscoting and stair rails were still intact. But the ballroom had been turned into a game room and bar/entertainment area and the kitchen had been remodeled into an open-concept style. But the fireplaces remained in every room and much of the house had been kept in the antique style. Even the light fixtures looked to be original.

"I'd looked at these before but they still amaze me," Marla said. "It's incredible it's still here, isn't it? It's strange, but this makes me feel even closer to Alaina."

The ladies agreed.

"You live in a house she lived in, and this was hers too. You and she are very connected," Ardie said, a knowing smile on her face.

Marla smiled over at her. It was as if Ardie understood exactly how she was feeling.

Everyone took photos of the house, then reluctantly moved on. They all felt connected to this house and like they were leaving a good friend behind.

"Holly Avenue is two blocks away, and Laurel is two more blocks. Should we go see Arthur's home on Laurel first then go back down to Holly?" Marla asked.

"Sounds good to me," Wanda said, and everyone agreed. The day was growing warmer and they were walking a bit slower.

"I'm getting old," Wanda complained. "I'm already winded."

"Good. It's not just me feeling that way," Rita said. "But I don't want to miss anything."

This made all the women laugh.

They turned and headed the four blocks up to Laurel, admiring the many older homes along the way. After going right on Laurel, Marla began studying the homes. So far, nothing looked like how she'd imagined Arthur's home. When they came to a pair of old, stone apartment buildings, Toni stopped them.

"The building on the left is where Fitzgerald was born in 1896," she said, looking at her papers. "His parents were living in one of the apartments here."

"There's a plaque on the column." Wanda pointed to it. They walked up the sidewalk and read the bronze plaque. It confirmed this was Fitzgerald's birthplace.

"Cool." Rita stepped back and took a few photos.

"It says on Zillow that these are condos now," Toni offered. "And they're expensive."

Ardie laughed. "I'll bet they are."

Marla looked down the street but most of the buildings looked newer. She turned in the opposite direction. "Maybe we have to go the other way," she suggested. "I see a few Victorians down that side of the street."

The group headed down the street and studied each house. "None of these look like Arthur's house," Marla finally said. "I suppose it could be one of these smaller Victorian homes, but I guess I imagined it was larger."

"There's nothing online or in my paperwork saying when any of these homes were built either," Toni said.

After walking up and down Laurel, they gave up. "Maybe it was torn down at some point," Toni said. "It's a shame, but it could have happened."

Marla was disappointed. She hated to think of Alaina's childhood home having fallen into disrepair. Unfortunately, nothing lasts forever.

The women walked back to Holly Avenue and began their search. The shade of the old trees along the sidewalk kept them cool as they studied the houses. Marla had a good idea where Hannah's second house was, but first they wanted to find the other one. They walked in the direction that Alaina had written in the journal and soon found themselves staring at a Victorian home with spindles on the railing of the front porch, just as Alaina had described.

"Do you think this is it?" Marla asked the group. She wasn't entirely sure. The house looked old and tired, and the yard was overgrown. She had a hard time picturing Hannah living here.

"I'm sure it looked a lot better when Hannah and Matthew lived here," Rita said. "After all, it is an old house."

Toni glanced around. "And I'll bet these other houses weren't here back then. It wouldn't have looked this crowded when Hannah lived here."

Marla nodded, discouraged.

"It's kind of a disappointment," Ardie said. "But I guess that's to be expected."

"Let's go find the other house," Marla said, trying to keep their spirits up. "I think I found it online and it's been well-kept up."

Everyone followed Marla as they walked down the street. She couldn't help but think she was walking the same path that Alaina had decades ago when she'd visited her dear friend. That thought warmed her heart. When Marla got to the end of the block, she turned and crossed to the other side. "What do you think of this one?"

The women stared at the house, smiles brightening their faces. The house was three stories tall, and very wide, with the turret going up all three floors. It was beautifully painted with elegant trim all around it.

"Well, now. This is more like it," Toni said. "And it's exactly as Alaina described."

"It's beautiful!" Rita stared at the house, looking delighted. "And so large. I can't imagine what it's like to live in such a big house."

Ardie chuckled. "Marla can, I bet."

Marla laughed. "Big houses are not all they're cracked up to be."

Wanda pointed to the lawn. "There's a For Sale sign. I can't even imagine what it would sell for."

Toni was already looking on her phone. "This house is no longer a single-family unit. It's broken up into three condos. The right side with the turret room is for sale." She whistled softly. "And it's not cheap, either."

As they admired the house, a well-dressed older woman came outside with a young couple. She smiled at the women as she said goodbye to the couple, then walked over to the group and looked at them quizzically.

"Are you all here to see the unit for sale? I thought it was just one woman coming."

"Oh, no, we aren't," Marla said hurriedly. "We were just admiring the house. It's beautiful."

"It is, isn't it?" the woman said. She raised her hand to shake Marla's. "I'm Dolores Finley. I'm a real estate agent."

"It's nice to meet you, Dolores." She shook her hand. "I'm Marla Madison. My friends and I were just touring the homes on Summit Avenue, and then came up this way to see a few. We know a little history about this home and wanted to see it in person."

Dolores's eyes lit up. "You do? Did a family member once own it?"

"No. Nothing like that. But a good friend of a family member owned it. She and her husband lived here when it was first built."

The real estate agent clapped her hands with glee. "That's wonderful. You have to tell me who it was. People love hearing the history of these old places. Why don't you all come inside and I'll show you around? My next appointment hasn't arrived yet anyway, so I have some time."

"Thank you," Marla said, thrilled to get a look inside. She looked at the group and saw the eagerness in their expressions as well.

They followed Dolores through the front door into a roomy entryway.

"This is the main entryway and the mailboxes are all over there," she told them, pointing to the left. "The house is broken up into three units, each having three stories. The one that is for sale is on the right." She glanced around, then said softly, "It's the most interesting unit because it has the rounded turret rooms. Follow me." She opened a heavy wooden door and they walked into a spacious living room. "This unit has four floors because there's a basement, too. They have a family room and game room in the basement, and this floor is the main living area, kitchen, and dining room. The next two levels are bedrooms—three in all—plus a bathroom on each floor. Go ahead and poke around."

The ladies walked around the room. It went in a circle, with a living room, small den, the kitchen, the dining room next to that, then the circular turret room. They all stopped there and gazed out the three, floor-to-ceiling rounded windows.

"Beautiful," Rita said with a sigh. "And cozy."

"I can see Alaina and Hannah now, sitting near the windows, hand-stitching baby gowns," Ardie said. "I love this room."

Emotion filled Marla as she gazed around, thinking about the two best friends in this room. There was a tall oak tree outside the window that had probably been much smaller back then and rose bushes outside the window. Carriages pulled by fine horses would pass by in the street as they sat there working.

"Isn't this sweet?" Dolores asked. "And each room has a fireplace. I'm so happy that they kept them. People have taken out the old fireplaces in some of these old houses. It's such a shame when they do."

"Yes," Marla managed to say, trying to hold her emotions in check. She was surprised how this room had affected her. Yet, she felt she knew Alaina so well that her connection to Hannah was strong too.

Dolores tipped her head. "So, tell me what you know about this house. I'd love to hear it."

Marla explained who she was and about the journal they'd found belonging to Alaina Madison and her friendship with Hannah Anderson who had once lived in this house.

"That's an incredible story," Dolores said. "And it goes along with the year this house was built. If we had the abstract, we would probably find the Anderson name in it."

"Does it still exist?" Marla asked, hopeful.

"I'm not sure," Dolores said. "And the state of Minnesota stopped making them mandatory years ago, so whoever owned the house in the eighties or nineties probably threw it away. So many people did."

Toni shook her head. "It's a terrible shame. So much history lost."

Dolores looked curiously at Marla. "Madison. Did your husband's family own Madison's Department Stores?"

Marla nodded. "Yes, but the last one was closed decades ago."

Dolores grinned. "I remember going to the store downtown when I was just a little girl. It was so fancy and had a huge toy department on the second floor. At Christmas, it was decorated inside and lit up like a fantasy holiday. It was every child's dream."

"I never saw it myself, but it sounds wonderful. My mother told me a similar story about her childhood. I wish I'd seen it," Marla said.

Dolores took them on the full tour, and by the time they were finished, her next appointment had shown up. They thanked Dolores profusely for allowing them to tour the house then headed outside.

"That was amazing!" Rita's eyes shone with delight. "It was fate that she was here right when we visited."

"I think you're right," Marla said, thinking the same thing. It seemed as if fate was on their side. Or maybe it was Alaina, somehow bringing them here at just the right moment. She'd written her journal for a reason. Maybe Marla was the one who was supposed to have found it. *Now I'm sounding as mystical as Rita does,* she thought.

They decided they'd played tourist enough for the day, so they walked the many blocks back to the café where their cars were parked.

"I'll see you all at my place on the thirtieth," Marla said. "With any luck, the weather will be nice, and we can sit outside on the patio."

The women all said goodbye and left, but Ardie hung back. "You seemed to be deep in thought back at the house. I think being so close to Alaina and Hannah was affecting you."

Marla's brows shot up. "Are you a mind reader? I was thinking about them and their friendship. It sounds silly, but I could actually feel them there."

Ardie smiled warmly. "It's not silly at all. This is quite a journey you're bringing us on. I think it's affecting us all—in a good way."

"Almost like it was meant to be? Me meeting you, joining the book club, and finding the journal?"

Ardie shrugged. "Stranger things have happened."

They both laughed, then hugged goodbye and drove away.

That night, Marla lay in bed thinking about everything they had seen that day. She glanced through her photos of Alaina and Nathaniel's house on Summit, but they didn't do justice to the elaborate mansion. Then she studied the pictures of Hannah's home. It was so beautiful. It was a shame it had been separated into three condos, but she understood why it had been. It would be much too expensive to maintain for one person. Still, it would have been wonderful if it had stayed exactly as when Hannah had lived there.

She was even more eager now to read more about what happened to Hannah and Alaina. They had become an integral part of her life since finding the journal. Maybe they had been the distraction she'd needed after Nathan's death. She was so thankful she'd met Ardie, and all the book club women. Everything new in her life was changing her. She felt more authentic than she had in years. Or, maybe it was allowing her to finally be the woman she used to be before she married Nathan and tried to fit into his life. Whatever the reason, she was happy where she was at this point in her life.

Chapter Nineteen

Alaina

Alaina sat with Margaret in the kitchen at her father's house eating a simple lunch of turkey sandwiches and iced tea. Even though she was now pampered with fancy meals at her own house, she still loved eating casually with Margaret at the kitchen table. But today, her mind was on more than the food. She was worried about her father and Margaret was also.

"He's seen the doctor, which was a miracle in itself," Margaret told her. "And the doctor told him it's most likely ulcers in the stomach. So, he's on a special diet of bland foods; bread, milk, broth, and such. And he was given some thick, white medicine to take when his stomach ached." Margaret shook her head. "But he still seems to suffer from pain and continues to lose weight."

Alaina frowned. Her understanding of ulcers was that they came from stress or worrying. Was her father concerned about the business? Was it in trouble? She hated that she no longer took care of the ledgers and bills. Then she'd at least know what the problem was.

She went home that evening with a heavy heart. Alaina was

concerned about both Hannah and her father. She'd visited Hannah the day before, and she'd looked so worn and pale. She'd been placed on bed rest by the doctor because he was concerned about her health and that of the baby. Hannah had taken it all in stride, and was making the best of it, but Alaina couldn't take it so casually. And now, this latest news about her father was troublesome. She'd never known her father to be anything but healthy. She wished there were more she could do.

"Did you see your father today?" Nathaniel asked her as they sat eating dinner.

Alaina shook her head. "No. He was at the factory, working. But I spoke to the housekeeper and she was very concerned. He isn't feeling well at all."

Nathaniel nodded. "I had noticed the last few times he's had dinner with us that he looks thin, and he doesn't eat much. Has he seen a doctor?"

She looked up at him and saw sincere concern in his eyes. After the incident over her leaving the house, she'd been upset with Nathaniel. But tonight, she saw he did care about her father, and that touched her heart.

"Yes. He's on a special diet and taking some medicine. They think it's a stomach ulcer."

"Ah, I see." Nathaniel took a bite of the roast beef. "Your father is an intelligent, competent man. I'm sure he will do whatever is necessary to get well. He has a grandson to think about now. I know how much he enjoys seeing him."

"Yes. He does," Alaina agreed, although she wondered what his underlying message was. That she shouldn't worry? Nathaniel reached across the space between them and placed his hand over hers. She looked up, surprised.

"You have every right to be worried about your father and

your friend," he told her kindly. "But please don't let your worry make you sick as well. Your son needs you. And so do I." He smiled at her, that handsome smile that made her heart melt.

"I'll try not to worry too much," she promised.

After Mrs. Hanson served tea and dessert, Nathaniel spoke again. "I was thinking we might spend a few weeks at Great Heron Lake again this year. We could rent the entire upper floor of the lodge, or maybe one or two of their larger cabins. I know the baby is too young to enjoy it yet, but it would make a nice family vacation."

"That sounds lovely," Alaina said, hiding her concern over leaving her father that long. But it was as if Nathaniel read her mind when he spoke next.

"Maybe your father could join us for a few days or a week. The fresh air and time away from work might do wonders for him. Don't you agree?" He smiled at her again, and Alaina couldn't help but smile back.

"That's a wonderful idea. Thank you for thinking of him."

"No need to thank me, dear. He's family. We take care of our family."

Alaina felt guilty that she'd questioned his motives earlier. Nathaniel did care about the people in her life. Wasn't this proof?

Two nights later, as she and Nathaniel were relaxing in the study, each reading a favorite book, Mrs. Hanson came in to deliver a note to Alaina.

"A young man dropped this off. He said it was important."

Alaina opened the note and read it. Her face creased as she took in the words.

"Is something wrong?" Nathaniel asked. "Who is it from?"

Heart pounding, she looked up at her husband. "It's from Matthew. Hannah has gone into labor early. He's afraid for her.

She's asking for me. I must go to her."

Nathaniel took the note from her and read it. "He says the doctor is there. What does he expect you to do? It's after nine o'clock. He can't possibly expect you to go running to their house at this time of night."

Alaina barely heard what he'd said. She hurried to the door and called for Mrs. Hanson. "Please have Mr. Hanson ready the carriage for me," she told the housekeeper.

"Absolutely not!" Nathaniel insisted, coming up behind Alaina. "You'll do no such thing."

Alaina spun around, stunned. "I must go. She's my dearest friend and she needs me. Matthew would never have sent for me if it wasn't urgent."

"He's not in his right mind, asking you to come this late at night. I won't hear of it. You can visit her in the morning. I'll not have my wife running around at night like some sort of trollop."

Alaina couldn't believe what she'd just heard. She turned to Mrs. Hanson. "Please. Ask your husband to ready the carriage. I must go."

The housekeeper stood there, uncertain, her eyes darting between Alaina and Nathaniel.

"Please! Hurry!" Alaina said.

"No," Nathaniel said with finality. "Mrs. Hanson, that will be all. Good night."

Mrs. Hanson nodded, then glanced at Alaina with remorse in her eyes. She turned and left. Alaina understood. She wasn't as important as her husband. Nathaniel paid their wages. She didn't.

Alaina spun angrily and glared at Nathaniel. "I'll walk there if I must. I don't care how I get there. I must be with my friend."

Nathaniel's eyes turned hard. "No, you won't. You'll not be

walking on these dark streets tonight. Do you understand?"

"She's my friend!" Alaina's voice rose in desperation. "Don't you understand? The baby is a month early and she's frightened. She needs me."

"There is nothing you can do for your friend. The doctor is there. You can visit her in the morning. You have your own child to worry about. I won't fight with you. You will not leave this house tonight."

Stunned and near tears, Alaina glowered at Nathaniel. How could he be so cold? So unfeeling? Without another word, she ran up the stairs to her room, where she locked the door before falling onto the bed and letting the tears flow.

Later, when Emma came in to help her ready for bed, she offered to go to Hannah's house and see if she could be of any assistance. Alaina hugged her and cried even harder. "I couldn't ask you to walk there at this time of night," she told her. "But thank you for being such a good friend. I'll go first thing in the morning. All I can do now is pray that everything will be fine."

Alaina paced and slept fitfully the entire night. She was so frightened for Hannah. And she was furious. She'd never been this angry with anyone in her life as she was with Nathaniel. She couldn't understand how he could be so cold. She'd thought she'd married a man who would treat her like an equal. Now, she realized she was no more equal to him than his servants were. Possibly, she counted even less than those he paid.

She rose with the sun and dressed hurriedly with Emma's help. Going downstairs in her coat and hat, she bypassed the dining room and headed straight for the kitchen where she found Mrs. Hanson.

"Please have your husband bring the carriage to the back door," she told the housekeeper.

"He's already on his way," Mrs. Hanson said. "I told him to be ready first thing this morning."

Alaina felt her emotions rise to the surface at the kindness in Mrs. Hanson's eyes. "Thank you."

Mrs. Hanson touched her arm. "I hope your friend and her baby will be fine. I've been praying for them."

Alaina did something then that her husband would have never approved of. She hugged Mrs. Hanson to thank her for her kindness, then she and Emma left the house.

When Alaina and Emma arrived at Hannah's home, she found Matthew in the parlor, his head in his hands. He looked as if he'd been up all night.

"Alaina." He rose and hugged her. "I'm so glad you're here."

"How is she? And the baby?" Alaina asked as she pulled away.

Matthew's already swollen eyes filled with tears as he shook his head. "We lost the baby," he said in a hoarse whisper. "A little girl. She was stillborn."

A gasp caught in Alaina's throat. Poor Hannah. How devastated she must be. "I'm so sorry, Matthew. How is Hannah?"

"She's not well." Tears streamed down his face. "She wasn't strong to begin with, despite bedrest, and she lost a lot of blood. She hasn't woken up since the baby came."

Alaina's heart lurched. She should have been here last night beside Hannah. Her dearest friend, so much like a sister to her, was suffering and had wanted her by her side, and she hadn't been here. Guilt enveloped her.

She turned to Emma and quietly asked her to see if Mrs. Harper could bring in tea and something for Matthew to eat. Then she sat on the settee next to where he'd dropped down and held his hand. "I'm so sorry, Matthew. I'm sorry I wasn't here. I wanted to be. Tell me, what can I do to help?"

He shook his head hopelessly. "There's nothing that can be done now except wait. The doctor has left, and a nurse is upstairs with Hannah. I feel so helpless." He turned to Alaina. "It's all my fault. She'd said she didn't want any more children, and I'd agreed. But it happened anyway. I should have been more careful. I should have let her be. I just love her so much. It's all my fault. If I lose her, I'll never be able to live with myself."

Tears filled Alaina's eyes. She held his hand even tighter. "You didn't do anything wrong," she said firmly. "She loves you, and she was excited about this baby. Don't blame yourself."

Emma brought in a tray with cups and a teapot along with muffins and biscuits and set it on the table in front of them.

"Here. You must have something to eat," Alaina told him. "Emma will pour you some tea. Please try to have a bite of food. May I go up to see Hannah?"

He nodded. "Yes. Please go see her. Maybe, if she hears your voice, she'll wake up."

He sounded so desperate that Alaina had to choke back tears. She headed up the stairs and into Hannah's room. A nurse in uniform sat by the bed.

"How is she?" Alaina asked quietly.

"She's been sleeping the entire time," the young woman said. She rose. "I'll give you some privacy. Please call me in if anything changes."

Alaina nodded and the woman left. She stared down at her friend, lying still under the covers. Her skin was as pale as a porcelain doll and her hair was mussed around her face. She looked so tiny—smaller than her usual petite self. The bed seemed to swallow her.

Alaina went to her side and gently smoothed Hannah's tangled blond hair. "Hannah. It's me. I'm here now. Will you wake up for me?" She swallowed back a lump that had formed in her throat. No movement came from Hannah.

Pulling a chair up beside the bed, Alaina sat and took her friend's hand. It felt cold to the touch. "I'm sorry I wasn't here last night. I wanted to be. Believe me, there was nowhere else I would have rather been than here with you. But Nathaniel wouldn't let me come. I'm so sorry, sweetie. I should have come anyway. I had no idea what you were going through. But I'm here now, and all I want is to see you open your eyes and speak to me again. Please, Hannah. Wake up. Please."

As her friend lay motionless, Alaina's heart slowly hardened toward Nathaniel. How dare he not let her come to her dear friend in her most vulnerable time. How heartless of him to insist she stay home. There were no excuses. She should have been here. If anything happened to Hannah, she swore to herself that she'd never forgive Nathaniel or herself for the rest of her life.

Matthew joined her and their vigil began. They took turns sitting with Hannah, waiting, hoping, and praying she would come back to them. Emma came and went, asking if they needed anything. The doctor visited, and a different nurse appeared for a shift change. Still, there was no movement from Hannah. By midnight, Hannah grew feverish, and by morning, she had passed.

A piece of Alaina died with her that morning. The young, innocent Alaina, who'd grown up alongside Hannah, full of hopes and dreams of a happily ever after. Hannah had been the bright, optimistic one between them. She'd kept things light while Alaina had been the serious one. Her best friend, her complete opposite, yet the one who knew her inside-out. All those sweet, childhood memories were shattered and lost the moment Hannah took her last breath.

Matthew was inconsolable. Alaina tried her best to stay strong for him and not add to his grief by breaking down. Her heart ached for the loss of her dearest friend, and guilt enveloped her for not being there when she'd sent for her. She would never have a last word with her friend, never see her beautiful eyes open or hear her sweet voice speak. It was all she could do not to collapse under the weight of her grief.

Matthew holed himself up in his den with a bottle of whisky, and Alaina let him. If he needed to drink away his pain, then so be it. The doctor, who was also a family friend, stayed to ensure Matthew wouldn't do anything drastic. The undertaker came and quietly took away the body to prepare it for burial. Matthew's parents were due that evening on the train from Chicago. They'd been sent a wire the previous day after the baby had died. Hannah's own parents had both passed away so there were no relatives to contact on her side of the family.

After ensuring the house was running properly and the children were being cared for by the nanny, Alaina left with Emma, exhausted and mentally drained. Sven had been summoned and drove them home. The grandfather clock in the hallway had just chimed six o'clock in the evening when she entered through the front door of her home. Emma helped her off with her cloak, hat, and gloves and both ladies were about to walk up the stairs when Nathaniel appeared in the doorway of his study.

"I see you have finally come home," he said flippantly.

Alaina stopped walking. "Go along, Emma. I'll be up in a moment."

Emma nodded and walked up the stairs as Alaina turned and stared hard at her husband.

"Yes. I'm home," she said, raising her chin defiantly.

Nathaniel appraised her. He was wearing his day suit, but

his jacket was off and his sleeves were rolled up as if he'd been working at his desk. *Of course he was working,* she thought. *That is all this man cares about.*

"You could at least have sent word you'd be there all night and day," he said. "You realize you have a house to run. And a child of your own to manage the care of."

"I understand my duties. Better than you can ever imagine. I'm going to my room. Good evening," she said stiffly.

As she turned to leave, Nathaniel stepped toward her and placed a hand on her shoulder. "How is your friend?" he asked, his voice softer now.

Alaina spun around and glared at him. "Dead. And so is the baby. I never had a chance to speak to her. I never had a chance to say goodbye. All because of you." She turned again and hurried up the stairs, not willing to speak another word to this man she felt she no longer knew.

Chapter Twenty

Marla

The book club ladies sat on Marla's outside patio around the lit firepit, each one speechless over the new revelation in Alaina's journal. The lake water lapped against the shore in the spring breeze and the freshly planted flowers all around the patio left a sweet scent on the air, but the women noticed none of it. They were all too absorbed in what Marla had just read.

"Poor Hannah," Rita said, her eyes watery with tears.

"Poor Alaina," Ardie added. "Losing her dearest friend and not being able to say goodbye."

"Nathaniel is a jerk," Wanda said angrily. "How dare he not allow Alaina to see her friend. She should dump him immediately."

Toni shook her head. "Not as easy in those days. Women stayed married no matter what men did. They were as much the property of their husbands as their homes were."

"Thank goodness some things have changed," Wanda said. "Because men haven't."

"Was Nathaniel a terrible person?" Marla asked, trying not

to judge him too harshly despite her own anger toward what he'd done. "Or just a product of his time? Maybe he truly thought he was protecting Alaina by not letting her go that night."

Wanda's brows shot up. "Are you defending that horrible man?"

Marla shook her head. "No. I'm as upset over what he did as you all are. I'm just trying to see it from his point of view. A good husband not only should have allowed her to go but also should have accompanied her there. But he was used to telling people what to do and getting his way. His flaw was his idea of propriety over his lack of compassion."

"Maybe," Ardie said, looking as if she were considering Marla's words. "But it's still so sad."

The other ladies nodded.

Everyone soon stood and stretched. The night air was cool, but it was beautiful out with the full moon shining over the lake.

"At least Alaina got to enjoy this amazing place at some point in her life," Wanda said, looking around. "I don't know how she ever forgave her husband, but we know they stayed together and lived here."

"Yes. This is gorgeous," Toni said. "What does the house look like from the dock?"

"Let's walk out there and you can see," Marla suggested. The women walked down the brick path and to the end of the long, wooden, t-shaped dock, with bench seats on the end. They turned around in the direction of the lit-up house.

"Glorious," Ardie said. "The lights through the big windows make the house glow in the dark like a candle."

"A really big candle." Wanda laughed.

"It's hard to imagine such a big house looking and feeling homey, but it does," Rita said. "You're so lucky to live in such a nice place, Marla. It's like being on vacation every day."

Marla nodded. "It is kind of like that. Sometimes." She gazed across the dark water to the point of land across the bay. The little cottage was lit up too but couldn't be seen well through the tress that protected its privacy.

"What's that over there?" Toni asked, following Marla's gaze.

"Oh, it's a cute little cottage house that I just adore. I've always wondered what it would be like to live there instead of in this big house. I know I should be grateful for what I have, but deep down I'm not a mansion-type of person."

"The grass is always greener," Ardie said with a smile and nudge to Marla's side.

She chuckled. "I suppose it is. I saw it once, though, years ago. They were having an open house, and I went to look at it. It's adorable. Just as I had imagined. I named it the Fairy Tale house because that's what it reminded me of."

Toni pulled her phone out of her pocket and started scrolling. "Is it on Bellwood too?"

"Yes. There's a long driveway that leads to that house. It's the only one on the point."

"Ah, here it is." Toni looked up at her with a twinkle in her eyes. "It's for sale. I thought I had seen it on the listings when I was looking up your house the first time I came here." She scrolled through the pictures. "It is adorable."

All the ladies huddled around her and looked at the photos.

"You definitely should buy it," Rita said. "I love it."

Marla laughed. "What would I do with it, though? I have this big house."

"Sell this one," Toni suggested. "I mean, if you really love the smaller one and would rather live there, why not? Or, you have the money to own both, I assume."

"Yes, I could, but that would be weird. My daughter would think I'd gone crazy if I sold this house. Although, she really doesn't want it," Marla said.

"Well, there you go. Move. It's as simple as that," Wanda said.

"I wish it were that simple." Give up the family legacy? It felt like a weight on her shoulders that she couldn't get rid of. But she also didn't know if she could sell it, either.

The group walked back to the house and the ladies readied to leave.

"Tell Mrs. Cooper we really enjoyed the food she made. It was delicious," Rita said. The other ladies nodded agreement.

"I will," Marla said. She still couldn't believe Mrs. Cooper offered to make food for her new friends. Marla was beginning to worry about the elderly woman. She was losing her edge.

Toni hugged her goodbye. "I'd be happy to show you the house 'officially' if you decide you want to see it."

"Thanks, Toni. I'll think about it."

Ardie hung back as the other ladies left. "How did the room that Dan and his crew worked on turn out?" she asked, looking curious.

"Come see for yourself." They walked through the kitchen and into the maid's room. Dan's crew had finished it the week before and it had turned out wonderfully. "It now looks like it's a part of the house and not something from 1970," Marla said.

There was now dark wainscoting on the walls that resembled the look throughout the house and cream-colored paint above it. New hardwood floors had been laid and a thick, sage and cream rug covered part of the floor next to the bed. The furniture was updated, and the bathroom looked wonderful with a creamy-white tile covering the walls and floor, dark cabinets, and a quartz countertop. Alaina had asked Mrs. Cooper to pick all the finishes, and she'd done a great job.

"How did Mrs. Cooper like it?" Ardie asked.

"It was all her ideas, so she loved it," Marla told her. "She said something odd, though, after it was finished. She told me that now it would be a nice bedroom for an assistant if I ever decided I would prefer one instead of a housekeeper. When I asked her what she meant, she said that everyone gets an assistant these days then hires a maid service. We already have hired maids who come in, so I wondered if that meant she was finally going to retire, and I should hire someone new to run the house."

"That would be nice, wouldn't it?" Ardie asked. "It sounds like Mrs. Cooper has never liked you that much. You could hire someone you get alone with."

"I know. I should be happy. But Mrs. Cooper has been in this house for decades. It would be odd to see her go."

Ardie laughed. "Oh, the problems of the rich," she said good-naturedly.

Marla grimaced, then laughed along. "I know. It all sounds so stupid, doesn't it?"

"No. It's just different from what the rest of us are used to."

After Ardie left, Marla cleaned up the kitchen and checked the patio to make sure the fire had died down. Then she walked out to the dock again and gazed around. The lake was still, and the moon reflected a silvery glow off the water. In the distance to her left, she could see the lights twinkling at the yacht club, but it was quiet. She turned to the right and gazed at the cottage tucked away in the trees. Like Jay Gatsby watching the green light at the end of Daisy's dock, she was constantly drawn to that cottage. She had been since the moment she'd seen it years ago.

"Maybe I should take a look at it," she said softly to herself.

"What could it hurt?" But she felt tied down to this house. It had been in Nathan's family for over a century. Did she have the right to sell it and walk away? She wondered what Alaina would have done if given the same choice. Maybe, when they read further in the journal, she'd find out.

Marla turned and walked back to the house, closing and locking the French doors against her desire for a different future than the one that had already been planned for her.

* * *

Saturday morning Reese showed up at the house with a bagged gown over one arm and pulling a small suitcase. Marla ran to meet her and hugged her tight.

"I'm so happy you came for your father's dedication," she said, smiling brightly. "Is it just you or did Chad come too?"

"Just me," Reese said. "Chad already had plans."

Marla took her suitcase and followed her up to her old room. "Are you and Chad still dating?"

"Mom. We don't really date. We've just been seeing each other. It's nothing serious."

"Isn't 'seeing each other' dating?" Marla asked.

"No. It's completely different."

Reese's room hadn't changed much since she was a teenager. Marla had toned it down a bit from the bright pink room with boy-band posters on the walls, and had changed out the bedspread and curtains, but otherwise it was the same. Reese's swimming trophies and horse competition ribbons were still on the shelves and high school yearbooks sat on the dresser.

"Ugh," Reese said, walking over to the yearbooks and touching them. "High school. Don't remind me."

"You loved high school." Marla sat down on the bed. "You were a straight A student, president of the class two years in a row, and prom queen."

"Yeah. I was a real winner," Reese said sarcastically. "Then we all leave the cocoon of high school and hit the real world in college. That's a slap in the face."

"College is the real world?" Marla teased. "I thought working was."

Reese hung her dress on the closet door. "I bought a new dress for the dance. Do you want to see it?"

"Of course."

She unzipped the dress bag and pulled out the floor-length gown. It was a gorgeous shade of deep blue with a scoop neck and a cinched-in waist from which the skirt fell in folds to the floor. The bodice had delicate beading that made it sparkle in the light.

"It's beautiful!" Marla exclaimed. "So sophisticated. I love it."

"Thanks. What are you wearing?"

"Oh, probably that black dress your father liked so much. You know. The one with the sequined bodice and the satin full skirt to the floor."

Reese's brows rose. "You didn't buy a new one?"

Marla shrugged. "It seems like such a waste for me to buy a new gown that I'm never going to wear again."

"But Dad always insisted you buy something new for the club dances. He knew that the women could be catty if you wore the same thing twice."

Marla smiled wryly. She had gone along with it when Nathan was alive because she knew it was important to him, but she really didn't care anymore what the women thought or said. "Oh, Reese. I don't care about all that. Let them talk. It's a lovely dress and it doesn't bother me if I've worn it before. It all seems so ridiculous when you think about it."

"Okay," Reese said, but she stared at her mother as if trying to figure her out.

"Let's go outside and sit. I'll make some drinks. It's beautiful out," Marla said.

As they walked down the upstairs hallway, Reese glanced into the old nursery. "This is completely different," she said. "I like it. It looks more inviting than it used to."

"Thanks. I thought I might change a few of the guest bedrooms too. I just finished that room so I haven't had time to decide what my next project will be."

They sat on the patio in the sun with iced tea and caught up. For once, Reese was more open about what was going on in her life and Marla enjoyed listening to her. They took a stroll down one of the lake trails, then both went to lay down for awhile before getting ready for the dance. Dinner was being served at seven, then the program and the dance. They were both ready and downstairs by six-thirty.

"You look beautiful," Marla said, admiring how stunning her daughter looked in the dress. It made her eyes appear an even deeper blue and her blond hair was up in an elegant twist. "Where did you learn to do your hair like that?"

"My first college roommate taught me. She was always playing with her hair. She ended up quitting college to go to beauty school," Reese said.

"It sounds like that was her calling."

Marla hadn't visited a salon since Nathan had died and her hair had grown out quite a bit. She'd curled the ends and brushed it back off her face.

"You look nice, Mom," Reese said. "Dad was right. That dress looks good on you."

"Thank you, dear."

They gathered their wraps and evening bags and Reese drove them in her car. It felt strange to Marla to be attending a club function without Nathan. They'd done everything as a couple. Most Saturday nights they'd gone for dinner at the club, and of course Sundays were for golf and then lunch. So much changed when he grew ill, and although they hadn't gone to the club together in a long time, it still seemed odd to her.

The valet helped them out of the car and drove it away, and Reese and Marla walked inside the club. The ballroom had been built in 1882 after the private restaurant had been added to the clubhouse. It was a grand ballroom, surrounded by large windows with chandeliers above, and a bandstand and gleaming wood dance floor. The club now used it for fundraising events, weddings, and other such gatherings, but when it was set up for a dinner and dance, it was at its most elegant.

Dressed in an emerald satin gown with matching jewelry, Vicki greeted the two women at the door. "Thank you both for coming," she said, giving them both air kisses. "I'm sure it's difficult coming here without Nathan, but we're so happy you did. We have a wonderful presentation scheduled for after dinner to honor him."

"Thank you," Marla said, smiling kindly at her friend. "We're thrilled that Nathan is being honored."

"Reese, you're getting lovelier with each year. Your father would be so proud of you," Vicki said.

"Thank you," Reese responded.

An usher showed them to their table, which was near the front of the room. They were sharing a table with Vicki and Catrina and their husbands.

"This might get annoying," Reese said softly to her mother.

Marla held back a laugh. She agreed completely. But they were there for Nathan, so she was willing to put up with Vicki and Catrina fawning over them. They were only the center of attention tonight because of Nathan; otherwise, no one would have given them the time of day.

The room began to fill up with couples in tuxes and designer gowns. Gucci, Tom Ford, and Chanel were prominent throughout the room as was Louboutin for high heels. Marla watched everyone as they blew air kisses to each other, each woman assessing the other to see if her dress was better or shoes were more expensive. It was a parade of money that Marla had never been comfortable with, and even though her closet could compete with anyone in this room, she really didn't care. If the women thought it was tacky she was wearing a dress she'd worn two years ago, so be it. She'd rather be tacky than phony.

As she pondered this, she wondered how she'd lived this way for so long. It was as if Nathan's passing had awakened her to the silliness of it all. The excesses, the cattiness. As she'd said to Reese earlier, it was all so ridiculous.

Some of Nathan's old friends stopped by the table to say hello. Nathan's best friend and lawyer, Anthony, dropped by for a moment to greet Marla and Reese with a hug. He was going to speak about Nathan at the presentation since he'd known him the longest. Marla liked and trusted Anthony and was happy to see him. In fact, everyone was polite and kind to her and Reese. The problem was that they all now seemed worlds away from Marla.

"Is everything all right?" Reese asked her mother. Marla had been staring off into space, pondering all these thoughts about her former life with Nathan.

"Oh, yes. I'm fine," she said. She moved closer to her daughter. "I was just wondering how I managed to live this phony life all these years. Do any of these people seem sincere to you?"

Reese looked surprised by her words. "I thought these people were your friends. You've known them for years."

"They were your father's friends. And for the life of me, I can't understand how a person who lived a quiet life like your father was able to put up with all this nonsense."

A small knowing smile appeared on Reese's face. "I used to wonder that too. Dad wasn't one to flaunt his wealth. He never bragged about his family lineage or their money. I don't know anything about the Madisons who came before us, but he fit in with this group so easily. It does seem odd now."

Their conversation was cut short when Vicki, Catrina, and their husbands, Marshall and Trevor, joined them at the table. A four-course dinner was served, and their table talk hovered around golf, tennis, and yachting. Marla nodded politely and answered questions directed at her, but otherwise, she found herself ignoring most of the conversation. She thought instead of Alaina and how she'd managed boring dinners like this. She thought of poor Hannah, dying so young, and Matthew, grieving the loss of his wife. She wanted to know what happened next. Did Alaina find happiness in the years to come? Maybe she'd loved the house at Great Heron Lake and grew old there. She thought about telling Reese about what she'd learned so far about the past Madisons. She hoped they'd have a chance to talk tomorrow before she left.

After dessert was served, Anthony stepped up to the podium. He rustled some papers he'd set in front of him, then moved the microphone closer and began to speak.

"Thank you to everyone for coming tonight. As you know, we're here to support our local hospital so it can continue to grow as our community grows. But tonight, we are also celebrating our good friend, Nathan Madison, whose family has been supporting the Great Heron Lake Yacht Club since it's inception. Tonight, we are honored to have Nathan's wife, Marla, and daughter, Reese, here with us to celebrate him." Anthony motioned toward their table. "The Madisons have lived adjacent to the yacht club since 1885. The very land the club sits on was purchased from Nathaniel Madison in 1880 and the club was built that same year. Since then, the Madisons have been members of the club and have supported it as it grew into the thriving gathering place it is today."

Marla listened as Anthony described how he and Nathan had learned to sail together at the club as well as play tennis and golf. He had several funny anecdotes of antics they'd shared in their childhood and teen years. She smiled as she listened, trying to imagine her Nathan as a young teen or even a young man. By the time she'd met him, he'd settled into a quiet life where the most excitement they had was drinking too much champagne at a club event. Yet, many of the people gathered here tonight had known him back in those days. That realization made Marla feel even more like an outsider tonight than ever.

"So, as a tribute to everything Nathan and his family have done for our wonderful club, we will hang this plaque in his honor in our club library near the painting of the original Nathaniel Madison and all the other honors given to his family throughout the years," Anthony said. "Let's all raise our glasses and toast our dear friend, Nathan Madison."

The entire room raised their glasses, and a few said, "To Nathan." Their respect and admiration for her husband brought tears to Marla's eyes. She hadn't expected to get emotional, but it was hard not to, considering how loved he was by this group of people.

Anthony stepped down from the platform and came over to give Marla a hug. "He will be greatly missed," he told her. She nodded, wiping away the tears.

After his speech, the band, that was nearly as big as an orchestra, began to play and the club staff started clearing the plates from the tables. Reese leaned toward her mother. "That was a nice speech, wasn't it? I had no idea Father or his entire family had done so much to support the club."

Marla nodded. "Your father supported many organizations with his family's money. And I've recently learned that his family was instrumental in starting this club. It's quite interesting."

Her daughter's brows rose. "Where did you learn that?"

"We can talk later," she said, gesturing to a young man coming their way. "It looks like someone wants to ask you to dance."

Reese turned in time to see an old schoolmate of hers standing next to the table. She smiled and spoke with him a moment, then left to dance a waltz.

Marla smiled. It was nice that Reese also had a place to go where old friends met. She'd never thought of the club that way before. But as the years went by, maybe Reese would return and reminisce about her younger years here.

"Anthony gave a lovely speech. Don't you think?" Catrina had moved her chair closer to Marla's so she could talk over the music.

"It was. Anthony is a dear. Thank you for thinking of Nathan and celebrating him tonight. And please thank the whole committee for me. It was very touching," Marla said.

"I'm so glad you're here," Catrina gushed. "I've missed you. I wish you'd reconsider playing golf and tennis this year." She turned to see where Vicki was then whispered, "Vicki can be such a bore. You know how competitive she is. I always had much more fun pairing off with you."

Marla did know how competitive Vicki was and she felt bad for Catrina, but not enough to join in at the club this year. "I'm sorry, Cat. Maybe next year. I just have to find my place on my own right now."

Catrina stared at her, looking confused. "What do you mean you have to find your place? You belong here. You've always been a big part of our club and community."

"I know. I have since I married Nathan. But now I wonder if there's something more for me to do. Something more important than playing sports or eating lunch out with friends. I truly enjoyed my time here with you and Vicki, but I need to find out what things I love to do now that I'm on my own."

Catrina looked disappointed. "I can't imagine what I'd do if I didn't have my friends here at the club or my activities. This is my life. It was yours too."

Marla regretted having said anything to Catrina about finding something new. Of course her old friend wouldn't dream of not being tied to the club. She still had a husband who was a long-time member and actively involved. She changed the subject. "I think I'll go see where they're hanging Nathan's plaque. I haven't been in the library before. I always felt it was off limits because the men gathered in there to drink."

"Oh, yes. Go ahead. I'll see you in a bit," Catrina said. She was already searching the room to see who else she could talk with.

Marla walked out of the ballroom and into the space between it and the restaurant. There was a lounge area and two hallways leading to the men's and women's locker rooms. She found the door to the library and opened it. Stepping inside, she was immediately greeted by a pair of dark brown eyes that looked very familiar. She walked closer to the fireplace, where, above it, hung a painting of a man who looked very much like her husband.

"You must be Nathaniel Madison," she said aloud, awestruck that she was looking at Alaina's husband. "How amazing that you and your great-great-grandson look so much alike." She studied the painting, taking in every detail. The dark, wavy brown hair, the expressive eyebrows, his prominent cheekbones and clean-shaven face. He was dressed in period clothing but looked very handsome. And his eyes. They looked warm, but serious. Marla understood how Alaina had fallen for this attractive, dynamic-looking man. But she could also see in him a man determined to get his way.

"Oh. I'm sorry. I didn't think anyone would be in here," a male voice said from behind her.

Marla startled, realizing someone else was in the room. She turned and found herself looking at a man she'd never met before. "Hello. I had just come in to look at the painting. I've never seen it before, and I was curious as to what Nathaniel Madison looked like."

The man tipped his head, studying her. "You mean to tell me your husband's family was responsible for this club being in existence, yet you've never even been in the library? That's odd."

She shrugged. "This club has a long history of men being in charge and this room used to be off limits to women. I guess I never even thought of coming in here." She studied the stranger a moment. He was tall and slim and his tuxedo looked to be custom-fit. His hair was dark and thick, although gray strands were weaving their way through it. His face was tanned, as if he'd already been out in the sun a lot, and his brown eyes looked kind.

"I'm sorry. I don't think we've met," she said. "I'm Marla Madison." She raised a hand to shake his.

He took her hand in his and bowed slightly. "Yes, I know who you are. But we haven't met properly. I'm fairly new to the club. I joined last summer. My name is Alden Pierce. It's very nice to meet you."

"It's nice to meet you too, Alden," Marla said. "What brings you to Great Heron Lake? Do you have family here?"

"Oh, no. No family. I came here one summer years ago and decided I would someday own a lake house here. Last year, I made that dream come true."

Marla smiled. She couldn't help it. His voice was deep and rich, the type of voice you'd hear narrating a documentary and that you trusted completely. Like Morgan Freeman or James Earl Jones. "Well, welcome to the area. I'm sure you'll love it here."

"I already do. Well, except that I feel I'll be an outsider for a long time, but I'll be so charming that everyone will eventually have to like me." He grinned and there was a glint of mischief in his eyes.

Marla nodded her understanding. "I get it. They don't accept new people readily here, unless you're related to someone they know. That way they can peg you. But I'm sure you'll fit in just fine."

They both turned and stared up at the portrait.

"So, this is the great and powerful Nathaniel Madison. He does look like he's in control, doesn't he?" Alden asked.

"Yes, he does. And from what I hear, he was a hardworking man who knew exactly what he wanted."

Alden glanced at her. "I suppose you know all about the family line."

She shook her head. "Not all of it. In fact, this is the first time I've seen a portrait of him. But I'm learning a lot."

"Hmm. That sounds intriguing."

Marla looked around the fireplace where plaques hung, celebrating other past members. There was one for an Andrew Tobias Madison given in 1983. She assumed that was Nathan's father. And another one for a Tobias Nathaniel Madison in 1950. An older one given in 1931 was to Arthur Tobias Madison. She smiled as she recognized the name. He would have been Alaina's son.

"A lot men with the name Tobias here, aren't there? Alden asked, gesturing toward the plaques. "Was that also your husband's middle name?"

"No. His was Andrew. But that seems to fall in line with the family names."

Alden nodded.

Marla turned in a slow circle and surveyed the room. It was small, like the size of a bedroom, and the walls were floor-to-ceiling shelves filled with books. A heavy hunter-green rug covered most of the floor. She could picture the men in 1890 sitting in the padded chairs or on the leather sofa or standing around, smoking their pipes and cigars and holding crystal glasses filled with amber liquid. This would have been the room where they'd be free to argue about politics or talk about business at their leisure, away from the women. She was sure that Nathaniel sat here, splendid in his best three-piece suit, pipe in hand, commanding the attention of everyone in the room. And he would have had it. A man that rich was always the center of attention.

"I'm sorry," Alden said. "Where are my manners? You probably wanted time to yourself in here. I will leave you to it." He headed toward the door.

Marla watched him reach for the door knob, then stopped

him. "Wait. No, I don't mind the company. I was just getting a feel for how this room must have been back in the 1800s. Don't feel you have to leave."

He walked back to where she stood. "How do you think it felt?"

"Stuffy," she said, grinning. "And filled with the hot air of so many men trying to outdo each other."

Alden broke out into a huge smile and laughed deeply. "I don't doubt that was exactly how it was."

"Why did you come in here tonight? What interested you?" Marla asked.

"I heard the part of the speech where he said that there was a portrait of the founding member, Nathaniel Madison, and I was curious to learn more about him."

"And have you satisfied your curiosity?" she asked.

"Oh, yes," Alden replied. "And I met a new friend in the process. So, I believe it's been a very satisfying evening."

Marla smiled and headed toward the door. She could feel Alden's eyes on her as he followed her out. She really couldn't say that it was an altogether unpleasant feeling.

Chapter Twenty-One

Marla

The day after the ball hadn't turned out the way Marla had hoped. Reese had risen at noon then ate a quick lunch and headed back to her place. Marla never had a chance to tell her about Alaina's journal or what she'd learned about Nathan's family. *Oh, well,* she thought. *She'd probably be bored with it all anyway.*

Since last night, Marla hadn't been able to get her chance meeting with Alden out of her mind. He'd followed her back to the ballroom, then disappeared for a while. When she'd thought he must have left, he appeared at their table and asked if she'd like to dance. She'd seen Reese watch him warily, and Catrina had looked stunned. Despite her daughter's obvious disapproval, Marla had accepted his invitation and they danced to one slow song together. He'd danced expertly, just as she'd imagined he would. They didn't speak, and after he'd escorted her back to her table, all he'd done was smile and said good evening, then disappeared. It had seemed like a dream, leaving Marla to wonder if she'd really met Alden at all.

But the two women at her table, as well as her daughter, would not let her forget that she'd just danced with the most sought-after bachelor at the club.

"Do you know who he *is?*" Vicki had asked, looking impressed. "He's one of the most successful investment gurus in the country. He's been a member of this club for over a year and hasn't once shown the slightest interest in any of the single women here."

"I had no idea who he was when I met him in the library," Marla had told them. "He just seemed like a nice man."

"Nice is right," Catrina had said. "And handsome, rich, and available. You're so lucky."

Marla had frowned at her friend, especially when she'd seen Reese's lips tighten into a thin line. "Cat. I'm not looking, and I'm not interested. I danced with a nice gentleman. That's all it was."

Both her old friends had looked disappointed that there was no more to gossip about, but Marla noticed her daughter had looked relieved, and that was all that mattered. After all, Nathan had only been gone for three months. The last thing on Marla's mind was finding a new husband—ever.

Now, as she thought about it, she still couldn't help but smile. Her friends were right. Alden Pierce was all those things. But most of all, he seemed to be kind and thoughtful, and had a sense of humor. And those were the things that meant more to her than good looks or money.

But the last thing she wanted was to be tied down to a man. She was enjoying being her own person right now.

That week, Marla decided to paint another of the upstairs bedrooms. It was a large guest room with another brick fireplace and an attached bath. She decided on a hunter green for the walls, which looked wonderful against the dark wainscoting. She pulled down the heavy draperies and replaced them with flowing floor-to-ceiling curtains of a lighter green to contrast the walls. She left the fireplace as it was, but hung a large, framed mirror over it, which gave depth to the room. She also bought a new comforter to match the curtains. By the time Thursday rolled around, the room was finished, and Marla liked what she'd done. It was a masculine décor, but it looked fresh and inviting.

On Thursday night, she dressed comfortably in a new pair of jeans she'd bought—this time in the women's department—and a silky black T-shirt. The women were meeting at Toni's house this week, so Marla grabbed the journal and headed out for the half-hour drive to her place.

Toni lived in a two-story townhouse in a large Victorian house that had been turned into three residences. As Marla pulled up in front, she was reminded of the house Mary Richards lived in on *The Mary Tyler Moore* show in the 70s. She chuckled to herself over this. Toni's last name was also Moore. It was a funny coincidence.

"Yes, I get that all the time," Toni said when Marla told her what she was thinking. "This house does look like the one from the series, but it isn't. And no, I'm not related." Her last statement made them both laugh.

Ardie was already there and laughed along. "I had teased her about the same thing," she said to Marla.

Soon, the other ladies arrived, and they all sat at Toni's dining room table which was on a platform in front of a bay window. They had a lovely view of the city.

"It looks beautiful at night," Toni said. "That's one of the reasons I bought it. Wait until the sun goes down."

They ate Chinese food from Toni's favorite restaurant, and

everyone caught up on each other's lives.

"How did the bedroom turn out?" Ardie asked Marla. "I loved that hunter green you bought."

"It turned out really nice. And the brick fireplace looks good against the green, so I left it. I think I'm done changing fireplaces. It's a lot of work."

"Mrs. Cooper will be happy to hear that," Ardie said with a wink.

"It's strange, but this time she didn't even blink when I said I was painting the room. Tonight, before she left, she asked which room I was painting next week. I guess she thinks I'm going to redo all the rooms." Marla shrugged. "Maybe I will."

"Well, that proves anyone can change no matter what their age," Rita said as she grabbed another eggroll.

"Not me," Toni said. "I love my life exactly as it is. I'm never changing."

Everyone laughed.

After eating, they got comfortable on Toni's creamy white sofa and chairs in the living room. Marla pulled the journal out of her purse.

"Who would like to do the honors tonight?" she asked.

"I'll give it a go," Toni said. "I hope her handwriting is easy to read."

Toni glanced at the page a moment, then began to read:

"Our love cooled like the silvery-blue frost on a frigid winter's day. Beautiful to look at, but too icy to touch. Respect, possibly, and admiration were still there. But love? Romance? All gone. Every time I looked at Nathaniel, all I felt was resentment for what I had lost and would never have again. My dear friend Hannah. And although

there were times when I thought I might be able to forgive him, something else would get in the way to prove that I had made a mistake in marrying him. One I'd have to live with for the rest of my life."

Chapter Twenty-Two

Alaina

Summer 1878

Alaina's world was shattered that spring. She attended Hannah's funeral with a heavy heart, and although Nathaniel was there by her side, she was not comforted by it. She'd not only lost her best friend, but she'd hardened toward her husband. Where once there was love, she no longer understood how she felt. They barely spoke, and she locked the door between their bedrooms to keep him out. It felt as if nothing could bring back the once-warm feelings she'd had for him.

For weeks after the funeral, Alaina visited Matthew and the children often to check on them, each time returning home saddened by Matthew's despair and the children missing their mother. She knew she could never be a replacement for Hannah, but she hoped the little ones saw her as a beloved aunt who cared for them.

All was not well with her father, either. Alaina was at a loss as to what to do. She visited him twice weekly, sometimes bringing along little Arthur to cheer him up. He was missing work often now, his pain too unbearable to withstand sitting at a desk or walking around his factory, talking with the workers. He left his manager, Jerome, in charge when he simply couldn't go in. Alaina was thankful there was someone they trusted who could run the business properly when her father could not. But she worried that her father's illness was much more than just an ulcer of the stomach, and made sure Margaret kept her abreast on anything she heard when the doctor visited.

In early June, as promised, the family went to the lodge at Great Heron Lake for a four-week stay. Nathaniel had rented two large cabins for their family and guests, and three smaller ones to accommodate their staff. Emma came along again, as did Nathaniel's valet, John, and little Arthur's nanny, Prudence Thompson. Prudence was an efficient, middle-aged woman with a solid resume and Alaina liked and trusted her completely with her son.

Nathaniel wasn't there the entire time. He took the train on Thursdays and stayed through the weekend, then headed back to the city for work late each Sunday. Alaina was fine with his schedule. She was more relaxed when he wasn't there.

Her father came the second week they were there. Alaina was relieved she'd been able to coax him into joining them. She hoped that the sunshine and relaxation would help him heal. And after a few days, he did look better with a little color from the sun and the fresh air. He spent a great deal of time sitting and holding little Arthur, who had truly become his greatest joy. But from time to time, Alaina would catch him staring off across the water, deep in thought.

"What are you thinking so intensely about?" she asked one lazy afternoon as she sat in a chair next to him on the deck.

Glasses of iced tea sat on the table and they were protected from the sun by a big umbrella.

Arthur turned to his daughter, a warm smile on his face. "I was just thinking how lucky I've been in my life. I have a beautiful daughter who cares about me, a perfect grandbaby, and I've lived a happy and prosperous life. What more could a man want?"

Alaina frowned at his using the past-tense. "It has been a good life, but you have so much more to look forward to."

Arthur nodded. "Yes, of course I do," he said, but his tone sounded resigned.

She reached out and touched her father's arm. It felt so thin under his summer suit jacket. "You'd tell me if you were dangerously ill, wouldn't you? Please don't hide anything from me."

Her father patted her hand. "I've told you everything I know. And I'm doing what the doctor has ordered. I've stopped drinking alcohol and smoking cigars and I've been following the diet he's given me." He chuckled. "How could I not follow it with Margaret on my back and controlling my meals? Nothing seems to make a difference, but I keep trying."

"Maybe you should see another doctor. Or a specialist. We could go to Chicago or New York. I could go with you," Alaina said with urgency. Nathaniel had offered to pay for her to take him elsewhere if it would ease her mind. She'd been surprised by his kind offer, but knew he was just trying to get back into her good graces. But she'd do anything, even take this offer of money from her husband, to help her father.

"Oh, darling. Please don't worry about me. I'm sure I'll be fine. And this week has been wonderful. I feel more rested than I have in years. Maybe that's all I needed—plenty of rest and fresh air. I'm just content in the knowledge that you're doing well and have a good life and a good husband to take care of you."

Alaina smiled and nodded, but she couldn't stop worrying. She didn't want to press her father, though, and upset him. She was also relieved that he hadn't picked up on the tension between her and Nathaniel. It was best if her father thought she was content in her life.

"You can stay here as long as you'd like," she told him. "I'd be thrilled if you stayed all month."

Arthur shook his head. "As tempting as that is, I won't take up your entire vacation. I also need to check on my business. Thank goodness for Jerome. He's been a great help while I've been laid up. I trust him explicitly."

On Sunday, she accompanied her father to the train station and hugged him goodbye. He felt frail and moved as slowly as a man decades older. "Please take care of yourself, Father. Contact me if anything changes."

He kissed her gently on the cheek. "You worry too much, my sweet daughter. I'll be fine. Enjoy your time here. It's a beautiful place. I can understand why Nathaniel wants to build here."

She waved as the train pulled away, but her heart felt heavy. Trying to think positively, she returned to the lodge where her baby boy and husband were waiting.

* * *

Alaina returned to the city in early July despite Nathaniel's suggestion that she and the baby stay another week or two at the lake. She was worried about her father and wanted to check on Matthew and the children.

She was up early on Monday morning and headed down the back staircase to speak with Mrs. Hanson before going into breakfast. As she came to the first landing, she heard giggling further down the stairs. Alaina stopped, wondering who it could be. There were whispers, and more giggling. She smiled. Apparently, someone in the house was carrying on a secret tryst, and she stood motionless, wondering who it might be. Surely not Sven and Tilda Hanson. They were too discreet to carry on this way at their age. Perhaps it was the young maid, Mary, and someone from the kitchen. But who? As far as she knew, there were no young men working in there.

Suddenly, she heard footsteps coming toward her and saw she was right. Mary came bustling toward her, her white cap askew.

"Oh! Ma'am!" She looked shocked to see Alaina standing there.

"Good morning, Mary," Alaina said, holding back a grin. Continuing down the stairway, she practically bumped into Nathaniel.

He was straightening his tie when suddenly he saw her. She stood there, frozen, hardly believing her eyes. He looked at her calmly, as if it was common for them to pass each other on the servant's staircase.

"Good morning, dear," he said. "I didn't know you used these stairs."

"Obviously." The word came out of her mouth before she even thought about it. He moved aside and she swept past him with all the dignity she could muster. He didn't follow her, but instead headed upstairs.

At the bottom, she stopped a moment to compose herself. Anger boiled up inside her at the indignity of his indiscretion. How dare he embarrass her this way, carrying on with a maid right under her nose. *Well, now I know who's warming his bed at night.*

Straightening her shoulders, she walked into the kitchen and found Mrs. Hanson. They discussed the menu for the week, and Alaina asked her to please have Sven bring the carriage around for her. As Mrs. Hanson turned to leave, Alaina stopped her.

"Why was Mary going upstairs instead of working in the kitchen this morning," she asked.

Mrs. Hanson tried to remain composed, but Alaina saw a look of disgust cross her face. "She has been promoted to upstairs maid. She went up to make the beds."

Alaina raised an eyebrow. "I don't remember making that change."

"No, ma'am. Mr. Madison directed it while you were away this summer."

Doing her best to hide her own disgust, Alaina nodded. "Thank you, Mrs. Hanson."

The housekeeper stood there a moment as if to say something but must have decided against it. She nodded also, then went about her work.

Alaina walked out of the kitchen and into the main dining room, then past the smaller breakfast nook. Out of the corner of her eye, she saw Nathaniel sitting there, drinking his coffee. She swept past the room, no longer hungry after what she'd just witnessed.

"Alaina?" Nathaniel called after her. She ignored him and went to the front door where Emma was waiting for her with her morning coat and gloves.

Nathaniel followed her into the entryway. "Are you not joining me for breakfast?"

She spun on her heal and glared at him. "I no longer have an appetite, after what I just heard."

He kept his cool, as she'd suspected he would. "Come, dear.

Let's discuss this over breakfast. Surely you aren't in that big of a hurry to leave."

"I'll breakfast with my father," she said. "Good day." With that, she slipped on her coat and gloves and headed out with Emma to the waiting carriage.

On the ride to her father's home, Alaina lost all her courage and practically wilted in her seat.

"What can I do to help?" Emma asked her, placing a caring arm around her shoulders.

She looked up into the eyes of her good friend. Because despite the fact that Alaina paid her to work for her, Emma was still, first and foremost, a friend. "Does everyone in the house know?"

Emma dropped her eyes. "I've suspected it. Others have gossiped about it. But Mrs. Hanson puts a stop to whispers when she hears the servants talking."

Alaina felt tired. So very, very tired. With all that was going on, between Hannah's passing and her father's illness, she now had to deal with this. Yet, what was she to do? Fire the girl? The mere fact that her husband had promoted Mary to upstairs maid while Alaina was away proved that she really had no power over the employees.

When he'd proposed marriage, Nathaniel had said he needed her clear head and organizational skills to run the house so he wouldn't have to. He'd said he wanted a partner in life, not some simpering female who couldn't hold her own. Yet, he'd undermined her authority over the household staff by moving a woman, a mere girl, really, upstairs so she'd be at his beck and call. Alaina felt powerless to do anything about it.

The carriage stopped at Arthur's house and she sat and stared at her former home with longing. She'd loved living there and working for her father. She'd felt in control of her own life and respected. Now, she was just another married woman whose husband did as he pleased, and she had no say.

Her heart ached.

"I'm sorry," Emma said, looking pained. "I had hoped it was just gossip. Tell me what I can do to help."

Alaina turned to her and patted her hand. "Please stay by me no matter what. I feel as if I have no one left to turn to."

Emma smiled warmly. "I'm not going anywhere. I promise."

"Thank you."

Sven helped both women down from the carriage and went back to his perch behind the horse. Alaina told him he could come back in an hour, but he declined. "I'm to stay with you at all times," he said. "Mr. Madison's orders."

Alaina was about to protest but realized it would be for naught. Sven had to obey his employer or risk being fired. "Well, then. Please pull the carriage up alongside the house and wait in the kitchen. Margaret will have breakfast ready by now."

"I don't want to be a bother, ma'am," he said.

"No bother at all, Mr. Hanson. Please. Go along. I can't bear to think of you sitting out in the sun waiting for me."

He smiled and bobbed his blond head, then did as he was told. Alaina and Emma made their way to the front door.

Margaret informed her at the door that her father hadn't gone to work that morning and was still in his bed. She'd left a tray with breakfast for him, but she doubted he'd eaten anything.

"He's worse?" Alaina asked, feeling panic setting in.

"I'm afraid so. The doctor was here yesterday, and considering it was a Sunday, I was very surprised to see him. But I'll let your father tell you the details himself," Margaret said.

Emma followed Margaret to the kitchen while Alaina

hurried up the staircase to her father's room. The day was going from bad to worse in a hurry and her heart beat faster with fear over her father's poor health.

She knocked on his closed door. "Father? May I come in?"

"Yes," came his feeble reply.

Alaina went inside. Arthur was lying up against a pile of stacked pillows and his tray sat beside his bed, untouched. He looked over at her, attempting a smile, but it came out as a grimace.

"Oh, Father," she said, moving closer to the bed. She leaned over and kissed him lightly on the cheek. He looked so frail, his skin stretching across the bones of his cheeks. His once thick hair looked thinner and grayer, and his skin was ghostly pale. Had it only been two weeks since she'd last seen him? He looked as if he'd aged twenty years.

"I'm afraid I'm being lazy today," he said. "I slept late and am still a little tired."

As she glanced around, she noticed he had a white hand-kerchief in his hand. She saw instantly that there were spots of blood on it. Her eyes grew wide with fear as she took it all in. "Father. Please. You must tell me what's wrong. This is more than an ulcer. I must know the truth."

Arthur sighed, his attempt to look stronger than he felt fading fast. "I didn't want you to worry about me, dear. And I didn't want to ruin your vacation at the lake. There is nothing that can be done for me at this stage and there was no reason to worry you."

A chill ran through her as she nearly fell into the chair next to the bed. *Nothing that can be done?* Those words tore at her heart. "What are you saying? What's wrong?"

Arthur reached for her hand and squeezed it. "Dear. The

doctor believes I have a carcinoma in my stomach. The pain has become much worse, and it's bleeding. The only recourse would be surgery, but in my weakened state, he feels I could not survive that either. So, all I can do is take care of myself as best as I can and wait."

"Wait for what?" she asked, not comprehending his words.

"I'm dying, dear."

Alaina saw her entire world crashing before her. First Hannah, then Nathaniel's betrayal, and now her father. Dying. How could she live without her father? He was the strong shoulder she could always turn to, the only man she trusted entirely to speak the truth. She squeezed her eyes shut and clutched his hand. *No, this isn't happening. It's a nightmare that I will awake from. I can't lose my father.*

"Alaina, dear. Please, don't cry. I've had a wonderful life. I married the women of my dreams and had a daughter any man would be proud of. And now, my grandson, my namesake. Don't cry for me, please, dear."

She opened her eyes and tears fell down her cheeks. Alaina hadn't even realized she'd been crying until she heard her father's words. "What will I do without you?" she asked, her voice shaking. "How will I go on without your strength and wisdom?"

Arthur smiled and his eyes lit up with love for her. "It was I who needed you, dear. You were my source of strength after your mother died. You've been the one I've leaned on to keep me strong and moving forward. What would I have done if you hadn't stepped in to run the household, or help with the ledgers when the finances had been tampered with from the previous bookkeeper? You are the strongest, smartest person I know. Never forget that. You can do anything you set your mind to. I truly believe that. Don't let a little thing like wearing a skirt while men wear trousers get in your way. You are a powerful woman. Use that power to make your life what you want it to be."

She stared at her father, stunned by what he'd just said. He thought she was the strong one. Then why was her heart breaking and her resolve fading as she sat here, watching her father wither away?

"Do you believe me?" Arthur asked. "Because I can't leave this earth peacefully unless you say you believe me. You are going to need all the strength you have to get through this life. I need you to believe that you have that strength. That you can do it."

From somewhere deep inside her, Alaina felt that determination that her father spoke of. Yes, she'd always been strong. But now, to be strong without those who loved her surrounding her would feel almost impossible.

"Believe me," Arthur said again.

Alaina nodded as she looked into her father's watery eyes. "I believe you," she said in a whisper. "I will be strong. I promise."

He nodded, looking relieved. Lying back on his pillows, he closed his eyes, his face looking peaceful for the first time that day as he fell into a deep sleep.

For the next few weeks, Alaina was at the house every day, sitting with her father. She was his go-between to Jerome, keeping him abreast on Arthur's health and answering any questions he had about the business. Jerome and his wife, Lisa, visited every few days, and Matthew also came to see Arthur when he heard the bad news. Alaina found herself crying in Matthew's arms the day he came, as they spoke quietly in the study. It was all too much for her, losing the two most important people in her life, and Matthew understood exactly how she felt.

"You will get through this," Matthew told her gently. "Believe me, I know. You have your baby to live for and your father's memory to keep alive. It won't be easy, but you can do it. You're the strongest woman I've ever met."

She shook her head as she wiped the tears away with a hand-kerchief. "Everyone keeps telling me how strong I am, but I don't feel it. I feel like I'm losing control."

"It's okay to lose control, but it doesn't mean you aren't strong," Matthew told her. "Hannah used to tell me stories of when you two were young. You were the one to stand up to the bully who teased Hannah in school. And you were the one to stop the gossips who wanted to ruin Hannah's reputation the summer you both were coming out. You were her strength, her hero. I know in the end, you will get through this."

She appreciated her good friend's words, but she didn't fully believe them. Luckily, she had Margaret and Emma to lean on. Nathaniel came often to the house, missing work to be by her side, which she thought was admirable, but she never felt she could lean on him for strength. He also hired a full-time nurse to sit with Arthur when he grew worse. It relieved both Marga-ret and Alaina from having to care for Arthur's physical needs, which gave him some dignity. And as his body grew frailer, Alaina moved into the house along with little Arthur and Nanny Prue, so she would be there night and day to watch over him.

On a warm August day, after having kissed little Arthur on the head and telling Alaina that he wanted to take a nap, her father fell asleep and didn't wake up. She sat with him, holding his hand as he took his last, ragged breath.

"Goodbye, Father," she whispered, as tears streamed down her face. Now, everyone she'd ever truly loved was gone.

Chapter Twenty-Three

Marla

There wasn't a dry eye in the group as Ardie passed the box of tissues around. Even Toni, who was always so reserved with her emotions, was barely able to read the last few words.

"Poor Alaina," Rita said, wiping away tears. "First Hannah, then her father. It's heartbreaking."

"And that stupid husband of hers, cheating with the maid," Wanda said angrily. "How unoriginal is that? He doesn't deserve Alaina. I hope she leaves him."

"I'm sure having an affair with a maid was quite common back then," Ardie said. "It'll be interesting to see how Alaina handles it. People didn't divorce as easily then as now."

Marla listened to her friends' comments but stayed silent. She felt so terrible for Alaina. She'd lost her own mother to cancer years ago, after months of suffering. But at least she'd had her husband, who'd been kind and helpful throughout her mother's illness. She, too, wanted to know how Alaina coped with the loss of her dad and Nathaniel's betrayal.

"This is like a soap opera," Toni finally said, brushing away a tear. "A Victorian Edge of Night." The other's laughed and their mood lightened.

"Well, I hope that something good happens for Alaina. She's a smart woman. I'm sure she'll soldier on," Rita said. She brushed back one of her red curls that had come loose from her hair clip.

Marla smiled. Rita's curls were as untamable as she was. Wearing a red blouse and a full, floral midi-skirt with ankle boots, she looked like a hippie from a bygone era. But Marla adored her as much as she did the others. They were all unique in their own way and made up a hodge-podge group that somehow fit together.

"Me, too," Marla said. "I hope she finds her happiness."

"May we all find our happiness," Wanda said, raising her wine glass. The other's raised theirs to toast.

Toni marked the page in the journal and handed it back to Marla. "You have an interesting history here. Do you have any photos or family records in the house? It would be fascinating to look those over."

"My housekeeper says there are portraits up in the attic. I suppose there might be photographs and such too. Maybe an old Bible with the family lineage inside it," Marla said.

"We should all explore your attic some day," Ardie said. "I'm sure it would be interesting."

"I think that would be great," Marla said. "I'm not too keen on going up there alone anyway."

"Oh, a creepy attic," Rita said excitedly. "Now that sounds like fun."

The ladies laughed and everyone got ready to leave. They all thanked Toni for hosting the get-together and headed for the door.

"I hate waiting another two weeks to learn what happens to

Alaina," Wanda said as she stood in the doorway. "Maybe we could get together weekly instead, at least for a while."

"I'm game," Ardie said. "How about every Thursday evening if that works for everyone?"

"Sounds good to me," Marla said. "In fact, why don't you all come to my place next week? We can go to the yacht club for dinner, then back to the house to read. My treat. They have good food there."

Rita raised her brows. "Oh, a yacht club? That sounds fancy."

Marla shrugged. "It is, but it isn't. Many of the members eat dinner in their tennis or golf clothes. We don't have to dress up."

The other women looked at each other, and Marla had the feeling they felt uncomfortable. She suddenly regretted her offer. "Or, we can just eat at my place. Whatever you want."

"I vote for the club," Toni said, always willing to try something new. "I'd love to eat there. I've heard the food is fantastic."

"I'm in," Ardie said with a smile.

"Sure. Why not?" Wanda said. "I don't mind hob-knobbing with rich people."

"It sounds great," Rita agreed.

They all left, and Marla drove home. When she arrived, she stood in the great room and looked around for what felt like the first time. She wondered if this was how the room had looked when Alaina had first come here, or if it had changed much. There was a lake painting over the rustic mantel of the fireplace, and other such smaller paintings with north country themes on the walls. Had those always been there? Maybe there used to be a deer trophy or a family portrait over the fireplace. She still found it odd that Nathan had never said much about his family. When they'd first married, she'd asked a lot of questions, but he'd always changed the subject, or said he didn't know. That seemed so strange, considering the history of his family. After they were finished with the journal, Marla planned on doing some research into the rest of the family.

The next morning Marla awoke to a very formal voicemail from Mrs. Cooper. The older woman said she wasn't feeling well and was taking the day off. This stunned Marla. She couldn't remember Mrs. Cooper ever taking a sick day.

Anita and Louise were due to come in for their usual cleaning day, so Marla stayed around the house until they arrived. She explained the situation to Anita and said to go ahead and do their usual Friday cleaning.

"Wow. Has she ever missed a day before?" Anita asked. "We've been coming here for three years and I can't remember her ever being gone."

"I honestly can't remember her missing a day either," Marla said. "Maybe I should check on her. She's getting up there in years. She might be really sick."

Anita nodded. "Maybe you should. I'm a little worried about her."

Marla decided she would, then realized that she didn't have Mrs. Cooper's address. She went to her office to look in the old filing cabinet where the employee records were kept. She found the address and wrote it down.

Deciding she shouldn't go empty-handed—and that Mrs. Cooper would probably stick her nose up at anything she made—Marla drove into their small town and stopped at the café. They were known for their homemade soups, so Marla decided to get a container of chicken noodle soup and a fresh cinnamon muffin. Then she followed the directions to Mrs. Cooper's house.

Mrs. Cooper lived on Bellwood Avenue, just as they did, but it was farther down the road where smaller homes and cottages resided. Nathan had spared no expense when he'd purchased the lovely little white cottage with black shutters on an acre overlooking the lake. Around here, lakefront property wasn't cheap no matter what the size of the home. A two-stall garage sat off to the side and the driveway was made of brick pavers. Pavers also lined the grass as a path to the front door. As Marla parked in the driveway, she admired the cute home. It looked neat and tidy on the outside. Rose bushes sat underneath the large bay window and the brick porch had black wrought-iron railings around it. It was as perfectly kept up as Marla would imagine Mrs. Cooper's house to be.

As she stepped out of her car, Marla wondered how the older woman kept it up so immaculately. Surely, after working all day, she didn't come home and work on this place too. She decided Mrs. Cooper must have a handyman and gardener to help her.

"Hmm. Or maybe our handyman and gardener work on her place, too," she said to herself. She wouldn't doubt if that was a part of Mrs. Cooper's retirement plan from Nathan.

She knocked on the door, then waited. A television was on inside the house, so she knew the housekeeper was here. Finally, the door opened. Mrs. Cooper, standing there in pajamas, a thick, fuzzy robe, and slippers, scowled at her.

"What on earth are you doing here?" she asked, sounding hoarse.

"I was checking to see if you were playing hooky," Marla teased. She raised the bag of food. "I brought soup."

The older woman did not look amused. But after a moment of staring at Marla, she finally said, "What kind of soup?"

Marla smiled. She knew she had her.

She walked inside the home and wasn't at all surprised by its décor. Mrs. Cooper had sensible furniture that wouldn't show dirt or stains or fade easily. The living room was to the right of the entryway where the big bay window was. The carpeting was dark gray, the walls were off-white, and the sofa and chairs were covered in a medium-gray twill fabric. The coffee and end tables were oak as was the large media cabinet across the room which held a good-sized television. The only color in the room was the burgundy tufted cushion in the bay window where a fluffy orange cat lay sleeping, curled up in a ball.

"You have a cat?" Marla asked, genuinely surprised. She couldn't imagine the fastidious housekeeper dealing with cat hair.

"Yes, I do. Why does that surprise you so much?" She stared steadily at Marla.

"I just never pictured you with pets," she said.

Mrs. Cooper turned and walked through a door that led into the kitchen. Marla followed, even though she hadn't been invited. The kitchen was large and faced the lake. Everything looked neat and new, like it was barely ever used.

"You have a nice view," Marla said, walking over to the French doors. "And a lot of light in here with all these windows. It's lovely."

Mrs. Cooper raised one eyebrow as she placed the bag Marla had given her in the stainless steel refrigerator. "You act as if you've never been here."

Marla turned and faced her. "I haven't." This seemed to surprise the housekeeper.

"Really? I always assumed you helped Nathan pick it out."

Marla shook her head. "No, I didn't. Nathan bought it all by himself. I didn't even know he'd bought it until he gave it to you."

Mrs. Cooper tilted her head. "I didn't know that. I guess I

always thought it was your idea for me to retire and live here."

"You thought *I* wanted you gone?" Marla asked, completely stunned. Even though she'd never gotten along with the house-keeper, she'd never told Nathan that she wanted her to retire. That had been his idea.

"I don't know. I guess I thought you'd encouraged it. I had no idea Nathan was the one to want me to retire." She walked over to the family room sofa and sat down, looking a bit dejected.

Marla sat in a chair opposite of her. "I don't think he wanted to get rid of you, if that's what you're worried about. He probably just thought you'd worked so many years that you'd want to retire."

"And do what? Spend quality time with my cat?" she asked sharply.

Marla shrugged. "I don't know. Travel? Visit with family? Relax?"

"That sounds hideous," she said with disgust.

Marla let out a laugh. She couldn't help it. Mrs. Cooper sounded so offended over Nathan wanting her to enjoy her life instead of working.

"You find that funny?" Mrs. Cooper asked.

"I'm sorry, but yes, I do. Most people can't wait to retire and relax. You, however, are adamant about not having time to relax. You're one of a kind, Mrs. Cooper."

Mrs. Cooper gave a small grin. "Yes, I am. They don't make people like me anymore. Everyone wants to have a good time. I like having a schedule and completing a job well-done. Being sick today was an utter nuisance to me."

"You're only human. You have to be sick sometimes," Marla said.

"Illness is for other people. Not me. My mother was ill for

years before she passed away. I supported her the entire time. I never wanted to be like her. Unfortunately, you can't stop the body from aging."

Marla nodded. "That's true. I didn't know your mother was ill for years. Mine died of cancer. I don't know if you remember that or not. It was a long illness too."

Mrs. Cooper nodded. "I remember. Your mother was a fine woman. I liked her very much. It was a shame that she died so young."

Marla tried not to look as shocked as she felt. She had no idea that Mrs. Cooper had liked her mother or thought that way. "Thank you."

They sat in silence for a while in the cozy little room where photos of Mrs. Cooper's past were displayed on shelves. Marla eyed a picture of what looked like a very young Mrs. Cooper with a very handsome, dark-haired gentleman with big, twinkling eyes. They looked happy. "Is that Mr. Cooper?" She pointed to the framed photo.

Mrs. Cooper glanced in the direction she was pointing and nodded. "Yes. That's Irving. That's a photo of him the year we were married."

"He's a handsome man. I don't remember him. Did we ever meet?"

"No. He passed away before you married Nathan."

"Oh, I'm sorry. Do you mind if I ask how he died?"

Mrs. Cooper grew still, a faraway expression in her eyes. Marla was immediately sorry she'd asked.

"He worked as a butler and driver for the Madisons. He died in the same car accident that took Nathan's father in 1983. He was driving at the time when another car swerved right in front of them and hit them head on. He was only thirty-six years old."

Marla's hand flew to her chest. "Oh, my goodness. I'm so sorry. I didn't know that."

Mrs. Cooper frowned. "Nathan never told you how his father died? Or that my husband was with him at the time? I find that odd."

"I know. I think it's strange now, too. I know very little about Nathan's parents or family at all. He never talked about the past and never would answer questions. I didn't think too much of it before, but now, I don't know why I didn't press him about it."

"Maybe it was all too painful to tell. Or so far removed by the time he married you," Mrs. Cooper said.

Marla wondered if she should ask questions now. Mrs. Cooper seemed to be in a thoughtful mood. Marla figured it was worth a shot.

"What was Nathan's mother like? I get the feeling she was a kind of free spirit."

Mrs. Cooper nodded. "She was. But she also believed in the old ways too. She was so full of life. Nathan's father, Andrew, had a devil-may-care attitude too. They enjoyed the family money and were never really serious about the family business. I felt that they were relieved when Nathan wanted to become a college professor. Once it was decided that he wouldn't carry on the family business, Andrew closed the last two stores. He'd been letting them close down until then anyway. It was a sad day when the last Madison's Department Store in St. Paul shut down. It was a premiere store to shop in from the 1800s until that day."

"I've been told it was in the 1970s," Marla said.

"It was 1975. The economy wasn't that good in those days anyway, so I suppose that's why they'd been closing stores across the country. But it was a beautiful store."

"Tell me more about his mother," Marla urged.

"She was a pretty woman. And sweet. Her name was Elenore, but everyone called her Ellie. She also loved to go to parties and dance the night away. And she used the pool quiet often. She loved swimming. But her greatest passion was painting. Her watercolor paintings didn't really go with the décor of the lake house, but she hung them in the hallway upstairs anyway. That's why she took down the portraits, so her paintings could go up there. She spent her days over by the French doors where the light was best, or outside in the summer, painting the landscapes, flowers, even still-life paintings of items she'd arrange on a table. She did a lovely one of an antique vase with a lace tablecloth under it and bunny salt and pepper shakers. It sounds odd, but the colors were soothing and made it beautiful. She gave it to me as a gift. It's hanging over there." Mrs. Cooper pointed to the dining room.

Marla stood and walked over to it. The vase was a rich blue and the background color was greenish-blue. Mrs. Cooper was right. Ellie had been very talented. The detail in the lace was so intricate, it looked real. She returned to where the housekeeper was sitting. "It's beautiful. How kind of her to give it to you."

"Like I said, she was a nice person. She donated her paintings to fundraisers and such. Other paintings hung in area businesses. I think she did it for the joy of it, not to make money. She didn't need money, after all."

"What did she do after her husband died?" Marla asked.

Mrs. Cooper sighed, remembering. "She was lost at first. They did everything together. But she still painted. And she eventually travelled with friends and was more involved with area charities. She continued living in the lake house until her death. She had cancer and died quite quickly. I guess they didn't catch it soon enough. It was such a shame."

"I wish I'd known her," Marla said. "Can I ask you how you managed after your husband passed? That was so tragic."

Mrs. Cooper raised her eyes to Marla's. "It was tragic. But the Madisons were very kind. They gave me paid time off, but I didn't really know what to do with myself. I spent some time with Irving's family, but then went back to work. It was right after that when I became the head housekeeper and moved into the bedroom off the kitchen. I didn't want to live in the little apartment alone that Irving and I had shared. And they never re-hired a butler, because their lifestyle really didn't need one anymore. There were no more big parties to take care of. Our staff shrunk down to me, another maid, and the gardener. We had a handyman we could call when necessary. It has stayed that way ever since."

"I'm sorry that happened to you," Marla said gently. "I'm assuming you had no children."

"No. No children. Unfortunately. That's why I took such great joy in your Reese. Watching her grow up made up for me not having one of my own."

"I guess I never thought of it that way," Marla said, suddenly feeling ashamed for the way she'd envied her daughter's closeness with Mrs. Cooper. "I know you two got along well, though."

Mrs. Cooper raised an eyebrow. "It annoyed you. Didn't it?"

She smiled. "Maybe. Sometimes. When she took your side."

Mrs. Cooper cocked her head. "You think I don't like you, don't you?"

Her question stunned Marla. "Well, I always got the feeling that you didn't approve of me."

"Hmph. I'll admit that I didn't give you such a warm welcome. And maybe I've always been a bit standoffish with you. But I did approve of you, after a time."

Marla wasn't sure if she'd been dissed or complimented. "Why didn't you like me at first? I tried my best to be nice to you."

Mrs. Cooper gave her one of her long stares. "To be absolutely truthful, I thought you married Nathan for his money." She raised her hand to ward off any protest Marla might give. "You have to admit that you were much younger than he when you married. It worried me. I'd known him since he was sixteen years old, so I felt protective of him. I know that was wrong. He was a grown man after all, but I did. I was afraid he'd married a trophy wife who'd rob him blind."

Marla sat back in her seat and crossed her arms. "You and everyone else, apparently. I hope you don't think that now."

"I don't," Mrs. Cooper said. "I haven't for a long time. He adored you, that was obvious. And you were always respectful of his wishes and even his eccentric ideas. You were an attentive mother to Reese and a good wife to Nathan. And the way you cared for him while he was ill was admirable. I have great respect for you."

Marla could hardly believe what she'd just heard. "Thank you," she said, at a loss for words.

"Well, don't let it go to your head. You can be sure I'll fight you every step of the way with any changes to the house. Unless the changes are my ideas, of course."

Marla burst out laughing. She laughed so hard, it made Mrs. Cooper laugh too, until the older woman began to cough.

Marla quickly got her a glass of water and Mrs. Cooper drank a few sips to calm her cough.

"I'd better leave so you can rest," Marla said. "I'm sorry I took up your time, but it was nice chatting about everything. There's just so much I don't know."

"Don't worry about it," Mrs. Cooper said. "I didn't realize Nathan never told you about his past. There weren't any deep, dark family secrets that I know of, so there was nothing to hide."

Mrs. Cooper walked Marla to the door. "I should be to work on Monday. I can't imagine how you're getting along without me."

Marla could never tell if Mrs. Cooper was being serious or wry. "Take all the time you need. I'll be fine. I didn't grow up with a housekeeper, you know."

Mrs. Cooper gave a small smile. "I forget that. It's just always been my job to make meals and take care of everything. I forget that someone else could easily do it too."

"Well, probably not as well as you do," Marla said. "I'm not saying you need to stay away forever."

"That's nice to hear," the older woman said.

As Marla walked out the door, Mrs. Cooper spoke once more. "You know, after you leave, I'll deny everything I've said today. I'll claim I was delusional with fever and cold medicine."

Marla chuckled. "I'm sure you will. Feel better soon." She waved and headed for her car.

Marla thought about her conversation with Mrs. Cooper all that day as she walked the trail by the lake then swam a few laps in the pool. She made herself an easy dinner and sat in front of the television watching her favorite home improvement show, but her thoughts were on Mrs. Cooper. She understood now the responsibility Nathan had felt for the housekeeper. She'd never understood before why he'd put up with her bossiness and how he'd just laugh when she'd tell him how to do something. He'd known her for decades, and she was as much a part of the Lake Heron house as he'd been. And their families were connected by the tragedy of his father and her husband dying in the car accident. She wished she'd known all of this before and wondered again why Nathan hadn't told her.

Maybe he thought it all belonged in the past, she thought. Whatever the reason, it had made for a very uncomfortable couple of decades for Marla around the housekeeper. Now that she understood Mrs. Cooper better, she actually didn't mind her so much.

It was funny to Marla how thoughts and ideas could change in an instant.

Chapter Twenty-Four

Marla

Thursday night came quickly. After the five women met in the yacht club's parking lot, they were shown to a nice table with a lakeside view. The hostess, Jeanette, was her usually polite self, but Marla felt several pairs of eyes on her when she sat down. It wasn't against the rules to bring friends who were non-members to the club, but many older members still frowned on it.

"This is some place," Rita said, glancing around. "It's very fancy, but you were right. People are wearing casual clothing. I don't feel too out of place."

Marla smiled at Rita, who'd worn one of her many floral midi-skirts and a bright blue blouse. She'd never fade into the background wherever she went, and Marla wouldn't want her to. She was perfect exactly as she was.

"Don't let their stares make you uncomfortable," Marla told everyone. "They stare at everyone, all the time. They're all probably trying to figure out exactly who each of you are and how rich you might be. It's their favorite gossip guessing game."

"They can't all be that bad, can they?" Ardie asked. She'd

worn a pair of black dress pants and a simple blouse and flats. She looked as nice as anyone else here.

"No. Not everyone," Marla admitted. "But sometimes it feels that way."

"Let's order and enjoy our meal," Toni said. "Ignore everyone. And look at that view. It's gorgeous. I'd love to live on this lake."

The women each ordered and shared a bottle of white wine. As they caught up over their salad course, Marla glanced up and saw Vicki and Catrina walk in with some of the other ladies from golf league. She'd forgotten that Thursday night was Ladies' League.

Vicki waved but didn't approach their table. Catrina followed suit. The women found a table across the room and sat.

"Friends of yours?" Ardie asked quietly.

Marla nodded. "Honestly, I'm not sure anymore. I sort of went bananas on them one day. I apologized, but I'm not sure they've gotten over it. Plus, I no longer play in golf league or tennis, and they think that's strange."

"Why did you stop playing?" Wanda asked. She'd worn a nice pair of jeans and a deep green blouse which was a great color for her. Marla hadn't noticed before how slender she actually was, since she usually wore loose scrubs. Wanda could certainly hold her own with any of the club members.

Marla shrugged. "I never really enjoyed it all that much to begin with. I played because Nathan did, and he liked spending time here at the club. It was also a way for me to meet friends when I first moved here. But ever since Nathan passed, I really don't care to spend my time that way anymore."

"I hate golf," Toni said. "I tried to play a few years ago because my then-boyfriend played. I never got the hang of it."

"I don't mind it," Wanda said. Everyone stared at her in surprise. "What? You don't think I can play golf? I used to play years ago. I would now, but I can't afford it and don't have the time."

"Well. You learn something new every day," Ardie said.

Everyone laughed.

After dinner, Marla led the ladies through the ballroom to the club library. "Here he is. The original Nathaniel Madison, hanging over the fireplace."

The women stood in a semi-circle around the fireplace and studied the portrait.

"He's quite handsome," Rita said. "He looks a lot like your husband."

"I know," Marla said. "I was surprised by how much they resemble each other."

"Well, that doesn't make up for the fact that he was a jerk to Alaina," Wanda said bluntly.

"No. It doesn't," Marla agreed with a smile. Leave it to Wanda to point out the truth. "And my husband was more understanding than he seemed to be."

"I would hope so," Toni said. She glanced around. "This is a neat room. So masculine, but cozy."

Marla nodded. "I'd never even been in here before until I heard there was a portrait of Nathaniel in here. This has always been considered a room just for the men."

"How archaic," Toni said, one eyebrow raised. "I hope that isn't true anymore."

"Not that I know of," Marla said with a chuckle.

"Oh, is this the plaque for your husband?" Rita asked. "Very nice."

"Yes. It was a nice gesture for them to do. Apparently, this club would never even exist without the help from the Madisons. It's kind of strange, when you think of it."

"But also something to be proud of," Ardie said, smiling over at Marla.

Marla agreed. While it seemed odd to her, she also thought it was a nice memorial to the men who'd helped make it possible. It was something Reese, and any children she ever had, could be proud of.

They left after that and went to Marla's house. It was chilly outside by the time they were ready to sit down, so they all found a spot on one of the leather sofas in the great room and got comfortable. Marla picked up Alaina's journal and began to read.

The days after my father's passing were a blur to me. There was the funeral to plan and I was grateful to have Margaret by my side assisting me. Nathaniel was very attentive during those difficult days and gave me full reign to do whatever I felt necessary to say goodbye to my father. I was grateful for his generosity, but felt that in some way, I'd be repaying him in one form or another when it was all over.

Chapter Twenty-Five

Alaina

1878

Those dark days following her father's passing were thankfully a blur to Alaina. While she remembered helping with the details of the funeral and reception, she mostly felt lost and unorganized through it all. Margaret stepped in to help her in any way she could as did Mrs. Hanson. Emma was by her side when she was needed, and gave her space when she felt she should. Nathaniel gave orders to everyone on staff to do as Mrs. Madison wished, no matter how big or small the detail. Alaina was grateful for his thoughtfulness, but wondered in her lucid moments at his motives.

The night before her father's funeral, Alaina went to her son's room and asked Nanny Prue to give her time alone with her baby. She sat and rocked the little boy to sleep, holding him tight against her heart. Little Arthur was so young still, only eight months. He was a busy boy, crawling and standing on his own, discovering new adventures every day. His hair was coming in dark and wavy, like Nathaniel's, but his eyes were bright blue, which she thought was extraordinary. She had no idea where those blue eyes came from. She'd never met Nathaniel's parents, as they'd passed away when he was a young man. Perhaps his mother had been a blond, blue-eyed woman. Or maybe it came from his father. She'd never know. But the Madison genes were strong in her son. He'd be a handsome man, like his father, but he'd bear her father's name. And, if she had any say in it, her father's demeanor and kind heart as well.

The next day she managed to get through her father's funeral. She politely thanked people for coming to the reception at her house and said all the right words. But her heart was splintered into a million pieces and she felt numb to it all. How she wished her dear Hannah were here to get her though this horrendous time.

After the mourners had left, she was ushered into the library by Nathaniel so her father's lawyer could read the will. She listened to very little of it, only nodding her head and wishing she could go upstairs and sleep. She knew that as her father's only child, she'd be the one to inherit everything. She would deal with it all later—her heart and mind weren't in it that day.

Two weeks after her father's funeral, Alaina awoke from her daze and began thinking about the future again. She'd spent a lot of the time locked away in her room, or in the nursery with her precious little Arthur. She'd reflected on everything in her past, from the loss of her mother to her most recent losses. She'd thought about her reasons for marrying Nathaniel, and her doubts about their relationship now. She realized that she had no one she trusted completely to turn to anymore. She was all alone.

That thought saddened her the most.

Emma helped her dress early that morning and seemed delighted that Alaina was finally going down to join her husband for breakfast. When she appeared downstairs, Nathaniel stood and held her chair while she sat, then sat down himself.

"I'm so happy you feel well enough to join me," he said solicitously.

She glanced up at him. "I haven't been ill, just sad."

"I understand," he told her gently. "And you may take all the time you need to grieve. I know losing your father was devastating for you. I feel his loss also. He was a great man."

His words touched her heart. She knew that Nathaniel had thought highly of her father, and she appreciated him saying so. "Thank you."

Mrs. Hanson served breakfast with a warm smile on her face. As they ate the fresh fruit, biscuits, and boiled eggs, Alaina addressed her husband.

"I'd like to speak with you sometime today about my inheritance. If you have the time, of course." She'd been told by Emma that over the past two weeks Nathaniel had worked most days at home in his study. It had been very unexpected, and she'd been appreciative that he'd felt a need to stay near her.

Nathaniel's brows rose slightly. "I'd be happy to speak with you after breakfast. Although, you needn't worry about your inheritance. I will take care of everything for you."

"But it's *my* inheritance," she said. "I should be the one to decide how best to handle it."

Nathaniel glanced toward the kitchen door, and Alaina became aware that he didn't want to speak where the servants could hear them.

"Let us enjoy our breakfast first, and discuss this later," he said courteously.

After breakfast, he led her to the study and closed the door. She seated herself in a chair in front of his desk and he sat behind it. She noticed that he had several ledgers and journals open and strewn about the desk, many of which had once belonged to her father.

"I've been looking over your father's business ledgers," he said. "I'm sure you're familiar with them, since you kept them so accurately for several years."

Alaina sat with her hands clasped in her lap, trying hard to stay silent. How dare he take it upon himself to look over her father's ledgers? They belonged to her now. She waited for him to continue speaking.

"Your father did quite well in his business, as you know. I'm thinking it will sell for a nice sum to someone who is already in the textile business and we can reinvest the money into the stores, or perhaps into a trust for Arthur." He glanced up at Alaina. "And I thought we'd sell the house too, although I wanted you to have a chance to go through all the furnishings and decide what you'd like to keep. I'm sure there are many things of sentimental value to you."

He smiled at her, as if he'd said something to be proud of. He was *allowing* her to go through the possessions that *belonged* to her now. Alaina seethed inside at the thought of it.

Sitting up straighter, Alaina said firmly, "I don't want to sell my father's business. Or the house, for now. I'll keep them for the time being."

Nathaniel's brows furrowed, as if he might become angry, but then he relaxed his features and smiled at her as one would a child who didn't understand the situation. "Darling. I understand that your father left all his property to you, but as your husband, I have the legal right to decide what to do with that property. While you were very efficient at balancing ledgers and accounts, you certainly aren't ready to make such important decisions as to whether or not we keep a business. Please. Leave it to me to decide."

Alaina stood and walked to the open window behind Nathaniel's desk. It was late September, and the day was unusually warm. She felt a trickle of perspiration run down her back, caused by the heat of anger welling up inside her. Very unladylike indeed. If she was going to win this argument, she knew she'd have to do it with intelligence and wit, while allowing Nathaniel to maintain his pride. She changed her tactic.

Turning around, she walked around the desk again and faced him, forcing a smile on her lips. "I only thought that keeping the textile factory might be a profitable business for you," she said gently. "You did buy a large portion of the products you sell from my father, as do other businesses across the eastern side of the country. Not only will you be able to stock your stores at cost, you'd make a profit selling to your competition. It seems like a lucrative situation for you all the way around."

Nathaniel sat back in his chair, watching her as she sat down daintily in the chair she'd abandoned moments before. He seemed to be considering what she'd said.

"That is true," he agreed. "I'd own the market in our area and beyond. But I have to admit that I know nothing about the textile business. I'm not sure it would be a good fit for me and my company."

"I know much about the business," she told him. "And Jerome, the manager, knows as much as my father did. He'd be the perfect manager for the factory. In fact, he's been running it for weeks alone, and has done a fine job."

"I see," Nathaniel said. "It might be something to consider."

Alaina thought she could actually see the wheels turning in his head. She held her breath, hoping he'd say yes.

"I'm not in agreement with you having anything to do with running the business, though," he said firmly. "You have a house to manage, a child to care for, and many other social and church functions to attend. I'll not have my wife slaving away, working at a factory."

Alaina's heart sank. She had so hoped to be a part of the everyday workings and decisions of the factory. "Perhaps I could still keep a hand in it by taking care of the ledgers as I used to do. At home, of course. It would save on paying a bookkeeper."

Nathaniel watched her intently, as if weighing his decision on her words. Finally, he spoke. "I suppose that will be fine. It's a sound business and you're right—Jerome has been handling it quite well. Let's give it a year and see where we stand after that. If the business continues to gain a profit, we'll keep it."

Alaina wanted to squeal with delight but held back. "Thank you," she said. "You won't regret it."

He stood and walked over to where Alaina was, sitting down next to her and looking her in the eyes. "But I have a condition to my offer."

Her smile faded. She should have known it wouldn't be that easy.

"I want us to go back to the way we were, before everything went so wrong in our lives," he said gently. He took her hand in his. "I'm sorry I was the reason you were unable to see your friend before she died. I take full responsibility for that. And you know how sorry I am about the loss of your father. I cared about him very much."

She dropped her gaze to their entwined hands and nodded. "What do you want?"

"You. I want us to be happy again. We enjoyed intimacy together before all of this happened. I would like us to go back to that. I loved how close we were. And I would like to have another child, if you're willing. Can you find it in your heart to let me in again?"

She stared down at the rug and contemplated what he'd asked of her. She appreciated his apology, but it still didn't help warm her heart to him. Still, he had conceded to keeping her father's business. She was a married woman, and she'd known she couldn't keep her husband at bay forever. But could she let him in her heart again? She didn't know.

Her eyes rose to his. She knew she had to say yes to appease him. But she had one more thing to ask of him. "We can try to return to how we once were, but now I have something to ask of you."

"Hmm," Nathaniel said, a grin appearing on his face. "I see you're quite the negotiator. All right. What is it you want?"

She sat up straight and held her head high. "I want the upstairs maid, Mary, to be dismissed at once." Alaina watched him intently but saw no sign of surprise written on his face.

"Of course," he agreed. "I will give her two weeks severance and a good letter of recommendation, though, if that is agreeable to you." He did not insult her by trying to deny there was anything between him and the maid, nor did he apologize for embarrassing her in her own home.

Alaina nodded. She didn't care how Mary left; she just wanted her gone.

"As for my father's house, I would like some time to go through everything before we decide what to do with it. If that will suit you," Alaina said.

"That will be fine. Take your time." He smiled then, that

devilishly handsome smile he was capable of. Unfortunately for him, she was no longer swayed by it. "I will give you a little more time to mourn your dear father, of course. But I am pleased we will once again be the happy couple we once were."

Alaina smiled back but said nothing. She'd gotten what she'd wanted out of the bargain. She guessed that was how it would be now between them. Forever bargaining for what the other wanted. But as a female in a time when women had few rights, it was the best she could do to survive.

* * *

Time went by swiftly for Alaina once she'd settled into her new role as owner of Carlton Textiles. She'd kept her promise to Nathaniel to place home, family, volunteering, and entertaining in the home first but also spent time working daily on the factory's ledgers. Once a week, she met with Jerome at the factory to discuss any issues that arose. He was a competent manager and a hard worker, and Alaina was thankful that she could trust him to work for the best interests of the company. She felt whole again, now that she was able to work, even in a limited capacity. And although she missed her father dearly, she was happy she could keep his legacy alive by being in charge of his beloved business.

After their "deal" had been made, Nathaniel had returned to his work as usual and was too busy managing his business to put any energy into the factory. Alaina didn't know if it was because he trusted her to run it smoothly, or he just didn't care how it was run. He didn't interfere except to look over the ledgers once a month to check how it was doing. He was always pleased with what he saw.

Alaina talked Nathaniel into extending Margaret's employment at her father's house until they could pack the items Alaina wanted to keep. For weeks after her father's death, Alaina set aside time to go through every room and pack the items she treasured. She had her father's desk from the study moved to her morning room on Summit, despite it being too masculine to fit into the room's delicate décor. Alaina had spent numerous hours sitting at that desk in the past, as had her father, and she wanted to have it for her own. She also boxed up things that had belonged to her mother and personal items of her father's. She put aside his gold watch to someday give to little Arthur when he was grown, and kept other mementoes for herself, such as the stick pin he'd worn in his tie and the wool jacket he'd worn at home when working at his desk. There were also old books, china dishes, family silverware, and other such items that she didn't want to part with. She gave away little mementoes to those who'd loved her father. A gold fountain pen to Matthew, a crystal vase to Margaret, a pair of her mother's earrings to Emma. Small things that meant something to her to thank those she cared about for being there for her in her darkest time.

When all was packed, the house did go up for sale and was bought by a young family quickly. Margaret went to work for Matthew as his housekeeper because Mrs. Harper had left. Alaina was happy Margaret would be there for the family. She would run the house expertly and with love, something that family desperately needed now that Hannah was gone.

Nathaniel's nightly visits resumed weeks after their conversation and Alaina accepted him back into her bed. While the passion had cooled between them, she couldn't say she didn't altogether enjoy his company. He was a kind and generous lover, and she took whatever closeness and comfort she could from him. By the time they went on their yearly vacation to Great Heron Lake in June of 1879, Alaina was expecting their second child.

On March 22, 1880, Ella Hannah Madison was born. She was a sweet, tiny little baby with a tuft of dark hair and bright blue eyes like her brother's. Arthur was a busy toddler by then, keeping Nanny Prue very busy, so Alaina hired a nurse just for Ella. But she stayed a very hands-on mother, unlike most of her counterparts, and spent time every day with both children, enjoying every minute of it.

Her life was full between work, home, and children, and that was the most a woman like her could hope for. She was content, and that was enough. Or so she thought.

Chapter Twenty-Six

Marla

As Marla set the journal aside, she thought about Alaina's words. *That was the most a woman like her could hope for.* Alaina hadn't been completely happy in her life but was content. She understood how the first Mrs. Madison had felt. Hadn't she also felt her life was content, but not happy? Marla had thought that was just something that happened after years of marriage. But now, she wondered if it happened for other, deeper reasons.

She looked up and was startled to see the other women watching her, as if waiting for her to say something.

"You were very far away just now," Ardie said.

Marla nodded. "I guess I was. I was contemplating Alaina's words. I found it sad that she felt she only deserved what she had, and nothing more. Yet, I can understand how she felt."

Wanda nodded. "It's sad, but I think a lot of women would understand her feelings. I know that I had those same feelings about my marriage before it fell apart." She shrugged. "Maybe that's why my husband cheated. Because he felt that way, too."

Toni sat up straighter. "You can't blame yourselves for how

you felt in your marriages. And you really can't say that you were responsible for your husband cheating, Wanda," she said firmly. "Marriages grow stale sometimes. And people settle, afraid to move on. That's why I'm not married."

"I had a good marriage. And a good life," Marla said. "But a part of me felt as if I gave up a lot to have this life. I lost my own identity in my marriage and became what Nathan wanted. I never realized it, until he passed. And, until we started reading Alaina's journal. She didn't have a choice how her life was run because men were in charge. I did have a choice, and I didn't utilize it."

"Sometimes the devil you know is better than the devil you don't," Rita said seriously.

The women all looked at each other, and suddenly burst out into laughter. "Oh, goodness. This is getting deep," Ardie said.

"Well, Alaina did stand up for herself and kept her father's business. Good for her! It stinks that she wasn't even in charge of her own inheritance, though, and had to fight for it," Wanda said.

"Yeah. Unfortunately, that was the way it was back then," Toni added. "But she was smart, telling him how he'd save money by keeping it. She was quite a woman."

The ladies soon left, promising to meet again the next Thursday at Ardie's house. Ardie stayed behind.

"Are you okay? You looked sad," she said to Marla as they cleared away the wine glasses.

"I'm fine. I didn't mean to bring up my personal issues. It's hard, though, listening to Alaina's story and not comparing it to my own. I mean, look at me. I have everything a woman could want. I live a comfortable life. I don't have to worry how I'll pay for my daughter's college or my house payment. I'm privileged.

But I always felt there was more to life than playing tennis at the club or throwing social events."

"Why didn't you keep working?" Ardie asked.

Marla shrugged. "I did for a while after we married. But then Reese was born, and I felt lucky that I could stay home with her. And I'm still happy I did, but now I wish I'd worked at least part-time. Not for the money, but as a way to stay connected to reality." She chuckled. "I am aware that I don't live in a normal reality."

Ardie laughed too. "Yeah, you have a pretty good one, that's for sure. But it sounds like you've done a lot of good, too. You said you used to run fundraisers for the community and the local school. That's important too."

"Yes, I suppose it is." Marla sighed. "I feel like I have no direction now. First I was busy raising Reese, then I was still busy with my husband, and then I spent over a year caring for him. Now, what am I supposed to do? Sit around here and wait for life to come to me? I just haven't figured out what to do with myself yet."

Ardie smiled. "I think you've done a lot since your husband died. Look at you! You've remodeled several rooms in the house, you went to a class to learn how to tile over a fireplace, you've made a whole new group of friends, and you've stood up to your long-time nemesis—Mrs. Cooper. You've come a long way, baby!"

Marla smiled wide. "I guess I have." She walked over and hugged her friend. "The best thing I ever did was meet you. You've changed my life, you know that?"

Ardie shook her head. "No, I didn't. You did. You've done it all by yourself and I am just here in the wings watching you grow. I think we both lucked out the day you walked into my paint department."

Marla's heart filled with warmth. It was so nice to know that she had a group of friends like the book club crew. They were all genuine, and that was what she loved about them. Ardie was right—she was slowly filling her life with new experiences and new friends. Maybe she just had to give herself time to figure out the rest.

* * *

Marla didn't work on any more decorating projects on Friday. Instead, she enjoyed the beautiful weather outside by taking a long walk on the trail along the lake. There was a large chunk of land that belonged to the state park where the trail winded through. Marla had access to it directly from her yard, and it ran beside the lake, then out around some of the private property, then back toward the lake. It was a two-mile hike one way, so she got a good amount of exercise by the time she went to the other end and back.

The day was warm, but a nice breeze blew in from the lake. It helped to keep the bugs away. As she walked, she passed others walkers as well, and some people on bikes. Many of the locals used this trail, and the tourists did, too. Their cute little town did bring in a lot of tourists in the summer.

"Well, hello there," a deep male voice said, coming toward her.

Marla had been thinking again of Alaina and her situation and hadn't noticed anyone heading her way. She looked up and was surprised to see Alden, in shorts and a polo shirt with sneakers. He looked just as nice dressed casually as he had in his tuxedo.

"Hello," she greeted him.

"It's good to see a familiar face out here." Alden stopped

when he reached Marla's side. "I don't usually see anyone I know when I walk."

"Do you walk this trail often?" she asked.

"Yes. But I usually take my walks in the early evening. I got sick of working today, though, and decided to enjoy the day."

"I usually walk in the daytime," Marla said. "That explains why I've never run into you before."

"Well, then. I'll have to change my habits and walk more in the daytime." He smiled at her, showing straight white teeth and crinkles around his friendly brown eyes. "Do you mind if I join you?"

"I was heading the way you came," she said. "I walk to the end then go back."

"Oh, I don't care which direction I walk. I just like being out here and enjoying the weather."

"Okay. Let's walk." She started down the trail with Alden at her side. "Is your house nearby?"

He pointed in the direction they were heading. "It's not far from here. I can access the trail from my property. It's a modest little home, but I like it."

Marla laughed. "When people around here say modest, they usually mean a medium-sized mansion."

"Oh no. My house isn't a mansion by any means. It's a three-bedroom, two-bath cottage. I have a large four-season porch on the front where I have a little woodstove set up so I can use it as my office all-year-round. I love working with a view of the lake."

"It sounds nice," she said, thinking about the Fairy Tale house she loved so much. "I wouldn't mind downsizing to a smaller place."

"The gossip at the club is you live in the big house near the yacht club," he said.

"Oh, yes. The gossip. They're good at that. But it's true. The Madisons have lived there since 1885."

"Wow. That's a long time. It's nice, though, that they've passed it down through the years. Many families find they can't afford such big homes a few generations down and sell them."

"Yes. My friends and I went sight-seeing around Summit Avenue in St. Paul. Many of those large homes are now apartments or townhouses. I can see where the houses can get to be too expensive. The Madisons were good with money, though. My husband was the last male heir to own the property."

"What about your daughter?" Alden asked. "Does she want the house?"

Marla smiled. It was nice he remembered her daughter from the club dance. "No. Not really. At least she says she doesn't."

He nodded. She figured as an investment broker, he ran into situations like this all the time.

"Have you always lived in Minnesota?" she asked, changing the subject.

"No. I grew up in a small town in Wisconsin. After college, I was hired by an investment firm in Minneapolis, so that's when I moved."

"I worked for an investment firm in St. Paul before I married," she said. "Maybe we crossed paths at some point."

Alden chuckled. "If we had, believe me, I would have remembered."

Marla felt a blush rise to her face. Goodness! No one had made her blush in a very long time.

A movement on the lake caught Marla's eye and she glanced up. "Look!" She pointed toward the lake. "A blue heron. Isn't it marvelous?"

Alden watched with her as the majestic bird skimmed the

water, searching for food. "They sure fly gracefully for such a big bird, don't they?"

She nodded. "I love watching the herons. Sometimes, I see one on the edge of my dock, standing as still as a statue. They're beautiful."

Alden turned to her. "Yes. They are." He smiled warmly at her.

They continued their walk and soon arrived at the end of the trail where Marla's yard opened to the lake. From here there was a good view of the house and of the sailboats docked in the distance at the yacht club.

"This is beautiful," Alden said, gazing around. "I hadn't realized you could actually see the yacht club from here."

"Just the sailboats," Marla said. "Thankfully, trees block the view of the club. Apparently, the original Nathaniel Madison bought up all this property in the mid-1870s and sold the yacht club their land. Many of the homes built past ours are also on land he once owned. He knew how to make money, that's for sure."

Alden grinned. "Some people have a knack for it."

Marla suddenly realized she was being rude. "Would you like a tour of the house?"

"Thank you, but I should get back to work. Can I get a raincheck, though? I'd love to see it."

She nodded. "Sure. Anytime."

He waved and headed back for the trail. A few steps away, he turned and said, "Maybe we could have lunch sometime at the club."

Marla stood still a moment, unsure. She would like to see him again, as a friend, but she didn't want to lead him on. She certainly wasn't looking for a relationship so soon after her husband's passing. "Sure. Maybe we'll run into each other there sometime," she said, then suddenly felt bad. It sounded like she was rejecting his invitation.

He nodded, waved, then headed off through the trees.

Marla felt terrible. Maybe he only wanted to be friends. Or, maybe not.

"Who was that gentleman you were talking to outside?" Mrs. Cooper asked as Marla entered through the French doors.

At least she called him a gentleman, she thought.

"Were you spying on me?" Marla asked with a sly grin.

The housekeeper stiffened. "Of course not. I was just passing the window when I saw you."

Marla laughed. "His name is Alden Pierce. He's an investment broker who moved here last year. He's a member of the yacht club."

"Hmph. How does he know you?"

"We met at the club dance last week." She waggled her eyebrows. "Apparently, he's a great catch, according to all the gossips."

"Great catch indeed. You'd better be careful. A young woman like you with all this wealth will attract men looking for money," Mrs. Cooper said.

Marla couldn't believe she'd heard right. "I honestly don't think Alden wants my money. He seems to have plenty of his own. But thank you for caring."

"I'm just doing what Nathan would want me to do," Mrs. Cooper grumbled, but Marla caught the small smile on her face as she left the room.

* * *

Marla had a lazy weekend for a change. She walked, sat outside with a book, and swam in the pool in the evenings. By Monday, she was bored and itching for a new project. As she was sitting in her office, going over ideas for decorating another guest room, her phone rang. She was pleased to see it was her friend, and lawyer, Anthony.

"Hi, Anthony. It's great to hear from you," she said into the phone.

"Hello, Marla. I hope all is well with you. I'm afraid I haven't been a very good friend of late. How have you been doing?"

Marla told him about her remodeling projects and how much she'd appreciated his heartfelt speech at the club dance honoring Nathan.

"I could have gone on and on," Anthony said. "You know how much I treasured my friendship with Nathan."

"I do. And he treasured you, as well. So, is this a business call or a friendly chat?"

"Both. But yes, I have something to discuss with you. I had a call from a group that wants to develop a piece of property down by the river in St. Paul. It's an old factory from the turn of the century they want to make into a big shopping area, apartments, and park. Apparently the Madisons own this property, which was news to me. But I called your accountant, and he confirmed that the Madisons have been paying the property taxes on it for decades. I never even saw it in the will."

"A factory by the river?" Marla asked, stunned. *No. It couldn't possibly be.*

"Yes. Did Nathan ever mention it to you? I'm thinking he didn't even know about it. It's prime property that's worth a pretty penny. I can't imagine why Nathan or his parents didn't sell it before this."

"He never said a word about it. Where exactly is it?" Marla asked. Anthony told her the address and she quickly looked it up on her computer. There it was. An old factory building on a large chunk of river property.

"Apparently, this area is slowly becoming an up-and-coming area for millennials," Anthony said. "The neighborhoods are being revitalized and young couples are remodeling and changing the face of the area. A developer wants to make this a place with shops, a coffeehouse, maybe even penthouse apartments on the upper floors of the factory. It sounds like a legit business deal and could be worth a lot of money for you."

Marla could only think of one factory that this place could be—Alaina's father's textile factory. But could it still be in the family after all these years?

"I think I'd like to go down and look at the property before deciding what to do with it," Marla said. "I've been learning a little history about the Madison family lately, and I don't want to sell anything until I know for sure what we have."

"Of course," he said. "I do have a tentative offer on my desk from them, just to give you an idea what it's worth. I'll email you a copy and you can look it over. Let me know what you think next week."

"Okay. I'll do that," Marla said. "Thank you, Anthony."

"That's what I'm here for," he said with a chuckle. They said their goodbyes and hung up.

Marla's excitement grew at the thought of the Carlton Textiles building still existing. And she owned it. She had to go see the property. And she knew who would want to go with her. She quickly texted each of her book club friends.

It's time for another field trip, ladies!

* * *

Early Tuesday morning the group of ladies met at a coffeehouse in St. Paul not too far from the factory. Toni hadn't wanted to be left out but was showing houses later that morning, and Ardie worked at noon, so they'd decided to meet at eight. Toni showed up perfectly coiffed and wearing dress pants, a blouse, and jacket while the others wore jeans, casual tees, and sneakers. Rita's tee was blue tie-dye and she wore her high-tops again. They looked like quite a group and got a few stares from the other coffeehouse patrons.

"I'm completely overdressed," Toni said. "But I have to meet clients at ten, so it is what it is."

"You look amazing," Marla told her.

"Yeah. Next time we do this, I'm wearing an evening gown." Wanda grinned.

Toni rolled her eyes, then turned to Marla. "So, you actually own an old factory. Do you think it's Alaina's?"

"I don't know. But I don't know what other factory the Madisons would have owned. I just can't believe it's still in the family."

"I'm so excited to see it," Rita said. They were sitting at a table eating pastries and sipping coffee. "Thank you so much for asking us to come along, Marla."

"I wouldn't want to do this without all of you," she said. "We're in this together." Marla meant what she said. She felt this story had helped bring them closer and they were all a part of it.

"This is a very up-and-coming neighborhood," Toni said. "Like your lawyer said. People started buying houses around here and remodeling them about ten years ago after the 2008 real estate crash. Flipping houses was just becoming a phenomenon then. They're good starter-homes for the younger crowd. I can see why the developers would want to take advantage of that by building up the area along the river."

They finished their coffee and everyone except Toni climbed into Marla's SUV. Toni followed in her car as they drove through neighborhoods in the light traffic. Within minutes, they were at the property. They rode down a small hill and turned left. There stood the tall building, facing the Mississippi River on an expansive lot of open land.

Marla parked close to the building and they all got out. Toni joined them as they stood there, gazing up at the large building.

"I never imagined it to be so tall," Wanda said, looking up at the three stories.

"No. I guess I thought it was one level," Marla agreed.

The building was made of brick and steel, and there were large openings where Marla guessed windows used to be but had long since been broken. The lower floor had larger windows, and the upper floors had smaller ones.

"I wonder if the rooms upstairs were offices or small work rooms," Marla wondered aloud.

"Or where the women sewed the fabrics. Maybe the down-stairs was for cutting and weaving," Toni offered.

"That could be," Marla agreed. She still didn't know for sure that this was the Carlton building. "Let's go closer."

They walked across the dirt and spotty grass toward what looked like the entryway. As they drew near, chills prickled Marla's spine. Above the main door, embedded in brick, were the words Carlton Textiles 1868.

"This is it. It's Arthur's business. I can't believe it," Marla said, tears forming in her eyes. It was incredible that after over one-hundred and fifty years this building was still standing.

Arthur's building. Alaina's building. And now, it was hers.

"I've got goosebumps," Rita said in a hushed whisper and everyone else chimed in that they did too.

"This is amazing. I mean, we were just reading about this from so long ago, and here it is," Wanda said. "We're looking at history, ladies."

They all nodded. They were. They were looking at Alaina's history, which was also tied to the Madison's history.

"If I had any reason to doubt Alaina's story, this proves it was true," Marla said, still in awe. "It's crazy to think my husband owned this building and maybe didn't even realize it. Only our accountant knew."

"Wow. That is crazy," Rita said.

"Do you think it would be safe to go inside?" Wanda asked, drawing closer to peek in the broken window. "There might not be anything of value left, but maybe something interesting is still there."

"I don't know," Ardie said, looking skeptical. "It might be dangerous after all these years. We don't know how sturdy it is."

"Yeah. We should stay out," Marla said. "But as soon as I have someone inspect it, maybe we could explore. I have no idea how long it's been out of use."

Toni turned to Marla and smiled. "Another piece of the puzzle has been found. This property will be worth a lot of money, especially since it's on the river."

"I know. But I want to make sure it's used for something worthwhile. I'm not going to sell it until I know more about the structure of the building. If it can still be used, it would be nice to fix it up and use it for something amazing."

Wanda grinned. "I like how you think."

Toni had to go meet her clients, so she took off and Marla

drove the other women back to where their cars were parked. She was still stunned at having learned that Alaina's factory was still around and was now hers. Marla couldn't wait to read more of Alaina's story.

Chapter Twenty-Seven

Alaina

After their daughter was born, Alaina's life fell into a routine of caring for little ones, managing the house, and work. She couldn't complain. She had beautiful, healthy children, a lovely home to live in, and work that fulfilled the part of her that needed to use her mind. The same year their little Ella was born, Nathaniel sold off a large chunk of the lakeside property he owned at Great Heron Lake to the Great Heron Lake Yacht Club. It was a huge coup for him. He'd seen the need long before anyone else had, invested, then made a small fortune from it. He kept a few acres for himself, still planning to build a summer home there soon.

The yacht club was built that spring and ready for the summer tourists. Even though Ella was only three months old, the family spent the entire month of June 1880 at the resort on the lake, joining in on the many festivities at the yacht club. Nathaniel was a founding member, and their biggest contributor, so he was a member of high importance. As his wife, Alaina was treated with great respect as well, and all the wives of the wealthy men who had joined wanted to be in her circle. This amused Alaina. She had no circle and she couldn't care less about yachting or attending club activities. But she did so for Nathaniel's sake, because it was extremely important to him to rub elbows with the wealthy and feel as if he belonged.

For the most part, Alaina spent as much time as possible involved in her father's business without shrugging her duties at home. She visited the factory once a week to pick up invoices and other paperwork and to meet with Jerome to discuss any matters of importance. Jerome was always polite and respectful of her opinions as her father had and they enjoyed a good working relationship.

When electricity came to St. Paul in 1882, their factory was one of the first to switch over to the new power source. Nathaniel had generously agreed that Carlton Textiles would profit from the change and allowed her to use the company's profits to do so. Electricity meant the factory could be open longer hours with better lighting, although Alaina was adamant that the women seamstresses not work the typical twelve-hour day. She changed the hours to nine per day so they could go home and be with family. It was a revolutionary concept for her time, but she found that when the women workers were happier and more rested, they actually performed better at their jobs.

That same year, Matthew remarried and sold the house he and Hannah had lived in, moving to one on Summit Avenue. His finding a new woman to share his life was bittersweet for Alaina. Because he was starting his life over, she felt she no longer had a place in his life anymore and respected that. But her last ties with her dear friend, Hannah—her children—were no longer in her life. She mourned her friend once more but knew it was good for Matthew to find love again and a new mother for his children. And because Margaret still worked for Matthew, Alaina rarely saw her anymore, either. Emma visited Margaret occasionally and brought Alaina news from time to time, but it wasn't the same. Nearly all of her past was gone, so her family became everything to her.

Since the birth of their second child, Nathaniel no longer visited Alaina at night. At first, she was relieved. She was a busy mother with young children and was too tired to attend to her husband's needs. But after several months had gone by, she began to wonder who was sharing his bed. She knew he had a healthy appetite for sex, yet he didn't rely on her to fulfill his needs any longer. He was polite and caring toward her in every way, at home and when they were out or entertaining. Watching them as a couple from the outside, one would believe they were very much in love. But in the privacy of their home, they were just two polite strangers who lived together.

In the spring of 1885, Nathaniel surprised her by requesting she go with him on a day trip on the train to Great Heron Lake. He didn't tell her why. She accepted, since she knew he was excited to show her something. The train stopped at the outskirts of the little village and a carriage was waiting for them. The driver took them out of town toward the lake. Soon, they were driving past the yacht club on the newly named Bellwood Avenue, then turned down a driveway.

"Where are we?" Alaina asked, gazing around her. The trees were thick here, but a path had been opened to create a narrow road.

"Don't you recognize this spot?" Nathaniel asked, his eyes sparkling mischievously. Alaina wondered what he was up to. They'd been married nine years, and although they were no longer intimate, they still maintained a friendly relationship. His respect for her had seemed to grow ever since she'd begun to run her father's business. He also acknowledged how well she was raising the children, and her great value at entertaining their friends and business associates. But today, he was acting like a child with a secret that he couldn't wait to spill, and this intrigued her. It was so unlike him.

Suddenly, the trees parted, and the property opened to a magnificent view of a house sitting atop a hill with the waters of Great Heron Lake laid out in front of it.

"Surprise!" Nathaniel grinned. "It's finished and ready for us to move in. Isn't it a beauty?"

Alaina stared at the house, completely stunned. She'd known Nathaniel wanted to build a summer house someday but had no idea he'd already been working on it. The carriage stopped in the driveway in front of the house as she took it all in. It was two stories tall but had dormers on the slanted roof indicating a full attic. The house was square shaped but on each end smaller sections jutted out. It was covered in white clapboard with black shutters on the windows. It looked more like a house in town than a lake cabin.

"Well, what do you think?" Nathaniel asked excitedly.

"It's lovely," Alaina told him. She gave him a smile. "And so big, for a summer cottage."

Nathaniel's smile widened. "Come inside. It's completely finished. I want you to see it."

He helped Alaina down from the carriage and ran his arm through hers, holding her close as they walked to the front door. It was a large, double door painted black, each with brass lion door knockers. They walked inside on the cool marble floor and Alaina was immediately taken aback by the room ahead of her. While the outside looked like a regular home, the inside had a lodge-style look. Dark wainscoting ran along the bottom half of all the walls and the upper areas were either painted or wallpapered. Exposed beams hung across the cathedral ceiling and a huge, stone fireplace took up a large section of the right wall. A buck's head with antlers hung over the fireplace mantel and the room held two full-sized sofas and several chairs in masculine colors of hunter green, brown leather, and deep burgundy.

Alaina looked up at the dead deer staring at her from over the fireplace. "Did you kill that?"

Nathaniel's brows puckered, looking confused by her question, then turned to where she was staring and laughed. "No, I didn't. The decorator thought it would look nice there. It goes with the style. How do you like it, dear?"

Alaina wasn't sure how to answer. She had always hoped that if he built a summer place, he would have asked her opinion on colors and decorating. But he'd had the entire house built and decorated without her even knowing. "It's very...large," she said. "And masculine. But nice," she added when she saw him frown.

"I suppose it is rather masculine," he said, surveying the room. "It's not like this throughout, though. Let me show you the morning room—your room. You'll love it."

He chatted on about how one of the most famous architects in the area had designed the home and he'd hired the most expensive decorator who had once lived in France. He seemed so proud of himself and all he'd accomplished without her knowledge. Alaina soon realized that he'd thought it would be a great surprise for her if he had done it himself, when in fact, she wished she'd been consulted.

"Here it is," Nathaniel said, opening the door. They had walked down a hallway off from the entryway to what looked like one of the smaller sections of the house. He beamed as he showed her the room.

Alaina glanced around. There were large windows on the back and side walls and a brick fireplace on the center of one wall. Dark wood wainscoting covered the bottom half of the walls, just like in the main room, and burgundy wallpaper with pink roses on it covered the top half. The floors were highly polished dark wood, and a large cream-colored rug with pink and blue cabbage roses sat in the center under a creamy-white settee. To her left sat a small desk, which she recognized immediately as her mother's desk. It was white and gold French Provincial with a glass topper to protect the surface. There was nothing in this room that Alaina would have chosen for herself. The wallpaper was hideous, and she much preferred her father's desk to this delicate one her mother had used. But when she turned toward Nathaniel, she saw he was so excited to see her reaction that she didn't want to disappoint him.

"It's lovely. A very feminine room," she said, feigning a smile.

"I had your mother's desk brought here from storage," he said. "I thought you'd like that much better than that heavy old desk of your father's."

Alaina loved her father's old desk, and she'd thought that Nathaniel would know that. Apparently, he did not. Nor had he asked her opinion.

"Come. Let me show you the rest of the house," Nathaniel said, guiding her out of the morning room and toward the staircase. Upstairs, there was a long hallway that also had dark wood wainscoting along the lower part of the walls and dreary wallpaper above. There was a nursery with a bedroom off of it for the nanny, plus six more bedrooms. The master bedroom was also decorated in masculine colors and her attached room was no lighter. The decorator hadn't thought of a women's taste at all when he chose burgundy paint above the wainscoting and dark rugs and counterpane.

"The water closets all have running hot and cold water," Nathaniel said proudly. "Very modern for a country setting."

Alaina nodded. The house was lit with gas lights, unlike the electric ones they'd had installed in the home on Summit Avenue. But it was nice to know the water closets were as nice as the ones at home.

After touring the upstairs, he showed her down the back stairs that led into the kitchen, which was surprisingly large and spacious.

"There's a room off the kitchen for the housekeeper," he said. "The rest of the help for this house can be locals who work daily. That way we won't have the cost of live-in help."

"That's a good idea," Alaina agreed. When they were at the lake, they didn't need a large staff because life here was less rigid and more casual.

He guided her out of the kitchen and back into the main room where there was a wide, heavy wood table and chairs for the dining room.

"I wanted the room big and open," Nathaniel said. "Then we can have dinner parties or even a ball here if we so choose. And look." He brought her to the wall of French doors that led to the back of the house. When he opened them, Alaina immediately saw Great Heron Lake just steps from a patio laid of bricks. The view was breathtaking.

"Imagine waking up to that view every day," he said, drawing her close to his side.

Alaina was surprised by his affection toward her. She knew he was excited and very proud of the house. And he should be. There was no other house yet on the lake as grand as this one.

His would be the one everyone would want to emulate. She knew how important his social status was to him.

"It's an incredible view," she said, smiling. "We will have many memorable family summers here."

Nathaniel turned to her and grinned. "Yes, we will. And we'll have a wonderful life here and in this community. The children can make the best possible friends here with children of people of quality. And you will enjoy the highest status of all the women at the club and in town."

Alaina laughed softly. "That sounds like a great much to accomplish over each summer."

"Not just summer. All year-round," Nathaniel said. "I plan on moving you and the children here permanently. This will be our main home from this summer on."

Alaina's smile faded as she stared, stunned, at her husband. "Here? You want us to live here all year-round?"

He nodded. "Yes. It'll be wonderful."

She looked out at the vast expanse of water as she let Nathaniel's words sink in. Move here permanently? He couldn't possibly mean it. She tried to remain calm as she turned to her husband. "What about the children's education? Arthur is seven this year and enjoys the school he's attending. And Ella will be able to start school this fall. The school here can't possibly be as good as the one Arthur attends now."

"I've already checked into it, dear," Nathaniel said matter-of-factly. "The normal school here is perfectly fine and when Arthur is ten, he'll be attending boarding school in St. Paul. As for Ella, the school here will be adequate. She can also go to a women's finishing school when she's older, if she so chooses."

"But what about my work at the factory? I go there at least once a week," Alaina said.

Nathaniel chuckled. "I'm sure Jerome can run the factory by now without your help. But if you feel you must go there, it's only a twenty-minute train ride and I can have a carriage waiting to drive you. Maybe you can come in once a week on your shopping day."

Alaina felt panic setting in. How could she talk him out of this terrible plan? Another thought occurred to her. "Are you going to ride the train daily into work?"

Nathaniel shook his head. "No, that would be wasteful. I'll stay at the house in town during the week then come out here on weekends."

"But what will I do out here alone all winter long?" she asked. Winters could be brutal as it was, but this far away from town the snow would make it even harder to get around. She didn't want to be imprisoned in the house throughout the winter.

"You'll have plenty to do, running the house, caring for the children, and socializing with the others who live here year-round. In fact, there are several very important families who make their home here. And the club will be open all year, too. They even plan on having a winter ball every December, just like we've attended in St. Paul. And they'll need talented women like you to organize their events."

Alaina didn't know how to respond. She'd run out of excuses, and Nathaniel seemed to have an answer for everything. He'd thought it all out very nicely. He'd hide his wife and family away in Great Heron Lake and have the big house on Summit all to himself. She had a pretty good idea what it was he wanted privacy for.

"Will Mrs. Hanson and her husband be coming out here or staying with you?" she asked.

"They'll be coming out here. You'll need a driver and Sven

said he'd be happy to help with home repairs of any kind and shoveling snow and such."

Alaina arched a brow. "So, you've already asked them?"

"Of course," he said nonchalantly. "I know how well you and Mrs. Hanson get along and I wanted her to be here for you."

Resentment rose in Alaina. How dare he inform the staff about this move before telling her. "Then who will take care of the house and you while you're in town?" she asked, her tone growing colder.

"Oh, I won't need much staff to attend my needs. I'm sure just about any of the staff can cook and clean for me. Don't worry about me. I'll be fine."

I'm sure you will be, she thought icily. *More than likely, the new upstairs maid will keep you well-fed and warm all winter long.* She couldn't believe she hadn't thought about it before. Even though she'd made him fire Mary, another young, pretty woman had been hired in her place. Alaina had liked this maid and hadn't noticed anything going on between her and Nathaniel. Now, she wondered.

Nathanial turned to face her, placing his hands gently on her arms. "Alaina, dear. I can see you're hesitant about this move. But I assure you, you'll love it here when you get used to it. And it's important to me, and my business. You'll be helping me which in turn, benefits you and the children. Your being a leader among the women here will show the men I wish to eventually do business with that we are an integral part of this community. There's a lot of money and prestige here, dear. I want that for you. For us. And for our children."

Alaina's shoulders slumped. She was just a pawn in his scheme to grow richer. That's all she meant to him. Someone to raise his heirs and make him look good. She'd thought she'd proven to him that she was worth so much more than that, but now, she felt defeated.

He took her silence as assent, smiled, and kissed her on the cheek. "You're going to love it here, Alaina. I promise. This will be a grand adventure."

And if I don't, what other choice do I have? Alaina thought sadly as they walked back through the house that she didn't feel belonged to her.

Chapter Twenty-Eight

Marla

"Now we know how she ended up in the lake house," Toni said, sounding disgusted. "It just irks me that she had so little say in her life."

"It must have been so frustrating for her," Rita added. "To be such an intelligent woman and then be banished to the country and told to be a good wife. She'd been, at least, content in her life in St. Paul."

Wanda yawned. "Sorry," she said, covering her mouth. "I'd love to hear more tonight, but I'm bushed. My daughter had soccer practice all day today and I was helping with water and snacks for the team. We have an out-of-town tournament this weekend and I'm going to be up to my neck in seventeen-year-old girls giggling and running around. I need some sleep."

"Sounds awful," Ardie said, laughing. "I'm glad I'm past all that. My son did basketball and baseball, and my daughter was in volleyball. I never knew if I was coming or going."

"My son was in baseball too," Rita said. "And made the traveling team in his teens. There's nothing worse than a van full of sweaty teen boys."

Everyone laughed.

"Have you thought any more about what to do with the factory?" Toni asked Marla.

"I have," Marla said. "I'm meeting with my lawyer tomorrow over lunch to discuss some options. I'd really like to use it for something that would enhance the community and give back. Maybe a homeless shelter for families to help them get back on their feet."

"There's a great need for that," Wanda said. "Or perhaps a shelter for battered women and their children. Not all shelters allow women and children to stay together. I can't think of anything worse than being abused by your spouse, then being separated from your child when you try to leave the situation."

Marla listened to Wanda with interest. She thought about Alaina, and how she'd been controlled by Nathaniel. It hadn't been abuse, but she'd still been treated like property even though she had a mind of her own. This had been Alaina's factory. What better use for it than as a place to help women?

"What a great idea." Marla beamed with excitement over the prospect of helping women in the community. "I'll have to do some research on it, but I think a women's shelter would be a perfect use of the building."

"I can give you the number of someone to talk to," Wanda offered. "I have several friends who work with the battered women's organization who'd be happy to help you."

Marla paused as she studied the woman before her. Had Wanda experienced abuse? Is that why she was so bitter toward men?

"The answer to the questions on your face are yes," Wanda said. "There are more reasons for my hatred of my ex than just his leaving me for a younger woman. She can have him. He wasn't a hitter, but the emotional and mental abuse was just as devastating. After I finally got away from him, I needed a lot of counseling to rebuild my self-esteem and confidence again."

"I'm so sorry, Wanda," Marla said. "I had no idea."

"Well, it isn't something I go around telling everyone, but I'm not ashamed of it, either. I survived a miserable relationship with help, and I know there are women out there who endure so much more than I did. I'm sure my friend would be thrilled to answer any questions you have about building a shelter for women."

"Thanks, Wanda. I'd love to talk with her."

Everyone left after that and Marla was the last to leave Ardie's. She turned to her friend. "Did you know about Wanda's past?"

She nodded. "Yes. I did. We all knew. I was happy to see her open up to you, too. It means she trusts you with her story."

A lump formed in Marla's throat. "I'm honored she told me too. I haven't had a group of friends like this since college. I mean, I had friends at the club, but they weren't as forthcoming and genuine as all of you. Everyone I've known over the past twenty years worked so hard to impress each other that you never really knew what was under the surface. I'm so thankful to have met this group."

Ardie hugged her. "We're all happy to have you as part of the group, too. You're the real deal, Marla. Not some stuck-up rich snob. You have a heart and soul and you care about people. Just the fact that you don't want to sell the factory, even though you could get a lot of money for it, but instead want to give back to the community, is amazing. You're a good person."

Marla thought back to the day Nathan passed away and how

unemotional she'd been. She'd actually felt relieved. Thinking about it made her feel guilty every time. "Not that good," she said. "But I'm trying."

* * *

The next morning, Marla had a productive conversation with Wanda's friend, Sheila Northbird, who was a women's advocate for a St. Paul shelter. She had plenty of statistics, advice, and resources for Marla to look up online to help her make a decision.

"Of course, the most difficult part of opening a shelter is getting the city to agree to let the property be used for that function," Sheila warned her. "If a developer has already received a green-light on using that property for a high-end apartment complex and stores, the city might not want to allow a shelter. Sometimes neighborhoods are against it, too."

"That's terrible," Marla said, shocked to hear this. "It's as if they think the women are the criminals."

"Exactly. They're afraid trouble will come to the neighborhood. That's only one part of the stigma of battered women that we need to change in this society. Women from all walks of life suffer abuse, not just the underprivileged. Please feel free to call me for help if you're able to move forward with this. I know plenty of people in power who support this cause. It helps to know the right people."

Marla thanked her and hung up. She pondered all the possibilities for the shelter as she dressed for lunch at the club with Anthony. She thought it would be nice to use the upper two floors for apartments large enough for women with up to three children, then use the lower floor for offices for counselors and advocates. It might also be useful to have a stockroom of clothes for the women and children, as well as someone to discuss job options if the women needed to find work. The place could be a transitional shelter, helping women with whatever they needed to get back on their feet and live a safe life.

As she walked down the stairs, she saw Mrs. Cooper coming out of the kitchen. Ever since their candid conversation the day the housekeeper was sick, Mrs. Cooper had seemed less rigid and more likable. Either that, or Marla was just getting used to her after all these years.

"Will you want me to prepare dinner for you before I leave tonight?" Mrs. Cooper asked.

Normally, the housekeeper would just make dinner and assume Marla was eating in. But now, she'd been asking first, as if she realized that maybe Marla didn't need to be waited on hand and foot anymore.

"Don't bother," Marla said with a kind smile. "If I get hungry, I can whip up a salad. I doubt I'll be very hungry after eating at the club."

Mrs. Cooper nodded. "Have a nice lunch," she said before walking back through the kitchen door.

Marla couldn't remember Mrs. Cooper ever telling her that before. Things were definitely changing.

Jeannette seated Marla at a window table and took her drink order of iced tea. She'd seen Vicki and Catrina sitting at a corner table the moment she'd walked in, and only waved at them. She really didn't feel like going over there to make small talk. They also didn't make an attempt to cross the space between them to say hello either. Marla figured it was for the best.

Anthony arrived, apologizing for being late. He kissed her on the cheek in greeting and waved at a few people he knew. Anthony knew nearly everyone at the club.

Today, though, he was all business as he settled in after ordering coffee. Marla relayed all she'd learned that morning about opening a shelter in the building, but the first thing on the agenda was to make sure the building's bones were structurally sound to remodel the factory.

"I can arrange an inspection of the building," Anthony said. "And I'll look into zoning to see if we can use the building as a shelter. If your contact has any friends on the city council, it would help."

"The factory has already been approved for the developers to build apartments there. This isn't any different, really. It'll be apartments and offices."

"Yes, but this is for a non-profit and it won't bring any revenue in for taxes. The city will be looking at that," Anthony countered.

Marla nodded. It was always about money. "I'll be paying property taxes, though. Even non-profits pay those."

Anthony smiled. "Yes, that's true. And that river property won't be cheap once it's been improved."

Marla smiled back and shrugged.

Turning serious, Anthony said, "You know, the developers are offering you a large sum of money for that property. You could always sell it and pick a different location if you want to donate money for a shelter. It might be easier."

"Yes, I know." Marla had thought about that too, but as far as she was concerned, it wasn't an option. "This building means something to me, though. I really want to see it turned into a place the Madisons would be proud of."

His brows rose. "But you didn't even know this building existed until recently. How could you feel so connected to it already?"

Marla chuckled. "I've been delving into a little family history and have learned a lot about the early Madisons. This building was important to the first Mrs. Madison, so it's important to me."

Anthony sat back and assessed Marla. "And money is no object?"

She shook her head. "Has it ever been for the Madisons?"

Anthony laughed out loud. "No. It never has been. And you know? I think Nathan would be so proud of you. He never gave much thought about the money and you know he always donated generously to the college. He'd be thrilled to know that you've found a cause to share the money with."

"Thank you, Anthony," she said. "You don't know how much that means to me."

The waitress came by and Marla asked if he was ready to order.

"Oh, I think I'll pass on lunch today, dear," Anthony said, patting his growing belly. "I'm trying to get rid of this girth. Orders from my doctor. I would like to live long enough to retire."

He packed up his briefcase and said a warm goodbye before leaving. Marla ordered the shrimp salad, and after the waitress left, she turned her attention to her phone. She was just finishing typing a message to Wanda, thanking her for connecting her with Sheila, when a deep voice asked, "Any chance I could join you?"

Marla looked up to see Alden standing there in a polo shirt and cargo shorts, looking as tan and fit as ever. "I didn't know you were here," she said, caught off guard.

"I just came in after a long, disastrous round of golf. I can't bear to sit with the men I played with because I was so terrible.

I thought you might be kind enough to save me the embarrassment."

Marla chuckled. "Then please. Sit down. I don't want you to feel any worse than you already do."

"Thank you." He sat and ordered a beer when the waitress came to the table. "And a burger and fries, please," he said before she left.

"I guess you don't have to watch your waistline," Marla teased.

"Nope. I'm naturally skinny," he told her with a grin. "So, why on earth are you sitting here all alone?"

"I wasn't," she said. "In fact, I was sitting with a very handsome gentleman just moments ago. Unfortunately, he had to leave."

"Oh." Alden looked disappointed.

"I just had a meeting with my lawyer," she said, seeing his eyes light up again. "We're looking into a new venture and he's going to do some of the legwork for me."

"Ah, I see. Still, you must have dozens of friends here. I can't believe any number of them didn't come to take the empty spot immediately."

Marla's smile faded. She glanced around, and saw Vicki staring at her, tight-lipped. A few other women were trying to be discreet about looking, but she saw them too. They were probably all jealous that she was sitting with the club's most eligible bachelor. "I'm kind of a pariah here these days. A single woman with her own money among self-proclaimed trophy wives. They have to be nice to me because of the Madison name, but they don't have to be my friends anymore."

Alden frowned. "That's terrible. But it doesn't surprise me. Women can be treacherous."

"Men, too," she added.

"Yes. Men too." He made a show of glancing around, then moved in closer to her and whispered. "Let's be pariahs together. After the way I played golf today, I'm sure they'll blackball me next year."

Marla laughed. She liked Alden. He reminded her of a character from an old movie. He was a genuinely nice person with a good sense of humor. She had fun when she was with him.

They talked about safe subjects over lunch. Nothing personal or too involved. She told him about the factory and what she was thinking of doing with it. He was intrigued.

"What a monumental task you're setting up for yourself," he said, looking awed. "Good for you! If you need donations, come to me. I'd love to help support such a project."

Marla liked his enthusiasm. And the more she thought about the factory project, the more excited she grew. It was a new beginning for her. Much bigger then just remodeling a room in the house. Now, she was looking at redoing an entire building that would be used to help others.

"Something is bubbling in that head of yours. I can see it in your eyes," Alden said.

"I think I've found my purpose," she said, suddenly realizing the magnitude of what she was doing. "Since my husband passed away, I've been spending my time trying to figure out what to do with my life. But this is it. I feel like I have something exciting to wake up for each morning now."

He smiled. "You're an amazing person, you know that? Most people would be thrilled to live a life of luxury in that gorgeous house of yours. Not you, though. You're willing to use your money and time to help others. I'm genuinely impressed by you."

Marla beamed. Yes, she could live out her life accomplishing nothing, rattling around that great big house. But she didn't want to. She wanted a purpose. As for the big house? She was beginning to think she knew what she wanted to do with that too.

Chapter Twenty-Nine

Alaina

Sadly, Emma decided not to follow Alaina to the Great Heron Lake house the summer of 1885. She'd fallen in love with a man who worked as a butcher in a local shop in St. Paul and they married that summer. Alaina was heartbroken to lose her closest confidante but was also happy for her. Emma had been the very last tie to her old life, and although Alaina had a husband and children, she felt a great loss.

They made the final move to the lake house in July amidst the scorching summer heat and humidity. Thankfully, the lake breeze through the open French doors helped to cool the house. Without electricity as they'd had in the Summit Avenue house, the hallways and rooms were darker, causing Alaina's mood to darken as well. She felt as if she'd gone backwards instead of progressing.

Poor young Arthur cried when he learned he couldn't return to his school in St. Paul, but Alaina assured him he'd make new friends here as she hugged his shaking shoulders and smoothed down his blond hair. He'd grown quite tall for seven years old with long, lean legs. Soon he forgot his worries while learning to man a sailboat with his club friends and swimming and playing endless games of tag in their large yard. Five-year-old Ella, still petite, her blue eyes bright under dark, thick lashes, made new friends as well with the younger girls. They strolled their dolls around in prams and also kicked their feet daintily in the water off the dock.

Alaina requested a tour of the school and brought the children along to see where they'd be spending their days. It was a nice building, and the principal assured her that it had been growing rapidly since so many wealthy families were beginning to move there permanently. It was becoming fashionable for the women and children to move out of the dirty city and live in the fresh air and wide-open spaces of this quaint little town. Alaina made it clear to the principal that any needs the school might have, be it supplies, books, or even additional teachers, her husband would be happy to donate the money. In fact, Alaina had taken Nathaniel's words to heart and made it clear all over town that the Madisons were there to help make the community a more prosperous place, and they could ask her for any necessary donations.

She immediately made good friends with the mayor's wife, Hedda Edling, who was also a member of the club, and invited the most prominent ladies over to the house regularly for tea. Alaina presided over many a lunch at the club, and if there was an event to be planned, she always offered her services. Soon, everyone in town knew and admired her, and with each donation she made, they adored her even more. After a time, Nathaniel would frown or wince when she'd ask for yet another large sum of money for the latest donation. She found humor in his discomfort. She felt it served Nathaniel right. Since he'd been the one to exile her to this lake house so he could spend time alone with his young maid, then she'd make him pay—right out of his pocket.

"I feel you may have taken my words too much to heart," Nathaniel said one autumn evening when Alaina asked for yet another donation for the school.

Alaina acted as innocently as she knew how, her brows raised and eyes wide. "I thought that was what you wanted me to do, dear. We're making important connections here and ensuring the Madison name is known to all. Your generosity is helping the school give the best education possible as well as the donations to charities about town. Would you prefer if I say no next time?"

He studied her a moment, as if gauging her sincerity, then shook his head. "Of course not. You have done a splendid job of making friends with all the right people. I wouldn't want to ruin that by becoming cheap, would I?"

Alaina just smiled and accepted the money.

Alaina made certain not to shirk her duties at the factory either. Twice a week, not once a week as Nathaniel had suggested, she boarded the train that took her to St. Paul then secured a cab to the factory. She was always accompanied by her new ladies' maid, a thirty-year-old soft-spoken woman named Velma Ogden, to make sure everything looked proper. On her bi-weekly trips, she'd confer with Jerome on any issues that had come up and tour the factory, visiting with the workers to make sure all was well. Afterwards, she'd collect the invoices and receipts to log in the ledger.

"The seamstresses are always appreciative of your visits," Jerome told her one day. "They feel more comfortable voicing their concerns through you."

"I'm happy I can make their working environment more

comfortable. Father walked the factory daily to make sure all was well, and I know that you do, too. He always said content employees worked harder. And he's right. We're looking at another profitable year already," she said, smiling.

"Thanks to your expertise," Jerome said.

"No. Thanks to your wonderful management. Nathaniel would never have allowed me to manage this place by myself, and if you hadn't been here, neither would the factory. I will be forever grateful for your unwavering devotion to my father, and to me."

Jerome smiled, looking embarrassed. "You also pay me well to do all this. Remember?"

"Yes, I do. But you'd do it no matter what. You're a good person."

Alaina was so grateful for the opportunity to own such a business. She made a difference in their city, supplying much-needed employment in a place that proudly treated their employees well and adding to the local economy. And in turn, she also provided Nathaniel's stores with quality merchandise which helped to keep his stores successful. It was a huge accomplishment for a woman of her generation, and she knew her father was smiling down on her, proud of her for continuing his legacy.

As the months wore on, Alaina was also grateful that the factory kept her busy over the long Minnesota winters. Often, the train would be delayed or cancelled because of heavy snow, and she'd miss her visit to the city. Sometimes she'd have to spend the night in the Summit Avenue house if she couldn't return home. Nathaniel kept a skeleton staff there, but it was sufficient during those emergency visits. And if she noticed any spark between the young woman, Krista Douglas, who'd transformed from upstairs maid to main housekeeper, and Nathaniel, she ignored it. It no longer mattered to her who her husband dallied with as long as it was kept quiet. Alaina was resigned to the fact that her life was full enough, with family, friends, and work, and she no longer needed the attentions from her husband.

A year after the move to the lake, Nathaniel sold the Summit Avenue house and purchased a three-story townhouse on the same street where he could reside during the week. He explained to Alaina that it hadn't made sense for him to own such a large home in the city any longer. Their lives were in Great Heron Lake, and since Alaina was working so hard to raise their status there, he had no need to put on airs in St. Paul any longer.

In the winter of 1886, they attended the first Winter Carnival in St. Paul as a family. Dressed warmly in their wool overcoats and boots, Alaina, Nathaniel, Arthur, and Ella wandered the grounds of Central Park just north of downtown where the very first ice castle was built. It was a spectacular site, built of blocks of ice from area lakes and rising to one-hundred and six feet tall. They all watched in wonder that night as the transparent castle glowed red with light from the inside as people dressed in their festive winter club uniforms held torches outside the castle. Clubs associated with curling, skating, tobogganing, and many other winter sports came from all over, even from Canada, to join in on the winter celebration. Arthur's favorite sight was watching the toboggans ride down the tall slide built just for that purpose, and Alaina marveled at the many crystal clear ice sculptures that decorated the lawn. It was a family outing that they all enjoyed and would long remember. Afterward, when they returned to the townhouse on Summit, they all warmed themselves by the fire and drank hot cocoa.

Alaina watched Nathaniel as he spoke animatedly to the children about all they had seen. He was good with the children, teasing and hugging them easily as his eyes shone with pride. She felt closer to him that evening than she had in years and realized that although their relationship had cooled, he was still a warm, caring father. For that she was thankful.

That evening after they had all retired, Alaina was surprised by a knock at the door that connected their rooms. She called out to Nathaniel to enter, and he did, wearing his nightshirt and robe. She'd been sitting on her chaise lounge, staring out the window into the night, reflecting upon the evening. Now, as she gazed at him, she was surprised to see longing in his eyes, something she hadn't experienced since before Ella was born.

"Am I bothering you?" he asked, hesitating as he stopped beside her.

Her heart quickened at the sight of him. She remembered their past intimate moments, and how close they'd felt to each other then. She had to remind herself that she wasn't the only one he'd shared his bed with, though. "No. I was just thinking about the night we had. The children enjoyed the carnival immensely. As I did. It was very kind of you to suggest we go as a family."

Nathaniel sat on the edge of her chair, near her knees. He made no move to touch her, only smiled at her, the lines around his eyes crinkling kindly. "I love spending time with the children. And you, of course. I do realize that I spend too much time away from all of you. But I also know that you understand. I'm building a legacy for our children. My hope is that they will never know what it's like to want for anything."

"They already want for nothing," Alaina said pointedly. "Except maybe their father's attention and time."

He nodded, his smile fading. He looked older, but of course they both had aged after ten years of marriage. Still, he was handsome despite the strands of gray streaming through his wavy dark hair.

"You've raised the children well," he said, gazing into her eyes. "And you've done more than I could have ever hoped to build up the Madison name in Great Heron Lake. Women admire you and everyone respects you. I'm so very proud of you, dear. And I appreciate all that you do." He reached for her hand and raised it to his lips.

His tenderness pulled at her heart. She hadn't seen him so transparent in a very long time. But she also had to guard her heart from being hurt again. "Thank you, Nathaniel. Your appreciation means a great deal to me."

He moved closer to her and gently touched his lips to hers. Pulling back, he said, "We've been apart much too long."

She reached up and cupped his face. Her body wanted nothing more than to feel his next to hers, but where would that lead? And what would it solve? "Do you truly respect me, Nathaniel, as you claim you do?"

"Of course I do," he insisted.

"Then please don't ask me to be intimate with you in the very same house as the other woman who shares your bed when I'm not here."

Nathaniel pulled back, stunned. But he didn't deny her words, nor lie to her. Instead, he kissed her hand once more, then stood. "You're right. I shouldn't insult you in that way. And I'm sorry if I've hurt you in any way." He bowed his head. "I do respect you, Alaina. And I do love you. Please know that."

She nodded, her heart clenching at his proclamation of love. She did know he loved her, in his way. But like all men of his generation, he felt he could also satisfy his needs elsewhere, and she would not stand for that.

"Good evening," he said. Then left the room.

For a long time after he'd left, Alaina wondered about her life. She was lucky to have a husband who didn't force himself on her, and who also respected her wishes. When he'd proposed to her, he'd said he'd wanted a woman who was strong and could think for herself. Well, that was exactly what he'd gotten. She wondered if now he wished he'd married a woman who wasn't as strong and would give in to his every whim. One who would ignore his affairs with other women and allow him in her bed, as well. She could never be that woman. In her mind, if he wanted her, he'd have to give up all the others. Sadly, she knew that would never happen.

* * *

When Arthur turned ten in 1888, he was enrolled in the most prestigious boarding school in St. Paul. Alaina was relieved that many of his friends from the yacht club were also attending. In fact, Arthur was very mature about the transition and had even been eager to go. He was allowed to come home on weekends, which he did at first with his father on the train, but soon, as his life became immersed in school and activities, he stopped coming home except for holidays. Alaina missed her bright, sweet son and doted even more on her lovely little Ella. Her daughter had turned eight that year and was also busy with school and ballet classes. She was already growing into a mini-version of Alaina, although she thought her daughter was much more beautiful then she.

That winter, as the women gathered at the yacht club to discuss the details of the winter ball, the mayor's wife, Hedda, brought up the subject of the Minnesota Woman Suffrage Association.

"I know many of you are members just as I am," she said to the group of affluent women gathered. "I propose we use the money raised from this year's ball to help fund the cause."

Alaina was intrigued. Of course she knew about the suffrage movement, and secretly supported it, but she'd never come across a group of women who were openly members.

"Do you think the men will balk at us using the money for that purpose?" a woman, whose husband had grown rich through the lumber trade years before, asked.

"The men just attend and never ask about the funds raised," Hedda replied. She winked at the group. "What they don't know won't hurt them."

All the women giggled. Alaina grinned. She was surprised that this group of well-to-do women were openly for women's rights. This placed a whole new layer to these women she'd thought were just spoiled wives of rich men.

After the meeting, she approached her friend Hedda. "I had no idea you were a member of the woman suffrage movement."

Hedda nodded. She had a mass of thick, blond hair piled high on her head and bright blue eyes. Even though Alaina estimated her to be in her late forties, her skin was still unlined and quite fair.

"I have been for years," she said. "As have many of the women I know with husbands in prominent positions. I'm surprised your friends from St. Paul weren't involved."

Alaina shook her head. "Most of the women I knew would have been afraid to go against their husbands' opinions, and most men I know are against women voting. But you can count me in. I've long thought that women aren't taken seriously enough and should have the same rights as men."

Hedda beamed. "Welcome to the cause, dear friend," she said.

"We can use every woman we can get."

That weekend, when Nathaniel and Alaina were eating supper after Ella had gone to bed, she brought up her support of the woman suffrage cause just to see his reaction.

Nathaniel stopped chewing for a moment and stared at her, then swallowed. "So, you believe that women should have the same rights as men? And the right to vote?"

She sat up straighter and looked him in the eye. "Yes, I do."

"And I suppose you'll be wanting donations for this cause, just as you've donated to nearly every cause in this town."

"Of course," she said boldly.

A small smile appeared on Nathaniel's lips, then he broke out laughing. "That doesn't surprise me in the least. And how lucky they are to have you on their side."

Alaina grinned back. Nathaniel was many things, but she appreciated his support of her activities. It made their family life so much easier.

Chapter Thirty

Marla

The women sat in the comfort of Marla's air-conditioned home as she marked her place in the journal and set it down. It had been a hot, sticky day and she was happy to relax in the confines of the cool house.

"Alaina was certainly a busy woman," Rita said. "We talk about women today having it all, but look at her. She ran a business, a home, and donated time and money to the community. Now, she's merged into the suffrage cause. Good for her!"

"She was amazing," Marla agreed. "Very progressive for her time. Yet, it seems that many women were like her. They just didn't get credit for all they did."

"Women have always been the backbone of society," Wanda said with certainty. "And as far as I'm concerned, have never gotten the credit we deserve."

"Here, here!" Toni said, raising her glass of white wine. The others clinked their glasses and they all took a sip. "And be sure to thank Mrs. Cooper for the delicious food. She really outdid herself. Can I steal her away from you?"

Marla laughed. "Yes. You can have her if she'll go. And believe it or not, she was actually happy to have people to cook for. Her job has become quite boring with just me to wait on."

She filled everyone in on how far she'd gotten with looking into using the factory as a women's shelter. "A building inspector is supposed to come out on Monday and give us a report. We're expecting it to be positive because the developers had been given the okay to use the building, so why not us? Then, we have to talk to the city about using it as a shelter. Sheila said she'd use whatever connections she has to help us make it happen." She turned to Wanda. "She's incredible. I'm so happy you connected us. I'm not sure I would have had the knowledge to do this without her expertise."

"She's a gem," Wanda agreed. "And if you can make this happen, you'll be adding a much-needed resource to the city."

The women planned on meeting in two weeks, because the Fourth of July holiday landed on the next Thursday. As everyone left, Marla asked Toni to stay behind.

"What's up?" Toni asked.

"Would it be possible for you to set up an appointment for us to look at the cottage across the bay? I'm seriously thinking of buying it, and if I can give you the sale, that's even better."

Toni's eyes lit up. "Sure. I'll call tomorrow and set something up. When do you want to see it?

"The sooner the better," Marla said.

The two hugged goodbye and Toni left. Marla took a deep breath. She was one step closer to making another monumental decision—possibly buying the Fairy Tale house. She hoped she wasn't jumping into everything too quickly. But it all felt right, and she was excited.

That evening, Marla went outside to sit on the dock before

the mosquitos came out. The weather had cooled, and the sun was almost down. She sat with her feet in the water and stared across the bay at the lights in the cottage. Marla wondered what it would be like, after all these years, to live in a normal-sized home instead of a mansion. She wouldn't need any help. She could cook her own meals and clean if she really wanted to. Well, maybe she'd have a maid service come once a week. But she could be self-sufficient. She might even be able to mow her own lawn and tend her own garden. Maybe. It would depend on how busy she'd be once work started on the women's shelter.

She would miss the pool, though. But then, she could always have an indoor pool built if she really wanted one. Other than that, she couldn't think of one thing she'd miss about this house. Not one.

Marla wanted to travel. She knew that for sure. She might even want to leave for a few weeks each winter to get out of the cold. She could go to Paris. She could have a Caribbean island home. Basically, she could have anything she wanted—she had the money to do it. But she had to be responsible about the money, too.

When she'd married Nathan, she'd thought he'd wanted the same things she did. But he was older, and he'd done all the traveling he'd wanted to before Reese was born. He became settled in his life. The university, the club, his friends, and home. That was all he'd wanted. And although she'd yearned for more, she'd been the dutiful wife who hadn't nagged him. She'd raised Reese, spent her days at home or the club, and spent Saturday nights with Nathan at the club having dinner with his old friends. She'd made his life hers. But now, she could do anything she wanted.

That seemed exciting and scary all at once.

Marla glanced up a the stars and spoke quietly to Nathan. "I hope you're okay with the decisions I've been making. It's been tough, but I'm finding my way. We had a good life, but now it's just me. It's time I think about what I want." She smiled as a group of fireflies twinkled nearby. "I love you, Nathan. I hope you're happy," she said softly.

Before going to bed that night, Marla texted Reese to ask if she was coming home for the Fourth of July. She suggested Reese could invite all the friends she wanted. The club always had a big picnic-style spread that day and set off fireworks over the lake in the evening. Personally, Marla preferred the fireworks display over the Mississippi River in St. Paul, but she'd never been able to talk Nathan into going there. But if Reese wanted to come for the weekend, she'd be thrilled to have her.

* * *

The next day Mrs. Cooper brought her tea into the morning room as usual. Marla was busy making a list of everything she'd like to have at the women's shelter and questions she had for Sheila about what services she thought would be the most needed.

"Good morning, Mrs. Cooper," Marla said cheerfully.

"Good morning," the housekeeper said. "How was your book club last night? Did your friends enjoy the food?"

Marla grinned up at the older woman. "They did, thank you. Everyone loved the food and said to thank you for it."

Mrs. Cooper waved her hand through the air as if to brush away the compliment. "It's my job to feed guests," she said brusquely.

Marla laughed. "Yes, but I appreciated it. Take the compliment. It's well-deserved."

Mrs. Cooper glanced at the list she was making. "What are you working on, if you don't mind my asking."

"I don't mind. It seems I own a piece of property on the Mississippi River in St. Paul where an old factory sits. I'm thinking of developing it into a shelter for women of domestic abuse. I want to make it a place where they can stay and find opportunities to re-build their lives. Also where they can bring their children to live with them while they're in transition."

Mrs. Cooper's brows rose. "My, that is ambitious. May I ask why you chose this particular cause?"

"A friend of mine suggested it. And I'd wanted it to be a place to help people. It seems fitting. Do you know that back in the late 1800s the first Mrs. Madison ran this factory after her father passed and was very successful? I felt she would appreciate it being transformed into a place to help other women."

The housekeeper looked stunned. "Really? How did you learn that?"

"I found an old journal of hers while I was remodeling. In fact, my book club has been reading it each week, learning all about her life. Her name was Alaina Carlton Madison, and she was married to Nathaniel Madison in the 1870s. So far, we've found that she was quite a woman with a mind of her own."

"That sounds very interesting," Mrs. Cooper said, looking intrigued. "Do you think I might be able to read it after you're done? I'd love to learn more about her."

"Of course. I'd be happy to let you read it." Marla beamed at Mrs. Cooper. She was thrilled that they could talk like this now. Before, she'd been afraid that the grumpy housekeeper would try to take it away from her. Now, she felt safe loaning the journal. She knew Mrs. Cooper would take good care of it.

"Breakfast will be ready in a few minutes," Mrs. Cooper

said, returning to business as usual. As she headed for the door, she paused, then turned around. "I think it's very admirable, what you're planning to do. Nathan would be quite happy with your plans, I'm sure."

Marla looked up at the elderly woman and saw sincerity in her face. A lump formed in her throat. Mrs. Cooper approved of something she was doing. It was the greatest compliment she'd ever received from her. "Thank you," she managed to say.

Later that morning, Marla received a call from Toni.

"Are you ready to look at the cottage? We can see it at one this afternoon."

"So soon? That's great," Marla said.

"Good. I'll come by and pick you up. I'm really excited to see this house. It looks charming."

They hung up and Marla actually felt like she was floating on a cloud. A few minutes later, though, her euphoria evaporated when Reese called her.

"Sorry, Mom. I won't be coming home for the Fourth. My friends and I have plans."

Marla sighed. She'd told herself that this might happen, but she'd really hoped Reese would come home. "That's okay, dear," she said, hiding her disappointment. "There's just so much I want to tell you. Maybe we could get together soon."

"Sure, Mom. What's so important?" Reese asked, although Marla could tell by her tone that she was in a hurry to get off the phone.

"We can talk later. I know you're busy. Have a fun time, dear," Marla said. After they'd hung up, she tried to remember what she'd been like at twenty. Had she ignored her own mother and just focused on her interests? She couldn't remember being that way, but maybe she had. Maybe all young people were like that. After Marla had married and had Reese, she'd spent more time worrying about her mother and had visited her often. And she'd been by her mother's side as she'd gone through her illness and then died. Marla hoped that some day Reese and she would be close like she and her own mother had been.

At one o'clock, Marla was waiting in the driveway as Toni pulled up. She hadn't told Mrs. Cooper where she was going, so she suspected the older woman was peeking out the window to see who was picking her up. That thought made her smile.

"You must be happy. You're grinning," Toni said as Marla slipped into the car.

"I am happy, but I was just thinking about Mrs. Cooper. I bet she's watching us right now."

"Then wave as we pull away," Toni said. Both women waved at the house and Marla thought she saw the curtain move in the morning room. They both chuckled conspiratorially.

Toni drove down Bellwood Avenue then turned down a narrow road. Along the way they passed a few other smaller homes like the cottage before coming to a long driveway. The trees cleared and there on the point, with the lake as its backdrop, stood the wood-framed, craftsman-style structure.

"It's just as I remembered it," Marla said, excitement welling up inside her. There was a brick path that wound its way up to the front door, which was still painted an orange-red. On one side of the door was a long, narrow stained-glass window. The wood siding looked in good condition, as did the dark green shutters and windows. "How old does it say this house is?"

Toni looked at the stat sheet. "It says 1907. The property is two acres and it has its own well and septic system. However, it can be connected to city water and sewer too."

"Let's go inside," Marla said, anxious to see it again.

Toni unlocked the door and they stepped inside. There was a small entryway with a coat closet on the left and a door to the two-stall garage on the right. Above hung a Tiffany-style light. There was a step-down from there to a large, open living room with a cathedral ceiling and a stone fireplace in the center. Large windows on the other walls let in plenty of light. The staircase wound its way behind the fireplace up to the second floor. The flooring was light wood with embedded dark wood accents.

"This is so cute," Toni said, glancing around.

"It's even cuter than I remembered," Marla said, falling in love with it all over again.

To their right was a short hallway that led first to a small bathroom with a shower stall, then to a first-floor bedroom. Toni opened the bedroom door. There were tall windows on two walls and the room was big enough for a king-sized bed with nightstands flanking it.

"This would make a nice office," Marla said, imagining the space with new furniture in it. "There's plenty of light and room for shelves."

Toni nodded. They walked back to the living room and stood in the center. The kitchen was on the one end, large and airy with big decorative windows up high over the sink. The cabinets were antique white with shiny black granite countertops. It looked like they'd added new appliances because they were all stainless steel. Between the living room and kitchen was an island with a second sink and an area for stools. Marla could imagine herself cooking in this kitchen and eating at the counter, enjoying all the natural sunlight.

"I love this kitchen," Toni said. "It's big but cozy. It's a great place for friends to gather and sip wine."

Marla chuckled. "Like book club friends?"

"The best kind." Toni grinned.

The living room was generous as well, with two nooks. One that had shelves and was the perfect spot to set a chair and read a book. Another had a bay window seat, a curtain pulled across for privacy.

"This is my favorite spot," Marla said, sitting on the window seat. "I imagine myself sitting here with my grandchild, reading Winnie-the-Pooh books."

"You'll have to talk to your daughter about that," Toni said, then laughed.

"I can dream." Marla sighed.

Off the living room was a full-length, four-season porch with large windows that opened. A cute, red, pot-bellied stove sat in the corner and on closer inspection, they found it was a gas heater. Perfect for cold winter days. The room had a stunning view of the lake. Marla stared out at the water, picturing herself standing here on a summer day as a gentle breeze blew in from the lake. Everything about this house felt cozy, a feeling she never had at the manor.

"Let's go upstairs," Toni suggested.

Marla followed her up the stairs to a landing that led to the master bedroom on the left and another smaller bedroom and bathroom around the corner. The master bedroom was large with beautiful built-in bookshelves on one wall. Attached was a master bathroom and through that was a walk-in closet.

"Can you imagine yourself in this bedroom?" Toni asked.

"Yes, I can. I love all the light woodwork and the tile in the bathroom is nice. That closet is amazing, too. I don't have a closet like this in my room now."

Toni's brows rose. "Really? The master bedroom's closet is small?"

"I live in the room next door to it," Marla said. "It was built in the days when husbands and wives didn't sleep together. The master has a huge closet, but mine doesn't."

"Oh." Toni looked surprised.

"I always thought of the master bedroom as Nathan's room, even though we shared it. It's the room he was ill in for so long. I can't see myself sleeping there anymore," Marla explained. She knew she didn't have to but didn't mind sharing that with Toni.

"I can certainly understand that," Toni said.

They looked at the other bedroom and the bathroom, which were both fine for guests, then went up the second set of stairs. At the top, on the side wall, was an adorable, small stained-glass window and a large skylight spilled sunlight into the room.

"This place has a lot of natural light," Toni said, looking impressed.

Marla nodded and entered the room. It was the space over the garage, and would make a great guest room or even a family room or library.

After the women were finished looking at the house and the garage, they walked the property outside. There were brick pathways around the house and out to the dock, and a brick firepit in the center of the lawn. The tall pines, oaks, and birch trees gave the property privacy without completely blocking the view of the water.

"This is a beautiful lake," Toni said, admiring it from the dock. "So crystal clear and with a nice sandy bottom."

"Yes, it is. I suppose that's what made it so popular," Marla said. She gazed across the bay and saw her house standing there, looking majestic. The mansion was beautiful, no doubt. But it had never felt like a home to her. And now, without Nathan and Reese there, it felt empty and cold. She turned and looked at the cottage. Everything about it said warm and cozy. It called out to her.

"What are you thinking?" Toni asked, coming up alongside her.

"I'm thinking that this seems more like a home to me than that big house across the bay."

"You know. They say you shouldn't make any big decisions the first year after you've lost someone," Toni said. "I'd hate for you to do anything you'd regret."

Marla turned to her and smiled. This woman she hadn't known just months before was now her friend, and she cared enough to warn her to be careful. Her heart swelled with affection for Toni, and all her new friends. What on earth would she have done without them?

"I've heard that, but I guess I'm not following it very well." She laughed. "I remodeled parts of the house. I've made new friends. And I'm on the path of starting a shelter for women. All in three months."

"You've been busy," Toni said, grinning. They both erupted in laughter.

"I love this house," Marla finally said when their laughter had died down. "I don't want to miss out on buying it. Who knows when it will come on the market again?"

"That's true." Toni looked thoughtful. "Well, you could buy it and keep it a while. From what I gather, you could afford to do that, right?"

Marla nodded.

"It's an idea. Don't sell the mansion right away and see how you like living here. You can always sell it in a year or two or keep it for a summer rental. It's a good investment."

"That's a good idea," Marla said. She turned with a huge

smile and hugged Toni. "Let's put in a bid. Full price. I don't want to lose it."

"Okay. That's not what I'd advise, but you're the boss," Toni said.

Marla looked at the house again and her heart soared. She was sure this was the right choice. Her mind was already spinning with what furniture she'd bring from the mansion and what she'd leave there when she sold it. Because in her mind, she was already leaving the big house behind. All she wanted to do now was look forward.

Chapter Thirty-One

Marla

Marla busied herself all week with writing up ideas and a business plan for the women's shelter. She wanted detailed ideas to bring to the city board when the time came. Before that, she'd hire an architect to draw up a design on how the building would look. First, though, she was awaiting a report from the inspector.

On Wednesday, she went for a long walk on the trail. It had rained the night before, cooling the weather down and pushing the humidity away. Halfway along her walk, she ran into Alden.

"Imagine seeing you here again," she said, smiling. "I thought you usually walked in the evening."

"I do." He came up beside her and matched her steps. "But it's been too hot and muggy this past week. I was glad it thunder-stormed last night and cooled the air. It's beautiful out today."

"Yes, it is."

"How is your new venture coming along?" Alden asked. "Have you heard from the inspector?"

"No, not yet. But he said it would take time to type up the report. All these things take time. I'm eager to get started, but there are a lot of hurdles to jump first."

"That's true. Especially when you're working with any form of government. They move extremely slowly."

They walked a while in silence, picking their way over the path. Alden finally spoke up. "Do you have any big plans for the Fourth? Is your daughter coming home?"

"No. She's not. She's working at a law firm for the summer and says she has to work the day after, so there's no way she can come. I'm sure she thought it would be boring spending the day with her mother."

"She's young. Most young people try to separate themselves from their parents. She'll come running for your advice when she marries and has children," Alden said.

Marla chuckled. "That's a long time off. She's working on a law degree, so she'll be in school for years."

"Oh. A lawyer. Smart girl."

"She is a smart girl. I'm very proud of her."

"You should be." He turned to look at her. "Will you be going to the club for their Fourth of July party? I was invited, but I'm not sure I want to go."

"I don't want to go either. If I really wanted to watch their fireworks, I could see them from my dock. To tell the truth, I was thinking of going into St. Paul to watch theirs."

"Really? Isn't that a crowded mess?" Alden asked.

She grinned. "I think I know of a spot where no one else will be to watch the fireworks." Feeling suddenly brave, she brightened. "Would you like to go, too? We could grab a bite to eat beforehand and then watch the fireworks."

"I thought you'd never ask," he said with a grin.

* * *

The next evening, Marla picked Alden up at his house.

"You're a very modern woman," he said as he slid into her SUV. "I think this is the first time a woman has ever picked me up."

She laughed. "Modern doesn't really describe me, but I like that." In truth, Marla had been nervous the moment she'd asked him to join her. She was worried he'd think she'd meant it as a date, and she wasn't sure she knew how to tell him that it wasn't. She wanted to keep things platonic between them, so he didn't feel she was sending him any romantic signals. It was too soon after losing Nathan for her to even think about another man.

They talked and joked as she drove into town, keeping the conversation light as she'd wanted. She pulled into a quaint little bar where she and Nathan used to grab a quick bite sometimes. It wasn't fancy, but it was nice, and they were seated in a booth in the corner.

After they'd both ordered iced tea, she said, "You can have a beer or wine since I'm driving. I don't mind."

He shrugged. "No. I'm good."

They both ordered burgers and fries, and after the waitress left, Alden glanced around. "This is a cute place. How'd you find it?"

"My husband and I have been coming here for a long time. Not so much over the past couple of years, but we used to. It's not too far from where I once worked or from the university."

"Ah."

"My husband preferred eating out at the club after he retired. We rarely came into the city then. But I like this place." She saw him nod then suddenly felt bad.

"Sorry. I guess it's uncomfortable talking about my husband," she said.

"No, no. Not at all. I understand completely. It hasn't been that long since he passed. You aren't expected to just forget him. You two spent a lot of years together, building a life."

"Yes. That's true. But we can talk about other things." She glanced around, suddenly feeling nostalgic. Maybe it hadn't been a good idea to come here after all. Too many memories. Her expression grew serious.

"Did you miss working after your daughter was born?" he asked.

This took Marla by surprise. "Well, yes, I did. A little. I was happy that I didn't have to stress myself out by trying to make time for Reese and work, but as she grew older, I missed it. By then, though, I was caught up in doing mother things, like fundraising for the school and the club and driving Reese to and from her different sports. The next thing I knew, she was grown and getting ready to go to college, and there I was, without a lot to fill my days."

"You could have worked then," he said.

She nodded. "I thought about it, but Nathan always told me it wouldn't be fair for me to take a job away from someone who actually needed it. I understood his point. So I tried to make myself useful in other ways."

"Wow. I guess that was one way to look at it," Alden said. "Not to be rude, but it sounds like your husband had some old-fashioned ideas about women."

Marla knew he was right—she'd realized that herself recently—but it annoyed her that he'd say that without ever having met Nathan.

"I'm sorry." He looked immediately apologetic. "I said the wrong thing and I can see by the look on your face that I crossed a boundary. Please don't be angry with me."

She sighed. "I'm not angry. In truth, yes, Nathan did have some very old-fashioned ideas. He hated seeing women wearing jeans, he didn't like television, and he only read the classics. One would call him eccentric. I went along with it because there was no reason not to."

"I'm sorry," he said again. "If it makes you feel any better, my wife was the one to leave me. She said I was boring. Can you imagine? Me? An investment broker. Boring?" He laughed.

She laughed along with him. She liked his easy personality. "Are you boring?" she asked lightly.

"Probably. I do like my work and tend to be a workaholic. But I also like having fun. I love to travel and try to go somewhere new twice a year. And I'm not a hermit like she accused me of being. I did join the club, after all. A hermit wouldn't do that, would he?"

"No. A hermit wouldn't join a club," she agreed. She was happy that he'd turned the conversation back to humor. It had become too serious.

After they ate, Marla drove them through the city and to the road that led to the factory. It was just growing dark when they turned down the deserted driveway. She backed the car up to the river.

"Where are we?" he asked, looking around.

"We're at my factory," she said happily.

"Ah. So, this is it." He studied what was left of the structure. "It looks like it's in pretty good condition for that old of a building. It hasn't fallen in or anything."

"I know. I'm almost sure the report will come back positive. These old factories were built to last. It would be a shame to tear it down."

"It would." He turned to her, his eyes full of admiration. "You're saving history here. And turning it into something positive. That's admirable."

She suddenly felt shy, dropping her eyes to her lap. She wasn't used to this kind of praise. "Thank you. Let's hope everything goes through and it happens."

He grinned. "I'm sure you'll make it happen one way or another."

His confidence in her abilities felt good.

They opened the back end of the SUV and sat on the floor. The night air was cool, but comfortable. Marla slipped on a sweater she'd brought along to keep warm.

Although the city bustled all around them, it was quiet in this deserted spot on the river. Lights from tall buildings reflected off the water and the bridges down the river were lit up like Christmas.

"It's beautiful down here," Alden said. "I've never been this close to the river, other than crossing the bridges. I had no idea how nice it was."

"Wait until the fireworks start up," she said. He sat only inches from her, and she could smell his spicy cologne. It smelled nice.

"Did you and your husband always come to town to watch the fireworks?" he asked.

Marla shook her head. "No. I haven't done this since I married him. We always went to the club."

He smiled at her, his warm eyes crinkling in the corners. She liked how friendly his eyes were. "Then I feel honored that you chose me to share this with."

She was happy he'd come too. It was more fun than if she'd come alone. And, if she were honest with herself, she enjoyed his company. He was easy to be around despite only knowing him a short time.

The fireworks began and the sky lit up in sunbursts of green, red, white, yellow, and blue. They were spectacular, and Marla marveled at their beauty. She felt twenty again, sitting on the shore of the river watching fireworks, just as she'd done with her mother when she was young and with her college friends later on. She hoped Reese was sitting somewhere similar, enjoying the show.

After the fireworks ended, Alden turned to Marla. "Thank you for bringing me here. They were beautiful."

"I'm glad you came. This was fun," she said.

He gazed at her a moment, and for an instant, she thought he was going to kiss her. She stiffened and pulled back. He gazed at her, looking confused, and she realized he hadn't meant to kiss her at all.

"Are you okay?" he asked.

"Yeah. I'm fine." *Other than feeling embarrassed for the way I acted,* she thought. "Maybe we should head home."

"Would you like me to drive us back? You know, to save my male ego and all."

She laughed, the tension she'd felt now gone. "Sure. I'll let you. I don't want to be the one to bruise your male pride."

"You could never do that," he said.

They were quiet on the way back to his house, and after he'd pulled into his driveway, he said, "This was fun. I hope we can go out together again."

She nodded. "I'd like that. As friends, of course," she added hastily.

He hesitated a moment before answering. "Of course. As friends. Goodnight."

"Goodnight."

Marla moved over to the driver's seat and watched Alden as he walked up the sidewalk to his door. She couldn't deny she felt an attraction to him. And she thought he felt it too. But she couldn't complicate her life right now with a relationship so soon after Nathan's passing. It wouldn't look good, or feel good, either. She hoped that Alden was a patient man.

* * *

The book club group met at Rita's home the week after the Fourth. As before, Rita was the perfect hostess. She'd made homemade pizzas with different toppings and salad. Marla thought it was delicious.

Rita offered to read the journal this time. Picking up the book, she began.

Working with the Minnesota Woman Suffrage Association has been an eye-opener for me. I always felt that women should be treated as equals but being around women who speak this out loud is refreshing. I've put a great deal of energy into it while still maintaining my work at the factory and at home. So far, Nathaniel is supportive. I'm hoping that will continue.

Chapter Thirty-Two

Alaina

Alaina's work with the Minnesota Woman Suffrage Association continued. She attended monthly meetings, learning as much about the suffrage movement as possible. Many legislatures, both local and statewide, were members of the yacht club and also good friends of Nathaniel. Alaina put on dinner parties, suggesting Nathaniel invite his political friends and then she'd invite Hedda and her husband, Albert, also. She was the perfect hostess at these gatherings, and when she saw an opportunity, she brought up the topic of a woman's right to vote. Often, it made the men at the table uncomfortable, or even angry, but she'd give Hedda the floor and let her speak her piece. After the first such dinner party, Nathaniel asked her if that had been her intention all along.

"Yes," she answered honestly. "We have connections, so why wouldn't I try to use them? You do the same thing every chance you get."

Surprisingly, her husband never grew angry at her over this. He'd just shake his head and grin. And when she'd bring up the subject of another dinner party and show him the list of invitees, he'd give her a knowing look, but not object.

His tolerance of her work with the suffrage association came to a breaking point, though, in the spring of 1889. The women's group planned a march on the state capital, and Alaina was front and center when they did. Prior to the march, she'd spoken with the women at the textile factory who she knew also belonged to a chapter of the suffrage group. Nearly every woman who worked there, whether it be in sewing, cutting, or weaving, belonged to the association, and they all asked for the day off to march. Alaina not only granted them the time off, but gave them pay as well, and offered a day off with pay to any man in the factory who agreed to march with the women. Surprisingly, several of the men said they would.

Jerome had taken her aside after he'd heard. "Does Mr. Madison know you've given such a generous offer to these workers? A paid day off to go march in a protest?"

Alaina stood her ground. "I'm a woman who helps manage this factory," she told him. "How can I not allow these women to have the opportunity to fight for what they deserve when I am doing so? Nathaniel will understand."

However, after the march, when Nathaniel saw his wife's picture in the newspaper along with the other women who'd marched that day, and read she'd given the women a day off with pay to march, he took the train to Great Heron Lake on a weekday to confront her.

"What on earth do you think you're doing?" he bellowed as he entered the house.

Alaina had been sitting on the sofa in the great room, reading, while Ella sat at the dining table, doing her schoolwork. Alaina looked up at her husband, unconcerned. "I didn't expect you home until Friday night," she said, rising.

Nathaniel glanced at Ella, then turned his eyes back to his wife. "I'd like to speak with you in the study." He spun on his heel and strode down the hall.

Sighing, Alaina followed. She settled herself on the settee as he shut the door behind them.

"Did you see this?" he asked, shoving the paper at her. "You're right there for everyone to see. And you even spoke to the reporter. What is this nonsense about you giving the factory workers a day off with pay to march in the protest?"

Alaina glanced at the photo. She smiled. She looked quite nice, standing there among her friends. Looking up at her husband, she became serious. "It wasn't nonsense. I offered them all the day off with pay to march. The majority of our workers are women. They deserve a chance to stand up for their rights."

Nathaniel stopped pacing and looked her in the eye. "I have been very tolerant of your suffrage work. But here, I must draw a line. You cannot associate my businesses with this movement. And we cannot afford to give people a day off with pay. It's ludicrous!"

Alaina raised one eyebrow. "Your business? Need I remind you that I'm the one who inherited the textile business and am the legitimate owner? That I'm the one who has made it profitable all these years?"

His eyes sparked fire. "You may have inherited it, but I'm your husband. I own the business and everything else. Just because I *allow* you to have a hand in it does not mean it's yours."

She rose, her skirts rustling as she shortened the space between them. She was not afraid of Nathaniel. "You *allow* me? How dare you? I'm the reason the factory is profitable, which in turn, makes your stores profitable as well. I'm also the reason so many people of great standing look up to you and our family."

She spun and walked back to the settee, trying hard to calm her temper. Taking a deep breath, she faced him again. "Need I remind you that it is women who shop in your stores? And it's women who run households and purchase the items for them. And must I point out that many on your staff of sales clerks are also women? *You* depend on *women* to buy your products and make your stores profitable. Just as I depend upon women to make the goods that sell in your stores. It would do you good to take a stance as I have for women's rights. Go against the male tide and do what you know is right. Because in the end, it will be the businesses that helped empower women that will profit when women's rights are granted."

They stood there in the masculine, wood-paneled room, staring hard at each other. She could see the wheels turning in Nathaniel's head. He was angry, but he wasn't stupid. She knew he was weighing what she'd said.

Finally, he spoke in a calm voice. "Please confer with me the next time you decide to do such a thing. I'd like to, at least, be warned."

She nodded curtly and left the room. She wasn't sure if she'd won, but she felt she'd made some headway.

The next week, after grumbles from his male managers, Nathaniel placed a sign on the front door of all his businesses. "Madison's Department Stores support the Minnesota Woman Suffrage Association."

Women flocked to the stores just to read the signs. Men grumbled but kept silent. Sales rose. Alaina's suffrage friends patted her on the back and complimented her on having such a progressive-thinking husband. Alaina just smiled and said nothing. There was no need to gloat on the outside, but on the inside, she was deliriously happy. She'd won.

* * *

The coughing began in late spring of 1889 and didn't let up throughout the summer. Nathaniel refused to see a doctor. "It's just a spring cold," he insisted. "Summer allergies." But as he lost weight and grew paler, Alaina began to worry.

"I'll not ruin our family vacation by worrying about a little cough," Nathaniel insisted, uncharacteristically irritated at Alaina.

She stopped bothering him the rest of June and into July as he spent time with the children. He worked with Arthur on his sailing and the two spent long hours out on the open water. The children played croquet with him on the lawn and they all swam in the crystal waters of Great Heron Lake. Alaina kept it to herself when she noticed Nathaniel breathing heavier than usual after a long swim or walk with the children.

By fall, Alaina was genuinely concerned about Nathaniel's health. He'd lost a lot of weight, even though he ate his regular meals. Despite spending time in the sun, his complexion looked sallow. And recently, she'd seen him using a handkerchief when he coughed. Sometimes, it looked bloodied. All his symptoms reminded her of her father's illness, and she grew frightened. On one of her bi-weekly trips to the factory that fall, she made a surprise stop at the townhouse and was shocked to see he was home, resting in the library.

"You are sick!" she exclaimed as she hurried to his side. She pulled a chair near his and sat beside him.

"Now, Alaina," Nathaniel said hoarsely. "Don't make a big fuss of this. I have a simple fall cold. I'm sure it will go away after a day of rest."

"This is no simple cold," she insisted. "You've lost weight and look pale. And I know that you've been coughing up blood. It's time you saw a doctor."

"To do what? Poke and prod me and not help in the least? We both know that physicians are useless," he said with disgust. "Look at what little they did for your father. Or for your friend."

Bringing up the pain of losing her father and Hannah did not deter Alaina from his issue. "We must find out what the illness is," she said. "It could be something infectious, like tuberculosis. You must see someone to learn more."

Alaina could tell she was getting through to Nathaniel. She knew he wouldn't want to transmit an infectious disease to their children. Finally, he nodded.

"I'll see a doctor to rule out anything dangerous," he agreed.

However, after several doctors examined him, none had the same diagnoses. One thought it could be a simple cold. Another said he showed signs of tuberculosis but couldn't be one-hundred percent certain. Yet another doctor thought it might be a cancer of the lungs. All prescribed fresh air, a healthy diet, and exercise.

Nathaniel, not certain what he was suffering from, confined himself all winter in the townhouse and did much of his work from home. He relied on his lawyer and store managers to do all his legwork. Some days were good, others were not. The children were not allowed to visit their father, but Alaina came often to make sure he was following the doctor's orders and to oversee the staff.

In early 1890, a medical doctor from the newly formed University of Minnesota Medical school came to see Nathaniel after he'd been recommended by a good friend. After thoroughly examining him, the doctor gave the opinion that it was not tuberculosis he was suffering from, but instead possibly cancer of the lungs.

"What can be done?" Alaina asked, hopeful there was a treatment.

The doctor looked grave. "Nothing, I'm afraid. My suggestion is to continue what you are doing. Perhaps go somewhere where the air is clean, continue to eat healthy, don't drink alcohol or smoke, and rest."

Nathaniel held back his anger until the doctor had left. "I told you doctors were useless," he growled. His outburst brought on a coughing fit and Alaina rushed to hand him a clean handkerchief and poured a glass of water for him to drink. After a time, he was able to breathe normally again.

"It's not the news we'd hoped for, but he could be wrong," Alaina said, trying to be optimistic. "The good news is that you're not contagious. We'll go to the lake house and you can be around the children again. The fresh air will be good for you."

Nathaniel shook his head and spoke seriously. "You realize I will not get better, don't you?"

"I won't give up hope if you won't," Alaina told him. "We won't know until we try."

Nathaniel agreed.

In March, despite there still being snow on the ground, Nathaniel allowed Alaina to take him to the lake house. He would have to run his businesses from there, through his lawyer and his assistant, Jonah Sanders, and with Alaina's help. Jonah was in his mid-thirties, tall and slim with dark hair. He'd worked alongside Nathaniel for several years as his right-hand man. He knew the business well and could be trusted to run things with instructions sent by Nathaniel.

That summer was different from the last. The children were busy. Arthur was now twelve and spending most of his time with friends sailing and swimming at the yacht club. Sweet Ella was now ten and swam every day under the watchful eye of her nanny, and attended ballet classes three times a week. Her favorite thing to do was walk the trails around the lake with Alaina whenever her mother could get away. Alaina tried to spend as much time each day as possible with the children, but she was also committed to caring for Nathaniel. John, Nathaniel's valet, was a great help when it came to Nathaniel's personal care, like shaving, bathing, and dressing, but Alaina was in charge of his medicine, meals, and routine of going outside for fresh air. With John's help, they'd bring Nathaniel downstairs each day to sit on the patio so he could watch the children swim or play. If it rained, he'd sit in his study for a time, reading or possibly doing some work at his desk. But as the summer wore on, and Nathaniel experienced more pain, he spent more time in bed, resting.

At first, visitors dropped by in the evening to see Nathaniel and Alaina. Hedda and her husband were regulars those first few weeks. She was a strong woman whose positivity was welcomed. Members from the club also came to visit, as did friends from St. Paul. But as the summer wore on, and Nathaniel's health deteriorated, he cut off all ties to the outside world. Nathaniel was a proud man and didn't want anyone to perceive him as weak. And that was how he was becoming—tired and weak. The doctor visited weekly, bringing with him the pain medicine that Nathaniel depended on to get through each day. On good days, Arthur would lie in bed with his father and play card games or read to him from his favorite classic novel. On bad days, Nathaniel slept fitfully and ate very little. It was actually a relief to Alaina when fall arrived. Arthur returned to boarding school and Ella was also busy with school. It relieved some of the strain put on Alaina after a summer of caring for everyone's needs.

Twice-weekly, Alaina took the train into St. Paul to visit one or more of the department stores and take notes that she'd bring back and read to Nathaniel. She began conferring with the managers of each store to let them know what Nathaniel wanted ordered, what was selling best, and what wasn't. She kept a close eye on the ledgers, seeing how each store was faring, then reported any profits or losses to her husband. She became his eyes and ears so he could continue to run his business, or at least feel he was. In truth, he was so ill that his concentration was spotty, and his answers didn't always make sense. By the end of October, Alaina was making most of the critical decisions about the stores on her own, but relaying orders as if it were Nathaniel's ideas. And she did an excellent job. Her keen eye and good business sense kept the stores running at a profit, and through the holiday shopping rush, she'd made good purchases that sold well. As long as the managers thought she was doing Nathaniel's bidding, they didn't balk at her giving them orders.

By the end of January 1891, Alaina knew that Nathaniel wouldn't be with her much longer. He was weak, in a great deal of pain, and hardly able to keep food down. She no longer spoke to him about business, other than to give him positive reports even though she was sure he didn't comprehend her words. No one saw him anymore, except John, her, and the children. Nathaniel was adamant about that.

Alaina, too, was exhausted. She worked non-stop to make sure his businesses were running smoothly along with her own. She'd given up doing the ledgers for the textile factory, but she still occasionally looked over them to make sure all was well. As she watched Nathaniel fade away, she knew she had to do something to preserve his businesses until Arthur was old enough to inherit them. And she knew what it was she had to do.

She sent a message to their lawyer asking for a copy of Nathaniel's will. It came via messenger, and she read it over carefully. He'd made no plan for the event of his early death. It only stated that Arthur would inherit the businesses, house, and other properties when he passed, and that there'd be money for Ella and Alaina's needs. Alaina realized that if she wanted to continue to grow the businesses so that they'd be there for her son when he was ready, she'd have to make sure Nathaniel changed the will.

On one of his more lucid days, she brought a document to Nathaniel that she'd had the lawyer draw up after a lengthy disagreement. It stated Alaina would be in charge of all business and property holdings until Arthur was of age. She sat on the side of Nathaniel's bed in the semi-dark room and gently took his hand in hers.

"Dear. We must have a serious conversation," she said softly. When his eyes turned to her, she hesitated a moment. He was rail thin, and his cheeks were sunken in his once handsome face. His hair had thinned considerably, and his skin was so pale, it was almost translucent. Despite the things he'd done in the past to hurt her, her heart went out to him. She would have gladly exchanged this shadow of a man for her robust Nathaniel despite their rocky relationship.

"We must think of what's best for our children in the event that you are no longer with us," she continued. "I've been successfully running the day-to-day operations of the department stores in your absence, and I'd like to continue until our son can take his rightful place. But you must sign this paper to be added to your will for that to be legal."

Nathaniel stared at her a long time, his brows furrowed. She wondered if he'd heard her and understood what she'd said.

Finally, he spoke, his breath heavy between words. "The men would never work for a woman."

Alaina winced. She knew it was true, but there was no other option. "I understand," she said calmly. "But you know that I'm as competent as any man with this type of work. I'm the only one who will look out for our son's best interests. Our family's best interest."

Nathaniel closed his eyes a moment, then opened them again. He nodded. "I believe you are."

Alaina brought the paper closer to him and read aloud what the lawyer had written. Then she placed a pen in his hand and held the paper against a book so he could sign. Nathaniel's script was shaky and almost unrecognizable, but it was good enough.

"Thank you," Alaina said, bending down to kiss his forehead. "I'll make you proud, I promise."

As she rose, Nathaniel reached for her arm and stopped her. "You were always too good for me," he said, his breath ragged. "I know that now."

Tears filled her eyes as she once again kissed his forehead. "I won't let you down," she said.

In early March, Nathaniel passed away in the morning with only Alaina at his bedside. After he'd breathed his last, labored breath, he was silent. Alaina kissed his paper-thin cheek, then stood and walked to the window. Drawing back the heavy draperies, she opened the window, letting in the fresh spring air.

"Now you can be free, my dear," she said, tears filling her eyes. She hoped his soul would soar to heaven and finally be at peace. Then she walked out of the room and down the long, dark hallway.

Her life would be forever changed.

Chapter Thirty-Three

Marla

A chill ran up Marla's spine as Rita read the words in Alaina's journal. It was almost as if she'd read the last moments Marla had spent with Nathan when he'd passed. She thought of that day and how she, too, had opened the window to release his spirit. She also thought about how relieved she'd felt. She'd told herself that her relief was over his no longer suffering, but she knew that wasn't entirely true. Part of it was that she would no longer be tied to the sickbed after all those months. She'd not only freed Nathan, but herself as well.

Alaina had felt the same. It was as if they'd led parallel lives.

"Are you okay?" Ardie asked, reaching over to touch Marla's shoulder.

Marla looked up, startled, remembering she was not the only one in the room. "Yes. Sorry. I guess that last paragraph hit me hard. Nathan's death was very similar. It's almost eerie."

Rita's eyes widened. "It is, isn't it? I mean, Nathaniel must have died in the same bedroom as your husband. And they had the same name. It's like history repeated itself."

Marla bit her lip and nodded. "I've felt that way about many of the things that happened to Alaina. I can relate to how she felt even though we've lived a hundred and fifty years apart."

"Ooh! I just had a chill." Wanda shuddered.

Marla laughed, breaking the tension in the room. "It's all just a coincidence, I'm sure." But none of the women looked convinced.

"You're all creeping me out," Toni said, shuddering. "Let's talk about something else. What did you all do for the Fourth?"

Each one recounted what they'd done. Ardie's family had gathered at her house then gone to the park to watch their local fireworks. Toni had gone to a park in St. Paul with friends to watch the fireworks over the river. Rita had attended an art fair that day and stayed home that night, and Wanda said she'd driven a carload of her daughter's friends out to pizza and to watch the fireworks.

"There's nothing crazier than a carload of seventeen-year-olds," Wanda said, rolling her eyes.

"What did you do, Marla?" Ardie asked.

"I drove down to the factory and watched the fireworks. It was the perfect spot."

"Alone?" the women asked in unison.

"That's doesn't sound safe," Toni added.

She shook her head. "No. Not alone. Alden came with me. We had dinner at a little pub then sat in the car and watched the fireworks."

"Alden?" Rita asked, glancing around at the other women. "Did I miss something? Who's he?"

"He's just a man who belongs to the club. I met him at the June Ball when they honored Nathan. He moved here about a year ago, so he's new to the area."

"And?" Wanda asked.

Marla frowned. "And what? We're just friends. We walk on the trails by the lake sometimes, and we had lunch once, but nothing else."

Toni raised her eyebrows.

"Nothing else," Marla reiterated. "It's way too soon after Nathan's passing for me to get involved with another man."

"Does Alden know that?" Rita asked.

"Yes. I'm sure he does," Marla said. And she was sure. Well, she thought she was sure.

* * *

The next Monday, Toni called with good news.

"The cottage is yours," she said excitedly. "They're asking for three months before closing to get everything out of there, which is pretty normal. As long as you're okay with that, it's a deal."

Marla was ecstatic over the news. "That's wonderful. Of course it's okay. I can't believe after all these years of loving that house it's finally mine."

"Congratulations!" Toni said.

"Thank you. And thanks for handling it. I can't wait to move in!" Marla walked to the French doors and gazed across the bay at her new house. Her house! She hadn't felt this excited over anything in years.

"Have you thought about what you're going to do about the big house?" Toni asked.

Marla wasn't sure. Reese said she didn't want it, but would she change her mind in a few years? "I'll have to talk to my daughter about it," she told Toni. "I'd like to sell it, but I can't if she has any hesitation. I think I'll hang onto it until spring and then if we decide to sell, do it then."

"Good idea. It's hard selling the family legacy. You could even rent it out summers if you want to wait longer. I hope if you do decide to sell it, you'll let me give it a try."

"I wouldn't ask anyone else," Marla told her.

Two days after the good news from Toni, she had more news from Anthony. "The inspection report came back positive. He says the building is sturdy and can be used. It's also far enough from the river by today's standards so there won't be any environmental problem with you building there. Now you can move ahead with a design and present it to the city."

Marla was overjoyed. "Thank you, Anthony. That's wonderful!"

"I admire what you're doing with that old factory, Marla. Not many people would give up a huge chunk of money to build a non-profit. I'm glad you're doing something you feel passionate about. Nathan would be so proud of you."

"Thank you, Anthony. That means a lot, coming from you." Marla sat back in her desk chair and glanced around the room, thinking of Alaina. She'd also be pleased with how Marla was using the factory. That thought warmed her heart. "I'll keep you informed of what's going on. Could you begin the paperwork for setting up a non-profit for me? I'm calling it the River of Hope House. I'd like to set up a foundation as well, called the Alaina Carlton Madison Foundation. That way we can collect donations for the shelter and possibly for future services if this grows."

"I can do that," he said. "You've really put a lot of thought into this, haven't you?"

"Yes, I have. It's all I've thought about since I decided to do this. I want to help women restart their lives. It's the least I can do, considering how fortunate I've been."

"I'll get the paperwork started," he said. "You have a lot of work ahead of you. I know you're up to the challenge, though."

She smiled to herself. She was. After years of using her time frivolously, she was ready for some hard work.

Marla had a busy week. She contacted Roger Simms for recommendations on an architect and he gave her a few names. He also put his hat in the ring to remodel the building, which made her smile. If it worked out, she'd be happy to use his crew for the reconstruction. He was honest and they all worked very hard.

After securing an architect, James Cromwell, to draw up the plans, she spent a few hours with him, giving him details of what she wanted the building to have. He said he could draw up some preliminary plans that would be enough for the city council to make their decision. If it went through, he could design more detailed drawings for her.

After that, she talked to the city secretary and asked to be placed on their agenda for the August board meeting. By the end of the week, she felt she'd accomplished a great deal. The book club had decided to go back to meeting every other week. The journal entries were nearing the end, and none of them wanted it to stop. Plus, summer was going by quickly, and they all had busy schedules. Now that Marla had something to focus on, she was keeping busy too. So, they'd meet the next Thursday at Wanda's house.

Friday night, Marla called Reese and asked her to have lunch with her in the city on Saturday. Reese tried to talk her way out of it, but Marla insisted. "I haven't seen you since the ball. Can't you take an hour out of your busy schedule to see me?"

Reese finally conceded. They met at the same little pub where Marla had taken Alden. Marla arrived a few minutes early and sat in a booth against the wall. Reese walked in soon after. She looked young and beautiful in a pair of shorts, a tank top, and sandals, her blond hair pulled up and her sunglasses resting on her head. Marla smiled. She remembered what it had been like to be young and carefree, as if you were on top of the world. My, but how things changed as the years flew by.

"Hi, Mom," Reese said as she slid into the seat across from her. "It's sure a scorcher out there today."

"A typical July day," Marla said. "Thanks for coming. I have so much to tell you."

Reese stared at her as if she found it hard to believe her mother had been doing anything interesting.

They ordered their food and both had iced tea. Reese sat back, looking bored.

"So, what have you been up to besides work?" Marla asked. "Are you still dating Chad?"

Reese sighed. "Yeah. Kind of. I mean, we see each other regularly. But don't go marrying us off yet, Mom. I have years before that."

Marla chuckled. "I know better than to even say the word *marriage* to you. I like Chad, what little I know of him. I'm glad you're still seeing him."

Reese eyed her mother. "I thought you had something interesting to tell me."

She grinned. "I do. I have a lot to tell you. First of all, believe it or not, Mrs. Cooper is warming up to me. Can you believe it?"

"Not really. But I'm glad to hear it. That must be why she hasn't called me in a while to complain."

"I wore her down with niceness," Marla said.

"You threatened to fire her, Mom. That wasn't nice," Reese reminded her.

"Oh, that wasn't a threat. Just an observation." They both laughed. Their food came and Marla continued talking.

"There have been some interesting things happening lately. When I was remodeling, I found a journal that belonged to the first Mrs. Madison who lived in the lake house. It's been a very fascinating read."

Reese looked intrigued. "Really? How long ago did she live?"

"The journal starts when they married in 1876 and so far, we're up to 1891. Her name was Alaina and she was a very interesting and independent woman for her generation."

"We?" Reese asked, looking confused.

"Huh? Oh. We're reading it aloud in the book club I joined a few months ago. The women have become quite attached to Alaina. Her story is so good. We're almost done, so I hope we find out how Alaina's story ends."

"Oh," Reese said. "I'm glad you're still meeting with your new friends. Do you still go to the yacht club, too?"

"Not so much. I've had lunch there a couple of times but that's about it. I think that part of my life is over. I've been moving on," Marla said.

Reese had brought a forkful of salad to her lips, but stopped and gaped at her mother. "Moving on to what?"

"That's why I brought up Alaina's story. Her father owned a factory on the Mississippi River here in St. Paul. I had no idea we still owned the building and property. I don't even think your father knew about it. Anthony called me about it a few weeks ago because a developer wanted to buy it. The ladies and I went to see it. It's really interesting."

"Oh. That's neat," Reese said as she took a sip of tea. "So, did you sell it?"

"No."

Reese's brows rose. "Why not?"

"Because I want it."

Her daughter looked stunned. "What would you do with it?"

Marla smiled. "I'm going to turn it into a women's shelter. This town has plenty of high-end apartments and strip malls. I wanted to use the building for something more substantial. Something Alaina would have approved of."

Reese sat back in her seat and stared at her. Marla could only imagine what her daughter was thinking. She probably thought her mother had finally lost her mind. "I don't know what to say. That's such a big project, but I agree. It would be a great use for the building. I just can't imagine where you got the idea from, though."

"You didn't think your mother was smart enough or motivated enough to do such a thing?" Marla asked, feeling downhearted. She didn't understand why her daughter thought so little of her. She was the one who'd raised her to be a strong woman. Yet Reese had such a low opinion of her.

"No. It's not that. I know you're smart. I just never pictured you taking on such a big project. I guess I figured you'd keep doing what you've done since I was little. Golfing, tennis, and club fundraisers."

"This is sort of the same thing, only bigger. I'm setting up a foundation to take donations and also supervising the shelter. Of course, I'll need plenty of help from women who know how a shelter works, and I have support from a wonderful woman willing to educate me. But I'm up to the task."

"But, Mom, is that how you want to spend your time? I mean, it'll be a full-time job just getting this thing off the ground, let alone running it. Is that what you want?" Reese asked, still looking shocked.

"Honey. What else am I going to do with my time? I'm only forty-six years old and I have years ahead of me to fill. I'm lucky enough to have more money than I need. And I have the ability to help the community. I'm not only up to the task—I'm excited about it."

"Wow. I'm speechless," Reese said. "I guess I underestimated you."

Marla grinned. "A lot of people have underestimated me for a long time. But I'm capable of doing so much more than people expected I could do."

"Then I'm happy for you," Reese said, sounding sincere. "I just have to get used to my mom being a powerful force."

Marla laughed. "I'm not quite that. But thank you, dear. I'd really love to show you the building. Can you take a few more minutes to come see it with me?"

Reese smiled, her eyes brightening. "I'd love that."

After they finished eating, they took Marla's car to the property which wasn't too far away. Once they'd parked down by the building, the two women stepped out of the car and walked up to the tall structure.

"This building is huge," Reese said, gazing up at it. "What kind of factory was it?"

"A textile factory. They made all types of household products like bolts of fabric and rugs and such. Alaina's father started it, and after he died, Alaina ran it for years. In fact, Alaina ran all the businesses her husband owned after he died in 1891. She was pretty amazing."

They walked up to the building and Reese read the inscription in the brick. "Carlton Textiles 1868. Imagine that. It was so long ago. So, would he be like my several-times great-grandfather or something?"

"Well, Alaina was married to your father's great-great-grandfather, so her father would be your great-great-great-grandfather."

Reese shook her head, looking amazed. "That's incredible. Why haven't I ever heard of these people before?"

Marla shrugged. "Your father wasn't much for talking about the family tree. From what Mrs. Cooper says, neither were his parents. But there's a portrait of the original Mr. Madison hanging in the library room at the club if you ever want to see what he looked like."

"What about Alaina? Is her portrait there too?" Reese asked.

Her question made Marla pause. Alaina and the other women had worked hard to help build the yacht club by raising money with fundraisers, yet none of them had ever been honored. "No, it isn't. But you know what? We may need to change that."

As they walked back to the car, Marla took the opportunity to tell Reese one more thing. "By the way. I bought a cute little cottage on the lake."

Reese's head spun in her direction so quickly, it was comical. "You what?"

Marla chuckled. "I'll explain it on the way back to your car."

Chapter Thirty-Four

Alaina

Alaina sat at the head of the conference room table adjacent to Nathaniel's private office. She'd called a meeting of the managers who headed up the six stores that comprised all of Madison's Department Stores. Six men sat around the table, staring back at her. They ranged in age from their mid-thirties to their sixties. Standing beside Alaina was Jonah, and in a chair along the side wall sat Paul Woodward, Nathaniel's long-time attorney.

It had been ten days since Nathaniel had passed, and a week since the funeral. Alaina had called the men together to announce the changes that were going to occur in the company. She knew they weren't going to like what they heard. She felt fortunate that Jonah had been overwhelmingly supportive of her when he'd heard she'd be running the businesses.

"I'll be happy to assist with anything you need," he'd said earlier when she'd met with him. "Mr. Madison spoke often of your expert business sense running the textile factory. I know you'll do a good job here."

She'd been relieved to hear that. And surprised. Nathaniel had spoken highly of her work? How wonderful to know that. That thought helped boost her confidence for what she was about to do.

Alaina had worn a simple, tailored black suit with a narrow skirt. She'd thought the men might take her more seriously if she looked serious. Now, seeing the six grim, unsmiling faces before her, she was glad she'd been conservative in her dress.

She stood, understanding the power of standing as others sat. The men rustled their chairs to stand also, as any gentleman would, but she waved her hand to indicate that they could stay seated.

"Thank you for coming on such short notice," she said. "And thank you all for attending my husband's funeral last week. He would have been pleased to know how well-thought of he was." She paused, then drew herself up even straighter. "I'm sure you're all concerned about the future of Madison's Department Stores. Please rest assured that all of your jobs are safe. Not only will the company still run as the finest department stores in the Midwest, but we will continue to grow and open new stores just as my husband had planned."

The men all nodded and looked relieved. They relaxed a bit and watched her with interest.

"There will only be one small change. As of now, with my husband's blessing, and until our son, Arthur, has completed his schooling and is ready to take over the family business, I will be in charge of the company."

For one quick second, the silence in the room was deafening. All eyes grew wide as they stared at her. Once the idea of a woman as their boss filtered through, though, the men began to protest and grumble. One man in particular, Walter Edmund, the elder of the group, stood to face her, taking it upon himself to speak for all the men.

"This is absolutely absurd," he said, puffing out his chest. "A woman cannot legally run a company."

Alaina stared steadily at him. He was a man in his early sixties, balding and portly, and he'd worked for Nathaniel since nearly the beginning. She'd had Jonah give her a background on all six of the managers, and their assistant managers, as well. Of all the men to protest, she had expected Walter would.

"It is legal for a woman to run a business," she said calmly. "And Nathaniel specified in his will that I would run this company. Mr. Woodward can testify to that." She glanced over to Paul as he stood from his seat.

"Yes. Mrs. Madison is the legal guardian and operator of Mr. Madison's businesses and properties until such a time as his son can take control," he said. Paul was an older man as well, and Alaina knew he wasn't happy with these conditions either, but he understood the law and had to follow it.

"Surely you cannot expect us, the men who've helped build this company, to take orders from you," Mr. Edmund said. "You have no idea what it entails to run such a business."

"On the contrary, Mr. Edmund," Alaina said calmly. "I've not only been managing my father's textile factory for the past twelve years, the very textile factory that Madison's Department Stores purchases many of their products from, but I have also been in charge of decisions for the stores over the past year during my husband's illness. I believe I do have the credentials to run this business properly."

"I daresay that making decisions while being backed up by Mr. Madison is not the same as running the business. I suggest that one of us, the managers, be allowed to move into the position of running the company until your son is of age."

Many of the men around the table nodded their agreement. Alaina began to walk slowly around the table, keeping her eyes on the men. They shifted uncomfortably in their seats. Everyone except Mr. Edmund, who stood stiffly, watching her. Alaina had seen Nathaniel do this very thing—walk around a room quietly, making people nervous. She felt she was accomplishing her objective by the time she was almost to the head of the table again.

"So, Mr. Edmund. You feel that I cannot supervise this company properly?" she asked.

He cleared his throat. "I feel it is not a job for a woman, yes."

She lifted her head haughtily. "And you refuse to work for a woman?"

"No self-respecting man would," he said.

Alaina smiled. "Then I will be happy to accept your resignation, Mr. Edmund. You are now relieved of your duties."

His eyes grew large as her words sank in. "What? You can't fire me," he sputtered.

"I believe I can," she said calmly. She eyed each of the other men at the table before continuing. "I'm sure that each of you have a well-trained assistant manager under you who would love the opportunity to become manager. If anyone else here feels they cannot work for me, please join Mr. Edmund as he makes his way out the door."

No sound came from the men. They sat there, possibly weighing their options and not finding they had many.

"How dare you, madame!" Mr. Edmund bellowed, his face turning red with anger. "You have no right."

"I have every right!" Alaina exclaimed, raising her voice. "Please be on your way, Mr. Edmund."

He glanced around the table for support, and when he found none, grabbed his briefcase off the table and stormed out yelling, "You will hear from my lawyer!"

As the door slammed shut, Alaina calmly returned to her seat at the head of the table. "I'm sorry that it had to come to that," she said. "And if there is ever a time any of you feel you cannot work for me, please feel free to leave. But I hope you won't. Your experience and expertise at running each store is highly-valued. I'd like to work with each of you to make Madison's Department Stores even more successful than they already are."

The men nodded, each looking scared to death to say anything.

"Wonderful," she said. "Shall we begin?"

* * *

Alaina was extremely busy those first few months as she took over Nathaniel's duties. Most importantly, though, she made sure she was home each evening to spend time with Ella, and also Arthur when he was home from school. Rather than living in the city, as Nathaniel had done, she took the train every morning and returned every night. It was stressful, to say the least, but she felt it was her duty to make sure the children knew she put them high on her priority list.

The first few weeks, Alaina spent time in each store working alongside the manager. She wanted to learn everything they did and understand what they expected of her. Jonah came with her and took notes on what she deemed important. The first manager she visited, a man in his forties, was not all that happy with her following him around and asking questions. But when he realized she wasn't there to tell him how to do his job, and she was open to suggestions for improving the store and sales, he slowly warmed to her. At each store, she found this to be true. She wanted the managers to feel she wasn't going to give orders—she was there to listen and make suggestions and offer solutions to problems. They all seemed very receptive of her after she'd spent time with each of them.

The assistant manager-turned-manager after Walter Edmund was let go was her biggest fan. He was a young man in his thirties named Arnold Krause, and he didn't hide his enthusiasm over the opportunity to show her he could manage the store.

"Do you have any qualms about working for a woman?" she asked him that first day they met.

He shook his head vigorously. "No, ma'am. My mother raised me to be respectful and my wife keeps me in line at home. I don't see any reason why I'd mind working for a woman."

She'd broken down into laughter at that, as had Jonah. The young Krause had looked confused at their mirth, then realized what he'd said and laughed too. After his honest answer, Alaina had a soft spot in her heart for the young man.

After she'd toured the stores, she set about looking over the notes that her secretary had typed for her. Alaina found humor in that. She had a secretary. And an office of her own. And a male assistant who did her bidding without any reservations. Oh, how she wished the women of the Minnesota Woman Suffrage Association could see her here. They might not have been able to win the vote as of yet, but she was breaking barriers every day for women.

The second thing she did after taking over was to have her father's desk moved from storage to her new office. She loved having a piece of her father's history with her as she broke new ground in her job. She knew he was smiling down at her, giving her the strength to make good decisions every day.

That summer was difficult, but Alaina did her best to balance work and family. She couldn't show any sign of weakness at work by not appearing there every day of the week. But she also needed to ensure her children were being cared for properly. Nanny Prue still worked for the family and was in charge of eleven-year-old Ella. But thirteen-year-old Arthur thought he was too old for a nanny, so Alaina hired a young man as his companion to escort him back and forth to the yacht club and other activities while ensuring his safety.

There were other changes that summer, as well. Alaina sold the townhouse in St. Paul and dispersed of the staff there. John Laraby found another position as a valet. Alaina had offered him the position of being a companion to Arthur, but he'd declined. She was sure he felt it was below his skill set. Alaina was thankful the Hansons still worked for her as she trusted Tilda and Sven completely. Neither seemed disturbed that she ran the house and business. They had their own cottage, that Nathaniel had built for them, just down the road from the house. Between their presence in the house daily, and Nanny Prue, Alaina felt confident that the children were among good people who cared about them.

When Alaina was finally able to attend a monthly meeting of the suffrage association at Hedda's home in late summer, she was surprised by the cold shoulder she received from many of the other members.

"Did I do something to offend someone here?" she asked Hedda later that evening after the meeting.

"No, dear. The women are a little put out that you've asserted yourself in a man's world and actually go to a job every day. They feel that it is unladylike for a women of your position."

She was stunned. "Are you joking? These very women who are fighting for a woman's right to vote are not supporting my right to work?"

"I understand how you feel, Alaina," Hedda said sympathetically. "I'm sure their views come directly from their husbands. Men fear women with any type of power. By calling it unladylike, it sounds acceptable to condemn what you are doing. It's just another way to keep women in their place."

"And do you feel the same way?" she asked her friend.

"Absolutely not. I'm so proud of you and what you're accomplishing for your family. You have to remember, though, that these women were raised in high society families and only believe that women below them work. Terrible, I know. But unfortunately, with the country club set, it's true."

Alaina found she was being ignored at the club as well when she'd go to watch Arthur compete in sailing contests or have lunch with the children in the restaurant. Women wouldn't return her greeting and men ignored her completely. However, the club didn't have the nerve to ask her to quit because it was her husband who'd been a founding member, and she owned the land that the club hoped to buy someday to make the club's property larger.

To hell with them, Alaina thought one day when she was treated poorly there once again. She didn't need these snobs. Her life was her own and she'd do as she damned well pleased.

That fall, Paul Woodward, her lawyer, resigned from her service on the pretext that he was retiring. She knew that wasn't true, because he still did legal work for others at the club, but she was fine with his going. She immediately went on a search for a new lawyer. She hoped she could find one who was younger and more open to working with a woman.

She interviewed several men at the office but could practically feel their contempt from their stares. She needed someone who would understand both personal and business law, and that didn't leave her with many choices. Jonah found other attorneys for her to interview, but still she couldn't find the right fit. When he suggested she speak to a gentleman named Edward Freburg, she wrinkled her brow, trying to remember where she'd heard his name before.

"He's a member of the Great Heron Lake Yacht Club," Jonah explained. "He's particularly versed in business law, but also handles family law. He's very well-respected."

Alaina nodded. Now she remembered who he was. She'd met him at the last dance she and Nathaniel had attended together. Freburg's parents were club members and he only occasionally attended events there. She was doubtful he'd agree to be her lawyer. His mother and father were among the people who felt she was no longer good enough for their crowd now that she worked.

She asked Jonah to set up a meeting with him anyway, and he did, but Freburg suggested they meet at the yacht club on a Friday afternoon since he'd be up for the weekend. She agreed, and on the appointed day, took the earlier train home and headed for the club.

Alaina was thankful the late afternoon crowd was light. The fewer people gossiping about her meeting, the better. She arrived early and asked to be seated at a table by the window with a view of the lake. No sooner had she sat than Mr. Freburg approached.

"Good afternoon, Mrs. Madison," he said, offering his outstretched hand. "I'm so happy we could meet."

Alaina accepted his hand and shook it, although she remained seated. "It's nice to meet you, too. Please, sit down. I was just about to order tea."

"Thank you. That sounds wonderful."

As he sat, Alaina studied him. He looked young, but she knew he wasn't much younger than her own age of thirty-four. He was tall and seemed to be in nice shape under his three-piece suit. He had thick, sandy blond hair and a handsome face with a square jawline. His eyes were a deep blue, and she noticed they didn't regard her with utter contempt. His gaze was friendly.

The waiter appeared with a tea service and another waiter brought a tray of small sandwiches, cakes, and cookies. Alaina took it upon herself to serve the tea.

"Thank you," Edward said. After taking a sip, he sat up straighter and asked, "What can I help you with, Mrs. Madison?"

She smiled. She liked that he wanted to get directly to business. "I'm looking for a lawyer to handle any business and personal dealings," she said. "We deal with many contracts from suppliers, as well as employee contracts. Issues come up during the year, and sometimes I would need legal advice."

"I see." He smiled. "And would this be a regular position or a retainer?"

"A retainer," she said. "You'd be free to work with other clients as well, as long as I could contact you when needed."

"It sounds exactly like the type of work I do," he told her. He placed a small sandwich on his plate and began to eat it. She liked that he didn't appear nervous around her.

"Would you be interested in the position?" she asked.

"Yes. Would I be working directly with you or do you have a manager who I'll be working with?"

Here it is, she thought. *He's thinking that he doesn't want to work with a woman.*

"You'll be working directly with me," she told him. "Will it bother you to work for a woman?"

His brows rose, but then he smiled. "Not at all. I take it that other male lawyers have had an issue with that."

"Everyone has had an issue with that," she said, sitting back in her chair. "And everyone has an opinion, from the manager I had to dismiss to the women in the suffrage association. Apparently, it's unladylike to work." She looked him in the eye. "Do you feel this way, Mr. Freburg?"

He shook his head. "Not at all."

"Well. That's refreshing," she said.

He chuckled, then apologized. "I'm sorry. I didn't mean to laugh. I'm sure you're running into all sorts of obstacles."

She grinned. "It's fine. I have to laugh about it sometimes or I'll burst. I have run into many obstacles. But for the most part, the men I work with seem to have accepted the fact that they're working for a woman, and some are even warming up to it. I was raised by a father who believed women were as intelligent, if not more intelligent, than men. He trusted me not only to take care of his finances, but also help make decisions with his factory. And my husband was more open-minded than most. I need a good group of people around me who are willing to forget that I'm a woman and get on with what is best for the business."

"Well, it might be difficult to forget that you're a woman," Edward said. "But I have no qualms about helping you do what is best for your company."

Alaina felt a blush rise to her cheeks. Surely, he hadn't meant his comment as a compliment. Still wearing her mourning black and looking quite plain, she doubted he was flirting with her. "That sounds wonderful," she finally said. "When can you start?"

"Right now, if need be."

She laughed. "I'm sure I won't be needing any legal advice

today, unless the cook has tried to poison me. It seems I am somewhat of a pariah here these days. They don't dare ask me to leave, though. After all, my husband helped establish this club."

"If it will make you feel any better, I'll let you in on a little secret," he said, moving forward in his chair and whispering conspiratorially. "My mother, who I believe has been snubbing you, was a working woman when she met my father."

"No," Alaina said, leaning in closer. "What did she do?"

"She worked in a hotel as a maid. My father worked there too, and that's how they met. It was his dream to open his own hotel, and together, they did. Now, he owns several of the most prestigious hotels in multiple cities. So don't let my mother and her cronies get you down. Many worked their way up from nothing. They've apparently contracted amnesia and forgotten those days."

Alaina placed a hand over her mouth, trying not to laugh out loud. She knew that she and Edward Freburg were going to get along quite nicely.

Chapter Thirty-Five

Marla

Marla and the other ladies had a good laugh over what she'd just read from the journal.

"What a bunch of snobs those women were," Wanda said. "But I do like that Edward character."

"Yes. He seems charming," Ardie said. "Perhaps a love interest for Alaina in the future?" She waggled her eyebrows.

"That's how I would write it if it were a novel," Rita offered dreamily.

Marla sat back and smiled. They were at Wanda's house, sitting out on the back patio enjoying the evening breeze after another hot July day. Wanda loved to garden, and since she had the entire summer off, she put her energy into her backyard. Plenty of flowering bushes and roses edged the fence line, birches and crabapple trees sat in the center, and large flowerpots thick with colorful blooms rested on the stone patio. It was a beautiful yard to escape to after a long day.

"I guess we'll see how it ends soon," Marla said, flipping through the last few pages left. "I'm hoping for a happy ending after all she's been through."

"Yes. We all need her to have a happy ending," Toni agreed.

"What about you, Marla? How is your project going? And I'm eager to hear—did you buy the house?" Ardie asked.

Everyone perked up, waiting for her answer as Toni smiled knowingly.

"I got the house," Marla said, bringing cheers from all the women.

"Congratulations!" Ardie reached over and hugged her. "I'm so happy for you. When do you move in?"

"Not for at least three months," Marla said. "And I might wait longer if I decide to do a little painting before moving in. I'll see how it looks after all their furniture is out."

"Are you excited?" Rita asked, clapping her hands together. "I know I would be."

"Yes. Very. It'll be strange, not living in that big cavern of a house anymore, but it'll be nice, too. I never really felt at home there. This place felt like home the first time I walked into it."

"Have you talked to Reese yet about selling the mansion?" Toni asked.

She nodded. "I did. Last Saturday we got together for lunch and I told her all about my plans for the women's shelter and even took her to see the old factory. She was impressed, which is big, coming from her. Then I hit her with the bomb that I'd also bought a house."

"How did she take it?" Ardie asked, turning serious.

"She was shocked. Then, after I told her about it, she warmed to the idea. She said she understood why I'd want something smaller. I asked if she'd like to keep the mansion in the family so she could have it later on. She was very adamant that she never wanted to own it. She said it was too large to maintain and she'd always think of it as the house her father died in. I can't blame her for that. I feel the same way."

"Wow," Rita said. "She does know her own mind. It sounds like she adored her father. I know I wouldn't want to live in a house where someone I loved died."

Marla nodded. "I won't even go in that room anymore. For me, it's a room of sadness, where I watched him wither away for months on end. There are just too many unhappy memories in that room, and the house now."

"Are you afraid his ghost will come and get you?" Wanda teased.

Marla chuckled. "No. Nothing like that. It's just a sad room. It always seemed sad to me. Maybe new owners can make it a happy space."

"I'm sure someone will," Toni said. "But you still have time to decide what to do with the place. Don't rush into anything. It hasn't been that long since your husband died."

"Yeah, I know. But this feels right. At least, buying the cottage feels right. And starting the shelter. Hopefully, everything will go well."

As Wanda refilled their wine glasses, Marla updated them on everything she'd accomplished with the shelter so far. "It's a waiting game, though," Marla said. "But I have the time to wait. There's so much to do to get this project off the ground."

"If you need any help, let me know," Wanda said. "I know a lot of people who'd be happy to donate their time to teach you how the system works. And you can even volunteer at a couple of places to get a feel for it."

Marla brightened. "That's a great idea. I'll call Sheila and see if I can shadow her or volunteer. It would be a big help to see how a place is run."

The next day Marla spoke to Sheila. She said she'd be happy to have her come to the shelter and work with her for a few days. "And you can volunteer for the hotline too, if you'd like. You'll want to have one at your place too. When women leave their husbands or boyfriends, they need help right away. So you'll want a toll-free number they can call any time of the day or night."

Marla had thought of that, too. It would be helpful to be trained on how to handle calls.

After talking to Sheila, Marla wandered into the kitchen. Mrs. Cooper was busy baking chocolate-chip cookies. "Oh. These smell good," Marla said. "Do you mind?"

"They're for you and anyone who visits," she said. "Help yourself."

Marla poured a glass of ice water and took one of the warm cookies. "Delicious," she said, sitting on a stool.

Mrs. Cooper studied her a moment. "Do you have something on your mind?"

Marla hesitated. She'd been dreading this conversation ever since she'd learned the cottage was hers. She didn't want to upset Mrs. Cooper, but she knew she had to tell her. "Yes. I do. I bought a smaller house on the lake. It's the cottage over on the point that you can see from our dock."

Mrs. Cooper stopped working and raised one eyebrow. "Really? That's interesting. What are you going to do with it?"

"Well, I plan on moving into it in a few months," Marla said.

"I see." The older woman resumed her work, carefully dropping dollops of batter on a cookie sheet. "Are you telling me you won't be needing a housekeeper any longer?"

"I'm not sure," Marla said truthfully. "I mean, you could still work for me there, if you want to. It's definitely a smaller home than this one, but if you wanted to cook for me, you could. Or, you can finally retire and enjoy life a little. I guess I'm leaving it up to you."

The housekeeper nodded. "Well, that's interesting. I'm sure a few months ago you would have been happy to be rid of me. What's changed?"

"You just grew on me, I guess." Marla grinned.

Mrs. Cooper's eyes slid to Marla. "Like mold?"

Marla broke out laughing. "No. Not like mold. I want you to work as long as you want to. And if you don't, that's fine too. I'm going to leave it up to you."

Mrs. Cooper placed a cookie sheet in the oven and set the timer. "What about this house? Will you close it up?"

"I'll probably sell it," she said.

The older woman's eyes darted up to hers. "Sell it? It's been in the family for over a century. What does Reese say about that?"

"She agrees with selling it," Marla said calmly. "She doesn't want to keep it for herself, either. This was Nathan's house, and all the Madisons who came before him. She said she didn't think she would ever feel comfortable in this space again after her father died here."

Mrs. Cooper shook her head. "Such a shame."

"I agree," Marla said.

"You do?"

"Yes. It would be nice to keep it in the family, but it would be a waste to let it sit here empty and rot for years, too. Houses need people to keep them alive. Maybe a new family will bring life back to this house."

Mrs. Cooper seemed to be considering this. "Maybe," she finally said. "Can I let you know later what I decide?"

"Sure. There's no rush. It'll be another three months before

I can even try to move into the cottage. Take your time." Marla stood and set her glass in the dishwasher. As she was getting ready to leave, Mrs. Cooper spoke.

"Marla?"

She spun around, surprised she'd called her by her first name. "Yes?"

"Thank you for thinking of me and giving me the opportunity to stay on," Mrs. Cooper said. She sounded sincere.

"You're welcome. And I mean it. I'd be happy to have you work there."

Mrs. Cooper nodded, then went back to her work. Marla smiled. She hadn't meant to invite her to work at the cottage but had done so anyway. And in truth, she was happy she did. Life would be strange without even a little dose of Mrs. Cooper every day.

Who knew she'd ever think that?

* * *

Marla's days went by in a blur. She spent time discussing her plan with Anthony as well as writing up her proposal for the city counsel meeting in August. She also shadowed Sheila at the shelter and trained with another woman on how to answer calls on the hotline. The first time she manned the line, she was nervous. But once she began taking calls, she grew more confident. Talking with the women was heartbreaking, but she felt good knowing she was responsible for getting them the help they needed.

"It's a difficult job," Sheila said after the first time Marla had managed the phone. "But it's rewarding. You have to be able to take the emotion out of it, though, and not bring that home.

That's not always easy to do."

Marla knew she was right. For days afterward, she thought about the calls she'd taken. She realized that not only would she need professional help available for women who came to the shelter, but she'd need to make sure there was help available for the volunteers and workers as well. There was so much to consider to ensure the shelter ran smoothly.

She talked to Alden about this when they took walks together. She no longer just hoped to meet him on the trail. They'd started calling each other to schedule their walks. She liked him. He was smart and kind, and he was a good person to bounce problems off.

"It sounds daunting," he said on a warm August afternoon as they strolled along the water's edge. "But I've no doubt you can handle it. Will you be completely hands-on at the shelter or simply managing it?"

"In the beginning I want to be hands-on, just so I understand the complexities of each position. After that, I think I'll be more of a manager, or maybe just involved in the fundraising. That will be a full-time job in itself."

He nodded. "I'm sure it will be. It'll be expensive running a place like that. But you know a lot of people with money, so that should help."

Marla grimaced. "That's true. I do. I hate the thought of begging the same people over and over again for money. I'm going to try to come up with community fundraisers that everyone can be involved in, not just the uber rich. But I'm way ahead of myself. I have to get the city's approval first."

"When is that meeting?"

"August twenty-first. Anthony is going to accompany me and so is James, the architect. I've written up a good plan with

Sheila's help. She's attending too. She knows a couple of people on the board. It's nerve-wracking just thinking about it."

"Want me to come for moral support?" he asked.

She smiled. Alden was fast becoming a good friend she could depend on, and that both warmed her heart and scared her. She wasn't ready to depend on a man. Maybe not ever. "That would be nice of you, but you don't have to. My friends are all going to be there, too."

"Aren't I your friend?" he asked, looking hurt.

"Of course you are," she said quickly.

He smiled. "Then I'll be there. I want to support you."

"Okay. Thanks." She looked down at the trail as they walked, wondering if she was leading him on in any way. She didn't want to do that.

"So quiet all of a sudden," he said. "What's wrong?"

She looked up at him. "I'm glad we're friends. But I'm afraid you might think it could lead to something more."

"I won't lie," he said seriously. "I'd love for our relationship to be something more. But I also know that your husband just passed and I'm not in any hurry. I don't mind being friends for as long as it takes. Or, forever, if that's what happens."

"Are you sure? There are a few eligible women at the club who have their eye on you."

He pretended to shudder. "No thank you. I wouldn't be able to keep them in diamonds and Botox."

Marla chuckled. "What makes you think I don't use Botox? My face could be full of it."

"Right. I can see when you smile your face hardly moves." He winked. "Let's just see where this goes. Until then, I'm happy to have a friend. You know, until I met you, I hadn't made any good friends here. You're the first 'real' person I've met."

She smiled. She liked that he was fine with keeping things casual for a while. Because if she were honest with herself, she really liked Alden and it would be easy to fall for him. She just needed to take things slowly.

Thursday night the book club met at Ardie's house where they caught up over a pot-luck meal everyone had contributed to, then finally sat down to read in her living room. Marla opened the journal and began to read Alaina's neatly-written script.

Once I became used to my routine of working each day, it was easier. Thank goodness for Tilda and Nanny Prue during this busy time. Arthur was at boarding school in town, which also helped, and I knew that Ella was always well-cared for by those two wonderful women. Oddly enough, my life was full of men. Men who worked for me, men who I dealt with to purchase items for the stores, and men in the banking and finance system. Sometimes, I'd visit the sales floor of one of the stores just to see other women who worked. Or stop by the factory to visit with the sewing women. It was refreshing to be around women who understood how hard it was to be a working mother. Because men didn't understand. They never felt guilty for not being there for their children. I, on the other hand, did, and battled that throughout the next few years.

Chapter Thirty-Six

Alaina

The first year after Nathaniel's death flew by and Alaina was stunned when the anniversary of his passing came along. She'd been so busy, she would have forgotten the date if she hadn't been reminded by Hedda, who inquired about the club honoring Nathaniel for all he'd contributed to the Great Heron Lake Yacht Club.

"That's a wonderful idea," Alaina said when Hedda approached her. "What do you have in mind?"

She explained that they wanted to honor him at the June Ball, and she wondered if there might be a portrait of Nathanial she could donate to hang in the men's library.

There was one, and Alaina happily donated it. It was a portrait of Nathaniel from before Alaina had married him, and he'd always hated it. "I don't even know why I commissioned it other than out of vanity," he'd told her that first time she'd toured the house on Summit Avenue. When they'd moved to the lake house, he'd had it stored in the attic. That was where Alaina found it.

The week before the ball, Alaina was in her office with Edward—with the door open, of course—discussing some legal matters regarding the possibility of opening a store in Des Moines, Iowa. She was no longer wearing her mourning black, but instead wore a cream suit with pinstripes and a ruffled blouse underneath. It felt good to finally be able to wear light-colored clothing again.

Edward smiled at her when their discussion concluded. "I hear they're honoring your husband at the ball this weekend."

"Ah, yes, they are. Will you be attending?" Alaina asked.

"I'm planning to. But I hate to go alone. I was wondering if perhaps you'd let me escort you."

Alaina sat quietly a moment, studying him, trying to read his intentions. She liked Edward. He was polite and fun to be around. They'd eaten lunch together a couple of times and he'd always been a gentleman. But it might be awkward to see a man socially who she was working with. Correction. He was working *for* her. Her silence must have made him guess her thoughts.

"I'd only be your escort. Very platonic. I'd be on my best behavior," he assured her with a grin.

"I appreciate your offer. It would be nice not to arrive alone, like an elderly aunt no one knows what to do with," she said.

Edward chuckled. "You're not an elderly aunt. You're not elderly. We'll have a good time, I promise."

"What if we meet at the ball and sit together?" she asked. "I'll have my driver bring me. I think that will look more proper than you coming to my house to pick me up. Especially since it is my late husband they're honoring."

"That will be fine. Very proper indeed," he said, amusement in his eyes. "I'll inform the hostess that I'll be sitting at your table. That way you won't have the embarrassment of explaining why."

Alaina folded her hands in front of her on the desk. "Thank you." She smiled. "I've been dreading this ball. Now, I think it might be fun after all."

The evening of the ball, Alaina was helped by Velma into the new dress she'd had made especially for this night. It was a deep blue satin with a scoop neck and short, puffy sleeves. White lace trimmed the neckline, waist, and hem, and she wore white elbow-length gloves. She'd asked for the dress to be made simple compared to the exaggerated styles of the day. Velma pulled Alaina's hair up in an elaborate style, leaving soft tendrils at the base of her neck. A silver comb with diamonds and sapphires decorated her chestnut hair and she wore the sapphire necklace and earrings Nathaniel had given her after Ella's birth.

"You look lovely!" Velma exclaimed as she studied her reflection in the mirror.

"Thanks to your expertise with hair." Alaina smiled graciously at her. Although Velma had been her ladies' maid for seven years, she hadn't became the close friend or confidant that Emma had been. Velma was quite competent at her job, though, and Alaina was grateful she'd found such a good worker. She didn't live in the house, and Alaina wondered if that was why their relationship had never grown closer than employer and employee.

Velma handed Alaina her small clutch and wrap. "Will you need help undressing tonight or shall I go home after you leave?"

"Go ahead home," Alaina said. "I'm sure I can manage. And thank you for staying late tonight."

"Yes, ma'am," Velma said. "Have a good evening."

"Thank you."

It was a lovely, warm evening as Sven helped her inside the carriage for the short ride to the club. Alaina stared up into the pale blue sky, reflecting on her life. She missed Emma. And

Margaret, and Matthew, and most of all, her dear father and Hannah. He life had been simpler in the days before she married Nathaniel. She didn't regret her marriage to him, because she had her beautiful children to show for it, but she still grew sad when she thought about all the people she'd lost. No matter how much she'd accomplished, she missed having loved ones to share it all with.

Upon arriving, they had to wait in a long line of carriages before they drew up to the entryway. Standing there patiently waiting for her was Edward.

He opened the door and helped her out. Smiling appreciatively, he said, "Good evening, Alaina. You look beautiful."

Alaina could feel the warmth of a blush rise to her cheeks. She knew then that this was what she missed. A companion who understood her, and appreciated her. Edward had understood her from the moment they'd met. It felt odd, suddenly realizing that here, as she gazed up at him.

She waved to Sven and he drove off. He'd be back later to pick her up after the event.

"You look very handsome, too," she said. His black tuxedo with long tails fit him impeccably, but his smile was his greatest asset. It was genuine and always lit up his eyes. This thought surprised her. She hadn't thought that way about a man, not even Nathaniel, in a very long time.

Edward offered his arm and she slid hers through as they entered the club's ballroom.

Music drifted through the large room from the band at the far end and the chandeliers sent shimmering light over the gleaming oak floors. The club had recently upgraded to electrical lighting, thanks to the tireless fundraising by the club ladies. The French doors on the far end were wide open and strings of lights brightened the outside deck that overlooked the lake. Tables draped in white cloths were set up with fine china and silverware on one side of the ballroom and the rest was open for dancing later.

They found their table and sat, and immediately a waiter delivered glasses of champagne.

Edward lifted his glass to her. "To a beautiful evening."

"To a beautiful evening," she said before clinking her glass with his.

Hedda and her husband, Albert, soon joined them along with two other couples who were ladies Alaina had known through her volunteer and suffrage work in town. Everyone was polite but cool toward Alaina, and she could tell they were dying to ask why Edward was sitting with her. After letting them stew a bit, Alaina finally said, "Mr. Freburg is my new attorney. He graciously offered to escort me tonight since I was coming alone."

The chill at the table subsided and warmed after that. Everyone must have decided it was acceptable for them to be seen together since they had a business relationship.

After the five-course dinner, Albert, one of the founding members of the yacht club, gave a moving speech honoring Nathaniel, then unveiled the portrait that would be hung in the library. After that, the band began to play, and the dance floor filled with couples.

"That was a lovely speech," Alaina told Albert. "Nathaniel would be honored to be thought of so highly."

"Thank you," the older man said, his eyes shining brightly. "Perhaps you will honor me with a dance?"

"Only if your wife doesn't mind," Alaina said.

"Go along," Hedda said, waving them away. "I'll be fine."

As Arthur led Alaina to the dance floor, she noticed that

Edward acted the gentleman and asked Hedda to dance as well. After a time, Edward cut in on Albert, and they happily danced far away from the other couple.

"Thank you for saving me," Alaina whispered, relieved.

"Albert is much too short for you. His eyes were in the wrong place." Edward grinned mischievously.

Alaina looked appalled. "That is quite disturbing."

"Me? Or Him?"

"Both of you." She chuckled and so did he.

Edward wasn't too short for Alaina, they fit perfectly together and he was a fine dancer. It felt nice being in his arms and twirling around the floor. Alaina felt alive again. All her cares and stresses melted away. It had been much too long since she'd felt that way.

As the night wound down, Alaina told Edward that she was ready to go home. He walked her outside and they saw Sven waiting with the carriage. Gallantly, Edward took Alaina's hand and kissed it.

"I had a wonderful evening," he said. "I hope you'll allow me to escort you to other functions as well. I'm sure there is a ball or two this summer. Or perhaps the Independence Day celebration they have here at the club."

"The children usually join me for the Independence Day festivities," she said. She felt he should know how important her children were to her.

Edward brightened. "Marvelous! The more the merrier. Shall I arrange to accidentally run into you that day right here at the club?"

Alaina laughed. She couldn't help it. Edward was so full of life and mischief. "I guess that could be arranged." She sobered. "It's been over a year since Nathaniel passed, but I'm in no rush to find another husband. I feel that you must know that before becoming too involved with me or the children."

Edward turned serious also. He held her gloved hand and his blue eyes met hers. "I understand. And I'm in no rush, either. Let's enjoy each other's company and see what the future holds."

She nodded. He helped her into the carriage and waved as she drove away into the night.

* * *

That summer Edward found ways to inconspicuously insert himself into Alaina's life and family. When she took all of July off from work to spend time with the children, he also took a month off and spent it at his parents' lake house. He invited Arthur to go sailing on his small yacht several times, much to the boy's delight. At fourteen, Arthur needed a male figure to emulate, and Alaina couldn't think of a better man for the job than Edward. He was always kind, polite, and a gentleman. Arthur hadn't had the benefit of his father's presence these past two years and it was beneficial that he had someone like Edward to spend time with.

In fact, Alaina was relieved at how well-adjusted the children were since losing their father. They had loved him, she knew, but he'd spent so little time in their day-to-day lives, she supposed they didn't feel the loss as deeply as one would think. In a way, despite it being sad, she was relieved it hadn't greatly upset their lives. At twelve and fourteen, they were at difficult stages and a deep grief for their father would have made things even harder for them.

The year moved on and Alaina was the happiest she'd been in years. She had her children, her home, and work that challenged her. But it was Edward who made all the difference. His presence brought joy to her life. He was all business and proper at the office and when they were in public, but he had a way of complimenting her that warmed her heart. He showed how much he cared in small ways, like sending her a card or flowers for no reason at all, being kind and attentive to the children, or simply listening to her when she became frustrated over a work situation. He never tried to tell her how to run her business, unless it was legal advice, and he always supported her decisions. He made her feel valued as an equal and wasn't afraid to let her know that was how he thought of her. It was both refreshing and endearing.

In 1893, The Minnesota Woman Suffrage Association had almost seen the passage of the right for women to vote, but the House didn't pass the bill. It was a huge defeat for women's rights after years of working toward that moment, and was discouraging for Alaina personally. After all the work she'd put into the cause, once again they'd been defeated.

In May of that same year, another disaster hit. The New York stock market had a sudden drop, causing it to crash in June as people panicked and sold out. As a result, banks closed, railroads stopped expanding, and businesses shut down across the country. It was all Alaina could do, with the help of Edward's advice and Jonah's knowledgeable management, to keep the stores in operation. Owning the textile plant was a saving factor, but she fought to keep that open, as well. It was impossible to obtain credit from banks, so she relied on her own savings and the profits from the businesses to keep the business lucrative. Her biggest fear was losing all the money she'd accumulated to date and not having anything to leave the children. It plagued her constantly.

"What if I lose everything?" she asked Edward one fall

evening after dinner at the manor. Ella had gone off to her room to study and they were alone in the great room.

"You won't," he assured her. "You've done a wonderful job so far of staving off disaster. St. Paul, thank goodness, is still a thriving community and thankfully not hurt as badly as the rest of the country. I know you can pull through this."

She gazed at him in wonder. "You're always so encouraging. I haven't had anyone believe in me so sincerely since my father."

"He was right to believe in you." Edward moved forward in his seat, closer to her. "Look at what you've accomplished since Nathaniel's death. Look at how you manage your family and home. Your children are doing extremely well, and your businesses are also. You're remarkable, Alaina. Why do you think all the women at the club envy you? You're accomplishing so much, all on your own."

"Well, not all on my own," she said. "I have you, and Jerome to run the factory, and Jonah to help manage the department stores. And Nanny Prue to help with Ella. And, of course, the Hansons, who keep this place running smoothly. I couldn't do all this without my friends and loyal staff."

"That's true." He laughed. "What would you do without me?" Tenderly, he kissed her cheek. "I hope you feel you cannot do without me, because I need you in my life."

She gazed into his kind eyes and knew she couldn't live without him, either. As much as she feared the thought of marriage again, and being owned by a husband, she did want to be with Edward.

"I'm happy you're in my life," she said. "Hiring you was the smartest thing I've ever done." She grinned mischievously at him.

"Oh, is that how it's going to be?" He winked, then he spoke more seriously. "When will you be ready to accept my proposal to become Mrs. Freburg?" He'd proposed to her once already and she'd told him she had to wait a bit longer.

"I just need more time. Marriage scares me. I was lost in my marriage to Nathaniel. Even though I was able to do some things I enjoyed, I always knew he could change my life without my permission at any time. He moved me to this lake house without even asking if that was what I wanted. I don't want to be owned again."

"I'd never own you," Edward said tenderly. "No one can. You have proven how capable you are at handling your life. I just want to share my life with you."

"A little more time. That's all I ask," she said softly as she raised a hand to caress the side of his face.

He kissed her lips in a way that made her want for more. "I'll wait as long as it takes," he assured her.

Knowing that gave Alaina comfort for the times ahead.

Chapter Thirty-Seven

Marla

"Marry him!" Rita exclaimed after Marla had stopped reading. "What are you waiting for?"

All the women laughed.

"She's afraid, and I don't blame her," Wanda said. "Nathaniel treated her like he owned her. Look at how he banished her to the lake house. She's enjoying her freedom. Good for her!"

"I understand how she feels, too," Marla spoke up. "I'd be afraid to marry again. My Nathan was a good man, but he had his idiosyncrasies. After he died, I felt lost. I hadn't created a life of my own, and he hadn't encouraged me to do so. Now that I'm building a new life, I'd hate to give that up for anyone."

"Who says you'd have to give it up?" Toni asked. "Not all men are like your husband was. You'd just have to make it clear what you want out of the relationship from the start."

Marla nodded but Wanda harrumphed. "Look who's giving marriage advice. Miss 'I'm never getting married.'"

Toni shrugged. "Even I could marry someday. But it'll be on my terms."

"Well, I'm team Edward for Alaina," Rita said. When everyone laughed, she asked, "That's a thing, right?"

"That's a thing," Marla said. "I'm team Edward too."

Before saying goodbye, Marla reminded everyone that the date of the board meeting was the twenty-first. They all said they'd be there. The night after that they were going to Marla's house for book club.

"Let's hope we have something to celebrate that night," Ardie said.

"I'm bringing the wine," Toni said. "Because I know we'll be celebrating."

* * *

The next day, Marla finished her proposal for the city counsel and added the legal papers Anthony had drawn up, along with the drawings from the architect. She put copies in a large envelope and personally took them to city hall so they could be copied and sent to the board members prior to the meeting. Afterward, she called Alden.

"I just dropped off the plans for the shelter," she told him. "I feel like we need to celebrate. Do you want to meet for dinner?"

"Sure. Do you want to go to the club?"

She hesitated a moment. Should they go there? Would everyone stare? Then she thought how silly that sounded. She was a member and so was Alden. Why shouldn't they eat there?

Marla agreed and they set a time to meet. Once home, she changed into a casual summer dress and sandals and pulled her hair up. Alden picked her up a few minutes later in his shiny black convertible.

"Fancy car," she said, getting in. "I don't think I've ever seen it before."

"This is the first time I've driven you anywhere." He grinned. "You drove the first time we went out, remember?"

She laughed. "That's right. I forgot."

They arrived at the club a few minutes later and asked for a table on the outside deck. It was a lovely night, warm with a light breeze off the lake. It felt nice to be outdoors. After they ordered their drinks, Marla saw Vicki and Catrina making a beeline for their table.

"Uh oh," she said softly.

"What is it?" Alden asked, looking around.

The women arrived at the table before she could warn him.

"Hello, Marla," Vicki said sweetly. "It's been a while since I've seen you around."

"Hi, Vicki. Catrina. How have you both been?"

Vicki answered for both of them. "We're fine. And I see you're doing quite well for yourself." She glanced over at Alden. "Hello, Alden."

Alden smiled and nodded but said nothing.

Vicki turned back to Marla. "What have you been doing with yourself this summer? It must be very lonely sitting around that big house."

Marla resisted the urge to roll her eyes. "I've kept busy."

Vicki eyed Alden again. "Yes. I see you have."

Marla's blood began to boil. She should have known the gossip squad would be upset that she was with Alden. She tried hard to stay calm. "Alden has been a great help with a new project of mine. Tonight we're celebrating."

"You haven't been having him help you rip down wallpaper and painting walls, have you?" Vicki asked, her red lacquered lips smiling wickedly.

"No. In fact, I've just sent in a proposal to build a women's shelter in St. Paul on property I own by the river. It's a huge project and I'm very excited about it."

Catrina spoke up for the first time. "A women's shelter? What kind of shelter?"

"One for women and their children escaping abusive relationships," Marla said. "I've been working with an advocate at another shelter to learn all I can about what's needed. I plan on building a place where women can live while they're getting their lives back in order. It's a very worthy cause."

"That's wonderful," Catrina said, beaming. She got a side-eye from Vicki for her effort.

"What would you possibly know about battered women?" Vicki asked, crossing her arms.

Marla couldn't believe how Vicki was acting. She'd thought they were still friends, after the June Ball. Apparently, that wasn't the case. "A lot, actually. You don't have to be an abused woman to understand a need when you see it. I think it's up to all of us who have privileged lives to help others. Don't you?"

Catrina nodded enthusiastically, but Vicki glared at her. Marla always knew that Catrina was the nicest of the two women, but it was very evident right now.

"Well, if anyone can accomplish raising money and helping those in need, you can," Vicki said. "One thing you know well is how to *find* money." She glanced again at Alden.

"I also know how to earn my own money," Marla said sharply.

"And look at you," Vicki continued, ignoring Marla's words. "A few months as a widow and already out with the club's most eligible bachelor."

"Are you two a couple?" Catrina blurted out.

Marla held back a laugh as Vicki gave Catrina a nasty look. "We're good friends, yes," she told them. "But no. We're not a couple."

"Not yet," Alden added with a grin.

"I see," Vicki said. "I guess we'll be seeing you around then." She grabbed Catrina's hand and practically pulled her away as Catrina called "goodbye" over her shoulder.

Alden looked at Marla and they both started laughing.

"What a pair they are," Alden said.

"And they used to be my closest friends." Marla shook her head, feeling sad. It was so hard for her to believe how quickly people could turn on her.

"I'm sure they're very nice people," Alden said with a grimace.

"They used to be. Or at least I thought they were. But now, everyone acts differently around me. Either they've changed, or I have."

"I'm sure you've always been the way you are. But maybe you just didn't see others as clearly as you do now," Alden offered.

She nodded. "These past few months have been an eye-opener."

He reached across the table and took her hand. "I like you just the way you are. And that's coming from the most eligible bachelor at this club." He winked.

"Lucky me," she said, laughing.

* * *

A week later Marla found herself sitting in the city hall meeting room, surrounded by her book club friends, Sheila, Alden, Anthony, and the architect, James. To her surprise, Reese came in also and sat down beside her.

"I can't believe you made it," Marla whispered, hugging her daughter.

"I came to support you," she said. "It looks like you have quite a cheering squad already."

"I can always use one more. Especially when it's you," Marla said, thrilled to have everyone she cared about supporting her.

The meeting began and the board members went through their long agenda. When they finally came to Marla's request, they asked her to stand and tell them a little about her proposal. She did, adding that the building had been in the family for over a century and she wanted it to be utilized for a good and useful cause. After she spoke, they asked a few technical questions that Anthony and James could answer.

The chairman spoke once all their questions had been answered. "Your proposal is a good one and we have much to consider. We'd like to discuss this further among ourselves, but as far as I can see, there shouldn't be any problems. We'll call you when we've made our decision."

Marla was overjoyed to hear that her plan had a good chance of being approved but forced herself not to get too excited. Everything could change if anyone brought up a complaint. "Thank you," she told the committee.

Afterward, everyone gathered outside the meeting room.

"It sounds positive," Anthony said. "Why don't we move ahead with the licenses and permits in the hope they say yes."

Marla agreed. She wanted to move forward and think positively. They all walked a short distance to a little pub and went inside for a drink.

"You did a great job in there, Mom," Reese said after everyone had been introduced and ordered. "I'm sure they'll okay it."

"I hope so," she said.

"They seemed impressed," Sheila told her. "I'm so excited for you. This is a wonderful thing you're doing."

When the drinks came, they all raised their glasses. "To success in helping others," Alden said.

"Now that's something I can toast to," Wanda added. And they all clinked their glasses together.

* * *

The next morning when Mrs. Cooper brought Marla's tea into the morning room, she asked how the meeting had gone.

"Very well, thank you," Marla said. "The board sounded positive about it. They just wanted to discuss it further before letting me know."

"I hope they approve it. There's no reason not to. It's a worthy cause," Mrs. Cooper said.

Marla brightened. "Thank you. I think it is too."

The housekeeper lingered a moment, then spoke. "I've been thinking about you moving into the cottage soon. I've decided that when you do, I'm going to retire."

"Oh?" Marla stared in surprise at Mrs. Cooper. "Are you sure?"

She nodded. "Yes. I would like to do a little traveling before I get too old. I've already registered for a cruise around the Caribbean in November. I've always wanted to see that part of the world. Next year, I may even take a European tour. It will wear me out, but it will be fun."

"Wow. That's wonderful," Marla said. "So it's official? You'll no longer be working for the Madisons starting in November?"

"Yes. I've been working in this house for fifty years. I think that's a good number to end it on. Don't you?"

Unexpected emotions welled up inside Marla. She walked over to Mrs. Cooper and hugged her.

"What is all this nonsense?" Mrs. Cooper asked, although she hugged her back.

Marla pulled away. "I think fifty years of service to one family deserves at least a hug."

The housekeeper laughed. "I guess it does. But you aren't rid of me yet. I'll be around a couple more months."

Marla smiled. "Good. I'd hate to have to get my own tea every morning."

Mrs. Cooper brushed her teasing aside with her hand and left the room.

Marla sat back down and looked around her. She'd been wrong about so many things. Mrs. Cooper wasn't such a bad person after all. She'd just misunderstood her. And this room, it wasn't Marla's office. It was Alaina's morning room, even though Alaina hadn't liked the wallpaper either. When Marla left this house, she'd be leaving behind decades of Madisons who'd called these rooms their home. But she was okay with that. It was time she had a space of her own, a place she could relax and enjoy her second act. She liked how that second act was shaping up.

* * *

That night, the women gathered at Marla's house for what would be the final reading from Alaina's journal. After snacking on an array of hor d'oeuvres made by Mrs. Cooper, they sat down in the living room on the cushy sofas.

"Are we ready for this to end?" Marla asked, glancing around at her friends.

"No," Rita said. "But everything has to end eventually."

Marla nodded. Then she began to read.

The years flew by so fast that I have rarely had time to write in this journal. So much has happened since I started it. I was reading some of the first pages and couldn't believe how much my life has changed, and I have changed. The businesses survived the Panic of 1893, hanging on as best we could, but it took years to recover and any thought of expansion of the stores was tabled. Arthur graduated from prep school in 1896 and continued on to the Minneapolis Business College for a degree in business and finance. He's grown into a handsome, studious young man of which I am so proud. And my Ella grew into a beautiful woman, who at age eighteen, I presented to society despite my mixed feelings about that tradition.

Chapter Thirty-Eight

Alaina

"I feel as if I am selling my daughter to the highest bidder," Alaina complained to Edward on an unusually warm day in late April of 1898. She'd rented a house on Summit Avenue in St. Paul for the "coming out" season. Edward was staying in a home that belonged to his uncle, not far away.

"You're not *selling* your daughter," Edward said soothingly. "She is happily attending the events and balls and will enjoy the attentions of several young, dashing men. Don't you remember how much fun you had during your coming out season?"

Alaina grimaced. "I had no fun at all. If it hadn't been for my dear friend, Hannah, it would have been excruciating. We had fun together, though." She smoothed her hand over her already perfect chignon that now had strands of silver running through it. Alaina smiled, remembering her and Hannah dancing with all the shy young men and then giggling over their clumsiness. How young and unaware they'd been, and how much fun they'd had together.

Edward stood up to pour himself another drink and kissed

her cheek on the way to the bar. They'd eaten at Alaina's home that evening while Ella, accompanied by her new ladies' maid, Tessa Carson, was attending a small get-together at one of the other young ladies' homes. Alaina trusted the young maid to watch over her daughter. Tessa was a smart girl of twenty-three who seemed to be enjoying Ella's coming out season as much as Ella was.

"The season has just begun," Edward said, handing her a glass of red wine. "Try to enjoy it. Ella is a smart young lady. She won't marry the first handsome man who looks her way."

"I won't let her," Alaina said determinedly.

Edward studied her. "Hmm. I understand why you're wary of marriage, but why wouldn't you want Ella to marry? If the right man comes along, that is."

She looked over at Edward, sorry she'd sounded so harsh. Over the years, he'd proposed several times and each time she asked him to wait. She was thankful he hadn't grown tired of asking, but she couldn't keep him waiting forever. "I'm not wary of marriage. Well, I am, but not of marriage with you. I'm just waiting for the right time. As soon as Arthur is ready to take over the business, and I know that Ella will be able to take care of herself, then I can look forward to my future."

He smiled, his sparkling blue eyes still gorgeous despite the creases that had begun to form at the edges. "I know. I only want what's best for you and Arthur and Ella too. I can wait."

Her heart warmed. She felt so lucky to have him in her life. "Ella has expressed a desire to attend a women's college. I'm encouraging her to do so. I wish I'd been able to continue my education, but women didn't back then. If my father hadn't taught me accounting and finance, I wouldn't be as successful as I am today."

"Oh, I think you would have managed if you'd wanted to."
Edward winked. "You're a pretty determined woman when you
want to be."

"True," she said with a grin.

Throughout the three-month coming out season, Alaina
and Edward attended many of the balls and dinners given for
the young ladies to meet eligible young men. Alaina watched
with interest as her beautiful daughter danced and conversed
with several handsome men, some a few years older than her.
She worried Ella might become infatuated with one of the older
men and hoped it wouldn't happen. She wanted her daughter to
choose wisely, and for Alaina, that meant waiting until she was a
little older than the tender age of eighteen to find a mate.

"Are you enjoying your season?" Alaina asked her daughter
one evening after they'd returned home from a dance. She sat in
Ella's bedroom and watched as Tessa combed out her long, dark
hair.

"Oh, yes, Mother. It's been such fun. Everyone has been very
welcoming and friendly."

Alaina smiled. Her daughter had the brightest personality
and was much more sociable than she'd been at her age. "I'm
happy you've been enjoying yourself. Has any young man caught
your eye?" she asked, quietly holding her breath.

Ella looked up in the mirror and caught her mother's eyes
with her own. With a mischievous grin she said, "I thought you
didn't want me to find a husband this season."

"Oh." Alaina was at a loss for words. She'd never actually
said that to her daughter, but perhaps her daughter had sensed
her feelings.

"Thank you, Tessa," Ella said. "You may go off to bed now."
Tessa nodded, said goodnight, and was gone, leaving mother and

daughter alone. Ella turned on her stool and faced her mother. "Is there a young man you have thought suitable for me?"

"Darling, I would never presume to choose a man for you," Alaina said. "That is your choice alone. And I have only said that you don't have to marry so soon because I want you to feel you have choices. You're so young. I don't want you to regret marrying the wrong man."

"I've seen the other mothers working fervently behind the scenes, encouraging their daughters to flirt with this or that man. You haven't pushed me in any one direction, and I'm thankful for that. There are a great many handsome men, but to be honest, Mother, not one of them interests me."

Alaina sighed with relief, making Ella laugh.

"Do you not want me to marry, Mother?"

"No, dear. I think it would be wonderful for you to marry when you're ready. I just don't want you to marry too soon. You've spoken of continuing your education. Or continuing dance. I'd be happy for you to do whatever pleases you."

Ella's eyes sparkled as she crossed the space between them and sat down beside her Mother. "To tell the truth, I'm looking forward to returning to the lake house and spending time with my friends there. I had hoped we'd be back before the June ball. I'd enjoy going to that this year, now that I'm old enough."

Alaina studied her daughter a moment. It had never occurred to her that Ella might have a crush on a boy she grew up with, or perhaps one of Arthur's friends. Or maybe she just wanted to go home with no other intentions. "I'd love to go home, too," she told her. "And we can certainly cut this season short and attend the yacht club's ball instead."

Ella brightened and reached out to hug her mother. "Thank you! I think that will be great fun."

* * *

The night of the yacht club ball, Edward escorted both Alaina and Ella. Arthur, home from school for the summer, also attended. Alaina watched her children from the sidelines as they danced with young people they'd known nearly all their lives. She noticed that Arthur preferred dancing with a lovely dark-haired girl who she recognized as Hedda and Albert Edling's daughter, Christine. What surprised her, though, was the attention Ella was giving to Adam, a college friend of Arthur who'd visited the house for the past two summers and was attending the ball. He was tall and lean with thick dark hair and a warm smile that he gave to Ella only.

"I guess I know now why Ella was so excited to attend this ball," Alaina said to Edward as they danced together.

"You mean her crush on Arthur's friend Adam? Are you telling me that this is the first you've noticed?"

Alaina's eyes widened. "You knew she liked him? Why didn't you ever say anything?"

He grinned. "Because I knew you'd want her to go through her season first just to make sure she didn't meet anyone else she preferred. And it was good for her. She learned a great deal about how to handle men these past three months. But I think her heart is set on this one."

"Well, I'm shocked. I thought he was just a friend. I had no idea she's been sweet on him this entire time," Alaina said, then frowned. "I do hope she still wants to continue her education first, though."

"He'll be in school a while longer. He's studying to be a lawyer. She'll have a couple more years to wait and decide what is right for her."

"That's good," Alaina said, relieved. "And will we be having a wedding soon for Arthur and Christine? I see they are quite close."

"Arthur is a smart young man. He'll want to finish school first too," Edward said. "But if it's a wedding you want, you do have an offer of your own."

Alaina moved in closer to Edward, their cheeks touching. "Soon, I promise," she said. "Soon."

* * *

Arthur graduated from the university in the class of 1900 and began working alongside his mother to learn the business. She started him in the textile factory under Jerome's tutelage, so he'd understand how important it was to their business. After that, he worked with each of the six managers in their stores, learning how the department stores operated from the ground floor up. She thought it was a good way for him to appreciate the hard work of all the employees so he'd be able to manage the stores with first-hand knowledge. To his credit, Arthur never complained. He worked hard and earned the respect of each manager as well as Jerome's.

Two years after graduating, he and Christine Edling were married in a lavish production set up by Hedda and Albert with a large reception of friends and family in the ballroom at the yacht club. Alaina adored Christine, and happily welcomed her into the family. She was a little hesitant of now being off-handedly related to Hedda, which made Edward laugh. Arthur and Christine made their home in a townhouse they rented on Summit Avenue, although Alaina knew someday they'd have the Great Heron Lake house as their own.

A year later in 1903, Ella married Arthur's friend, Adam

Draper. She'd spent two years studying art and dance in a local women's college before becoming his wife. Alaina liked Adam. She thought he made a good match for her daughter. He set up his own law firm across the river in Minneapolis and they bought a lovely house in a new neighborhood.

"Both children are grown and married," Edward told Alaina not long after Ella had moved out with her husband. "You're running out of excuses not to marry me."

"Soon," she said with a smile. "Soon."

In 1905, I handed over the business to Arthur, Alaina wrote in her journal. I was fifty-one years old and it was time. I set aside two acres of property on the lake for myself and built a cottage on it where I could live each summer. Arthur and Christine moved into the lakeside mansion and Ella and Adam joined them there every summer. I had accomplished what I'd set out to do. I'd kept the family business running successfully to pass on to my son. I'd also taken some of the profits from my father's textile factory to set up a trust fund for future Madison women so no one would ever have to marry for money just to survive. I want the women in this family to have a choice to do as they wish with their lives. I was finally able to. I can only hope that my descendants will be able to also.

My life is once again changing, and I look forward to what is to come. I will leave this journal in a place where hopefully, years from now, someone will find it. My hope is that whoever reads it will learn something from my mistakes and my accomplishments.

June 1905

Chapter Thirty-Nine

Marla

The ladies all stared at each other, their eyes wide, after Marla had read the last words in the journal.

"I have chills," Wanda said, rubbing her arms.

"But we don't know the end," Rita said, looking crestfallen. "Did she marry Edward? How many grandchildren did she have? Did she travel? Did she regret giving up the business so young?"

"We know she had at least one grandchild otherwise Marla's Nathan wouldn't have been born," Ardie said with a chuckle. "But I'm just as curious. What happened? Why did the factory close? When? There's so much we don't know."

Marla wanted to know the answers too. She remembered that Mrs. Cooper had said there were old photo albums up in the attic. "I think it's time we visit the creepy old attic and look for our answers."

"Let's go!" Wanda said enthusiastically.

Toni shuddered. "I hope it isn't too creepy."

Marla grabbed a flashlight from the kitchen and they all followed her upstairs. At the end of the long hallway was a door.

Behind it was a narrow set of stairs that led up.

"Goodness. This is eerie," Ardie said.

Marla switched on the light that swung on a cord from the ceiling. They walked up the stairs until they came to the top. The attic was large with a slanted roof. A round window was on one end but otherwise there was no light. Since it was dark outside, the window was no help anyway.

"I know there's a light around here somewhere," Marla said. She searched with her flashlight, finally found a cord, then pulled. Dim light filled the space.

The attic was packed with old furniture, dress dummies, trunks, and boxes. Marla began searching the writing on boxes to see if she could find the scrapbooks. Wanda opened one of the large trunks, and gasped.

"What? Did you find a spider?" Toni asked, backing away.

"No, silly," Wanda said. "Look! These clothes have to be from Alaina's era. Or at least Ella's." She pulled out long dresses, puffy-sleeved blouses, and floor-length skirts. They were all faded and wrinkled, but the women could tell from the fabric and buttons that they were of high quality. Deeper down, she found hats of all sizes, then a ball gown.

"It's emerald green!" Wanda exclaimed. "Isn't that the gown Alaina wore to the June ball she attended at Nathaniel's home?"

"Yes, I believe it was," Rita said, growing excited. "It's beautiful."

They all marveled at the lovely clothes, then continued their search for photo albums.

"What are the odds we find another journal?" Ardie asked.

"I can't believe she wrote the one and didn't keep writing journals. But that would have been at the new house she built, wouldn't it?" Marla said.

"Unless her son brought her things here after she died," Toni suggested.

After pushing a few boxes aside, Marla saw one marked "Photos – 1900 – 19--. The two last numbers had been smudged and faded. She pulled it to the center of the floor so they could all gather around.

Rita placed her hand on the box to stop them. "Wait! What if she died young? Do we want to know?"

The women stared at each other a moment, then Marla spoke up. "That would be sad, but I'd still want to know what happened."

They all nodded agreement. Marla opened the box and peered inside. There was a stack of old scrapbooks and other loose photos in cardboard folders. She lifted out the first scrapbook and set it on her lap as everyone drew closer. Opening it, the cover page was handwritten "Madison Family 1900." She turned the page and there was a large black and white photo of a young man with light hair and a nice smile. Underneath it was printed: Arthur Madison, University Graduation.

"He's so handsome," Rita said. "He's exactly as I imagined him."

On the facing page was a young woman wearing a ball gown. Her dark hair was styled in an elaborate updo and she wore white gloves up to her elbows. She was petite and slender, and simply gorgeous. The name "Ella Hannah Madison" was written underneath.

"She's so beautiful," Marla said, amazed at the family resemblance. "Her facial features remind me so much of Reese."

Everyone exclaimed over her photo. They began going through the pages. Most of the photos were professional ones taken at dances, balls, or events. They recognized some as being taken at yacht club dances. Arthur and Christine's wedding photo was in there, as was Ella and Adam's. They stopped a moment when they realized a picture of an older woman and man, dressed up and smiling, were Alaina and Edward at Arthur's wedding.

"She's lovely!" Marla exclaimed. After all this time, she couldn't believe she was finally looking at Alaina. "She's just as I pictured her. How could she ever have thought she was plain?"

"She's beautiful," Toni said. "And Edward is quite handsome. Lucky her." She grinned.

Several pages in, Toni gasped and pointed. "Marla! Look! The house she's standing in front of. That's your cottage."

Marla's eyes went to where Toni was pointing. Alaina was standing in front of the Fairy Tale house, smiling broadly. Underneath it was written: "My New Home."

Goosebumps ran up Marla's arms. "Alaina built the cottage? The cottage I bought."

Toni clapped her hands with glee. "This is amazing. I guess you both have very good taste."

"Isn't it weird?" Wanda asked. "I mean it's cool and all, but just think about it. You and Alaina's lives are very much the same. And now you're going to be living in her other house. Don't you think it's odd?"

"Maybe it's not as much odd as it's fate," Ardie offered. "I'd bet that Alaina had many happy years in that cottage. And you will too." She smiled warmly at Marla.

Marla smiled back. She continued to turn the pages as the women drew in closer. A photo dated 1905 showed Alaina and Edward, dressed up nicely with her holding a bouquet. Underneath the date was written: "Our Wedding Day."

"She married him," Rita said. "That makes me so happy."

"What a wonderful ending. Or should I say beginning for

her," Ardie said. "Keep turning. Let's see what else happened."

As Marla turned the pages, Alaina's life unfolded before them. She and Edward had honeymooned in Europe. Photos of Ella's first baby, a little girl, then of Arthur's baby boy then a baby girl. More trips for Alaina and Edward. They went to the pyramids in Egypt, on safari in Africa, and to many sites around the United States, like Niagara Falls and New York City. There were newspaper clippings about World War I and local boys who hadn't come home. And then an entire page of newspaper articles in 1919 when women had finally won the right to vote in Minnesota elections. Alaina had written across the top of the page: "We did it!"

"This is absolutely incredible," Ardie said happily. "We know now that she had a great life with a man she loved and admired. I'm so glad she had a happy ending. She worked hard for it."

Everyone agreed. Marla wanted to look through all the old albums in the box, so she asked if everyone would help carry them downstairs. As she pushed the empty box aside, she noticed something leaning against the wall with a sheet over it. "What's this?" she asked aloud. Setting down the albums, she pulled up the sheet and there, staring back at her, was a young Alaina in a framed portrait.

"Look everyone!" She brought it out under the light. "It's a painting of Alaina when she was younger."

Alaina's chestnut hair was up in a lovely style and her eyes looked kind. She was a stunning woman. All the women exclaimed how beautiful she was.

"You should bring that downstairs too," Wanda said. "It really should be hung somewhere."

Marla nodded. As she studied it, though, a thought occurred to her. "I agree. It should be hung and admired."

Ardie grinned. "What are you thinking? Maybe at the shelter?"

"No. I think it's time Alaina got credit for all her hard work. I'll let you all know as soon as I find out if it can be done."

After carrying down the albums and painting, the ladies soon said goodnight. Marla placed the painting of Alaina on the fireplace mantel in the morning room. As she stared up at it, she smiled and said, "I have the perfect place for you, Alaina. Just you wait and see."

* * *

The next day when Mrs. Cooper brought in her morning tea, she stopped and stared at the painting. "Who is this?"

"Alaina Madison. She was the first Mrs. Madison to live in this house."

"She was quite stunning, wasn't she?" Mrs. Cooper asked.

"Yes. And she was just as interesting as she was beautiful." Marla handed her the journal. "We finished this last night. It's an incredible and inspiring story. When you're done reading it, I want to give it to Reese. She needs to know about the strong women she comes from."

"Thank you," Mrs. Cooper said, admiring the antique leather cover. "I can't wait to read it."

That day, Marla made a call to the board president of the yacht club. After much discussion, despite his hesitation to grant her request, he finally did. The Madison name still held a lot of weight at the club, and she hadn't been afraid to use it.

That afternoon, as she was going through more of the photo albums, her phone rang. The city council chairman called to tell her that they had decided to allow her to move forward with the shelter.

"Congratulations, Mrs. Madison. We all admired your willingness to use your building and land for this project. You have a good team around you and we look forward to seeing the shelter once it's in operation."

Marla could hardly contain her excitement as she thanked him. After she hung up, she ran into the kitchen where Mrs. Cooper was making her lunch and blurted out, "The shelter is a go! The city approved it!"

"That's wonderful!" Mrs. Cooper said. "Congratulations!"

"Thank you. I'm so excited. I have to call everyone. What a great day!"

Mrs. Cooper smiled. "Maybe you should calm down a little before calling everyone."

Marla laughed. She called Alden first, her daughter, then Ardie, and went down the list of her friends. They all agreed they needed to get together to celebrate.

After Marla had made her calls, Mrs. Cooper set her lunch plate on the counter and handed her a glass of red wine. "A little something to celebrate with," the housekeeper said.

"You have to join me." Marla wanted to share her special moment.

Mrs. Cooper pulled a plate from the fridge as well as a full wine glass for herself. "Don't mind if I do," she said, sitting down beside Marla at the counter.

Marla chuckled. Of all the accomplishments she'd made over the past few months, she thought that maybe becoming friends with Mrs. Cooper was her biggest one.

"Cheers," Marla said, lifting her glass.

"Cheers to you," Mrs. Cooper said, then clinked her glass to Marla's.

Epilogue

One Year Later

Marla stood at the entryway of the River of Hope House greeting the many people who'd come for their official opening. Managers from other shelters as well as those who worked for crisis centers had come to see what services they were providing along with city officials and members of the press. Before they opened for official business, Marla had wanted people to see the type of place River of Hope House was and understand what they were offering.

All her book club friends came, as well as Alden, and Reese, who brought along Chad. It had been a busy year of making decisions, filing for numerous licenses and permits, and just getting through the day-to-day issues of remodeling a building the size of the factory. And through it all, Alden had been there by her side, helping her when things got tough, giving her advice when she asked, and just listening when she needed an ear. She didn't know what she'd have done without his calm presence in her life.

Last November, she'd moved into the cottage and hadn't

regretted it at all. She loved her new, smaller living space. She felt instantly free of the weight of the mansion the minute she moved out. It had always been too big and too much to worry about. The only thing she missed was the pool, and she'd already decided that was the one big expense she'd splurge on with the money from the sale of the mansion. In early spring, Toni had listed the Great Heron Lake home for her once she knew for certain that Reese didn't want to keep it in the family. To her and Toni's delight, it had sold for a ridiculous amount of money in early June. A family with two young children had purchased it, and that delighted Marla. She hoped they'd bring love and laughter back to that home and enjoy it for years to come.

After the sale, Marla had donated half the money from the house to the non-profit foundation she'd set up for the shelter—the Alaina Carlton Madison Foundation. That, along with the many donations she'd received from businesses and generous individuals would help keep River of Hope House running for quite some time. Marla also had several community fundraisers already set up for the coming year to supplement their funds. She loved her new job working to fund the shelter. It was rewarding knowing she was helping women rebuild their lives to move on to a better one.

Marla had also talked the yacht club into donating money to the foundation from the proceeds of this year's June Ball. Escorted by Alden, she'd attended for two reasons—to promote the shelter and to dedicate something to the club, with the chairman of the board's permission. That evening, she'd stood up in front of everyone and told them the story about a woman who'd been the wife of one of the founding members of the club. A woman who'd dedicated her time, money, and support to the club and the growth of the town of Great Heron Lake while it was still in its infancy.

"We've given the men credit where credit was due throughout the years. But we've forgotten what the women of this club have contributed to continue its growth and existence," Marla said. "As the women today of the Great Heron Yacht Club put on fundraisers to keep this club running, expanding, and maintained, the very first women of the club did also. They dedicated their time and expertise to organize fundraisers for such things as building this gorgeous ballroom, buying new docks, purchasing the land to add the golf course in 1912, keeping the club afloat during World War I and II when most of the men had gone to war, and keeping it open even during the Great Depression when so many had lost their wealth. It was their determination to continue the legacy of this club for their families and their grandchildren's families to enjoy. And that is why, in honor of all the women who contributed to the club for over one-hundred and fifty years, I'd like to dedicate this portrait of Alaina Madison, wife of Nathaniel Madison, to the Great Heron Lake Yacht Club. I believe she's earned the right to have her portrait hang beside her husband's inside the library, because without women like her, this club wouldn't exist today."

The board chairman stood and unveiled Alaina's portrait for all to see. Everyone clapped, and soon, all the women in the room stood, giving Alaina, and themselves, a long-overdue standing ovation for all that women through the years had accomplished.

Afterward, everyone came to Marla's table to compliment her speech, and thanked her for honoring the women, past and present. She'd been astonished by everyone's praise and how emotional the women had become. But she understood how they'd felt. The women had never been appreciated for their contribution before, and she was happy that she'd been able to do that through Alaina.

"It looks like you've brought this club into the twenty-first century," Alden had said with a grin.

"It's about time," she'd said.

And now, as she stood at the shelter, greeting guests and answering questions, she could feel the spirit of Alaina with her. She had a feeling Alaina, and even her father, Arthur, would be proud of what she'd done with the building. She wouldn't be standing here today if they hadn't stood in this very building over a century ago. That thought warmed her heart.

"What are you thinking about with that faraway look in your eyes?" Ardie asked, coming up beside Marla.

She smiled at her friend. "I'm thinking about Alaina and her father, and all those who came before us who helped us get to where we are today," Marla told her. "And about you, too. I don't think I would have done any this if I hadn't met you that day at the store when I didn't even know how to paint a room."

"Oh, wow. I highly doubt I'm responsible for all this," Ardie said, laughing. "You would have found your way here without me. That's for sure."

Marla shook her head. "I don't think so. It was all a series of events. And you and Toni and Wanda and Rita were all there with me, every step of the way. If I'd continued with my old life after Nathan died, I never would have found the journal, and I never would have been inspired by Alaina and all of you. I'm so happy to have shared this journey with you and the other ladies. You're a true friend, something I desperately needed then, and still do."

"I think we're all the better for it, don't you?" Ardie asked. "You did this all yourself, but I'm glad I was with you through-out the entire transformation. You've inspired us all to be even better people. I think I made a great decision that night I asked you to be in our book club." She grinned.

Marla hugged her. She was thankful for her new friends and had learned to appreciate her old friends as well. They had all come through for her, even Vicki, donating to the shelter and being proud of her and all she was accomplishing.

That night, Marla invited the book club ladies to the cottage to celebrate. Reese and Chad were staying the night there, and Alden was there too. Mrs. Cooper dropped by also, to congratulate Marla and visit with Reese.

Marla pulled Reese aside in the kitchen as they were pouring the wine and handed her Alaina's journal.

"What's this?" Reese asked, looking confused.

"It's your past," Marla said. "Alaina Madison's journal. I think you should read it. She was an amazing woman. She's the one who set up the trust fund for future Madison women, so they'd never have to depend on a man to take care of them. And every woman who's inherited it has also done the same for the next generation. It's your turn now. Someday, you'll be the one to leave the money to your daughter or granddaughter."

Reese looked stunned. "I'd never thought about where the money came from before. I just took it for granted it was family money. She did this all on her own?"

Marla nodded. "Yes. She had no way of knowing if times would change and women would be supporting themselves. But she was a woman with ideas ahead of her time. I hope you'll read it."

"I will," Reese said solemnly. "And Mom?"

"Yes?"

"I'm very proud of you. You've accomplished so much this past year. You amaze me."

Tears filled Marla's eyes as she hugged her daughter. "Thank you, dear. You don't know how good that makes me feel to hear you say that."

They brought a tray of filled wine glasses into the living room and everyone took a glass. "Here's to the River of Hope Home," Alden said.

"Here, here!" the others cheered as everyone took a sip.

"So," Rita said a while later as everyone sat around the cozy living room. "It's been a few months since we've gotten together for book club. What book are we going to read next?"

"Anyone have an old journal laying around their house?" Wanda asked, laughing.

"Maybe my Mom should start remodeling the cottage. She might find another old journal around here," Reese chimed in.

"You never know," Marla said.

Everyone laughed as Alden wrapped his arm around Marla.

-End-

About the Author

Deanna Lynn Sletten is the author of MISS ETTA, MAGGIE'S TURN, FINDING LIBBIE, ONE WRONG TURN, NIGHT MUSIC, and several other titles. She writes heartwarming women's fiction, historical fiction, and romance novels with unforgettable characters. She has also written one middle-grade novel that takes you on the adventure of a lifetime. Deanna believes in fate, destiny, love at first sight, soul mates, second chances, and happily ever after, and her novels reflect that.

Deanna is married and has two grown children. When not writing, she enjoys walking the wooded trails around her home with her beautiful Australian Shepherd, traveling, and relaxing on the lake.

Deanna loves hearing from her readers.

Connect with her at:

Her website: www.deannalsletten.com

Blog: www.deannalynnsletten.com

Facebook: www.facebook.com/deannalynnsletten

Twitter: www.twitter.com/deannalsletten

Made in the USA
Columbia, SC
26 March 2020